# BLOWBACK

## BLACK CIPHER FILES

LISA HUGHEY

Lisa Hughey

ISBN: 9781452485249

Print ISBN: 978-1-950359-10-3

July 2011



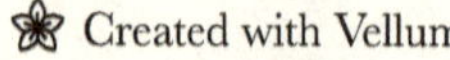 Created with Vellum

# PROLOGUE

*I* was recruited by the NSA at fifteen.

It seems young, I know. But, I was ripe for it. All they needed was the carrot.

Revenge.

As I lay in the cold sterile hospital bed, anonymous government men whispered, "Come work for us."

I ignored them, lost in a haze of agony...and grief. The beep of the machines barely registered. Constant pain splintered through my leg and arm.

Help us catch the terrorists who killed your family. Your mother, father, brother.

All dead. Even with my eyes closed, damn, I could hear the whoosh as the armored car went up in a fireball, smell the burning flesh, and feel the impact of my right side hitting the limestone steps. The only reason I wasn't dead now was because I'd been throwing a tantrum.

A silly, childish tantrum had saved my life.

In my hospital room, the radio murmured with the top song of the day, Cutting Crew, singing about dying in their arms. Those foolish singers had no clue.

They didn't kill you.

I wasn't dead. I knew that. But in an instant my world had shattered. I'd watched my family blow up. Despair settled over me, weighing me down.

Come work for us.

I could have resisted. Did resist. Unable to make an effort to do anything but drown in an abyss of pain.

You can help stop this from happening again.

What did it matter? They were dead, all dead. Then, with a logic designed to convince me, they succeeded. *What if they get your little sister?*

Fear crystallized in my heart. Not Bella. Not her too. I couldn't bear it.

Work for us. Train with us, they murmured. We'll keep Isabella safe.

I would do *anything* to protect my little sister. And so I said yes.

My childhood was over, as dead and gone as my family. To keep Bella safe, they told her I died too. The NSA became my life. I trained, attended college, learned the business of espionage, excelled in the business of revenge.

The only one who knows about Bella is Carson, my handler. I keep tabs, mostly electronic, on Bella. Without his knowledge, of course.

I don't want anyone to use her against me.

Then again, I don't exist.

# CHAPTER 1

*B*lowback (blo′ bak) *n.* A deadly, unintended consequence of a covert operation.

Eerie blue light penetrated my consciousness first. The regulated thump-thump of tires pounded in my head, echoing with fierce resonance.

*Where the hell was I? Why did I feel like this?* I kept my eyes closed, knowing pretense was paramount to my survival. Wherever I was, it wasn't normal.

Ha. My life would never be normal.

I tracked back to my last memory. I'd hooked up with a guy. Had relatively indiscriminate sex with him.

I inhaled shallowly, carefully, not wanting to give away anything. I still smelled like sex. Really great sex.

I wanted to smile but kept my expression lax.

I'd longed to stay in that bed. Sleep with him. Just sleep with the comforting warmth of another human being. The ache had been so intense that as soon as he dozed off--I left.

*That* was my last memory.

"You can stop pretending."

I continued to fake sleep. I didn't know that male voice.

It was bland, not angry, but with a slight smirk, as if he knew something I didn't.

"You should be awake by now. We calibrate our doses very carefully."

That statement raised so many questions, I decided to comply with his unspoken request and let my eyes drift open. I calculated we were moving at a speed of about thirty miles per hour. Suburban, blacked out windows, bulletproof glass. The blue light came from the interior dome in the big SUV.

"The light is to protect your eyes. The drug affects your pupil's ability to dilate and contract."

*What drug?* I kept silent.

"Not very curious, are you?"

My last conscious memory was from the motel off of 295 near Alexandria around nine in the evening. It was pitch dark out now, so I'd been out for awhile.

Lucas. Could the guy have been a plant? Possible. Since he was my last clear memory, it made sense.

I sifted through the spaghetti of my brain. For the past two days, I'd been undercover, shadowing Staci Grant's life. Last night, I'd encountered Lucas Goodman, who'd been looking for Staci and thought he'd found her when he found me. The sexual heat between us had been instantaneous and mutual. A few sweaty hours later, I'd left, confident my movements as Staci had been tracked. My cover had been working.

They'd kidnapped Staci.

Excellent.

I was right where I needed to be.

Now I needed answers. My task was to discover why CIA, DIA, and NSA agents were being kidnapped, the method of interrogation, and who was doing the kidnapping. The answers would be coming. I just had to be ready.

I settled into the backseat of the car to wait, taking in details. Mistake number one. They hadn't taken my ring, so the satellite audio transmitter should work. I twisted the unusual ring with my thumb and pressed the citrine stone twice. I was now sending voice-activated recordings back to Carson.

Mistake number two. They'd cuffed my hands, in front, but left my legs unshackled.

They'd taken my government firearm but missed the knife in the sheath at my waist. Mistake number three. Always, always check everywhere for hidden weapons.

Although my mind was the most powerful weapon I had.

My watch was gone and my government-issue GPS with it. Slouching to the side, I got a better view of the dashboard panel. My kidnapper had conveniently supplied me with another GPS system, live and tracking.

Coordinates. Latitude–47. Longitude–122. I was in the Pacific Northwest. I looked out the misted window to see a reflection of the Space Needle and pinpointed my location as Seattle. I was a long way from Virginia.

I returned my gaze to the kidnapper. Subject was male, small head, blond hair gelled into little spikes, crescent-shaped birthmark below his right ear.

The car rolled to a stop. The rocking intensified my queasy stomach. I ignored it.

"We're here."

*Here* was a warehouse near the water. The guy wasn't rough but the sudden motion as he lugged me out of the SUV caused my stomach to roil.

I breathed in the cold, damp air through my nose, trying

to quell the nausea. As he led me toward a semi-truck trailer, I noted the parking lot was empty except for one other truck and a car, too far away and too dark to make out details. The warehouse, constructed with long cinder block walls interrupted by doors at twenty foot intervals, was to my left and behind me.

The trailer was modified from a regular shipping container, doors locked up tight in the back, with another entrance on the side. It looked as if the stairs were all one solid block which could fold up into the interior of the trailer.

The recessed entrance looked exactly like an old-fashioned front door complete with screen door. A porch light flicked on. The screen door wheezed open as a dark-haired woman in a white coat stepped out onto the platform.

The light behind her filled the doorway with shadows. I couldn't make out her features but I caught a furtive movement, the light illuminating her hand as she tucked a syringe into her pocket.

"Thank you. You can go now." She nodded regally to the man holding me. Her melodic voice held a hint of Asia, probably second-generation American.

He promptly let go of my arm and walked away. They must believe that the plastic restraint cuffs would be a big deterrent to resistance. The click of his heels echoed in the silence as she stared at me, her hands clasped tightly in front of her, so tightly her knuckles showed white.

There was something in her stance--tension, stress? I eased back a step.

"Welcome." She put a hand on the railing and took a step down. Then she hesitated and glanced back at the open doorway. "We won't hurt you."

I thought about the syringe in her pocket. *No thank you.*

I'd had drug resistance training but honestly I didn't want to put it to the test. At least, not yet. Although if that scenario became unavoidable and they pumped me full of drugs, the transmitter in my ring guaranteed I would get the information Carson and the NSA needed.

All of the kidnapped agents had an unidentified drug in their bloodstream and unknown consequences from those drugs. We had no idea what national secrets they'd given away or what kind of long-term effects were possible from the drug cocktail most likely in that syringe. My job was to get myself kidnapped, acquire the drugs, identify the perpetrators, and get out before they could accomplish their objective.

I wobbled as if unsteady on my feet and eased back two steps, assessing my position.

As the Suburban left, the beam from the head lamps shone on her. The shape of her face and the tilt of her eyes marked her as Chinese. Lines of strain curled around her mouth, the expression was supposed to be a smile but came off as more of a grimace. "Come with me."

I don't think so.

I'd expected the kidnapping, the intel suggested that Staci Grant would be next. I'd planned to resist at first. I didn't want to make it too easy for them to subdue me. Carson was supposed to have a team on standby waiting to capture the kidnappers after I completed my objectives. But since we hadn't planned for a cross country abduction—all of the other kidnappings had been local and accomplished within a matter of several hours—it would most likely take a little time before the extraction team got here.

If they got here.

I pivoted and ran for the warehouse door nearest me. Her footsteps rang on the metal steps as she followed.

"She's getting away." A man's shout, older, deeper, slightly frantic, registered as I reached the door. Two against one. More difficult, but not impossible. Woman, older man. Until I saw his physique, I couldn't judge who was more dangerous.

"I've got it," the woman replied and sprinted toward me.

I yanked on the handle, flung the door open, and slid inside. The heavy metal swung shut with an ominous clang.

Obviously, the drugs were making me melodramatic.

The warehouse was dimly lit. Industrial metal lights hung from the ceiling, their muted pink glow making the surroundings blurry. Metal shelving separated the concrete floor into long, wide aisles. Three tiers of jumbo shelves housed wooden pallets of goods. I stood at the end of one aisle.

I hustled over two aisles, pulling the knife from the sheath at my waist as I went. The restraint cuffs at my wrists took a few swipes before slicing clean through.

I grabbed some small ceramic rice bowls and shoved them into my jacket pockets. Mistake number four. They'd let me keep my jacket.

The door banged open.

"Don't let her escape." I could hear the man huffing, and a rhythmic thumping noise as they pursued.

"She won't escape," the woman replied grimly from somewhere behind me.

I stalked down the industrial cement aisle, my footsteps silent. Glancing around, I searched for another way out.

"Please don't try to escape, Agent Hunt." The man's plea had a desperate edge to it.

My legs faltered. I wanted to stop, stand rooted to the floor. Only training kept me moving.

He'd spoken my real name. My *real* name, not the cover I was using for this assignment. So who did they really want?

Me, Jamie Hunt, NSA agent? Or Staci Grant, CIA officer?

I had assumed they kidnapped Staci. Apparently I'd been wrong.

I had more immediate problems. My plan to eventually let them 'catch' me rapidly shifted as details clicked. This was not like the other abductions.

Counting on the insertion team to pick me up after this additional snafu was too optimistic. I didn't like the deviations from their prior kidnappings. Something was wrong.

They were going to find me if I didn't get it in gear.

Up. I could go up.

The metal shelving had slats in the girders that would work. I monkey-climbed up the structure, like I did the rock climbing wall at the NSA gym. The climb wasn't difficult. The rough metal edges should have been hell on my hands, but I climbed without pain.

When I reached the top, I stared at the mess of cuts and traces of blood on my fingers. It should hurt more.

"Come now, Jamie. This won't hurt a bit." With a hint of Irish in his voice, the placating words betrayed his place.

The slight echo could be distorting the sound, but I had a bead on his position. He was one row over and halfway down the aisle. No other footsteps, so no guards. Hopefully.

A break between pallets came into view. Squeezing between shrink-wrapped bottles of Windex, I paused. With the knife I ripped through the plastic then grabbed a bottle of cleaner and stuffed that in my jacket as well.

"Resistance is futile." The guy moved closer, the thump muffled on the cement floor. "Always wanted to say that."

"Wait until we restrain her." The white-coated lady was in front of me now. Both were near the exit. Excellent.

I kept quiet, peering around the pallets, searching for a way to move over a few rows. Even one would be beneficial.

Paranoid years of studying exits everywhere gave me an edge. All warehouse stores were basically the same, so another row or two over should be a set of doors.

"Your nearest exit is blocked off. You're trapped."

Ah-ah-ah. Never give up any information.

"Come now. We've got to get to it. I don't have time to waste." He said irritably, "The others were not this difficult."

"The others were unconscious," the woman muttered.

I spotted an electrical cord drooping down across the aisle. I jumped up, pulled the cord down, and then tugged to make sure it would hold my weight. The tension indicated enough support. A deep breath and a Tarzan swing later, I landed on top of the shelving across the aisle.

I tossed the bottle of Windex over two more aisles.

"Where *is* she?"

"We'll get her," the woman soothed. "The drugs should be messing with her perception."

*What drugs?* Were they the same drugs they'd given to everyone else? My coordination hadn't suffered. So far the only thing off was the halo around light, my blurred vision, and an increased tolerance for pain.

Any hope of letting this mission proceed was gone.

I tiptoed across the top of the pallets working my way to the end. I'd be out of here in a minute. Although once I got out, I'd have a new set of problems. This guy knew my *real* name.

I waited behind a pallet of Veuve Cliquot champagne about thirty feet up.

The woman guarded my planned exit door, hands in her pockets. Holding the syringe? More funky drugs or something lethal? I had no intention of getting up close and personal with that needle.

"We aren't going to hurt you." The guy was nearing the end of the row. "You'll be happier when we get through with you."

"Shush," the woman hissed.

"Susan, girl, it doesn't hurt anything to tell her. She won't remember anyway." He treated her like he was indulging a child.

"Never influence the data with your own conclusions. You taught me that."

The man responded analytically, "Obviously Agent Hunt's physical abilities are fantastic. Can't wait to get her in the lab, run some tests."

Lab? Could that be what the truck out front was? Some sort of rolling laboratory. Why? And why bring me all the way to Seattle? Everyone else had been kidnapped close to their home base and only gone for a few hours.

Somewhere a cell phone rang. The woman paced in front of the door, her heels rat-a-tat-tatted a quickening rhythm, transmitting her nerves.

"Shit, shit, shit," she whispered. In a louder voice, she said, "They'll be back soon. We may have to abort."

Great. We were going to have company. Time to go.

I sheathed the knife. I couldn't risk planting it in one of them. I might need it later. Reaching into my jacket, I pulled out the rice bowl. Perfect.

"Nonsense. Agent Hunt," he called imperiously, "Do you feel you have any weaknesses?"

"I think we should wait," the woman burst out. "Refine."

"No time," he growled. "The program is in place."

"But--"

"Remember your incentive."

"I'm hardly likely to forget." I heard the grim resolve in her tone. "I will do what has to be done."

While she was resolute, he seemed fanatic. Agents with a mission were dangerous; fanatics with an agenda difficult to identify were unpredictable and unstable. Not a good combination.

He thumped closer. I chanced a look. He was older but not old. Maybe early to mid-50's. But the cane was definitely for use, not effect. He glanced left, then right. "Come on out, love."

Not a chance. I had to trust my instincts and assume my cover had been compromised.

"We've got Lucas Smith."

Lucas Smith? The guy I met yesterday? The guy I'd had the most incredible sex with? Plant or collateral damage?

A momentary loneliness stabbed through me, so powerful I had to ignore it. They were fools if they thought they could use Lucas against me.

A professional would have known better.

With one deep calming breath, I centered myself. I calculated the distance and angle of trajectory before launching the bowl. The rice bowl swooped in a neat arc and knocked out syringe lady. Susan. I filed the name away for later.

She crumpled to the floor with a muffled oomph, the ceramic dish clattering to the ground beside her.

"Susan?" His footsteps scuffled closer, the thump of the cane more pronounced. "Look, we won't hurt Lucas. As long as you come out."

Sorry man. National security comes first.

"Interesting," he murmured. "Our research shows that a woman's weakness is caring about the fate of others, most especially a threat to someone they care about. Why isn't this working with you?"

His casual tone and clear disassociation from his actions was chilling. A weird shiver worked through me. I shrugged the sensation off. He was still giving too much away.

As he rounded the end of the aisle, I launched the other rice bowl. His body hit the floor with a thud, and his little wire-rimmed glasses and cane tumbled onto the cement.

"Then you shouldn't have chosen some guy I just slept with."

If they'd wanted to use coercion, Bella would be the only leverage that would work against me. My heart bulleted out of my chest at even the possibility that Bella was in danger. My knees wobbled and I found my balance against the bottles of champagne.

They hadn't mentioned Bella. No one knew about her. She was safe.

I pushed away from the pallet, climbed back down the girders, then jumped the last few feet. I wanted to kick the door open and make tracks. I wasn't waiting for the extraction team. Company was coming. I forced myself to slow down and assess.

I examined the cane, but it was just an ordinary wood cane, no hidden compartments or weapons. I checked his pockets. No i.d. That would have been too easy. Then, I grabbed the syringe from the woman and tucked it in my jacket pocket. We needed chemical analysis on that liquid ASAP.

I also needed transpo. Rifling through the woman's lab coat, my fingers closed on a key fob. A set of Lexus keys. Just what I needed.

"Nice ride," I murmured.

Eyeing the door, I checked for any kind of trip wire. The guy in the Suburban should be long gone. Hopefully.

I pushed open the heavy door. No alarm sounded, so I was safe for another minute. As I eyed the lightening sky, the door slammed shut. A sign, Closed For Inventory, fluttered against the door.

The parking lot was deserted, except for a Costco delivery truck and the Lexus SC320. I headed for the car. I needed to get out of Dodge.

Tires squealed, warning me--getting away wasn't going to be as easy as I'd hoped. A black SUV pealed around the corner and rocked to a stop in front of me. The passenger door popped open and the driver yelled, "Get in."

My gaze skimmed over tousled dark blond hair, a straight jaw dusted with light stubble, and sensuous lips pressed together in a firm line.

Lucas Goodman.

My last memory before lights out happens to show up right when I'm escaping. How convenient.

A little too convenient.

"I don't think so."

"There's no time." Impatience darkened his gunmetal eyes.

Nice touch, but I wasn't buying. I fingered the syringe in my pocket. "What are you doing here?"

"I'll explain later." He revved the engine. "Get in."

"You were a lot less evasive when you were trying to sleep with me."

"I had a lot more time."

The metal door to the warehouse banged open. Syringe lady, her hair askew, staggered into the edging dawn. The overhead light poured down over the doorway, defining the pistol in her hand. The Lexus was too far away.

My options narrowed.

Lucas...or syringe lady.

I vaulted onto the leather seat as the first shot rang out. "Drive."

# CHAPTER 3

The SUV leapt from zero to seventy-five.

I now knew two things about Lucas Goodman, he was hell on wheels in *and out* of bed.

Susan, the syringe lady ran for her car, shooting as she went. I calculated the angle of her arm and the direction of the weapon barrel. "She's aiming at the tires."

He wrenched the steering wheel, zigging then zagging. The motion rocked my stomach as thoroughly as the truck and I swallowed back bile.

He drove like a pro. We flew over the sidewalk, screeched sideways and revved up the hill, engine straining toward the ramp to the highway. The GPS voice bleated, "U-turn if possible", and The Boss belted out *Born to Run* on the radio.

How appropriate.

"We're going to have company," he said.

I pulled her keys from my pocket and jangled them. "Not unless she kept a spare set with that weapon."

He shot me a grin, his eyes glittering.

I whipped the syringe out.

His grin disappeared, his gaze went back to the empty road. Lucas shifted his shoulder against the driver's door and propped his elbow on the console, opening up as if he had nothing to hide. "What do you want to know?"

I wanted to know so many different things that they jumbled in my brain, scrambled because underneath the anger and bravado, a part of me was pleased to see him.

That made me scowl.

I was a long way from Virginia. I asked, believing I'd hear a lie, "How'd you find me?"

"It's not like you went to Oz." Lucas avoided my question, but he hadn't lied. Interesting.

I waggled the syringe.

"Right. I put a tracking device in your shoe."

"You what?" No way.

"When you went into the bathroom, I planted a tracker."

"Why?"

"I had a feeling you'd be hard to pin down. And Staci is the only lead I have right now."

Something about that statement bothered me, but I couldn't quite figure out what.

"I needed to make sure I talked to you again about Johnny."

"The kid in the picture you showed me?" John Wishbone. Some kid who was the pretext for contacting Staci. Originally I'd thought he was the contact for getting kidnapped. I'd been sure when I got into the hotel room there'd be a welcoming committee.

As far as we knew, and they were admitting, none of the agents had any sexual contact before or during their kidnappings.

Instead we'd stumbled into the room and spontaneously combusted. And then I'd left and been kidnapped.

"When I packed for my trip, I brought along contingency trackers. Just in case you refused to speak with me at first contact."

I stayed silent, analyzing that statement. Instead of refusing to speak to him, we'd ended up in bed together.

"After our...interaction, I knew if I closed my eyes, you'd be gone," he volunteered.

The uncontrollable need to refute his assessment bubbled up. "You don't know me."

His body stayed relaxed and loose, but his gaze skittered from rear view to side mirror checking for tails. "Honey, until a year ago, I *was* you."

"You couldn't know--"

He shifted again, curling both hands around the steering wheel, pressing his shoulders against the seat. "Yes. I could."

He couldn't know me. No one did. "So you woke up and thought, hmmm, I guess Staci's headed West. I'll hop a plane to keep tracking her."

Right.

He hesitated. "No. I watched you."

"You were asleep."

"I'm a light sleeper. The door closed, the sound woke me up."

Spell it out for me. "And...."

"I watched you walk back to your car from the window. I saw them tranq you."

"Who?" I still couldn't be sure Lucas wasn't involved. Was the whole kidnap/syringe/rescue a set up to get me to trust him? Perhaps his 'rescue' designed to make me relax my guard. "And how?"

"They double teamed you. One guy came out of the

liquor store and shot the dart, another guy was in the car. They had you inside their car in five seconds. Very practiced. Very smooth."

Well-rehearsed. Well-explained. Unless he was one of the guys who took me down. I paused a moment, tucked the keys and syringe back in my right pocket as far away from him as I could.

"What did they look like?"

"Pros."

The single word raised more questions.

The only thing I clearly remembered was getting up, pulling on my clothes and the piercing sense of regret when I left.

The hours in his arms...I'd felt better than I had in a long time. His scent permeated the car, triggering a rush of yearning suspicion should have wiped away.

But being seduced into treason by a warm male body was not in my game plan.

Who was this guy?

"So, being the white knight you are, you immediately rushed over--"

A red flush stained his cheeks. "I found you didn't I?"

"How exactly?"

"I used a GPS tracker to follow you. At the airport, I finagled the flight plan out of a contact."

"Commercial airport?" Private jet. Not military. More privacy, less paperwork. "What if they'd filed a false flight plan?"

"I still had the tracker on you."

"They could have killed me."

"If they'd wanted you dead, you'd be dead." He flattened his lips and I tried to forget the unbelievable things his mouth had done to my body.

I focused back on my problems. "Did you get any identification on the plane?"

"Partial I.D. number, no other identifying marks."

I needed to assimilate and plan. I had no i.d. for a commercial flight. With one phone call I could get NSA air force transport back to Maryland, but I didn't want anyone else tracking me.

I needed to be anonymous a little longer. At least until I could get in touch with Carson and get the syringe contents analyzed. If we could identify the chemical composition, we'd be closer to capturing the people responsible for the kidnappings.

First things first. I rolled down the window, then tugged off my shoes. Wedged between the heel and the sole was a tiny tracker. I pinched at the device, mentally wincing as tiny cuts on my fingers cracked, burning like acid. I ripped the tracker out of my shoe and flung it out of the car.

Under the pretense of watching the device fly away, I hung my head out the window. Cool morning air whipped against my cheeks, the wind blew away traces of nausea and the medicinal odor of drug-induced sweat.

"Damn. That set me back some serious cash." He sighed.

"Too bad." My mind moved at a million miles a minute. "We'll have to ditch the car. I'm sure they've got a trace on the license plate right now."

"She wouldn't have been able to get a clear look. I smudged dirt on the plate."

Nice.

Who was this guy? Not just a regular private investigator, clearly, since he'd followed me across the country.

"Did you rent it under your own name?"

He ignored me—which I didn't like.

I checked the mirrors again, scanning for followers but the morning horizon was thankfully bare.

"My turn," he said.

I don't think so.

"What's in the syringe?"

"Nothing you want injected in you." Snappy, evasive. I liked it.

As remnants of the kidnapper's drug wore off, adrenaline rushed through me. Blood pumped faster through my veins, spreading euphoria.

"You don't know," he said.

It wasn't enough to make me crash but it brought reality back. What *was* in that syringe? "You tell me."

He could have been involved in my abduction. I had nothing to prove he wasn't, except gut instinct. And since I kept remembering the sex, my gut was suspect.

"No idea." He checked the GPS again. "What did they want?"

I reviewed the kidnapping. Maybe I'd run too soon. They hadn't asked about the NSA, CIA, or other agents. They'd only mentioned Lucas.

I couldn't quite cross him off my list, even if this setup seemed too elaborate to be real.

My stomach roiled. The urge to hang my head out the window swelled. I squared my jaw, unwilling to let him see my handicap.

"You okay?"

Dammit. He'd noticed.

"Fine." Or I would be. As soon as I got this mission back on track. I may have aborted the initial plan but my overall goals remained. To discover who was abducting field agents, why, and then capture the abductors. Copping the syringe was a bonus.

Six CIA and NSA agents had lost hours of their lives and no one knew what had happened in those lost hours. Traces of Rophynol, a date rape drug, and a Sodium Pentothal derivative, nothing cutting edge, which was surprising, had been found in their bloodstream.

There were no known connectors between the abducted agents. They were both men and women, from different agencies, from different divisions within the agencies, and with different skill sets.

Two agents were dead. The real Staci Grant had been killed in a prison uprising in Afghanistan, although only a select few people knew she was dead, and Brad Johnson had been brutally murdered by a suspected double agent.

It was unclear if the abductions had played a role in exposing the two agents, but the odds that the two agents' deaths were unconnected were zero.

National Security was at stake: agents, secrets worldwide may have been compromised.

The government didn't know.

It was up to me to find out.

First I needed to know what was in my bloodstream. Was it the same combination used on the other abducted agents? "You have any spare syringes lying around?"

"Fresh out." He hesitated. "We could buy a disposable storage container and get a urine sample, when we can stop."

We couldn't stop. Yet.

I ran through possibilities. A urine sample would have a limited time window to capture analysis of substances. And I had no lab source near here.

"Sweating, upset stomach." He paused, lifted a hand to my face, and curled his fingers around my chin.

It was the first time he'd touched me since I'd left that

hotel room. The rush of pleasure as his callused fingertips brushed the tender curve of my cheek unsettled me.

His gray gaze bored into mine, concern etched in the slight crimp of his brow. I wanted to shift, look away, but somehow it was imperative to stand my ground. I held motionless against the silent query.

He released my chin, returned his gaze to the road. "Pinpoint pupils."

The matter of fact analysis threw me again.

"Any other symptoms?"

I gripped the keys in my balled fists and experienced a stab of pain as sensation returned. I hadn't noticed while I'd been climbing.

Higher tolerance for pain. "No comment."

Based on my symptoms, nausea, sweating, vision, pain tolerance--I'd been given some sort of opioid. But since I'd had resistance training, I shouldn't be so affected.

"Ever heard of Oxycontin?"

I sorted through my drug knowledge. Slow release pain medication. Frequently used for terminal cancer patients. "Yeah."

"Abuse is on the rise. Popular street drug, hillbilly heroin," he said.

Available by prescription or on the street. Difficult to trace. I wouldn't know without some sort of chemical analysis. "Possible."

He cleared his throat. "If they ground it up, it could have been fatal." And I knew I must have imagined the emotion I heard there.

"As you can see, it wasn't." And I didn't have time to worry about it.

I needed to go through the evidence I'd swiped from the warehouse, but not in front of my chauffeur. I deliberately loosened my grip on the keys, and felt a ripple in the metal design of the key fob. Possibly a manufacturing seam but could it be something more? Her keys lay in my pocket like a cement-booted body at the bottom of the river.

I needed my cell phone. I needed a STU-3 secure line and a chat with Carson.

My badge was gone.

Damn. I was going to be red-badged.

Worst case scenario: They had my keys, my car, my badge. The thieves could infiltrate Crypto City, NSA Headquarters, with the registered car. As long as they didn't try to bring explosives past the canine unit, they'd get through the security gatehouse.

But even with the badge, they couldn't get far. Visitor turnstiles wouldn't be a problem. But to access top clearance areas, a retina scan was mandatory. And since I still had both my eyeballs....

"All our secrets safe?"

Even as I sorted through possible security breaches, I couldn't miss the bite of sarcasm. I declined to answer. Looking around, I noted we'd spent the last twenty minutes driving south on I-5. "Where are we going?"

"Where no one will think to look for you."

I still wasn't sure Lucas Goodman was clean, but at the moment, he was my best option. If he was involved, I needed to stay with him, figure out how to identify the people from that warehouse. If he wasn't part of the conspiracy, I was using him, plain and simple.

"Where's that?"

"My place."

I tracked back to our...encounter, yesterday. He'd said he was from San Francisco.

"No, I wasn't lying."

"San Francisco?"

"Here we come."

Perfect. I had an NSA bolt hole stashed with disguise and identification at the Greyhound Station at 1<sup>st</sup> and Mission. If it looked like he really wasn't involved, I'd lose Lucas Goodman after we crossed the Bay Bridge.

I could pick up my new i.d., get back to D.C., get that liquid analyzed, and figure out what the hell was going on.

# CHAPTER 4

en hours on the road, two rental car switches and no sleep. We'd had no visible sign of pursuit. It should be safe to stop for a few minutes.

I needed caffeine and I needed it now. "Coffee."

"About Johnny—"

"We've been over this." *Ad nauseum.* I couldn't help him find John Wishbone. I wouldn't help him. Each time he brought up the kid, I gave the same response. His consistent requests for information had *almost* convinced me that Lucas Goodman had nothing to do with my kidnapping. "No."

Lucas rubbed fingers with blunt-tipped nails over his face, his hands rasping against the blond stubble of his beard.

"I need to find him," he pressed. "And Staci Grant is my only lead."

I never explain myself. Never. Yet fatigue strummed across my nerves and I felt inexplicably compelled to elaborate. "I can't."

His head bobbed once in understanding, but the set of

his mouth telegraphed his intent. "I will convince you to help me."

Not in this reality. "Whatever gets you through the day, pal."

"What gets you through the day?"

*Bella safe.* The answer popped into my mind like a psych word association. That's the only truth that made life worth living.

I compressed my mouth, not wanting the thought to escape. Staring straight forward, I shifted in the bucket seat of the compact car. We'd traded down about three classes since the SUV.

I scanned the highway again, but nothing looked out of place. But I had a bad feeling.

A low-level buzz, something wasn't right. I couldn't relax my guard. And I'd feel a lot better if I were more in control.

"Would you like me to drive?" Pleasant, soothing and probably annoying as hell.

"Nope." His response was far too cheerful.

"You're sure?" An edge I didn't want crept into my voice. I was used to being the one in the driver's seat. Literally.

"You're not on the rental car agreement."

Lame, very lame.

He laughed, a rough wheeze of breath. "Okay. So that was lame."

He had the disconcerting tendency to voice extremely similar thoughts. It made me wonder....

Honey. A year ago I was you.

Since he seemed to understand my thought process, I knew he'd need more. My assets and informants were afraid of me, of what would happen if they messed with me. I'd blown that by having sex with him.

It's difficult to scare someone who has seen you naked.

"You can trust me." I used my 'I'm a harmless little female' smile hoping that would work.

"Right." He flipped the blinker and sped down the exit ramp. "Like you trust me?"

The smile, the tone hadn't worked. To be honest, I'd have been disappointed if it had. I had to offer something.

I poured sincerity into my words. "I won't ditch you." Not until San Francisco. I needed the ride. And, the timing of his appearance bothered me. So I might as well try to figure out why. Pure coincidence? I didn't think so.

"I don't trust you. You wouldn't trust me if our situation was reversed." He zoomed up to the order box of a fast food restaurant. "Maybe if you explain why you're sticking with me, I'll believe you."

I snorted. This from a man who planted a tracking device in my shoe.

"Large coffee, two creams and three sweeteners, please."

"Right." He rolled down the window and spoke into the box.

Four p.m. in Podunk, California. My unease grew.

I deliberately slowed my breathing. The muscles in my neck were so tense a blind man could have seen them. And, even tired, Lucas Goodman was anything but blind.

After our word association game, I needed to check on Bella. Now.

"Ask if they have a library with internet access."

He eased the Ford Focus up to the window and asked about a library. The cashier, obviously Latino, responded, "*No bibliotecka, esta una cibercafé.*"

Internet café. Wow. Hadn't seen one of those in a long time, but in this rural town with a significant amount of migrant workers, its existence made sense.

I leaned toward the open window, ignoring the rush of heat as my breast brushed against the hard plane of his chest. "*Donde esta las cibercafé?*"

The cashier rattled off directions in Spanish.

"*Gracias.*" I shifted back to my own seat, careful not to let our bodies touch again.

"Did you get all that?" he asked.

"Yeah." As Lucas pulled away, I repeated the directions in English.

"I take it you want to go there."

Not want to. Had to.

I shrugged, trying to shake off this blossoming unease. "I'd like to check email." And I wanted to see if my suspicions about the key fob were correct.

"Find out if security has been breached over in Crypto City?" I didn't imagine his snide tone now.

Crypto City was the term for NSA headquarters. But Staci Grant was an adjunct lecturer for the Department of Arabic Language, Literature, and Linguistics at Georgetown.

If you dug deeper, she was a recruiter for Islamic Fundamentalist groups in the U.S.

And if you had top level, and I mean top level, security clearance, you knew Staci was an agent for the CIA. Nowhere was the NSA mentioned.

Suspicion blossomed *again*.

I delayed by taking a sip of hot coffee. The burning liquid did nothing to soothe my tight throat. After his little bomb, the adrenaline kick-started me far more quickly than caffeine would.

"What's Crypto City?" Playing dumb didn't suit me. I could do the part, but I didn't particularly like it. Stupidity was more effective when I sported a slinky dress, high heels, and no bra. A guy's IQ tended to go south along with his eyes.

In day-old designer jeans, a sweater, and post-drugging breath the effect was largely wasted.

He pulled up in front of the café. "I saw your NSA badge."

My NSA badge with Staci Grant's name? When?

"After." His gaze poured over my body like warm oil. "When I planted the tracker."

Suddenly, I was back in that hotel room, where he'd trailed his hands in the same path his eyes now traced. All the blood in my body pooled low, throbbed between my thighs. Even knowing I didn't quite trust him, my body ached for that physical connection with him again.

His eyes were as hot as my body and helplessly, I glanced down to see the bulge in his jeans.

I couldn't afford the distraction, the mistake.

I clenched the door handle, forcing myself away from the edge of insanity.

I never had more than one sexual encounter with a man. Never. No attachments, no emotional weapons for extortion. I needed to stay secure. For Bella.

I never broke my rules. But I was tempted.

And that pissed me off. "I'll be right back."

He slammed the car door shut as I yanked the glass-fronted door to the café open. Someone had spruced up a tired old diner with red and white toile curtains. The linoleum had seen better days, so had the chrome stools and Naugahyde booths in cherry red.

A silver-speckled curved counter held desktop setups with internet access. My fingers itched to get at a keyboard, but not until I unloaded Lucas.

He dogged me, invaded my personal space, then whispered, "What's your real name?"

He couldn't know I was undercover as Staci. I curled my body away from him. "Privacy."

If we didn't sit down soon we'd draw the attention of the other patrons. Five for Fighting crooned about not being superman and espresso and steamed milk scented the air as I waited for him to make himself scarce.

"On one condition."

Tension hummed through me. I could disable him, but we needed to be forgettable.

"What?"

"You answer ten questions."

"One."

"Eight."

"Three."

"Six."

"Five."

"Deal." He sauntered over to a booth far away from the counter.

I finessed the keys. Sometimes being a techno-nerd comes in handy. I hack into computers for the fun of it. Not much else to do when you live alone, work alone, survive alone.

I accessed Bella's email, watching her instant message her friends about where to party tonight. For just a moment, I imagined her primping in front of a mirror, playing with eye shadow and lip gloss. Her life was fun, carefree. All the things I'd given up.

Something within me eased. Bella was safe.

I touched a finger to the screen. *Keep safe, baby girl.*

I erased the footprints from my illegal foray. I'd made sure Bella was safe.

I glanced quickly at Lucas but he was reading a paper. With a furtive movement, I examined the key fob, eyeing the seam. Pressing on the symbol in the center, the end popped off. I'd been right. The fob hid a computer flash key. I shoved the key into the USB port, accessed my secure and encrypted site and with a few clicks uploaded the scientist's information on the fob to my untraceable storage account.

I wanted to take a look at the information I'd found, but the tingling at the back of my neck hadn't gone away. It was growing stronger. Something was definitely wrong.

I wiped away the connection info on the hard drive.

Lucas stood, cased the café. He felt it too. We'd been in one place far too long.

He strode over to me. "Time to go."

"Yeah." I was already moving.

We jumped in the car in a synchronized maneuver. Lucas gunned into the back alley, just as a big black Suburban plowed into the parking lot at the diner.

"Duck."

I was one step ahead of him.

Tracking device, most likely on me. Pretty sure it wasn't him. We'd switched cars twice, different rental companies, different makes and models. We'd alternated between local roads and freeways.

At the last place, he'd paid cash and used an ID that identified him as Mark Wesson.

I dove into the backseat and started stripping.

Everything came off. Jacket, jeans, sweater, bra, underwear, earrings, knife, even the transmitter ring got rolled into a bundle.

I saved the syringe. I really wanted to hold onto the key fob/flash key but since I'd already uploaded the information to my storage account, it would have to go. I memorized the design; a silver inlay of a caduceus, a typical symbol representing doctors, set in black onyx.

As Lucas cruised down the main street toward the highway, he rolled down the window. "My fantasies of you naked again weren't quite so public," he said conversationally as he tossed everything into the flowering bushes that divided the road.

"Can't go South." Just in case he didn't get it.

"Going North."

Excellent.

We shot up the ramp onto the highway.

"The engine in this tin can can't beat their souped up truck."

So much for forgettable. We were in deep sh–.

"Shit. You sure know how to show a guy a good time. Are they going to catch us?"

Ah-ha. Maybe this is the point where he 'lets' them catch me. And again they try to get me to 'save' him.

I lifted my head above the seat, peering out the back window but the highway, full of pick up trucks and compact cars, was blessedly empty of dark blue Suburbans.

"Have you got a weapon?"

"Duffel bag," he said. "Who are they and why do they want you so badly?"

I ignored him. Besides, I had no idea.

I rifled through the duffel and pulled out a 9mm Glock. It would come in handy. I placed it gently on the back seat.

"I hate to ask...but do you have anything else to take off?" His gaze was glued to the rearview mirror.

I snuck a glance out the back. I could see the SUV. Three quarters of a mile back. The gridlock would keep them there momentarily, but we didn't have much time.

"Nope." I was stark naked.

"Have you got an implant?"

"Honey. These puppies are real." But, shit marie, what if they had access to my implanted, government-issued tracking beacon? I set the Glock on the seat and rummaged through his bag again. "Nail scissors?"

"Doc kit."

I pulled the small scissors out. "Get off at the next exit and turn around."

I inhaled deeply, filling my lungs while I probed the base of my hairline. Breathing through my nose, I felt for the tiny scar on the back of my neck.

*Gotcha.* I split the tiny scissors open.

This was going to hurt like hell.

# CHAPTER 5

With a clean slice, I opened up my skin.

Warm blood trickled down my back as I dug with the tip of the scissors and fought not to pass out. Finally, I got the tiny chip in my slick fingers.

I was right. It hurt like hell.

"Roll down the window and toss this out at the bottom of the next exit."

I handed him the bloody lump of tissue and silicon.

"Jesus, that's disgusting."

Yes. It was.

He sped down the ramp, launched the beacon out the window, and did a fast u-turn to get back on the highway going south again.

I ran my fingers along the seams of his duffel looking for any kind of unusual bump or irregularity in the stitching. I didn't think they were tracking him but it didn't pay to overlook details.

Satisfied, I rummaged through his duffel and found a sock. First, I rubbed at my blood-stained fingertips then jammed the cloth against the gouge in my neck.

I grabbed a white t-shirt, soft from use and scented with bleach, and tugged it over my head. He didn't have any extra pants. Only some boxers.

There was something very intimate about wearing his underwear. "No tighty whiteys, huh?"

"You already knew that."

I ignored the rush of heat, as the memory of peeling his boxers down muscled thighs, his erection hot and smooth in the palm of my hand, burned in my brain. I vaulted into the front seat and cranked down my window. The late afternoon breeze cooled the sweat from my face.

Traffic on the two lane highway was heavy but cruising at sixty-five miles an hour. Factory workers, leaving the bars after tossing back a few cold ones, and business people with suit jackets off and rolled up sleeves, competed to see who would get home first.

I assessed the traffic, the open median, and the waning sun. A potential nightmare to shoot through but I could, if needed. The weight of the Glock settled in my cut-up hands. I adjusted my grip for maximum efficiency.

We would pass them in a second.

I saw the two men in the Suburban just as Lucas jerked the car into the right lane. He'd spotted the sniper rifle too. Clear shot into our car.

I lunged for the window crank, but it was too late. A dart punctured Lucas's neck.

"Same kind--" He slumped over.

I grabbed the wheel, then crawled on top of him, wrestling to keep the car straight. The driver's seat of a Ford Focus is not made for one large person. Forget about two regular-sized people. Lucas's head lolled on my shoulder, while the dead weight of his body pressed against my back. Between his bulk and my height, we were jammed in.

"Too bad they couldn't have caught up with us while we were still in the SUV."

No answer. I hadn't really expected one.

He wasn't dead. I could feel the slow, somnolent rhythm of his breath along my neck.

My heart pounded against my rib cage, thudding in double time, booming as if it would leap clear out of my chest. My hands tingled with adrenaline as I gripped the steering wheel in my left and his Glock in my right.

I needed three hands. Still holding the weapon, I steered with the heel of my right hand and contorted to reach around and yank the dart out of his neck. My gaze shot to the rear view mirror, waiting for our company to find us again. As soon as I could, I pitched the dart out the window in case it housed a homing beacon.

So far, the Suburban, the only vehicle I'd spotted, wasn't behind me. Hopefully, I wasn't up against team surveillance.

Time to exit.

Fortunately, I'd planned to get off the freeway again and had already mapped out a route along country roads. I took the second exit and coasted down the ramp. At the bottom, I turned away from the town proper and the smattering of fast food restaurants and gas stations.

The road quickly turned rural. Grids of fruit trees lined the state route, with the occasional oasis of farm house and out buildings set back a few hundred yards.

I should dump Lucas.

It would be easy. And expedient.

My gaze roved the open landscape, searching for a good place to leave him. After the last eleven hours I'd determined he really did just want information on the kid, Johnny Wishbone.

He'd wake up eventually. If the dart had the same drug

I'd been given, he'd be a little woozy and have a slight sensitivity to light, but basically fine.

Unless he had some adverse reaction.

Unless it wasn't the same drug. I couldn't be sure. And somehow a sense of responsibility I didn't want to have, smothered me.

After about thirty miles, I drove through a small town. A feed store, general store, restaurant and bar all rolled into a single establishment sat on one corner and a gas station on the other. I checked my speed appropriately and knew this was the perfect spot to unload him. But as I crossed through the minuscule town, I left Lucas where he rested, his weight pressing uncomfortably against my back. I estimated I had another hour or so before he woke up, less assuming the dart had been meant for me.

I forced myself to think logically.

Something was seriously out of whack. I had people shooting at me with tranquilizer darts instead of bullets. People tracking me when it shouldn't be possible, followers with high profile tracking capabilities. Two abductors who acted like scientists not like spies.

Lucas stirred, much sooner than I'd anticipated. A muted groan rumbled from him, pleasantly scrambling my insides. His arms curved around me, snug against my ribs, and his sandpapery cheek rubbed my shoulder.

A feeling I couldn't identify curled through me like a warm sip of whiskey.

Pleasure.

My body fairly hummed with it.

I pushed away the traitorous yearning and focused on a safer emotion. Relief. He could pull his weight now. "Excellent. You're awake."

I felt caution return to his body as his mind cleared. "I'm too old for this shit."

How old are you? I wanted to ask but it was irrelevant and revealed a weakness I couldn't afford. Especially now.

"Thirty-four."

He'd done it again. Answered my unspoken question. He removed his arms from my waist, and without the comfort of his embrace, I felt bereft.

Lucas drew his finger lightly along the curve where my neck met my shoulder. "Holy...heck. That's where the beacon was?"

I shrugged.

Lucas pressed a gentle kiss against my shoulder, reminding me of when my mother used to kiss my aches and pains away with nothing but love.

The fact that I softened at the brush of his lips was annoying and disconcerting. I couldn't afford any weakness.

He stretched, arms over his head, chest hard against my back. His erection swelled against my thinly clad buttocks.

"Lift your hips up." The slight rasp in his voice betrayed him.

I complied.

He leaned over and pulled himself into the passenger seat. Cloth rustled against skin in an erotic whisper.

No time for that.

I focused on the road while Lucas eased the shoulder strap across his body, the click of metal into the buckle loud in the silent car.

"Buckle up."

I shot him an 'Are you crazy?' look.

He grinned, gleaming with amusement. Lucas leaned over, his forearm brushing my breasts as he pulled the belt across my body. I'd fended for myself since I was fifteen. Yet here he was, trying to take care of me. The notion was foreign.

"I suppose I should be grateful you didn't just dump me while I was unconscious."

Yes. He should.

I already wondered why I hadn't.

He stretched again, muscles and joints popping. "You escaped and took out two people after being doped up like this?"

My blood iced.

He'd only seen the woman. My right hand eased toward the grip of the Glock.

"Two?"

He lifted a brow, an easy smile on his face. "So far they seem to be working in pairs, so I assumed you had a deuce on your tail in the warehouse. Am I wrong?"

"You were right." His explanation made sense. Unobtrusively, I removed my hand from the weapon's resting spot. "How far to your place?"

He peered at the road. "Where are we?"

I named the route and gave him our distance to the main highway.

"Hour and a half, maybe two." He rubbed his hands over his eyes. "Question time."

I'd promised to answer five questions. Didn't mean I couldn't pick and choose which five.

"The NSA doesn't have field agents. It's just a bunch of techno-nerds sitting in remote outpost towers eavesdropping on enemies or allied neighbors."

If he wanted to believe that then let him. "That's not a question."

"Right." He rubbed his hands against his eyes again.

Probably feeling the effects of the drug. I ignored any sympathy and tamped down on my relief that he was fine.

"So you're an NSA field agent?"

I yawned.

"I wouldn't have answered that one either, but you can't blame a guy for trying."

He was silent for a moment which, I had figured out, meant his brain was ticking along. I forced myself to relax.

"You aren't Staci Grant. Her cover is a CIA legend."

A legend is a cover story crafted and developed over years.

Staci Grant was a real person with many layers. On the surface, she was a wealthy woman who occasionally taught college students. Just below the surface, she steered potential recruits toward terrorist organizations. Her position on campus giving her access to young students.

Another layer down, she worked for the CIA, tracking recruit information. And even further down, she recruited for the CIA. Very few people at the CIA knew she worked for them. Her entire life had been one big cover.

But he couldn't know that. He couldn't.

The agency had spent years crafting her cover story. As part of the Joint Special Collection Service, the CIA occasionally used clandestine personnel and techniques to assist the NSA. Both agencies had known Staci's occupation and CIA cover might come in handy.

Intelligence confirmed that the real Staci Grant had died in a prison uprising in Afghanistan around two months ago, as a prisoner, her cover intact.

I had to ask. Had to. Why would he even think Staci Grant was a cover? It had taken *years* to construct.

I kept my tone casual. "What makes you say that?"

"I can spot a manufactured background file."

It was more imperative than ever that I keep in character. This entire mission was already a goat fuck, but if something in the file gave me away, I needed to know.

I wouldn't let him see my insides were churning. I leaned back against the driver's seat. I'd known he wasn't just a private investigator, but how could he figure out a manufactured cover? "Huh. How?"

"I was in the business."

"Was?" Anything to keep him talking while I assessed this information. I realized I hadn't taken him seriously. I was still underestimating him. And that was dangerous. Who was this guy?

"I got out." His voice was tight and low.

I couldn't imagine getting out. The NSA, my job, my calling, my obsession almost, was my life.

"Question number one." Lucas reclined in the seat as if the answer wasn't of importance. "What is your real name?"

My real name? The name of the moment. Staci Grant. Whose street profession was terrorist recruitment.

Through her we'd arrested, detained, or followed hundreds of potential individual threats to the country.

Suddenly I put it together. Lucas had been looking into Staci Grant because of his...missing person.

I smiled. "Staci Grant."

Lucas sighed. "Fine. I'm going to keep my five questions in reserve."

"Four."

"Five. You didn't answer the first one."

# CHAPTER 6

As we cruised across the San Francisco Bay, the nighttime lights on the bridge dipped and curved upward, sparkling in the early evening sky, competing with the stars in the clear fall night.

We seemed to have lost our tail from the diner. However I wasn't counting on them staying lost. We'd switched off driving and Lucas was at the wheel again. I'd learned what I could from him. As soon as we crossed the bridge, I was gone.

I cleared my throat.

"We're almost there," Lucas answered my unspoken question.

Great.

The itchy twitchy feeling in my gut intensified. I couldn't wait to get to a phone and call Carson. Then I needed an internet connection to dig into the coded information I'd uploaded to my online filebox. And a lab to analyze the contents of the syringe.

Lucas exited to the left and sped around the curve. "My place isn't too far."

I flexed my hands, then wiggled my fingers. The syringe rested against my spine, loosely trapped between the elastic waistband of his boxers and my back.

I glanced at the street. The buildings were mostly industrial interspersed with apartment buildings and several small takeout restaurants in a row. Storefront lights bathed the street with soft white glow. Small lighted signs in basic black and white advertised in English and Spanish, Cantonese or Vietnamese depending on the food.

Almost time.

I inhaled slowly, centering, waiting for the perfect moment. We were in the right lane next to cars parked along the curb. He looked at me again and I directed him back to the traffic. "The light's about to turn green."

As the light changed, I shoved open the car door. Lucas grabbed at the boxers but I escaped and slammed the door shut then sprinted for the alley around the corner. I thought for sure I would hear cursing or shouting, but only a few irritated honks followed me.

No Lucas.

I eased along the dumpsters, ignoring the cool sensation of concrete against my bare feet. The back doors to three restaurants were propped open. Resisting the urge to hurry, I deliberately slowed my breathing and ignored the prickly pins and needles piercing the balls of my feet.

At the second restaurant, I found what I needed. Lockers. I waited until the bell over the front door jangled, listening to the two employees chatter as they moved toward the front, and then I slipped inside. I lifted the latch on the locker and pulled out a black sweatshirt and an extra pair of black and white checked chef pants. No luck on shoes.

After closing the locker quietly, I slipped out the back. I tugged on the pants, found a spare twenty in the pocket, and zipped the black sweatshirt all the way up then flipped the hood over my hair. The elastic of the waistband dug into my belly button, hugged my back, and I registered the syringe was gone.

Shit.

I reviewed the last few minutes and realized it had fallen when Lucas grabbed the boxers. I'd have to worry about the syringe later. My immediate goal was shoes.

At the third restaurant, I picked up a pair of clogs. Someone had taken them off right inside the back door, probably a leftover habit from home.

I made tracks out of the alley, back the way I came, just in case Lucas waited at the opposite end. When I exited the alley, I was in the clear. No Lucas, no car.

I hustled down the sidewalk wanting to get to the bus station to pick up the identification and money I had stashed there.

The sidewalks were nearly deserted as I approached the bus terminal. Rather than head right in, I walked around the block once taking note of the people and cars along the way.

I hadn't had any followers for awhile, but I didn't want to assume anything. Hidden in the shadows of the underpass, a scruffy homeless man glared at me the second time around, spreading out his blanket in a territorial move.

"No worries. I've got a place," I said softly, wanting to reassure him and not draw any undue attention.

I hurried inside, secure no one watched the exits. Keeping my head down, I quartered the room surreptitiously, feeling as if something was off.

First, I found the payphone, made the collect call, and waited for Carson to pick up. But he didn't answer, which was very, very strange.

I left a brief, "We need to talk," and hung up.

I'd get my bag and try Carson again.

I went to the bathroom where I'd stashed the locker key and found it attached to the underneath of a baby changing station, right where I'd left it.

As I headed toward the lockers, tension rose within me. Something wasn't right. I slowed, needing a moment to assess.

The station was crowded. There must be several buses getting ready to leave. I couldn't have timed it better if I'd tried. I stood at the information board pretending to look at arrival and departure times while checking out the reflection of people in the plexiglass booth on my right.

That was when I saw them.

Two guys in suits were positioned at either end of the locker section, their gazes constantly roving. In a restaurant, bar, office building they'd have blended right in. But in the Greyhound station, they stood out.

Shit.

With the certainty of years in the field, I knew. They were waiting for *me*. I had several options.

One. Go for the locker, hope I was wrong, and get my stuff.

Two. Get the heck out, and come back later to retrieve my stuff.

Three. Forget my stuff and get out.

I had just hung up the phone, so there was no way they'd traced the call and gotten here that fast. If those men were waiting for me, someone had access to a hell of a lot more than my beacon. NSA field training stressed having bolt holes in bus stations. Prior to 9/11 we'd used airports, but because of security issues, we'd switched to bus terminals.

The fact that there was a team here was even more disturbing. So far, I'd been tagged in three cities. That took manpower and, more importantly, money.

What in the hell was going on?

I didn't even glance at the lockers as I turned away and headed for the closest exit. I made sure to slow my steps rather than hurry, not wanting to draw any attention to myself.

But as I pushed open the glass door to Second Street, I could feel eyes upon me. Listening to the pounding of feet, rustling of clothing and the swell and fall of voices behind me, I knew I'd been made.

I shoved the door closed and took off running for the steps. The clogs were too big and not the best shoes for sprinting. My feet clomped along the broken sidewalk.

White light from the street lamps spread down over the sidewalk, keeping it well lit and safe for passengers. As a means of trying to evade pursuers, it sucked.

If I could make it to the underpass where I'd seen the homeless guy, I'd have a chance in the shadows. Assuming my followers didn't have any hearing.

A deaf man could hear the racket I was making with the shoes.

The rubber-soled shoes of my pursuer squeaked on the cement. He was gaining. On the upside, it was too risky to shoot at me on the street.

I swerved under the pass. The shoes had to go.

"Here you go." I kicked them toward my buddy and whispered a quick sorry when he grunted.

I tore around the corner, running parallel to the underpass bridge. At the intersection ahead, a line of cabs waited for fares. I curved to the right, away from the terminal and sprinted toward the last cab at the back of the line.

Illegal but hopefully the cabbie would agree to take me.

Behind me, I heard a solid thud and then inventive cursing. My homeless friend must have slowed the guy down.

I ripped open the door to the cab. "I need a ride."

"It will cost you extra," the cabbie barked. "I can get fined for this."

"Okay."

I had twenty bucks and no syringe. There was only one place to go. Good thing I'd flipped through his wallet when I'd examined his duffel. I gave the cabbie an intersection in Lucas's neighborhood and slunk down in the seat. I wanted that syringe back.

He switched the meter on and took off.

I waved the twenty at him. "Run the meter for five bucks worth, get me as close to that intersection as you can, and the rest is yours."

<h1 style="text-align:center">CHAPTER 7</h1>

*I* wanted that syringe back.

I'd walked the last six blocks to Lucas's townhouse. He wasn't home yet, so I waited in the shadows on his cement steps.

Darkness blanketed the sidewalk. Old fashioned street lamps illuminated the cement in little pools of light, but kept the garage entrance fairly dark.

The Ford Focus cruised down the street. I straightened and slipped into the shadows near the garage door. Lucas punched a code into the electronic gadget aimed at his garage. The car idled as he waited for the door to rise. If there was a perfect time for an ambush, it was now.

Not the time to let down my guard.

My heartbeat slowed and I settled into familiar alertness as the single barn-like door rose. I slid into the garage quickly.

Pure fluorescent light, shockingly bright in the blackness, shone in my face like an interrogation floodlight. I squinted against the strong rays.

Lucas angled the car in with a burst of gas. The garage door started rolling down before the car even bumped the pvc pipe designed to stop it from hitting the wall.

He shut off the engine and opened the door slowly. I knew he'd seen me. He probably expected me. "We need to talk."

Not a chance.

Lucas sighed and stepped out of the car, the syringe nowhere to be seen.

"Just give me the syringe." I figured reasoning with him was the only way to go. In a day, I'd lost half my evidence, my competence and my confidence. But I'd never let him see that. "And I'll be out of your way."

His gaze cut to the back seat of the car. "No."

The duffel.

I reached for the back door.

He grabbed my wrist in his left hand, clenching so tightly his fingers whitened. "No."

I thought about arguing. I thought about physically attacking, but he looked pissed.

And I had no idea why.

The puzzle of his anger tugged at me when I shouldn't even care. I needed to focus on who was coming after me-- and what was in that syringe.

"You'd be better off if you just let me go." We both knew I wasn't talking about my wrist.

"I can't." His fingers loosened on my wrist, his thumb rubbing against the pulse gently. "You need help."

Nope. I needed a phone, a computer and a place to regroup and reassess. And I would find one--alone.

As soon as I got the syringe back.

I tugged my wrist away from his grasp and the sweep of

his thumb against my pulse. I grabbed the door handle to the back seat, yanked it open, and reached into the back seat for the duffel bag.

I monitored his movements while I scrabbled through the duffel. Lucas took two steps to a refrigerator in the corner. He keyed a passcode into a panel on the front and the refrigerator popped open with a hiss.

He'd out maneuvered me. I hit my head on the door frame as I tried to squeeze back out of the car. I caught a glimpse of some wine bottles, as he tossed the syringe inside then shut the refrigerator door with a snick.

Fuck. I'd let him distract me.

"Open it." I swung the duffel forward and back, bursting and sparking with electric fury.

I'd fucked up my mission. Since escaping, I'd almost been captured, twice. I'd lost evidence. I had to pull it together. Irrationally, the syringe represented the chance to reverse the course of this mess. If I could just get it back, things would return to normal. Or as normal as my life was.

He lifted his hand as if to touch me.

I knocked away the tender gesture.

"They had access to your tracking beacon," he stated gently. "Either you have a government agency after you or someone sold you out."

Yeah. Tell me something I don't know.

I needed that freaking syringe. And I needed to know what was so important they'd have multiple surveillance teams in place. And who the fuck they were. "Open the refrigerator."

He put his hands on his hips. "It's an eight digit alpha numeric code. It will take you longer to crack it than it will for me to take a shower."

"Shit."

"Let's go." He pivoted toward the door.

Not a chance. I swung the duffel out and around, watching as it arced toward Lucas's traitorous head.

He ducked.

Fortunately, I'd seen his muscles tense and checked my swing. Otherwise the momentum would have spun me around.

He faced me and fell into a ready stance, his hands in blades. Martial arts training. Figured.

"I should have dumped you in the boonies when I had the chance." I feinted to the side, dropped the duffel and kicked it back toward the car.

"Why didn't you?" One hand went behind his back to ease his Glock from his pants. He placed it carefully on the counter behind him, his gaze steady on mine.

I shrugged. I still didn't have a lock on why I'd kept him with me. And as this mission spiraled into a complete cluster fuck, I lamented my uncustomary breakdown in judgement.

What the hell had I been thinking?

"Open the door," I demanded.

I didn't want to advance until he was locked into a smaller space. To make it difficult to evade, I shifted nearer to the fridge and boxed him into the corner. I hadn't glanced at it but Lucas knew where my focus lay.

"It's state of the art."

I shot out my heel in a forward kendo kick.

He twisted, his thigh taking the brunt of the kick, his calloused fingers grasping, almost holding my foot.

I danced back, trying to keep his attention fractured. Then, with the other foot, I lashed out.

Again, he blocked my move.

In quick succession, I kicked three more times. Each time Lucas blocked my move, safely, gently, making no attempt to counter-attack.

He whispered, sharp and focused, as if he could will me to back off, "I am not your enemy."

He sure as hell wasn't my friend.

Each time he grabbed my bare foot, his fingers trailed along the bottom in what felt strangely like a caress.

I retreated. This wasn't working. He wasn't engaging. "I'll shoot it open," I said, testing him.

"The lock is explosion sensitive. Any kind of device or blast from a bullet will cause a backup lock to activate."

Sure.

"Steel butterfly bolts along the inside walls will bore into pre-drilled openings and twist to secure." His shrug was for effect because the calm truth in his eyes convinced me. "You shoot the lock and it will take longer than trying to crack the code."

I glanced around, noting a multi-drawer tool chest in the corner, chock full of screwdrivers and wrenches of all sizes. Perfect. "Why so high tech?"

His eyes gleamed in the bright glare of the garage lights. "I really like gadgets."

Right.

Since I couldn't shoot it or blow it up, I'd just dismantle the damn thing. It would take time, but I needed that syringe.

"Truce?"

I contemplated his hand, held out in an imitation of good will.

"Look. I need a shower. Then I might have a solution to your syringe problem."

I deliberately put my hands on my hips. "Give it to me and I won't have a problem."

"Later." He grinned and used the hand I'd ignored to gesture at the car. "In case the diner guys noted the license plate, you want to disable the tracking box in the Focus or you want me to do it?"

Huh. My brain must be rattled. It should have been my first priority. Dammit. If this mission was a disaster, the fault was mine. I'd been distracted and off balance since it started.

"I'll do it." I yanked the connection wires, shutting off the device that would track location, accidents, speed and whatever else the rental company wished.

While I disabled the box, he reached behind his neck and pulled his bloodied shirt off in a smooth one-handed move, leaving his gun hand free.

Then he tossed the shirt in a garbage can just to the right of the washer and dryer. The ripple of muscles in his abdomen had my mouth going dry.

His skin had been gloriously smooth. The urge to reach out and stroke him was intense. I curled my fingers into a fist.

"I've got one shower. We can take turns." He dug into his pocket for keys. My body reacted to the bulge outlined by the soft denim he wore. He was trying to distract me with sex. I knew it and still my brain took a moment to process.

"It's your place. You go first."

"And they said chivalry was dead." He unbuttoned his jeans, his thumbs hooked in the waistband.

I swallowed the shot of desire. Waiting until he had his jeans at thigh level, I struck out with a kick designed to unbalance him.

Lucas, damn him, anticipated the move and grabbed my

foot, turning the maneuver back on me. I slipped to the floor, jerking him with me.

He grinned as he toppled onto me, kicking out of his pants as we fell onto a square of carpet. "Let's get this over with. You are not getting the syringe. Yet."

His heavier weight pinned me. I tried to ignore the sultry heat of his bare chest pressing against my breasts. That momentary hesitation cost me, and I lost the chance to disable him with my knee.

Lucas slid one large hand beneath the elastic waistband of the chef's pants and boxers, the hot press of his palm against my naked skin startled me again.

Erotic memories clashed with fight instinct.

The remembered pleasure evaporated as he spoke. "Do I have to steal your pants as insurance, so you don't leave again?"

"I'm not going anywhere." Without that syringe.

He smiled at me--a conspiratorial smile--as if we had some secret just between the two of us. "I know you want the syringe. I think I have a way to find out what's in it."

Did my need to know what was in the syringe outweigh the caution never to trust anyone? Focus on what you can control.

Something about this whole mission was...off. I should have stayed at that warehouse and gotten shot up with whatever was in the syringe in Lucas's refrigerator. I'd never disobeyed a mission directive before. In a sense I hadn't, but I sure hadn't followed the parameters that had been set up either.

"My friend's background is from the DOJ crime lab in Sacramento," he continued trying to persuade me.

I was already shaking my head. I couldn't afford the scrutiny of credentials needed to get into a government lab.

"She does private work over in the East Bay now. No major security measures." He assessed me steadily.

"What's in it for you?" I kept my tone even, mild.

"Information."

I must be mistaken about his reluctance. "About...."

"My missing person."

Ah yes. The kid. The man didn't give up.

"Okay." Since I didn't know squat about Staci beyond the basics of her cover information or about Johnny Wishbone, I figured I was safe in agreeing.

I caught the gleam in his eye before he subdued it. He thought he'd played me. Whatever.

"Let's go," I said.

"Shower and food first."

"Time's a wasting. Are you going to let me up?"

He rolled off to the side. Smart man. If he'd pushed up I wouldn't have been able to resist a sharp jab to his balls. Just on principle.

He tugged his jeans back up. He'd set me up.

Worse, I fell for it.

I glanced at the counter. The Glock was gone.

Lucas opened the house door, punched another code in the alarm box, and started up the stairs. "Grab that duffel, will you?"

Unable to resist, I tugged on the handle of the refrigerator door. Locked.

Then I prodded at the keypad. Nothing.

Running my fingers along the side seams of the refrigerator door, I tested the hardware. The hinges were interior. I was screwed.

I had two choices. One. I could head for the toolbox. Two. I could search the place looking for another way to get that refrigerator door open.

Staring at his butt in the worn denim, I snagged the duffel and bounded up the stairs.

I pulled my gaze back to his face as he said, "For what it's worth...when you search my place, try not to make a mess."

And he headed for the shower. Casual as you please.

# CHAPTER 8

*I* should have never let Lucas get the drop on me in the garage. My reactions, my thought processes were off. Perhaps as a result of whatever they'd used to knock me out? It was something I'd have to explore later. I needed my focus back. Now.

I tossed his apartment quickly and efficiently, looking for anything that might help me get that refrigerator open before he finished showering. Like...an instruction manual, but I found nothing.

His desk was Mission style, big, heavy, and scarred. A pile of unopened mail, addressed to Lucas Goodman, lay on the corner. The drawers held nothing but office supplies. No files, no warranty cards, no clues.

I moved away from the desk and on with my search.

He had a collection of Mexican blankets scattered around the room. One was thrown over the back of an overstuffed leather chair and another over the arm of a worn, lived-in sofa.

He liked to read, any kind of suspense, mystery or thriller based on his bookshelves. He had a few favorite authors for whom he chucked out the extra change for hardcover. I'd thumbed through some looking for potential hiding places, or an earmarked alpha numeric code, but all I found was he had a tendency to bookmark with receipts and he always paid in cash.

Lucas Goodman had told the truth. At least about the apartment. And I still couldn't trust him.

Then I saw the other books. *In Spanish.*

I flashed back to the drive-thru in Podunk. Obviously, he hadn't been completely honest.

I moved into the kitchen and quickly rifled through his refrigerator. When the pine floor squeaked, I turned toward the arched doorway.

"Find anything in the icebox?" he asked lazily.

I hadn't. Not that I expected him to hide anything there. He was too clever. But I hadn't even found any food, and I was hungry. Frustrated.

The rough material of the chef's pants scratched at my abused body. The odor of stale peanut oil wafted from the black sweatshirt, permeating everything. Suddenly, I couldn't take it anymore. "Can I borrow some clothes?"

He sauntered over to the counter, invaded my personal space, and slowly reached out. I tensed, planning a defensive move, but his finger only stroked a stray tendril of hair. The clean scent of soap and something spicy wrapped around me, elevating my need to wash away this grime.

"Shoot. Here I was thinking I could keep you naked and chained to the sink."

I shivered at the heat in his eyes. His verbal prodding, meant to keep me off balance, was working. I held firm against the temptation to answer with a not so subtle shift of my hips.

"Pass."

He twisted his finger around a strand of my blonde-streaked hair. "What is your natural hair color?"

"Question number one?"

"Call it a...toll to get in the shower."

"I don't know." It changed frequently. Depending on my cover. I had no idea what my natural color might be. Somewhere between blond and brown. My father....

My father had been blond. My mother's hair had been coal black. Funny to remember that. I didn't let myself remember my parents very often. It hurt far too much.

I also remembered my parent's admonitions never to give up any information, no matter how trivial. I'd broken their rules without even thinking about it.

I turned toward the bathroom.

"Jesus." His fingers wrapped around my forearm, gentle as he stopped me.

"What?"

"There's blood on this." He touched the napkin I'd jammed over the open cut in my neck when I'd lifted the new clothes. "It's going to hurt when I pull it off."

Oh brother. Like it didn't hurt when I did it? I reached around and yanked the paper off. "All done."

He smiled but his eyes were sharp, lethal. "I guess you're a 'get it over with' kind of girl."

"Woman." I hadn't been a girl for a very long time.

He grabbed a dishtowel, soaked it with warm water, and dabbed at the sore skin. It felt like he was stabbing my neck with a knife.

"I know this hurts. I'm sorry."

I shrugged.

"Always the tough one." He pressed a kiss to the exposed curve of my neck. The gesture was tender and completely unexpected. And very, very seductive.

"I'll get that shower now." I pushed away from him before my body and mind could betray me. And to remind myself that I couldn't trust him, I turned back. "*Adios.*"

He acknowledged my verbal parry with a nod. "Guy's got to keep something in reserve."

I wondered what other secrets he had tucked away.

* * *

The shower was quick and intense.

As the hot spray hit my neck, I dug my toes into the vintage octagonal tiles of the shower floor. Thank God the beacon had been implanted shallowly.

I rushed through dressing, rolling the sleeves of his cotton dress shirt up to my forearms. I left the top three buttons undone, letting my considerable cleavage play peekaboo with anyone interested in looking.

I'd take any distraction I could get.

His jeans weren't all that large on me. Dammit. At least the extra room in the waist gave me ample space in the small of my back. I just needed a weapon.

Lucas's ongoing tenderness kept suspicion in the front of my thoughts. Why hold on to the syringe? There didn't seem to be a logical connection between him and my abductors

but--I couldn't rule it out and I couldn't let down my guard.

Lucas sat at the desk, flipping through unopened mail. He glanced up as I entered. "You ready?"

For what?

"Dinner." He stood swiftly. "It's not far."

I flexed my right hand. Out? He only had frozen french fries in his freezer and moldy spaghetti sauce and a full container of fuzzy leftover Chinese vegetables in his fridge. But he must have seen my instinctive denial.

"Even if I had any food, you wouldn't trust anything I'd give you to eat."

He was right. And I was starving. I didn't even want to calculate how many hours since I'd eaten.

"We'll go out." He grabbed a jacket and tossed it to me. "You pick--Mexican or Chinese."

I loved Mexican food. It was hard to find a decent Mexican restaurant at home, but even then I only allowed myself to go to the same place once every six months. I paid in cash and altered my appearance, just to be safe.

I couldn't stand Chinese food. "Chinese."

"Excellent." He shrugged on a jeans jacket.

If I pushed too hard about the syringe he'd make me wait longer. I knew it but I still couldn't waste an opportunity to attempt to retrieve it. "We should bring the syringe with us."

"Not yet." Lucas smiled and strode over to the door where I waited. "I don't go back on my promises."

I shrugged. It had been worth a shot.

Lucas set the alarm and locked his door. "It's safer here. Locked away."

We walked down the steep hill to a main thoroughfare. My gaze roved the still crowded city street, checking constantly for anything suspicious, out of the ordinary.

Traffic buzzed along, a Muni bus door hissed closed, music spilled from an open apartment window.

Lucas registered the same innocuous sounds and deemed them unimportant too.

I followed him along a cracked sidewalk. It was clear from our journey Lucas walked this way regularly.

An elderly man huddled on a stoop, a paper bag in his

hand. He wore a cardigan with thinning patches to protect against the crisp fall night, a thin gold band around his left ring finger, and pink cheeks with tiny broken blood vessels. "Evening, Lucas."

"Nice night, Mr. C."

He saluted us with the bag. "Sure is. You enjoy it with your lady friend now."

Cool air from the Bay whipped through the corridor of apartments and storefronts, chilling me. The scent of garlic and basil poured out of a transom exhaust from an Italian restaurant.

I registered a noise. In the same moment, Lucas grabbed my arm, pulling me out of the missile's path as a kid with a bright red mohawk, skateboard wheels scraping along the concrete, whizzed past.

Not a threat.

My heart pumped blood through my veins, filling my body with fight instinct. I took a deep breath.

There's no way they could track me here. I'd disabled the car tracker, the beacon was gone, I hadn't made any phone calls since leaving the bus station. They must not have followed me to Lucas's place. Unless Lucas was the reason they'd stopped.

I spotted another old man, slightly younger this time, on a bus bench, staring at us. Newspaper, bulky jacket, multiple hiding places for weapons. I tensed.

"Missed you last night, my boy." The old man winked at me. "You musta been busy."

Lucas waved. "Musta been."

After the third person greeted Lucas by name, I shuddered. "Why not just hang a sign around your neck with your name on it? You're a breeze to track."

"I don't have anything to hide," he said neutrally.

He might not have anything to hide, but I did. I wondered what such an open life would be like. I didn't have that luxury. Would never have it. Based on the background he'd hinted at previously, his open lifestyle seemed like a blatant flaunting of good judgement.

"Why do you do it?" The question burst out before I even thought to stop it. Shit. I couldn't possibly care, could I?

"It?" he countered, amused.

I pressed my lips together, refusing to elaborate. He knew what I meant. I couldn't look away, searching for a chink in his seemingly ironclad nonchalance. I really wanted to understand.

Lucas sighed. "I was tired of living in the shadows."

"Shadows work," I defended.

He was silent. I didn't think he was going to answer.

"There are big ways to live and small ways to effect change," he said slowly. "I'd tried the big and frankly that didn't work out very well...so I'm focusing on the small."

I couldn't miss his inference. We turned onto a less busy side street, traffic more muted and pedestrians few and far between.

Finally, I gave in. "Okay, okay. Tell me more about the kid."

# CHAPTER 9

"John Michael Wishbone is eighteen."

"Legal."

"His mother asked me to look for him after he disappeared."

"He's a big boy." What was the problem? He was eighteen, plenty old enough to take care of himself.

I waited, knowing he'd volunteer the information when he got around to it. So far, nothing raised any flags. Kid took off. Mama wanted him back.

I thought back to when I was eighteen. I'd been learning about anti-aircraft missiles and studying five different languages, burying my grief about my family in learning to protect my sister.

"Kid probably just wanted a little freedom. This mother sounds a bit overprotective." I ignored the pang of longing, the wish for a mother who'd been around to be overprotective. No one had worried about me in a very long time.

I sensed him stiffen. I glanced around quickly, but didn't see anything out of the ordinary. My gaze went back to

Lucas. His face was still, impassive. That's what clued me in to how disturbed he was about this kid.

"Why doesn't the mother just wait for him to come home?"

"He's not a typical eighteen year old. His father--" He stopped, his voice devoid of any expression but his eyes were tortured. "Was killed in the collapse of the Twin Towers."

Ouch. That kind of hurt I understood. Of course, I'd pushed away the devastation of my parents' death and immersed myself in learning everything I could about avenging them.

"He'd been depressed, moody. He was on medication and in therapy, then suddenly, he stopped."

Wish someone had thought to give me happy drugs when my parents bought it. Then again, maybe they hadn't on purpose.

The angry wail of a fire truck ripped through the night air. I blinked, did a quick recon of our surroundings.

A trio of women in business suits spent an inordinate amount of time staring into a shop window. But, when a fourth woman came out loaded with shopping bags, I relaxed.

"He started hanging around with ME's, young men of...Middle Eastern descent."

"Maybe he was trying to understand their culture." Or learn the enemy. The thought popped into my head before I could censor it.

"His mother wasn't happy with his choice of friends. But he was eighteen and he'd stopped needing all the other forms of coping. He seemed to have a purpose. The new friends seemed to give him a focus."

But what had the focus been? Despite myself, I was intrigued.

"He was in a car accident with minor injuries. They decided to keep him overnight for observation. Hospital officials told his mother a woman visited her son in his room and twenty minutes later, he checked himself out. And disappeared."

I waited. But Lucas seemed to be done.

"No trace?"

"None."

Jesus. It was as if this kid had replicated my life. Except I hadn't had a mama at home to worry about me. A pang echoed in my chest. I shoved away that traitorous longing for *someone* to care.

"What's wrong?" Lucas slowed, going to high alert, his body tensed and ready to fight.

"Nothing," I said abruptly, totally unsettled he could pick up on my mood shift. "Girlfriend?"

"No."

"So he ran away." I shrugged, struggling for no reaction. Happened all the time.

He eyed me knowingly. "I don't think so."

"Why didn't the mother call the police?"

"She was worried about the consequences."

"Consequences?"

He hesitated, so I nudged. "I need to know all the facts if you want my advice."

"She was afraid of a kind of John Walker Lind type lashback. She didn't want her son in prison for the rest of his life."

"Why would she think that?"

"The son of a slain FBI agent joins a terrorist cell."

I raised a brow. So Lucas's missing boy had a Fed for a father. Those headlines would sell a lotta newspapers. I finally connected the dots. The mysterious woman who visited the kid had a name. Staci. Shit.

"Staci Grant is the one who visited him in the hospital," Lucas said calmly.

That posed a serious problem. Staci Grant was dead.

And I had only assumed her identity two days ago, which meant one of two things. Either the agency had two people undercover as Staci--unlikely.

Or someone outside had decided to take over her 'trade' since she was gone.

"When did this happen?"

"Can't refresh your memory, Staci?"

I gave him a blank stare. "I never visited this kid."

"Three weeks ago."

"You need to work on your PI skills if it took you this long to track down the wrong person."

"You aren't the wrong person," he said patiently, ignoring my slam. "You also aren't Staci Grant, but you're the closest thing to her."

In that respect he was right, but he still had a snowball's chance of help from me. I'd never even heard of this John Michael Wishbone kid. "What is it you think I can do for you?"

"Check the files at the NSA and see if any branch of the government has a record of him--in any capacity."

"What do you mean?" Spell it out for me, Lucas.

"I want to know if he is training at a terrorist camp in Africa under his own steam or...."

We stopped in front of a bright yellow sign with red letters flashing: The Lucky Dog.

I watched him swallow hard, then purposely looked away from the conflict I sensed in him. "Or?"

"Deciding to work for the government as an undercover terrorist trainee," he said tightly.

The possibility had crossed my mind. I could even see how whoever had recruited him would have done it. Probably very similar to my own recruitment.

Avenge your daddy.

"I can't help you," I replied calmly, held his gaze steadily while I lied. "I'm just a simple adjunct lecturer at Georgetown."

"You have the connections," he insisted.

"Is this the place?" I deflected his attention away from the request.

"I'm surprised by now you haven't figured out that I won't give up."

I pushed open the door, effectively ending our conversation. The guy behind the podium greeted Lucas by name then eyed me speculatively.

He looked to be in his mid-fifties, although sometimes it was hard to judge. He still had a head of thin black hair combed to one side, and a wide smile with one gold filling on the left eye tooth.

The little man bowed slightly and led us to a table in the back. "What will you allow me to serve you, Mr. Lucas?" He spoke in Cantonese. I translated roughly. My Cantonese is a little rusty.

"The usual, times two," Lucas replied in Cantonese. He shot a glance at me, then switched to English, "Trust me. This will be heaven."

As long as it didn't send me to hell, I'd be happy.

Lucas leaned over to whisper in my ear. "I'll taste it first."

The man glanced between us, his eyebrows raised. "I am happy to meet your lady."

I could have sworn Lucas flushed.

He spoke quickly and fluently in Cantonese while I waited and pretended not to understand. Something about a favor and a car.

The man bowed again. "As you wish."

Within five silent minutes, a waiter came out and served us family style. Huge plates of Kung Pao chicken, fried rice and a vegetable dish that looked suspiciously like the fuzzy carton of leftovers in his fridge.

"I bring you vegetables. Good for you, Mr. Lucas." The waiter bowed.

The Chinese food was surprisingly appetizing. True to his word, Lucas tasted everything first. After he proved the food was safe, I dug in. The sauteed green beans and chicken packed a punch. I sipped the green tea from our communal pot and hoped Lucas hadn't developed an immunity to any kinds of drugs. I let the warm liquid slide down my throat, cooling the heat of the spicy peppers.

The waiter handed the bill to Lucas along with a set of car keys.

Lucas paid, thanked the man in Cantonese and led me toward the back exit. The unexpected move unnerved me. I didn't want to go through that door.

The men here could all be plants. The Lucky Dog could be a front for something more sinister. To try to get me to trust Lucas. But to what purpose? I must be losing my mind. Maybe the drugs I'd been given were inducing a case of paranoia.

On the other hand, I never trusted anyone. I never worked with anyone and I was in the unusual position of needing to work with him until I got the damn syringe back.

And if I was honest with myself, I had this blind spot, this weakness about Lucas Goodman that I couldn't seem to shake. I stopped him before he opened the door to the alley. "I held up my end. Now it's time to get to a lab." And test the contents of the syringe.

"We're on our way." His tone was expressionless but something in his voice had me taking a closer look. He was frowning. But not at me--it seemed to be at himself. "And once we're done at the lab, you owe me."

"Fine." I shrugged off the need to make sure he was okay.

Lucas yanked open the door to the alley. He said forcefully, "I just want to find Johnny."

Maybe Lucas was closer to this kid than I'd thought. "Why?"

Lucas usually moved with a fluid grace, an unconscious easy lope. His stiffness gave away the depth of his unease as he strode toward a car in the alley. "Money."

But I didn't believe it. His apartment didn't scream money but it didn't scream, 'I'm poor, I need money' either.

"Try again."

"You've got your secrets." He stared at me over the hood of the car and smiled grimly. "I've got mine."

* * *

WE RETURNED to his apartment in the car borrowed from the Lucky Dog's owner.

Lucas had given me a black-haired wig in a chic bob. Out of somewhere he'd found a spandex dress in basic black and a push up bra in the right size.

After I slithered into the dress and adjusted the wig, I went out into the living room. I looked down at my shrink-wrapped body, then back at him. "You go out in drag often?"

His lips quirked but he offered no explanation.

He wore an understated suit in an interesting shade of olive green and glasses tinted another color green shaded his eyes. We were bland enough that the guards wouldn't remember many details.

Lucas's gaze traveled over the length of my body, lingering over the cleavage. My nipples beaded and desire throbbed low in my belly. Not happening again. I waved my hand in front of his face. "Hello. My eyes are up here."

"And they are a picture to look at too."

My body wanted to warm at his smile but I refused to give in to the attraction. I had much bigger problems than a wayward sex drive.

I wanted the syringe back. Now. "Syringe."

"Right before we leave." He went into the back bedroom.

Frustration sizzled along my nerve endings. I plucked at the skintight dress. "Couldn't you have come up with something less revealing?" I muttered.

Lucas's voice drifted through the doorway. "Yeah, but this way I get to enjoy the view."

"Is there an Office Depot around here?"

He walked back into the living room. "What do you need?"

Sharing information was a foreign concept for me, but I couldn't see anyway around it. "Untraceable cell phone." I needed to contact Carson. He was my control and I'd been out of contact, since the loss of the ring, for hours. After my last experience with the pay phone at the bus station, I didn't trust using a landline.

"I have a couple of those pay-as-you-go cell phones with phone cards."

"Registered to you?"

He just looked at me. Okay. So he wasn't stupid. I knew that. I also knew that I never trusted anyone.

*Could* I trust him? Maybe...but I wasn't going to. "I'm sure there's an Office Depot along the way."

"Right." Lucas looked at me for another second before turning away. He didn't try to change my mind, which conversely did make me more inclined to trust him.

"We've got a lot to do." He glanced at the titanium steel dial of his watch. I tried not to notice the strength in his wrist and failed. "What first, the lab or the store?"

The time was nearly eleven. My first priority had to be getting this solution to a lab. The store might be closed. The phone would have to wait until later.

"Lab."

"The lab is out in Livermore." He picked up the keys we'd gotten with our bill.

Livermore. East Bay. Lots of government contract work. "How long will it take?"

"About an hour, maybe less, this time of night."

"Will your friend be there at this time of night?"

He swung open the door to his garage and gestured with a courtly sweep of his hand. "I already called. She's meeting us there."

"You didn't give her any specifics over the phone, did you?"

He just looked at me with a small bit of censure in his gaze.

"Turn around." He keyed in the code to open the refrigerator. The keypad was silent, no beeps I could recall and re-enter myself.

True to his word, he pulled out the syringe and handed it to me.

"Just like that?" I questioned, suspicious.

"Look at it," he said drily. "It's the same."

His words spooked me. He really could read me. The feeling was strange and extremely uncomfortable. So I took his advice and examined the syringe carefully. It was the same.

Going over to the bins opposite the door, he grabbed several containers. "Sterile evidence cups."

I set the cups on the counter.

Efficiently I uncapped the syringe. I looked at the needle. Serious size. The liquid gleamed innocuously. I wondered what they had wanted to inject into my body.

In the course of my training and my work, I'd taken plenty of drugs that were bad for me. I could speculate until I was blue in the face. I needed more than speculation, I needed identification.

I squirted the liquid into two equal portions in the evidence cups, screwed on the lids, and tucked them into the little black sequined purse. I saved the syringe. It was possible we could get prints off of it, but not likely.

"Ready?" he asked.

Before we left I needed to get into character. Tight black dress, fake eyelashes, and full makeup. Hmmm, southern charm school.

I smoothed a hand over his sedately patterned tie, drawing his gaze. Then, I thrust my shoulders back and straightened my spine and tossed my head in a flirty move. The act lifted my breasts, pulling his gaze right where I wanted it.

"Let's go, sugar."

# CHAPTER 10

At almost midnight, the lab parking lot was deserted. Powerful halogen lights illuminated the blacktop as Lucas drove slowly into a visitor parking space.

The Lucky Dog's Ford was a nondescript sedan, somewhere between tan and beige. Lucas angled the car, parking so the license plate would be in the shadows and impossible to identify on security camera tapes.

"Don't get out. I'll come around and open your door, like a true gentleman."

Lucas sauntered around the front of the car and opened my door with a sweeping gesture. Leaning over, he held out his hand and gently pulled me out. "By the way, Mr. Lee has strict instructions to report the car stolen if we're not back by a certain time."

Shit. There went that plan.

I sashayed to the glass-fronted doors with Lucas trailing behind me. What I wanted to do was punch something. Every time I had some semblance of a plan, he figured it out.

How the hell did he do that?

I must have looked perplexed because he answered as if I'd spoken.

"Remember. I was you." Lucas pressed an intercom button beside a numeric keypad.

Through the bullet-proof glass, I saw the security guard, maybe twenty-one, with peach fuzz on his chin and a buzz cut flipped up at the forehead. He sat behind a fake wood, half-circle console monitoring the cameras.

"Lab is closed." The tinny voice announced from the intercom.

"Thanks, but we're not here for the lab. We're driving through and stopped to see a friend of ours. Barbara." Lucas zeroed in on what would put this infant at ease and hitched up his pants so his white socks and black shoes showed beneath the hem. Very non-threatening, easy going, everybody's happy. "She told us she had to work late, but we could stop by before we headed down South."

"One minute, sir."

I tilted my head, examining my fingernails. I pretended to frown over a chipped nail while I peered through the cover of my eye lashes, searching for any other cameras than the one aimed at the door. I found two more. One on each corner of the building, doing a sweep of the parking lot.

I stayed to the side and slightly behind Lucas, using his body as a shield.

The buzzer sounded.

I was one step closer to finding out what was in that syringe.

As we entered the lobby, the guard stood, puffed out his chest, hands on his hips, drawing attention to the gun belt resting low on his waist.

"I'll have to ask you to sign in."

"No problem, son." Lucas signed two names with a flourish.

Fred and Betty Stone. Are we heading back to Bedrock after this?

Lucas rubbed his index finger over an eyebrow, drawing the guard's eye to a large gaudy gold ring on his right hand and away from his smirk.

"I'll need to see identification."

Shit. My brain must be fried. No i.d.

Lucas reached into his back pocket and flipped open an alligator skin wallet. As the guard leaned over to look at it, Lucas diverted his attention by talking and gesturing with his hands.

"Barb's an old friend. So glad we could touch base with her." Lucas snapped the wallet closed as the steel-reinforced door to our left swung wide open.

The guard was trying to figure out if he should ask to see it again or let it go. Nice moves.

A woman, Barb presumably, strode toward us in a pristine lab coat and nylons. Her high heels tapped out an even rhythm on the black granite floor, except for a tiny falter when she saw me.

She was gorgeous, with skin the color of a frothy latte, large chocolate brown eyes, and a pixie cut of thick black hair. High cheekbones brushed with blusher and full lips painted a soft amber subtly emphasized her beauty. She'd taken the time to do her makeup before we got here. When she smiled, her focus on Lucas was warm and very friendly.

"So good to see you." She kissed him on the cheek.

Although her smile didn't slip, as she turned to me, she assessed me with sharp interest and not a shred of welcome.

As Lucas draped his arm over my shoulder, I cursed him

silently. He'd slept with me yesterday. How long had it been since he'd slept with her?

I saw the 'oh shit' realization hit him.

Time for damage control. Barb needed to be put at ease. I needed her expertise. I shimmied out of Lucas's light grip and walked cautiously toward her, hands out.

"Barb, sugar, I'm so pleased you could fit us into your busy schedule."

"Anything for you and Fred." She held my hand in a fierce grip, her knuckles white.

I hugged her stiff form and whispered in her ear, "Get us somewhere private."

"I can't take you on a tour. Security, you know. But there is a visitor's lounge." She hustled us to the steel door. Then she swiped an employee badge through a reader, punched in a series of numbers, and practically shoved me through.

As the door shut behind us, I noted the security cameras along the ceiling. The hallway was wide with dark grey industrial carpeting, startlingly white walls, and very bright halogen lighting. Interspersed at regular intervals were light grey doors, all with keypads and magnetic card readers to grant access, and cameras aimed at each entrance.

"Do y'all have a little girl's room?" I patted the tips of my wig, staying in character in case there were cameras I couldn't see. "I need to use the facilities."

"Sure." Barb turned a corner, tugging me with her and Lucas trailing behind us. At the end of the hallway was an open lounge with a water fountain, a row of chairs, and a door that didn't need clearance to access.

As we approached the doorway, Lucas looked as if he was going to follow us right into the visitor's bathroom. I turned away from the camera and glared at him.

"I'll wait right here." He dropped into the chair, picked

up a magazine from the little end table, and pretended to read while shielding his face.

Barb and I slipped into the ladies room. Casing the sparse room with linoleum floors and white walls for surveillance equipment, I got right to the point. "No cameras in here?"

"No." She crossed her arms over her chest in a classic defensive posture. "Why should I help *you*?"

"What did Lucas tell you?"

"You have a chemical you need identified." Her voice was hostile.

I improvised a quick plan that would, hopefully, win her sympathy. "Look. Lucas offered to put me in touch with you and I'm doing him a favor in return."

She snorted and her gaze trailed up and down my body. "I'll bet."

"Are you two...ah...tight?" The question popped out before I could censor it. None of my business. And no bearing on my mission. So why the hell had I asked?

"No." She sure wanted to be. It was right there in those high heels and face sparkling with makeup. The wave of relief that went through me was unwelcome.

I wanted to get away from Lucas Goodman. He was a distraction I couldn't afford.

"What kind of favor?" Barb narrowed her eyes at me.

So Barb was going to play hard ass. Fine.

I hated negotiating. It was so much easier to work with intimidation. But I didn't have anything to hold against her at this point.

"He really needs my help with a missing kid."

"Johnny?" Barb raised her eyebrows and paced around the two stall bathroom.

"Yes." She knew the kid. Even better. I twisted the point as hard as I could. "I'm his only lead."

Pretending indifference, I pulled a tube of bright peach lipstick from the little purse and efficiently slicked my lips.

She watched me in the mirror. "You hurt him, and I'll have to hurt you."

The threat was delivered in such an even tone it took a minute to penetrate.

"Excuse me?" This powder puff thought she could take me? I held back a smile but a glimmer must have come through.

"I'm not kidding."

Whatever. If she wanted to think she was playing rough, so be it. I appreciated that she'd go to the wall for Lucas. It made it her eminently likable. "Okay."

She held out her hand. "Give it to me."

I slipped the cup from my purse. "You can analyze this...off the books?"

"I can put it through the GC/MS computer." She arched a brow, waiting for me to ask.

While I knew Gas Chromatography/Mass Spectrometry computers existed, I'd never needed one before. It also wouldn't hurt to give Barb the stage for a second. "How does it work?"

Barb tucked the cup into her lab coat pocket. "Simply put, the machine breaks down the chemical components of a substance and gives a precise chemical analysis of all the elements."

"The machine will tell you *exactly* what is in the liquid?"

She hesitated. "It will break everything down and give specific analysis, if available."

I noted the qualifier. "How long?"

"I should be able to have a preliminary answer in the next few hours."

Even better. Finally something was going my way.

"One thing," I said, placing my hand on her arm to emphasize the point. "Don't share the results with anyone, don't show it to anyone. It's a matter of national security."

Barb looked skeptical as she peeled my fingers off. "Where should I call?"

"We'll call you."

She nodded. "Lucas has my number."

"Why don't you give it to me. Just in case." In case I was able to ditch him. I was sure I could finesse the results out of her if need be. I capped the lipstick and dropped it back into the little bag as she rattled off her number. "Thank you. I can't tell you how much I appreciate this."

"Anything for Lucas."

I had a momentary pang of regret, knowing I was going to let her down, but I pushed away the softer emotion. I didn't have room for softness in my line of work. Softness could get you killed.

"Better get back out there before Fuzz Face gets suspicious."

She snorted with laughter.

We burst out of the bathroom, startling Lucas. He straightened from his slouched position in the chair and eyed us nervously. "You two look friendly."

"Just a little girl talk." Barb unobtrusively flexed her arm muscles and grinned.

He shuddered.

I could tell she was anxious to start the analysis and I was just as anxious for her to get started. But we had to make it look good, so we chatted about nothing for a few minutes, then she took us back to the front lobby.

As she kissed Lucas goodbye, she whispered, "I'll start right away."

She hugged me under the watchful gaze of the security guard. "So wonderful to see you both, we must get together for lunch next time you're in town."

Sure.

"Best time to travel. At night like this. You miss all the traffic," Lucas boomed out for the benefit of the guard.

Barb stood at the door and waved as we breezed toward the Ford.

Fatigue tugged at me. Drugged unconsciousness was no substitute for good REM sleep. As far as I knew Lucas hadn't slept either.

"You want me to drive?"

He paused, bent down, pretending to check the tires. Then he stood and gave me a look. "It would be out of character for me to let Betty drive."

As I slid into the passenger seat I said, "You are going to have some serious making up to do with Barb after tonight."

Lucas threw a startled glance at me. "We're just friends."

Not if old Barb had her way.

I wished I could relax now. Half the liquid was on its way to being analyzed. The other half was safely tucked in my purse. I hadn't had any pursuers in the past four hours. A record at this point.

But tension wound around me like a coiled snake. And I waited for the next strike.

* * *

WE'D RETURNED THE FORD, removed our disguises and changed back into the jeans and shirts we'd worn to the Chinese place. Only one task remained.

We stood in Lucas's garage, staring at the rental car. No one had located it while we'd trekked to the lab.

I needed to get the hell out of here, but every time I turned around, Lucas contrived some new way to keep us together.

I could take the rental car. But the license plate could be on a watch list and I had no money for gas. In the other bay of the garage was a nondescript white van. It looked like a plain delivery van on the outside. No logos or distinguishing marks. A little beat up but nothing that would spark a person's memory two seconds after seeing it.

I'd have to take the van.

I opened the passenger door and pretended to inspect the inside. Unobtrusively, I tucked the purse with the evidence cup and liquid into the console between the front seats. I had to make this look good. "Nice digs."

"Thanks."

I slammed the van door shut and gestured to my getaway vehicle. "Loan me your van and some cash. I'll get it back to you."

"I'd never see you again." He backpedaled. "And I'd never get the information about Johnny."

Never see me again? Not a bad thing in my mind. He already distracted me more than I was comfortable with. I was ice woman. No one got to me. And here I was considering Lucas's feelings, brooding that he wouldn't find Johnny. I didn't like it.

"We should turn the car in near Sacramento." Lucas dismissed my request.

How did he know I'd thought the same thing?

"It's the logical choice. Makes it look like you're heading East," Lucas continued.

Which I would be. I'd pretty much figured out I didn't

want to draw any attention to myself until I had the lab results.

We needed to wipe down the car. If they captured latent prints from the cushions or the trunk, they might be able to get a usable print and tie the rental back to Lucas. My prints were not in any registered government database. But what about him? "Are your prints registered?"

I expected him to answer yes.

He stared hard at the bins on the opposite side of the garage, then cut his gaze to me. "I used to be FBI."

That meant yes. It also meant I had a load more questions I should ask. But in his face I saw something that made me pause. Clearly, his departure from the FBI was not a move he'd chosen.

The clues had been there from the start. Lucas wasn't just a P.I. with lots of gadgets. Johnny's father was with the FBI and Lucas was connected to him. He needed to make sure no one could trace the car back to him. I didn't want to bring him any more grief.

And those were not my problems.

Lucas climbed into the van, disappeared for a moment, then came back out and handed me a pair of thin latex gloves. He snapped on his own and began efficiently wiping down the rental car, eliminating our prints.

"I'll drive the car," he said. "It's registered to a man. We don't want to draw any extra notice."

I couldn't refute his logic. "Okay."

"You can drive the van."

Perfect. He'd done exactly what I wanted without even negotiating.

Lucas handed me a Motorola walkie-talkie. "For communications. Five mile radius."

I crawled in and looked around. A curtained partition

shielded the back of the van from view. Curious, I pushed aside the black fabric.

The walls held wire bins in a grid pattern. The bins held a variety of different surveillance items. Cameras, telephoto lenses, film, wire taps, flashlight, gloves, evidence bags, more costumes and disguises. Wigs hung from pegs on the grid.

A small refrigerator was bolted to the floor behind the passenger seat. I reached in and grabbed a bottle of water.

The incredible thirst still plagued me. I took a long draw. The crisp water woke me up a bit. In the back right corner, he'd installed a pee tube. Men had it so easy. I eyed the small receptacle then looked back at the smaller mouth of the bottle. In a pinch, the pee tube would work.

Lucas rapped twice on the hood of the van.

Showtime.

As the garage door lifted, I finalized my plan. When we were close to Sacramento, I'd split off and take the van. I had to hope he wouldn't report it missing. With all the supplies in here, I guessed there'd be money someplace.

I shoved down a pang of regret. There was no room regrets in my life.

Traffic was nonexistent. We made the drive to Sacramento in about forty minutes, checking in via the walkie-talkies. I was getting antsy to break away. Only five more minutes and we'd hit downtown Sacramento. Then, I'd be outta here.

Lucas buzzed me. "Check your purse."

He wouldn't. I looked over at the small sequined purse. It was flat. I snatched it up and yanked on the zipper.

The evidence cup, with my liquid, was gone.

# CHAPTER 11

*D*amn him.

"So was that what you were after all along?"

"Don't be paranoid." He huffed out a long suffering breath. "I could have refused to open the fridge and been sitting at home instead of roaming the freeway in the middle of the night."

True.

"You there?"

"I'm still here," I snarled. "Where to?"

We decided on a place to return the car. The airport was out. Too well-lit and too crowded. Lucas, the all-knowing, remembered a return place near the Capitol.

I followed the Focus, fuming the whole way. Two blocks from the return lot, I killed the engine and crawled in the back. His van was equipped with a drop down tube like the scope on a submarine. I tracked Lucas through the viewer. He parked the car on the edge of the rental car lot near the shadows.

"Gloves." I reminded him with the walkie-talkie, annoyed with myself for even caring.

"Still on." He popped the hood on the rental car and fiddled with the black box. "I need your help to reactivate the tracking system in this box."

I walked him through the process. Out of habit I checked my wrist for the time, but I didn't have my watch anymore. I glanced at the digital clock in the dash. Two eighteen a.m.

Lucas finished with the car and slammed the hood into place. Then he skirted the edge of the lot and dropped an envelope with the keys in the nighttime return slot. Keeping his head down and shoving his hands in his pockets, he sauntered down a side street.

I waited patiently, keeping my gaze on the well-lit parking lot. It would be interesting to see what happened next, if anything.

A quiet knock came from the back door. I peered through a tiny peephole.

"Let me in. I hear a car coming," Lucas whispered harshly.

I wrenched open the back door, yanked him in and slammed it shut. I wanted back to the surveillance scope. Pronto.

A black Suburban squealed to a stop at the rental car place. Two men jumped out and ran onto the lot. It was two twenty-six.

Lucas already had the telephoto lens on the camera. He snapped quick pictures of the license plate and the man who was, at the moment, jimmying into the car we'd just returned.

One spoke into a tiny cell phone. Another hopped back in the Suburban and drove off, turning down the side street Lucas had walked down, searching for us.

The man in the lot pulled out a fingerprinting kit and started dusting the inside of the car.

"That didn't take long."

"Eight minutes," I answered absently, still staring through the tube.

Carson and I needed to have a serious talk.

The man took a long look around. The instinctive urge to duck was strong but I held immobile. Lucas continued to snap away.

Maybe the license plate on the Suburban would yield a clue, but I doubted it. My luck hadn't been running that good. I already had suspicions about who was after me. I just needed to narrow it down to specifics.

"That answers that question."

Lucas looked away from the car. "What's that?"

"They're still after me."

"Us," he said.

We waited in tense silence while my thoughts fragmented and coalesced into patterns, ideas, searching for an answer that felt right.

I was stuck waiting. I needed the analysis on that liquid and I'd really like to get a look at the files from Susan the scientist.

My number one suspect was the United States government. No one else had the resources to pull off a search and surveillance of this scope.

I just didn't know which agency.

Or why.

Although I found it hard to fathom that the NSA might be conducting surveillance missions against itself, I couldn't rule it out. It didn't make sense. And yet, someone had access to our policies and training procedures.

The Suburban left but neither of us moved. Lucas sacked out on the little cot underneath the bins.

"Want to join me?" he asked lazily, his eyes closed and a small smile on his face.

I tried not to remember the last time we'd shared a bed. But the image of him sprawled across the white hotel sheets, his tanned torso gleaming with the sheen of a bout of hot, sweaty sex, wouldn't leave my mind.

I swallowed the lump in my throat. "No."

I wondered if he used his van for rendezvous of a more personal nature. I couldn't figure out the snap of jealousy zipping along my veins. "Quite the setup."

"It serves its purpose."

"All the comforts of home?" I crossed my arms underneath my breasts.

Lucas squinted up at me. "Mostly."

He tossed a blanket to me. I spread it out on the floor and sat down on the hard corrugated metal. "Half an hour."

"That's what I figured."

We needed to wait to leave. The two men had only been gone about fifteen minutes. Chances are they were lurking somewhere close in case we were still around.

"I'm not tired." He set his watch for fifteen minutes. "I'll take first watch. You take the first nap."

I nodded.

"Use the bed." He got up and moved to the peephole in the curtain at the front.

I lay on the soft mattress and let his body heat, still trapped in the plain cotton sheets, warm me. The thought was not soothing at all and yet, I still managed to sink into a gentle sleep.

I woke up to the steady thump of the tires on a road. I

snapped awake, unlike the last time I regained consciousness in a moving vehicle.

Sitting up quickly, I shoved my hair out of my eyes. I burst through the black curtain and into the captain's chair on the passenger side.

Just in time to see a sign for Reno.

The first hint of sun pinked the sky, spreading from the dark outline of the Sierra Nevada mountains.

He'd let me sleep. I stretched, finally feeling like myself again. As annoyed as I was, I must have really needed the rest. Perhaps I was still feeling the effects of the drug.

The drug.

I needed to touch base with Barb. She might want to check in with Lucas when I called, so I asked nicely instead of snarling, "Why are *we* in Nevada?"

"Don't you have to get back to Washington?"

"Yeah." I really, really didn't want to spend three days driving across the country in a van with him.

"I propose we pool resources." Lucas kept his gaze on the highway. "I'm just going to follow you back to D.C. whether we go alone or together."

I blinked, still a little foggy from sleep.

What would it take to get rid of this guy? Of course, if I admitted to myself, I wasn't trying super hard. And I had more pressing problems than one 'hard to get rid of' private investigator.

"I want to call Barb."

"You two bond in the ladies room?"

I shot him a dirty look. "She thought she might have preliminary answers for me."

Lucas gestured to the glove compartment. "My cell phone is in there."

I pulled it out and started punching in numbers.

He glanced, eyebrows raised. "You know her number?"

"She told me in the bathroom."

"And you remember?"

"Auditory memory retention. Sort of like an auditory photographic memory." I shrugged. "It's the way my brain works."

I waited for the inevitable 'huh' or 'wow' which translates to: *freak.*

"Cool."

The only other person who thought it was cool had been my older brother. A wave of sadness crashed through me. My brother and I had fought with the fervor of two teenagers, each convinced we were in the right every single time. But I'd loved him.

I shoved away the tender memory. Once I had results from Barb, I could try to call Carson and give him an update. It concerned me that he hadn't answered the phone last night when I'd called. That in itself was unusual.

There were far too many questions and no solid answers. And the itchy feeling at the base of my neck was getting worse. Because of the far reaching arms of whoever was after me, the urge to check on Bella again was growing.

When I'd gone to work for the NSA, they'd given me a new name and wiped my record clear of any next of kin. No one was supposed to know about Bella but me and Carson.

But whoever was after me had access to so much. What if they had found my sister?

I had to get a handle on the situation. I climbed in the back for some privacy and called Barb's cell. She answered on the first ring.

"Hi." She sounded breathless.

"It's Betty."

"I know. I recognized the number." Barb paused. "How's Fred?"

She was firm but not confrontational. "He says hello," I answered mildly.

"I want to hear his voice," she demanded.

Good thing I hadn't dumped him.

"Tell your *friend* hello," I called out to Lucas and held the phone up.

"Hey babe." He sounded cheerful and far too confident.

I put the phone back to my ear just as she said, "Have you completed your favor?"

Jesus, I felt like I was back in Catholic school with the nuns. "I'm working on it. Any luck on your end?"

"Do you want the good news or the bad news first?"

"Bad news."

"There were actually three different chemical compounds in the liquid." She paused.

"That's bad?"

"The machine couldn't identify one."

"Oh. Okay." I dropped down onto the cot.

"Not okay. This machine is state of the art. Brand new technology. Any registered drug, chemical compound, even illegal substance should be recognized or categorized. And this machine didn't have an answer on the one."

I thought about the implications.

An unknown drug.

"Can you analyze the chemical composition? Figure out a class of drug or similar compounds?"

"Already started on it." Barb crunched something loudly in my ear.

"What were the other two?"

"Rophynol, which is a drug that renders your brain

impaired and usually causes you to forget. Commonly known as a date--"

"Rape drug. Yeah. I know it."

"And sodium pentothal."

Truth serum. A fairly tame version, as with the right connections there were far more dangerous psycho-pharmaceutical, truth-inducing drugs available.

The findings were consistent with the information I already had. The likelihood I'd been abducted by the same people was high. The damage potential to the U.S., even the world, espionage community was astronomical.

I shuddered.

Barb said, "Not a great combination. No matter why they're dispensing it, this is a bad cocktail. Not to mention I have no idea how it would work in conjunction with the unidentifiable compound."

As I dug through a disguise bin and pulled out a knock-off Anne Klein watch, I considered the implications of an unknown drug.

"How long should I give you on this other drug?"

"At least a day."

"Any ideas?"

"I have a few hypotheses. But honestly in science, it's better to keep an open mind."

I sighed. "Okay."

"Can I ask a few questions?" I could hear her curiosity, challenged by the lure of the puzzle.

"You can ask." I tucked the phone between my ear and shoulder and strapped on the fake pink snakeskin watch.

"Our government or someone else's?"

I hesitated. I had no conclusive proof. Just my own suppositions. Then I decided in this case I needed to share. "My guess. Ours."

She blew out a breath. "Okay. That gives me a starting point. I may want to consult on this."

I thought about the people who were after me. "No."

"But--"

"Not an option."

"At all?"

"No."

"Okay, Betty. Call me in about twenty-four hours."

"Thanks," I responded with sincere appreciation. "I owe you one."

"No. You owe Lucas. And you'd better pay up before you call back." Hardass Barb was back.

"Hey, what's the good news?"

"I lied. There isn't any."

# CHAPTER 12

*L*ucas wanted to know about the contents of the syringe. The desire was there in the tension of his hands gripping the steering wheel, but I wasn't going to play. He had a long wait.

He held out for a good ten minutes. "Could she help?"

I hesitated. Just because I wouldn't tell him the contents didn't mean I couldn't dangle information. Just enough to satisfy without any real substance.

"She needs more time."

He blew out a breath. "I couldn't help but overhear."

"Like you couldn't help abducting me?" I taunted.

Only his whitening fingers on the steering wheel gave away the depth of his anger. "Do you think you were raped?" he asked bluntly.

His question startled me, my voice rose, my gaze shot to him. "What?"

"Rophynol," he responded tightly, staring out the window at the morning traffic.

Inexplicably touched by his worry, I answered softly, "No."

He nodded and his fingers loosened. "What next?"

My next step had to be another look at the information from the flash key I'd obtained at the warehouse. And Bella. I wanted to check on her. As soon as possible. "I need to make a stop."

"What do you want?"

"I'll know it when I see it."

I found what I wanted about twenty minutes later. God bless being connected twenty four seven. A McDonald's with a computer bar with desktop setups and internet access. Impersonal. Anonymous. We pulled off I-80 and into the parking lot.

Lucas tapped his watch. "Ten minutes."

"Okay."

Lucas stayed in the van, ready in case we had company.

Inside the restaurant, I set up at one of the public computers and twisted my body so the security camera couldn't capture my keystrokes or the screen information.

The online storage account was registered with a false name and a black credit card. There was absolutely no way to trace back to me. I opened the .zip file I'd uploaded from scientist's flash key to find several file folders: Test data. Subject data. Empirical data. Sequencing.

Based on their document designation, they were all standard documents and charts. But when I tried to open a file, the password requirement stopped me. With a few keystrokes I was into the encryption program log. It would take hours to break into this, assuming I could. Something about the encryption program seemed familiar but I didn't have time to analyze it right now.

This was supposed to be a quick stop only. Especially since they tracked me to the cafe after my last online attempt. Although I was pretty sure that was through my beacon, this job had me totally spooked. I was on edge about Bella for no real reason. They couldn't find her. Everything that had happened to me could be explained by great surveillance work and logical conclusions based on evidence input.

But I needed to see for myself that Bella was okay.

The slot machines in the McDonald's lobby clanged with someone's victory. The irritating noise jangled my already tense nerves.

The ding-ding-ding beat in my head. *Quick, quick, quick.*

I hacked into the Georgetown University system chat room Bella tended to frequent.

She wasn't online now, but she had been, late last night. She'd instant-messaged with someone new, a boy, for about an hour before insisting she had to get to sleep. She had a big math test today.

For a moment, I let myself wonder what it would be like to see her in person. I'd seen photographs, once or twice when she'd emailed them to friends.

But I hadn't seen her, touched her, hugged her, since I was fifteen years old.

I could imagine her calling me for help with her Advanced Calculus homework. Although perhaps not. Bella was as gifted in math as I was, maybe more.

Her conversation with this new boy, Donald, had lasted a long time. I made a mental note of his screen name, DonnyBoy. It wouldn't take too much to find out his real name.

Then I'd check him out.

I'd done it before. I may not have been able to see or touch her in thirteen years, but I was still very much a part of her life and I was going to protect her. No matter what.

As I read through the archive of their messages, an ache spread through my chest.

DonnyBoy: How'd your parents die?

Bella: Car accident.

DonnyBoy: That must have been tough. How old were you?

Bella: Almost six.

DonnyBoy: Wow.

There was a break in the time stamps.

DonnyBoy: You there?

Bella: I saw them. I was watching from my bedroom window. I wasn't allowed to go.

DonnyBoy: What happened?

Bella: One minute they were there. The next...they were gone.

DonnyBoy was different. She'd never spoken of this to any of her other friends online. She was talking about our family. What she remembered of our deaths. She glossed over the details. A car accident.

The horror of watching us die.

I didn't know she'd seen us.

I thought back to that day. I'd been in a fine tantrum, annoyed because my parents didn't approve of my first boyfriend. We'd always been isolated, a tight-knit family unit. I'd wanted to experience life beyond their restrictions and innate reserve. I'd wrenched open the car door and stomped back up the beautiful limestone steps.

Ironically that was what saved me.

The concussion from the blast threw me halfway underneath the shaded porch, so the shrapnel only hit the back of one leg and a little bit of my side.

I skimmed the messages until another caught my attention.

Bella: I thought that maybe my sister was okay. But she was gone too. I was pretty wrecked.

DonnyBoy: I'm sorry.

Bella: Hey, nothing years of therapy couldn't fix.

But I could see the pain beneath her flip words. *Years* to get over our deaths.

I reached out as if to touch the screen.

DonnyBoy: Geez. I'm sorry.

Bella: The worst part was my parents were arguing before they left.

DonnyBoy: Was it something important?

Bella: About some tie company or something like that. It doesn't sound important now, but they were really angry.

DonnyBoy: That sucks.

Bella: I'll tell you what. It taught me one important lesson. I never go away angry. And I never go to bed angry. Speaking of bed. better go. Big test tomorrow.

"Hey. You okay?" Lucas jarred me out of my memories. I jerked my head up to see him standing in front of the computer, keys in hand.

"Fine." I cleared out the computer, fiddled with the software to erase my footprints.

He glanced around the crowded highway stop. "Ready?"

I checked the watch on my wrist. I'd gone over the allotted time. "Yeah."

I rubbed the center of my breastbone. Near my heart. I ached with a fierce, intense regret.

"What's wrong?" Lucas's blunt question jerked me back to the present again.

I didn't answer.

I hadn't had time to get quiet and morose the last time I checked on Bella. No time to fall into my usual funk after touching the fringes of her life. Like the whisper of a ghost, she never even knew I was there.

I knew it was for her own good.

But deep down inside, in that place I barely acknowledged existed, I ached for real contact.

A real hug. A real conversation.

Lucas slid his fingers down my forearm until he rested his hand against my palm and meshed our fingers, twining us together.

That simple human touch undid me.

I wanted, I craved, I would have bled to keep the warmth of his hand in mine.

To show him that bit of vulnerability, that little weakness, was unacceptable.

"Just tired." I disengaged our hands and fought the urge to rub my palm over my breastbone again. "Let's get going. I need to find an Office Depot."

"Don't you like to live dangerously."

I smiled as he wanted me to do, knowing full well the danger lay not in doing my job, but in wanting his touch.

* * *

WE'D BEEN TRAVELING for hours. The GPS system had no Office Depots or Staples for over two hundred miles. We were almost at the Nevada/Utah border.

I wanted to call Carson. Now.

Again Lucas seemed to read my mind. He gestured to a bin on the wall in the rear of the van. "Use one of my extras."

I was tempted, but something held me back. I didn't want anyone to trace me to Lucas. I wasn't sure if I was protecting him—or leaving myself an out.

Finally I found an office supply store near West Wendover.

I fiddled with the GPS system, searching for an average street name. First Avenue. I plugged in the street name then looked around for a house number.

McDonald's—58 Billion Served.

58 First Avenue.

Worked for me.

I needed a first name. "What was the name of your first girlfriend?"

He closed his eyes, and with a reminiscent little half smile, he patted his open palm over his heart. "Sarah McBride."

Was she really that great? I should ignore him but somehow, in that second, the need to know was greater than my need to show indifference. "Was she really that great?"

"There's nothing like your first romantic love." Lucas stared at me for a minute. "Come on. You can't tell me that you don't remember."

I shrugged. I didn't want to remember.

"Who was your first boyfriend?"

Jorge Somebody. The reason I'd been throwing a tantrum. Jorge had wanted to take me out, without a bodyguard and my father had said no. It wasn't safe in the little South American country where we were living. You aren't safe, my father'd said.

You're too overprotective, I'd railed.

I'm cautious, he'd countered.

Stifling, I'd retaliated. You isolate us.

It's for your own good, he'd stated firmly. And that was that.

*That's* why I'd been throwing the tantrum the day our car blew up.

My father had been right after all. It wasn't safe.

Lucas nudged me with his foot. The contact was completely non-threatening and yet it touched off a fear in me. "Give me a name. It's not like I'll be able to use the information to get any goods on you."

I gave the English version. "George."

He opened a bottle of chilled water. "I bet you broke his heart."

"I doubt it."

I hadn't ever gotten to tell Jorge no. The place and time of our potential date had gone unnoticed while I lay in a sterile bed in a hospital no one knew about.

Pushing away the disturbing memories, I shoved open the door to the van.

Unfortunately, mid-morning Fall in Nevada meant sweltering heat. I stepped out of the van into a dry, oppressive heat of over ninety degrees and hustled into the store.

I wanted a change of clothes, a seriously cold Frappuccino, and a shower. The little sponge bath I'd given myself earlier had done nothing to improve my mood.

I headed straight to the phone aisle, Lucas following.

On an end cap I found the paperwork for buying an untraceable phone. I could activate a number, use the prepaid phone card, and toss the phone when I finished.

I found an empty counter and grabbed a pen. Pretending to stare off into space, I looked at the stacked boxes of paper.

HP, Hammermill.

Sarah Hammer. Perfect.

I filled out the form with my fake name, then pressed Lucas for a few bills.

"Can you spare an extra hundred?"

"You think you'll need that much air time, Sarah?"

I ignored him. "I'll pay you back."

He gave me a long serious look. "Yes. You will."

He wasn't talking about money.

I stuck out my hand, palm up. And suddenly I was thrust back to being fifteen again, asking my father for money, wheedling for enough to go buy an outfit or to hang out with my friends--along with my bodyguard.

Pain speared. I swear I could hear his voice. "Don't spend it all in one place, punkin."

I'd roll my eyes and leave out my hand, palm up.

I forced my thoughts back to the present and blew out the breath I'd been holding.

Fortunately, Lucas hadn't seemed to notice my lapse. He opened his wallet and peeled out five twenties. "There you go."

I curled my fingers around the crisp bills and headed for the checkout and away from the painful memories plaguing me.

No Frappuccino. I snagged an icy cold coke, paid the bill and walked outside. "Privacy."

His face broke into a wry smile. "Something I can help you with?"

I gave him a 'get real' look.

"Can't blame a guy for trying."

My defenses were down. I needed a reminder of who I was, who I'd fought to become. So these weak feelings would go away. "Privacy."

"Okay. I'll leave you in the van and I'll take a walk over to Bargain Barn and score us some new clothes." He jangled the keys in his pocket. "Don't take off without me."

I looked around pointedly. We were in the middle of the desert, right off the freeway. The assortment of fast food joints and discount shopping was an oasis in an otherwise desolate sea of dirt and tumbleweeds.

Besides, at this moment, he was the only one I trusted. Of course, I had no intention of sharing that with him.

"Cash only," I reminded him.

"I know." He rolled his eyes at me then jogged off to the store.

I slipped into the van and dialed into a secure location. After a series of beeps and tones, Carson answered his office line.

"Yeah." The familiarity of his gruff voice centered me.

"Hey."

"Hallelujah." I heard the tap of his pen against his cherry desk. "Where are you?"

"On the road."

"Last address I had for you was in California. Then you stopped calling." Carson's code for my tracking beacon. He spoke as if his line wasn't secure. Taking his cue, I formulated what I needed to say. We only had a few minutes before my position could be triangulated.

"I had to have surgery...and didn't want to bother my friends." I placed the emphasis on friends, hoping Carson would pick up on this. "Cousins, either."

"Family?" The U.S. government was my family. The contemplation in his voice threw me.

"Yeah. They were really happy to see *me*." I hoped he'd get the emphasis on me. If he read the transcripts from my ring transmissions, he would know that the man had used my name, not Staci's but it bore repeating.

"Do you need me home right away?" Could I get transport? He could arrange it within two hours.

Instead, he confirmed what I'd already suspected. "The

road is fine. Take your time. See the sights." That way he could see who was interested in my absence.

Worry gnawed at me and an unrelenting feeling that something wasn't right.

"How's my package?" My sister. Bella.

"Good, good." Carson asked, "Any other news?"

Nothing else I could share over a possibly tapped line. I thought over the transmissions he would have received through my ring before I had to toss it on the side of the road. He knew about the syringe, Lucas and John Wishbone. Everything else would have to wait. "I'm good."

"Do you need supplies?"

Cash. I thought about how every time I'd hit a public location, there'd been someone waiting. Then I thought about Lucas. He was my ace, as long as no one knew about him. "We've got it covered."

That should tell Carson I still had company.

I really should get off the line but I hesitated. I thought about Barb, about the liquid, about how much I owed Lucas Goodman. One thing couldn't wait. "One favor?"

"Anything." The fervor in his voice threw me.

"I'm going to send you a name."

"Okay." He paused. "And?"

"Find out what you can for me."

"Is this related?"

"No."

"I'll check it out." He paused as if he were going to say something else. "Stay safe."

I disconnected the call and texted John Michael Wishbone to Carson's cell. As I waited for the text to go through, I wondered what that note in his voice had been. With anyone else, I'd have thought fear. But that didn't make any sense.

# CHAPTER 13

"What's your real name?"

As I'd done every other time he'd asked, I answered, "Staci Grant."

We'd been back on the road for hours. We'd crossed into, and out of, Utah with little fanfare. At just past midnight, I was driving. I'd managed to avoid talking by taking turns sleeping and driving, but Lucas had just woken up.

Darkness cocooned us in an intimate bubble, the only light from the glow of his laptop.

"Give me a bone. Something." He had a miniature laptop on his knees. "Come on. I'll give you hair color as question number one. I know Staci's cover is a legend."

"What would make you say that?" Yeah, we'd been over this before. Now I knew him better. And I wanted more information.

"I have a sixth sense about these things. I could always spot a manufactured identity."

"Even legends?" I referred to identity covers that were painstakingly created over years.

"Legends are harder, but yeah. If I felt the identity was off, it usually was."

Interesting. I wonder what could he tell me about Staci Grant? "You have 'people tracking software' on that?"

"I subscribe to a service." He tapped something else into the computer.

"You have internet capability?" I eyed his laptop.

"Yup."

"Why didn't you tell me?"

"You wouldn't use any computer that could footprint back to you. And wireless isn't very secure."

He was right so I let it go.

"Did you track Staci with that software?"

"Yeah."

"And what did it tell you?"

"She lives in a townhouse in Alexandria, Virginia. She's an adjunct lecturer in Department of Arabic Language, Literature & Linguistics at Georgetown and does volunteer work in Afghanistan for an international foundation dedicated to de-mining."

So far nothing unusual in his findings. "What else?"

"She drives a Lexus."

"Yeah." I remembered the ride. Staci's was cherry red and hot. "Love that car."

I would never drive anything that flashy. I had a Honda Civic, in an unremarkable light blue.

"The word on the street is," Lucas said, his gaze still on the laptop screen, "that if you're interested in supporting a terrorist group, Staci has connections."

Interesting. His information was dead on. Staci Grant's cover was as a known recruiter. "You didn't get that from your software," I said mildly.

"I also called in a few favors."

A giant tumbleweed, caught in the high beams, whipped across the empty highway as I waited for him to drop his bombshell. It was discomforting to realize I already knew him well enough to figure out one was coming.

"Staci Grant died a few weeks ago in Afghanistan."

Now, he'd shocked me. *Very few* people had access to that information. I lifted a brow and turned toward him. With a lazy smile, I tilted my head. "That seems to be misinformation since I'm sitting right here."

"Cut the crap." His jaw tightened, emphasizing the hard lines of his face. "I worked with your cousins in Counter-Terrorism. I investigated Staci as part of a task force—until we were told to back off very politely by the CIA. I did surveillance on her for a month. You aren't her."

He'd known Staci? Now he'd really surprised me, but I kept my foot steady on the pedal and fingers loose on the wheel.

I figured the game was up. Maybe I should be more suspicious, but although he hadn't told me he'd actually known Staci, he had been honest about knowing I wasn't her since he'd rescued me.

"Why didn't you say so earlier?"

"I didn't want to spook you." Lucas grabbed his Coke from the holder in the dash. His fingers curled around the plastic cup. I tried to forget what those fingers were capable of. But memories crowded my mind, reminding me in high definition detail.

For the first time ever, I regretted my policy of only having sex with someone once. But I lived by my rules and I never broke them.

As I reviewed my situation I wondered...did it really matter if I held back my name? With his contacts he could likely get it on his own. But if I pretended to give something up, Lucas just might be able to help me. I wanted to check out this guy Bella had instant messaged. She didn't usually reveal personal information.

If I wanted his help, I had to give Lucas something. Based on the past fifty-nine hours, I was reasonably sure he wasn't involved in my kidnapping.

"Jamie Hunt."

"What?"

"You heard what I said," I answered. Jeez. The guy bugs me for two days and then isn't paying attention when I finally give in.

"With an I or a Y?" He tapped something into the computer.

"I.E."

"Short for anything?"

"No."

"Middle name?"

"Jean."

He rested his hand on my forearm. And just like the first time he'd touched me, a powerful shiver rippled through me.

I kept my gaze on the road, but I could feel him watching me. He leaned over, his breath warm on my cheek. His lips caressed the soft skin below my ear. "I know how hard that was for you."

"I'm...cautious."

He laughed, warm and rich and pleased. The rumble caused little quivers along the back of my neck. "No kidding? I would have never guessed."

I swatted him away. His actions rattled my brain and I needed to focus. Now that I had given something, he owed me.

"Can you look up a name for me?"

I could feel his gaze upon me. I imagined some censure but I must be wrong. You didn't get something for nothing. He'd worked for the FBI, he knew how the game was played.

The FBI. Cousins. All of the sudden his earlier comment, *I worked with your cousins in Counter-Terrorism*, clicked into focus.

I jerked the van onto the shoulder in a spew of rocks and dust. The headlamps shone over an expanse of empty highway.

I forced the words through gritted teeth and a clenched jaw. "You listened to my conversation." With Carson. My private conversation. The sense of betrayal caught me by surprise.

"Yeah. I did." He took the opportunity to lean over and kiss the curve of my neck.

"Stop trying to distract me with sex."

"This isn't sex." Lucas jabbed the button for the interior lights. The look on his face was pure frustration. "This is a connection."

"Hah."

"Don't you feel it?"

"Not a thing."

"You are *such* a liar."

Of course I was. That was what I did. I lied to everyone. All the time. Sometimes...I even lied to myself.

Lucas curled his palm against my cheek. "Every day is a gift."

I humphed. Every day is an obligation.

His gaze bored into mine, intense and unwanted. "In your line of work, life is a gift. You should know that as well as I do. Connections, intuitive understanding like this doesn't come along every day. Hell, sometimes it doesn't come along in a lifetime. But right here, right now, we have a connection."

I ignored him. I didn't do connections. I didn't have relationships. I did one night stands. I purposely directed my gaze out the window.

"Do you really think that I would have ridden halfway across the country for just anyone?" Lucas turned my face toward him, his eyes gleamed in the moonlight. "We have something here."

I scrunched my eyes shut.

"Something that transcends mere physical attraction. And to ignore that is a criminal waste."

"If this is your way of talking me into bed again, it won't work." Stronger, more persuasive men had tried.

And failed.

Of course, I'd never felt the pull I felt with him. "When did this miraculous connection occur? When you were trying to find your missing boy?"

He was silent for a minute, then said softly, "Somewhere between you sneaking out of the hotel room and trying to take me down in my garage."

I snorted.

"Do you really think that I slept with you to get information about Johnny?"

Yeah. I did. He had a boatload of guilt about this kid. I might not know why but it was clearly there. And as much as he wanted to find the kid, he was afraid of the answers. "Actually, I believe sleeping with me was a pretty good way to delay getting information."

I scored a direct hit with that one. But somehow I didn't feel so great.

"That is exactly what I am talking about."

"What?"

"You know me." He thumped his chest. "Me."

I didn't want to know him. Beyond how he could help me, I didn't want to know him at all. He was a distraction. An inconvenience.

And to want someone like I wanted Lucas was bad. That kind of wanting got people hurt. Even killed.

So I ignored him and pushed away all the longing his words invoked. I couldn't afford to have needs or wants.

I shrugged him away. "How?"

Disconcertingly, he understood right away. "The radio has a two-way deal."

"Show me."

He reached over and pressed the volume knob twice. "A parabolic microphone transmits to a small ear piece." He pulled a tiny listening device out of his shirt pocket.

"What kind of a range does it have?"

"I managed to scavenge through the racks at Bargain Barn while you were on the phone."

Pretty far.

Lucas toyed with the tiny earpiece in his callused fingertips. "Who were you talking to?"

I'd spoken to Carson in code. Lucas clearly had understood part of the conversation since he referred to my cousins. But he shouldn't be able to extract any more information than that.

I pulled the van back on the highway. Toward Maryland. Ending the conversation.

I had to protect my sister. That was my life. My purpose. My obligation.

"I guess that means you aren't going to share with me." He ran a finger down my arm. "When you're ready. I'll be here."

I wanted off of that topic right now. If he'd listened to

my conversation with Carson then he knew I'd asked about Johnny. So it was fair game to ask about Bella's IM guy. "Georgetown chat room. Screen name: Donny Boy."

"We will talk about this again." Then he huffed out a short sigh. "You looking because of your cover? Or yourself?"

I couldn't bring myself to lie to him. Not right then. So I didn't answer. I wasn't going to have Lucas anywhere near Bella.

He sighed. "Let me see what I can come up with."

I should be trying to find some link between myself, the other abductees and the kidnappers. But my hands were tied until I got back to NSA Headquarters in Maryland.

My impatience built.

Whenever I got too impatient, I imagined myself in Bella's life. This new boy was definitely important. I spun a fantasy of Bella as a radiant bride with a white tulle wedding gown while strains of Pachabel's Canon played by a string quartet. She'd have a perfect life. Two children and a house in the country with a porch swing and flowers by the front door.

If he checked out.

We'd been traveling for over twelve hours today. And when I started imagining Bella's perfect future, I knew it was time to take a mental break.

"Got a name."

Excellent. Was he going to share?

"Donald Christian."

That was fast. "What else can you get for me?"

"Basic background check--Initial information, credit problems, address, arrest warrants will come up right away. If you want more detailed information like an asset check it will take a day or so."

He waited. Patiently.

"Detailed, please."

"Initial info, coming right up."

Lucas twisted on the radio. Dave Matthews wailed about the space between wrong and right while Lucas punched away at his laptop.

"Huh."

That didn't sound good.

"We've got a small problem."

Shit. "What?"

"There are two Donald Christians at Georgetown. Do you have any other information?"

"No."

"You want a check on both of them?"

"Yes, please."

"That was easy." He punched some more keys, then said casually, "So you going to let me help you with your other problem?"

"I don't have any problems."

If you didn't count the fact that someone, either within the government or with covert government backing, had kidnapped me and planned to shoot me up with mind altering drugs.

"I'll offer you my take on the situation," he said calmly. "Your abductors were Feds."

By my count, I'd most likely been tracked by at least three separate agencies. The agency who nabbed me originally, no clear indication of which one. Then the DEA dropped me off in Seattle.

And the guys in the bus station were likely local Secret Service. It made sense. Their office was on the Embarcadero just a few blocks away.

That kind of multiple agency, tag team surveillance took

high level coordination. And approval. The only pair in the whole equation who didn't fit were the man and woman in the warehouse. They'd let me escape far too easily.

"With access to the frequency of your personal homing beacon."

Yeah, yeah. Okay, so I definitely had problems. Nothing I couldn't handle.

"I guess we aren't going to talk about this," Lucas said. "You want me to drive?"

"Not yet." I wouldn't sleep now. Too many questions. "Why don't you get some more rest."

I didn't want him looking at me, probing, testing for weakness. Showing me we did have some sort of connection. That he really could pick up on my thoughts, my emotions. Me.

"I'm pretty much wired." He took another sip of Coke, then started messing with his computer again. "Can I borrow your phone, Sarah? I want to check messages at my office."

"Sure." I tossed him the cell phone. His request intrigued me. "Is it just you?"

"Yeah."

A loner. Like me.

"How do you do surveillance?"

"If I need to, I contract out with another friend of mine. Most of my cases are internet tracing."

"Really?"

"I can work from anywhere. And I get most cases through referrals."

"So, you like it?"

"Pays well."

"Beats a government salary, huh?"

"Yeah." But his voice had a closed off sound. Hidden

pain.

Another thought occurred to me. If he did most of his work on the computer..."Why the van?"

He shrugged. "It's a toy."

Men and their toys?

"So is internet searches what you're working on now?"

"I've closed out most of my current cases. It usually only takes a few hours to a day to trace these back to their source."

"You have a lot in the pipeline?" I wanted to get a handle on how he had the time to drive to the East Coast-- unless that was his intent all along.

"No."

I should try and finesse the answer but I didn't think that would work with Lucas. "Did you plan this trip?"

"Well--"

I waited, cruising along the mountains of Wyoming. I wasn't sure but I thought he was trying to figure out how to tell me something I didn't want to hear.

"I knew this wasn't a half day fix."

"Did you consciously clear your schedule?"

"The answer to your questions are...sort of and no." He stopped punching numbers into the cell phone and shifted to face me. "I had hoped finding Johnny wasn't going to be as difficult as I imagined."

"You were wrong?"

He blew out a breath. "Yeah."

"Have you checked out the kid's associates?"

"His mother didn't have any last names."

"None?"

"Nope." He hesitated. "I'm running lists of first names from his school and the gym he works out at but it's a slow process."

"Anything at his home?"

"His room was clean." He rubbed a hand over his face, his fingers rasping along the dark blond stubble. "Too clean."

"It had been wiped?"

"No incriminating scraps of paper. His laptop was gone. His desktop computer was too clean. Someone had obviously taken the time to go in and delete anything that could be traced back to them."

"It could have been Johnny."

"I thought of that but his mother thought someone had been in the house *after* Johnny had his accident."

"Huh." It sounded slick. Too slick.

"These guys are organized and efficient." He dialed. "That's why when Staci Grant started making purchases and being seen, I jumped on a plane. Fast."

Which really did explain how we'd hooked up.

Lucas said, "I need to see Staci Grant's file on Johnny Wishbone."

"I promise you. I did not get that boy out of the hospital."

"I know that."

"But we need to figure out who did," I said.

"Yeah."

"Your only lead is Staci Grant?" The woman I'd been impersonating.

"Staci Grant, a dead woman," he said intently.

Definitely dead. She'd been decapitated. "According to the reports."

"So someone out there is impersonating Staci Grant."

"More than someone." I thought of myself. "Two someones."

# CHAPTER 14

*I*'d slept like the dead.

Lucas had let me sleep far longer than I'd asked. Again.

I couldn't remember the last time I'd slept that hard and the cot in the van was far from comfortable. I refused to acknowledge that I'd felt safe in his company.

Absolutely refused.

I'd had sleep deprivation training and I'd still hit a wall last night. "What is the deal with you?" I sat up in the cot and glared at the back of his head. "Don't you ever sleep?"

"I need very little sleep. Always been this way." He bit into some sort of biscuit with egg and sausage. It smelled fantastic.

We were parked at a truck stop somewhere in Nebraska. Flat plains and acres of wheat fields gave way to a morning sky and wide open space.

"Most of the time it's a good thing." Lucas fell silent.

I knew what he meant. Usually, I could take or leave sleep. Sometimes staying awake gave you too much time to think. About the decisions, the mistakes. In the dead of night, when silence surrounded and darkness crept in, doubts, regrets and hindsight could make you question every moment in your life.

Fortunately, the dawn came every day without fail.

As the sun climbed over the road, wisps of rose and sunshine yellow bled into an expanse of blue, and possibilities lived.

Possibilities for peace, possibilities for hope, possibilities that today would be different.

"Yeah." I crawled up into the passenger seat. Jeez, I wanted a shower. "How about we stay at this truck stop and grab a quick shower?"

"I'm a grown up. I only camp if I have to." He grinned, with a wicked light in his eye. "How about a nice motel with real plumbing and a soft bed."

I didn't want to waste the time.

"Four hours." He looked at me steadily over the edge of his breakfast.

Did I want to be trapped in a hotel room with him? No. Absolutely not. On the other hand, maybe I could use his software while he slept.

"Only if you let me use your laptop."

I grabbed the biscuit from his hand and took a healthy bite, chewing slowly, practically daring him to say no. "Deal?"

He peeled my fingers from the biscuit. "Deal."

In twenty minutes, we had checked in, parked around back, and Lucas had crashed on the single Queen-sized bed.

It wasn't easy to ignore the sleeping man. He lay sprawled on his stomach across a hideous bedspread in a faded, circa 1970, avocado and orange motif.

Lucas clutched a puffy pillow under his head, his biceps rippled against the taut t-shirt, his back muscles clearly defined by the pull of the thin cotton. A peep show of skin where the shirt had come free of his jeans at the base of his spine, taunted me.

He didn't snore exactly. The sound was more of a soft exhale. His back rose and fell in a slow, easy rhythm which I found extremely erotic.

I remembered the last hotel room we'd shared with exquisite clarity and I found the similarity disconcerting.

Memories of his body sliding into mine, the thick, hard length of him, the rub of his chest hair against my breasts, and the solid muscle of his thighs between mine.

I rubbed my hands over my arms and ignored the fact that my body tingled in places better left alone. If he awoke and exerted any kind of coercion right now, resistance would be impossible.

Because he was right. We have a connection. I didn't want anything to do with it, but my wishes didn't make the feeling go away.

The best I could do was ignore the intense pull.

The bedside clock flipped and I realized I'd wasted a chunk of time, staring, remembering. I focused on the laptop and signed on to my storage account.

Get your head back in this mission.

From the intel I'd been given, six agents had been kidnapped. I had backgrounds but no names. No obvious links in their service records. They had been stationed all over the world, specialized in different areas. And while there might be overlap between one or two, nothing jumped out at first glance.

Men and women.

No major links between training classes.

No childhood background similarities. There had been a

fair amount of public service in the family history of some abductees. But not all.

I couldn't see any obvious link. But until I got back to Crypto City and went into the files there, I was stalled.

I'd been told my mission was to identify and capture the kidnappers. But perhaps my mission had just been to test the information network of whoever was behind the kidnapping. But then, why lie to me?

I opened the files stolen from the woman, Susan, in the warehouse and studied the encryption again. Something familiar nagged at me. I'd seen this code before. I kept trying to break into the encryption. I was missing a key link, which was especially frustrating as I knew I'd seen this code before.

My heart, my brain iced as I looked at the commands.

The NSA had their own code writers and the pattern was very distinctive. This file code was similar to an encrypted file I'd played around with at the office. That meant, either someone had broken the encryption program or someone in the NSA was actually behind the kidnappings. But what would be the point in that?

My mission was VRK, Very Restricted Knowledge, the highest clearance possible. Which meant only a few key people had access to the information.

The President. The National Security Advisor. The Director of Homeland Security. The Director of the NSA. Carson. And me.

I'd been involved in several highly classified missions in the last year. The information stored in my brain would be top secret for years if Congress had their way. So...what was specific about my current mission?

The man at the warehouse had asked about being compromised, but that wasn't a danger. As long as no one knew about Bella, nothing would convince me betray my country.

Bella.

The need to check on her again mushroomed.

I was being irrational, but worry spread like a cancer feeding on healthy tissue. Something was out of whack.

I found Bella in her favorite chat room. Donald was there as well. Her sudden connection with him had me worried, since I didn't know enough about him. He might be a perfectly nice kid.

DonnyBoy: How'd you do on the test?

Bella: Got an A. Advanced Calculus is my best subject.

DonnyBoy: Wow. Maybe you could help me sometime. I have a really hard time with math.

Bella: Sure. What are you up to today?

DonnyBoy: I'm meeting some friends at a coffeehouse. Wanna come?

Bella: Thanks but I've got to study for my English exam.

DonnyBoy: You sure do study a lot.

Bella: I need to do good.

I dropped the thread of their conversation and started tracing his email address back to its source. There must be footprints to lead me back to his server and computer which would lead to the right Donald Christian.

Then maybe I would have answers.

Like who the hell he was and what he was doing with my baby sister.

"Who's Bella?" Lucas's rumbling voice came from behind me.

Only years of training held me immobile.

My throat constricted, muscles seizing like a boa tightening for the kill. I swallowed several times before I could answer.

"Just some girl Donald Christian is hitting on."

I couldn't look at him, terrified he'd see the fear in my eyes. No one knew about Bella. No one except Carson.

Unless I'd been compromised when they'd drugged me.

"Since you're awake, why don't you get in the shower." Deliberately, I leaned back against his arm, bringing my cleavage into the range of his gaze. I went for provocative on purpose, trying to deflect his attention away from Bella.

But he ignored the move.

"In a sec." He leaned over to scrawl Bella's email address on the hotel stationary. "We should check her out."

"Not necessary." I minimized the screen with a casual stroke of my finger.

"Can't hurt."

But it could. Somehow I would have to get rid of that information without making it look obvious.

"Shower?" I had to get him away from the subject of Bella and I would use any means. I toyed with the neckline of my t-shirt, running a finger along the fairly deep V.

His gaze dropped to my breasts. And away from the computer. Just like I'd wanted.

My nipples tightened in response. Which I definitely didn't want.

Jeez, he affected me.

Lucas shifted, propped against the fake wood desk and raised one brow lazily. "You offering?"

Tempting. Too tempting.

I remembered the feeling of rightness I'd found in his embrace...and the way I'd run from it.

He leaned over bringing his face even with mine. Tension arced between us, hotter than the Indian Summer sun rippling off the hotel parking lot. I couldn't tear my gaze away from the promise of heat and heaven in his gunmetal eyes.

I saw the kiss coming, didn't stop him.

Nothing was going to happen. I had strict rules. I'd never broken them and I wasn't about to start now. But I wanted this kiss.

I craved his touch in ways far too needy. For one moment, I allowed him entrance.

For all the heat in his gaze, the touch of his lips against mine was soft and somehow pure. He didn't plunder. He tasted, sipped at my mouth.

He trailed his fingers along my nape and then cupped my neck. Sensation tingled. His other hand held my chin, as if he knew I would back away.

Our breath mingled. He nibbled my lips with a tenderness somehow more shocking because I could break his hold, but hadn't.

This was a kiss of intimacy, not passion. Passion simmered below the surface, but this embrace wasn't the wild coupling we'd indulged in before.

I clenched my hands into fists. The temptation to reach out and touch him a hunger within me. A hunger I needed to deny.

I broke away and cleared my throat.

"I'll take that as a no." His voice wasn't quite steady.

"You take the shower first."

"Sure." He walked to the bathroom, unbuttoning his jeans as he went.

I breathed deeply, held the breath in, waiting.

"Jamie."

I jerked my gaze back to Lucas as he stood silhouetted in the bathroom doorway.

"Yeah?"

"I'm not going away." He closed the door with a secret smile.

While Lucas took a shower, I placed another cell call to Barb.

"'Lo." Her voice was raspy. Unless I was mistaken, she'd been mostly asleep.

It was nine o'clock in the morning California time. "Up and at 'em."

"Go to hell."

"You struck me as an early to bed, early to rise kind of girl."

Her jaw popped as she yawned in my ear. "Just got to bed."

"Boyfriend keeping you up?"

"I wish."

I suddenly realized I might have put my foot in that one. She'd made it clear that she'd be happy to have Lucas but he wasn't biting.

"Give me a minute."

I waited impatiently. "Any luck?"

"Yes. And no."

Again with the yes, no. "Spill."

"Did you help Lucas?"

I thought back to my conversation with Carson. "I'm using all the resources I have to help him."

"Let me talk to him."

Oops. This probably wouldn't go over well either. "He's...ah, in the shower."

There was silence on the other end, then she spoke tightly, "It seems to be some sort of...mood or behavior influencing drug that possibly affects the brain. I've never seen anything exactly like it."

Mood or behavior influencing drug. I tensed.
"Like LSD?"

"Lysergic Acid Diethylamide is mood altering, frequently inducing strong mood swings and paranoia. The effects of a single dose usually last around twelve hours. This is different. It has an element that may change at the cellular level."

"What does that mean?" I listened to the running water and waited.

"It means...I don't know." There was frustration in her voice. "It looks similar to some gene therapy drugs I've seen."

"Give me more."

"Have you ever heard of the Human Genome Project?"

"Pretend like I haven't."

"The Project mapped the entire DNA sequence of humans, identifying and classifying which genes influenced or directed all aspects of human function."

"So...."

"One of the things discovered was that the body has ways to turn on and off cell function. If a cell is methylated it will block certain functions."

"Go on."

"With recent gene therapy if compounds are injected into the body using nanotechnology it can actually reverse or change how the body and brain react to stimulus."

"What cells are being changed?" I rubbed the back of my neck. If cells were being changed, to what purpose? Did the changes wear off like an...aspirin or were they permanent? "Can you be more specific?"

"I need more time," Barb snapped. "I think I've got an idea but I need to do more research."

I calculated how long we had left on the road. One day. We could make Maryland in the next twenty four hours.

"Okay. I'll call tomorrow." I said goodbye and hung up.

Tomorrow I could get to Crypto City and Carson could answer my questions about this increasingly complex series of events.

The shower shut off.

And I could finally be rid of Lucas Goodman.

I ignored the fact that the idea of getting rid of Lucas wasn't as appealing or comforting as it should be.

CHAPTER 15

We were finally back home.

We'd hit the Beltway about an hour ago, right in the early afternoon, and traffic was still heavy.

"So...where should I drop you?" I asked casually.

"Right where you're going, honey."

Too much to hope he'd go to a hotel. I hadn't figured he'd fall for it, but it was worth a try.

"I really don't think that's a good idea."

"And I really don't care." He rubbed at his face, looking as tired as I felt.

I didn't have any more time to waste on his guy. "What if I promise to get you the information?"

"Nope."

I'd known he would push. I'd do the same. "Let me see what I can find out." I called Carson at the office but there was no answer. Carson updated his voice mail hourly if he was in the office or in a meeting. When he didn't have contact details it meant he was out of the office.

"My contact seems to be out of pocket right now." I fiddled with the radio and mentally calculated another way

129

to get rid of him. "Why don't I drop you at a hotel and call you on your cell when I've got the information you want?"

"You are not out of my sight until I get the information about Johnny."

I gave up for the moment. "Fine. Let's go." We'd check out Staci Grant's house, see if we could find files, anything there. I gave him detailed instructions to her townhouse in Alexandria.

When he pulled off at the exit where we had originally hooked up, I turned my head sharply. What was he doing?

"A little different than last time." He grinned, then shook his head. "Relax. I just want to see if the car you were driving is still there."

Good point.

I really must be tired. As we pulled into the liquor store where I'd been kidnapped, I glanced cautiously out the window and then checked the rear view mirror before getting out of the van.

"No signs of the abduction."

I hadn't really expected any. But no sign of Staci Grant's Lexus either.

"Bummer about the car," he said.

For a moment, I mourned the loss of the truly fine vehicle. "Yeah."

Without any further words, we got back in the van. I deliberately didn't look toward the hotel. The memories of our encounter in that room already occupied too much of my thoughts.

When we arrived at Staci's, Lucas circled the block, looking for parking.

The neighborhood was quiet, quaint and picturesque. The cobblestone street was lined with established trees, old curbs, and pristine rowhouses. Big urns overflowing with fall flowers perched on clean porch stoops.

Nothing seemed out of place or unusual. The very normalness was somewhat disconcerting. Nothing bad ever happened in a neighborhood like this.

"I don't want to be too far away from the van."

Finally Lucas found a space off the alley behind her townhouse. By silent agreement, we maintained surveillance for half an hour before moving in. No one seemed out of place. No one seemed to be watching the house.

Her backyard was a long narrow strip of grass edged with a picket fence and freshly-planted fall flowers. Mums, maybe?

As I got out of the van, it struck me again that someone had gone to an awful lot of trouble to keep up Staci Grant's life.

"Doesn't look like she's been dead for seven weeks," Lucas murmured in my ear.

His hot breath stroked my neck. I ignored the shiver of awareness rippling through me.

We strode down the brick path toward the back steps.

A Weber grill sat near steps leading down to a basement entrance. Adorned with hanging pots of geraniums and droopy trailing greenery, an iron railing edged the stairway down.

The backdoor had a screen, but the kitchen window was free of curtains. A striped blue and white awning hung suspended over the dining room window. Through the lace curtains, a warm light promised us welcome.

A surreal quality shrouded the house, as if someone had stepped out to the store or gone for an afternoon walk. Not been dead and gone for almost two months.

It was a very creepy feeling.

I'd shadowed Staci's life but I hadn't stayed in her house. So when we got to the door, I realized…"No keys."

"Look at this place," Lucas whispered. "There's probably a key under the mat."

I lifted the edge of a woven flax mat with pictures of flowers printed on it. No key.

But he was right. This was the kind of place where someone would hide a key. We spread out. I tilted a giant cobalt pot by the steps while Lucas edged his fingers around the rims of the hanging pots.

"Pay dirt." He pulled grimy fingers and a key out of the middle pot.

Within minutes, we were inside. A house alarm bleeped quietly in the warm glow of the dining room light.

Lucas pulled on a pair of gloves and rubbed away his prints from the key. I pulled on a pair of latex gloves I'd lifted from Lucas's van, then punched the security code I'd been given into the pad.

"Good thing you know the code."

"Yeah." I'd been given the code in my briefing before I assumed her identity.

Staci Grant was supposed to have been kidnapped. Instead I had been kidnapped. Lucas was searching for information in relation to his missing kid who was checked out of the hospital by Staci. Her name linked the events of the last few days.

If anyone came after us, the basement would be their most likely point of entry. "I'll take the basement. Keep your ears open."

"Wait." Lucas pulled his weapon from the holster clipped to his belt loop.

No one was here. I could feel the emptiness in air that should be stale but was scented with cinnamon and coffee.

However, if he wanted to play macho man, I'd sit back and enjoy the show. He turned the knob slowly. The muscles in his arm bunched as he tried to pull the basement door open.

I licked my lips, watching the play of muscle in the dim light. The man really did have fine arms. As he stepped back, my gaze shifted to the seat of his jeans. He had a world class ass as well.

"Locked."

"Hmm." No flower pots around. I knocked on the door lightly. Reinforced steel.

"Steel door. And look at this lock." Lucas tucked his weapon back in his holster and bent down to look at the shiny, *new* lock. "This is state of the art."

I tried to keep my eyes on the lock, but once again I was distracted by the curve of his butt.

Extremely unprofessional.

The wheeze of a screen door snapped my focus back.

He straightened, but I was already relaxing.

"Neighbor," I said quietly. I could see a woman and hear children tumbling into the yard to the left.

He nodded. "Let's stay together."

"Upstairs."

If there was that much overt security on the basement door, it was a decoy. Nothing important would be down there. The logical conclusion was Staci Grant's legitimate files for the University were down there. We could check on that last.

The dining room was decorated with an antique table and chairs. The chairs had lion claws for feet and gracefully curved arms. A giant breakfront with ornately carved lion's heads supported a massive marble top against the far wall.

Three foot tall silver candle holders flanked the ends of the sideboard.

No one would store critical information in this room. It was too open. Too available and too easy for the world, or at least neighbors, to see in.

"We're going to be awhile."

"Yep."

We headed to the staircase taking care to avoid the plate glass window in the front living room. I eyed the furnishings for potential hiding places.

She had original artwork on the walls. A beautiful oil painting of a mosque in dark yellow hues hung over a rich cordoba leather sofa. Two wing chairs in butter flanked a delicate end table. A plasma television hung in the far corner with state of the art electronics, DVD, speakers and a sub woofer huddled below the screen like cubs around a mama bear.

I envied the slick entertainment system. Mine was functional but utilitarian.

Polished wood floors gleamed beneath an antique Persian carpet. A deep blue burkha, the traditional dress of Muslim women, was mounted and framed in mahogany.

"No obvious hiding places here." Lucas bent and ran his hand under the leather sofa. "Unless she had files sewn into the stuffing of the sofa or chairs, this room is a bust."

The DVD and CD collection in the cabinet would take a few hours to go through. On the way out, I'd pick them up. They could be viewed at my apartment.

I crept up the stairs behind Lucas. At the top, I assessed the layout.

Two bedrooms. One bath, obviously renovated.

Lucas stood in the doorway and whistled. "Nice room."

Staci had expanded the bath most likely using all of a

large bedroom to do it. A decadent Jacuzzi tub dominated the room.

He gestured to the Travertine floor. "Marble costs a small fortune."

Battered metal pots, full of ferns and orchids, clustered on the two foot ledge behind the tub.

Sunlight poured in through a tube skylight, reflecting off an ornate scrollwork mirror. A small linen closet held towels, sweet smelling bath salts and a horde of cosmetics.

I picked up a bottle of lotion, unscrewed the cap, and sniffed. Gardenia.

"There won't be anything regarding Johnny in this room." Lucas conveniently reminded me of the reason he was here.

He wasn't my partner. He wasn't my friend. He brushed by me, his body rubbing against mine. I forcibly reminded myself, he couldn't be my lover again, either.

The sooner I got rid of Lucas the better off I would be. "I'll keep a lookout," I said brusquely.

There were two bedrooms, one master and an office complete with a computer set-up on elaborate mahogany office furniture. Crown molding and framed maps of the World decorated the walls. Bookshelves held books on diverse subjects with a large section devoted to Middle Eastern studies. Not surprisingly.

Lucas came into the room. "In plain sight. Her files have got to be somewhere."

"Maybe." This woman was sophisticated and world-traveled. I needed to get a better sense of Staci Grant but not in the same room as Lucas.

"I'll take the master bedroom."

Shades upon shades of yellow with touches of purple and burgundy colored the walls, the carpet, the bed. Rich velvet pillows mounded at the base of the intricately carved wood headboard. Tapestries of beautiful scenes from the desert to the sea graced the walls.

And on the foot of the bed, finally, was my clue.

The pattern of quilt was plain but the materials ranged from the finest shimmering silk to jewel-studded velvet. Layer upon layer of color and richness all sewn into an exquisite package.

This was the key to Staci Grant.

Simplicity hidden in extravagance.

Where would she hide her private files? I had no doubt Lucas would find files in the office. But I didn't think they'd have any useful information for him or me.

I looked in the mirror hanging above the bed. Files closest to her heart and mind.

Under the bed? I looked. No trapdoor.

I opened the closet door, and flipped on the light switch. Rack upon rack of simple clothes in rich fabrics crowded the room. Against the opposite wall, wainscoting detail was mostly hidden beneath wall-mounted shoe racks.

I went back to the bedroom, turning out the light and closing the door softly. But as I stared at the intricate tapestry on the far wall, my mind calculated square footage and angles.

Even with the closet, there was room between the walls.

I lifted the tapestry above the bed. Nothing. A television sat on a chest across from the bed beneath another tapestry. As I gazed at it, I knew.

Going to the bedside table, I found a remote control. The first button turned on the television.

The second, a stereo.

When I pressed the two buttons together, I heard a panel slide somewhere in the closet.

Bingo.

I set the remote back on the table, and glanced out the window just in time to see two garbage men coming up the sunlit brick path.

We had trouble.

# CHAPTER 16

"*L*ucas?" I called softly.

"Yeah."

"Pack it up." I checked the room making sure it looked undisturbed. "And get in here fast."

"On it."

He hustled into the bedroom as the security alarm dinged. I'd been right. Staci Grant wasn't getting special garbage treatment.

I yanked him inside the closet. "I pressed some buttons on the t.v. remote and heard something slide open. There's got to be a door in here somewhere."

Lucas fumbled through the clothes feeling for a door or open space. I pushed at the wall with the shoe rack. Nothing. But when I tugged on the rack, the entire panel swung forward exposing an opening.

"They're almost up the stairs."

"Yeah." We stepped inside, pulled the shoe rack back and it clicked back into place, just as we heard footsteps in the hallway.

Narrow stairs went up. Attic room. I couldn't wait to get

into her stuff.

"Too risky." The brush of his breath tickled my ear.

I nodded.

We had to stay right there in a space designed for one person. My shoulder blades pressed against his chest and my bottom snugged against his hips. And a part of him I knew I'd never see again.

Apparently his body hadn't gotten the memo. The hard ridge of his erection rubbed against my butt. Heat steamed through me. My nipples pebbled annoyingly.

"Got any discovery fantasies I can help you with?"

I could hear the laughter in his quiet whisper, but had no safe way to retaliate because the men entered the master bedroom, arguing loudly.

Hopefully, the garbage detail didn't know about the secret room.

"We should have never gone to lunch together," the first guy said disgustedly. "They're long gone."

"Maybe not."

"House feels empty." He flipped on the television. "We shoulda just double parked when the alarm went off."

"Quit bitching." The man with the gruff voice opened the closet door.

If the guy in the bedroom kept pressing buttons, the guy in the closet was going to get quite a surprise.

Drawers rolled open. "Get a load of this chick's lingerie." He was literally a wall away from us.

Lucas shifted bringing his left hand up my side and around to press on my stomach.

Dammit, this wasn't the time to be copping a feel.

He moved again, and his lips brushed my cheek. What the hell was he thinking?

"Unless someone is hiding in that drawer, cut it out."

Lucas tensed. That was when I felt it. He'd pulled his weapon out of his holster. He'd only been trying to protect me...us.

"Holy Jesus. Is that missing the crotch?"

"Yeah." The first guy whistled and slammed the drawer shut. "Let's run a quick check up here. But my guess is the basement. That's where they'd be. It's the only logical place. What with the lock on the door and all."

"Did you just stuff those panties in your pocket?"

"Guy's got to have some excitement in his life."

"No way is your wife putting those on."

"Who's talking about my wife?"

Their voices faded as they thumped down the stairs. But Lucas and I were stuck. We were going to have to stay here until they left.

I should be able to relax now. Instead I got more tense. He pressed against me again. Now I knew he was putting his weapon away. But God, as his erection prodded into me, all the blood rushed from my head.

I leaned forward trying to get away from him, my torso pressed against the wall, my cheek turned away from the sliding door.

"You feel incredible." His breath tickled the back of my neck. He'd leaned forward to whisper in my ear.

I knew a dozen defensive moves to make him crumple over and puke his guts out. But I didn't dare try one, just in case the sound carried down the stairs. I jabbed my elbow into his stomach, not hard, just hard enough to get his attention. Instead of the soft oomph I expected, I hit solid muscle. He'd anticipated my reaction.

He moved his hands around to cup my elbows, then leaned into me further. "You should have told me you wanted to play," he murmured.

Before I could retaliate, his lips touched mine at the corner.

It was a butterfly touch. The tip of his tongue traced my upper lip. Then he pressed soft, tender kisses along my jaw. The little nip of his teeth on the sensitive lobe of my ear shivered through me.

The sensation was sweet. And erotic.

His fingertips trailed up and down my forearms. Goose bumps rose on my flesh as the gentle touch tingled through me.

I couldn't move. In that moment, I didn't want to.

He had to stop. I couldn't afford the weakness flowing through me. "What do you think you are doing?" I whispered harshly.

"Passing time?" The lilt in his voice gave him away. He was laughing. Again. His thumbs brushed agonizingly close to the fullness of my breasts.

"You're breaking my rule."

He cupped his hands around my breasts, fingers playing with my nipples. "Rules were made to be broken."

I inhaled sharply. The scent of him surrounded me, embraced me. "No."

His hands slid down my abdomen. Somehow he knew exactly where to press his fingertips against the flat plane of my stomach. He stopped just short of the low waistband on my hips. "No?"

"No more."

With a sigh, he slid his hands up to rest against my rib cage. Even that innocuous touch aroused me.

"What is your rule?"

"Once." I gritted the word out.

"Once what?" His tongue licked at the curve between my shoulder and neck.

"I only have sex with someone one time."

He was silent for so long I thought he was going to let it drop.

"Ever broken it?"

"No."

His hands slid from my body. "Ever wanted to?"

I didn't answer. I had never even thought about it, until Lucas.

The air was warm, heavy with the scent of arousal. Ripe sensuality hung in the tiny space. With every breath, I remembered the feel of him possessing my body.

"Right," Lucas said, nodding his head toward the attic steps. "You notice anything?"

He shifted gears quickly. Damn him.

I should be pleased. He did as I asked. But perversely, his compliance annoyed me. Was it so easy for him to stop? Was it all just a game? How could he get into my head in such a short time? Well, I wouldn't show it. I'd focus on here and now.

I stared at the dark wood steps lined with an ancient Persian runner. Ignoring the quality of the carpet, I looked more closely at the wood treads. They were spotless. Huh.

"No dust."

"Yeah." He leaned against the other wall, away from me.

I hated that I missed his warmth. Damn him.

"Someone is going to a lot of trouble to keep up this place."

Very strange. Impatience built. I wanted to see what was

at the top of those steps. But we had to wait at least another half hour.

"Maybe Staci is still alive." If that were the case it was going to be interesting to explain to her why we were in a clinch in her secret room. And if she was still alive, why was the NSA having me impersonate her...and why would they lie to me? "Interesting scenario."

"I know Staci Grant is dead," Lucas said.

"Maybe it wasn't her."

"I saw the report from the prison where she was captured." His voice was grim. "Supposedly there were pictures...her head was missing."

I wouldn't ask how he'd seen something that had to be highly classified. And yeah, I'd seen the same report. "Her head was missing—"

"Tatoo. A distinctive one," he replied shortly.

"Ever heard of Photoshop? All I'm saying is we can't be sure." I argued. But we had more pressing problems. "So who would be keeping up this place?"

"CIA maybe." He huffed out a strong breath, the warmth hitting the back of my neck, sending a shiver through me. I knew he wasn't trying to be sexual. Damn him. He was just frustrated.

"Why'd they pick you to impersonate her?"

I had assumed Carson had chosen me because Staci and I had similar builds and I had Arabic skills. I was decent at reading fusHaa, written Modern Standard Arabic. I did much better with Romance languages but I could speak Educated Spoken Arabic albeit very rudimentarily.

A control panel bleeped at the top of the steps, the light glowing red after the intruders reset the alarm. Finally, the slam of the front door reverberated through the house. We could move. I'm not sure who shot up the narrow attic stairs faster. Me or Lucas.

Good. So he wasn't as indifferent as he pretended.

At the top of the steps, I paused and Lucas jostled me, pushing me further into the twenty by thirty foot room.

"Don't turn on the lights yet," I cautioned. The boys from the bedroom could still be watching outside.

Then I noticed the leaded glass circle window, visible from the street, had been blacked out. No light would seep through.

I flipped on the light. In one corner was a state of the art computer set-up. No visible internet connection. She wouldn't use wireless. Too insecure. So Staci Grant didn't have internet access up here.

Probable. If she wanted a totally secure, secret system.

I'd save the computer for last. I prowled the room, quickly surveying the contents. Woven tapestries in varying hues, hanging by simple wood rods, adorned the walls.

At the end opposite the stairs was a ten by ten mat. A rack with weights and sparring equipment butted against the wall. A stack of white towels sat on a weight bench.

I walked over to the towels, picked one up, and inhaled slowly. No scented detergent, but they didn't smell musty either. They smelled...clean.

"Someone comes here regularly," Lucas said from right behind me.

I jumped, inside. "Yeah." Outwardly calm, I set the towel down precisely on top of the others and turned. "Let's get started."

Before they came back.

We both crossed to the desk and I turned on the computer. I entered the same password as her house alarm doubting it would work. To my surprise—the computer brought up a series of icons.

Afghanistan.
Africa.
Indonesia.
Pakistan.
U.S.

# CHAPTER 17

The file icons listed were known countries with terrorist camps. The numeric file, I had no idea.

I didn't want to get any more involved in his search for John Wishbone, but Staci and Johnny were linked somehow. So I had to ask. "Would Johnny Wishbone have gone to work for an Islamic Jihad group?"

Lucas was grim-faced and silent. "I don't know."

It seemed improbable for the son of a 9/11 victim. But it also seemed unlikely Staci would identify John as a possible recruit for a group like that.

He yanked open the file drawer and started flipping through file folders coded with Arabic names. He opened one file at random, scanned the contents and then replaced it quickly. I tried to focus on my own information gathering, but I couldn't help but notice his morose countenance.

I clicked on the United States icon.

A list of files with both letters and numbers came up. Initials and dates possibly. But after twenty minutes of clicking on file names I realized while the password might get me into her computer, it didn't grant access to any coded or sensitive information.

"Any luck?"

He closed a file folder slowly. "Not exactly."

"This could take years."

Fortunately, Staci Grant was meticulously neat and ordered. In the drawer to the right of the keyboard, an organizer separated pens, clips, scissors, tape and other office supplies. In a matter of minutes, I copied the files on the hard drive to a large capacity flash key.

"Let's get out of here."

"Yeah."

I shut down the computer. Before I could reach for the flash key, Lucas had wiggled the device free and tucked it into his jeans pocket.

We closed up the attic, reset the remote panel. Peering out the office window, I saw a nondescript sedan with two men inside, facing the front of the townhouse. "Still there."

"Can't trip the alarm." Lucas eased cautiously down the narrow stairs, with me following.

The men in the sedan obviously had a link to the alarm system. After closing the hidden access door, we went into the master bedroom. I checked the windows. "Sensors here."

"How does the person keeping up her place get in and out?" Lucas murmured.

I dug through the bedside table. A stash of magnets and double stick tape were in the second drawer. I held them up.

"There's a possibility," Lucas said thoughtfully.

"Yeah." I taped the magnet near the wireless alarm sensor. "Get ready to run if this doesn't work."

Lucas nodded. "Meet back at the van."

Circumventing her alarm system was ridiculously easy. I

wondered why the items were in Staci's drawer. Had she put the low-tech devices there before she died? Had she thought someone was monitoring her?

I raised the window slowly. Lucas eased out onto the striped awning protecting the dining room window and slid down the heavy canvas. I climbed out, closed the window and slid after him.

So far, so good. No shouts. No gunfire.

I dropped to the brick patio and crouched. The tall bushes hid us from the mother and toddlers playing in the yard next door.

As we crept toward the van, I saw it.

Staci Grant's car.

The late afternoon sunshine gleamed off the polished chrome of her Lexus, parked in a visitor spot in the alley. My gut cramped at the innocuous sight of her car, far away from where it had been abandoned after I'd been kidnapped.

Someone had brought the car back.

I should check the car and see if my missing weapon and badge were there. Too risky. I would have to come back later.

My gaze shot to Lucas, still creeping toward the van. He hadn't noticed the car.

As I reached the van, he smiled at me, a smug twist of his lips. "Where to?"

Just because we'd found her files didn't mean he'd found his information. Instead of frustration or annoyance, I was curiously relieved. I wasn't getting rid of him yet.

Where to? There was only one place left to go.

Home.

CHAPTER 18

I refused to think about the difference between my apartment and Staci Grant's home.

I never stayed in one place very long. I'd been in my current apartment complex for about five months. Almost time to move.

No roots. No ties. No way to connect me with any specific place or person. My mail was diverted multiple times before going to a post office box. The utilities were included in my rent and I paid every month in cash.

I didn't even keep the NSA current on where I lived. I file change of address paperwork about five months after I move in and right before I move out. In fact, I'd just sent the form in last week to change to my current address. Knowing the bureaucracy of the agency, the change should go thru when I was already at my next place.

Lucas pulled the van to the curb adjacent to the parking lot of the complex, then gestured to the boxy, nondescript building. "Your place?"

"Yeah." I knew he'd give his opinion and it wouldn't be good.

149

"Nothing significant around, completely indistinguishable. This complex could be in twenty different cities." He shook his head. I tried not to mind. It was perfect for my needs. Quiet and impersonal.

"I used to live in a place like this."

I thought about his apartment in San Francisco, the neighborhood, the neighbors, their interest in him, and shuddered. I had no contact with my neighbors. They probably wouldn't recognize me in a line up, which suited me just fine.

Before getting out of the van, I stretched and watched for any off behavior. Lucas stared out the window. "See anything suspicious?"

I didn't.

The parking lot, mainly deserted, was separated into sections by small patches of grass. A cement walkway bordered with some moldable shrub led to the building's entrance. Most of the tenants worked during the day, some traveled and were gone for extended periods.

"Nope."

"Me either." He twitched. "Can't tell if I'm just jumpy or if my skills are rusty."

I popped open the door of the van and waited. If anyone were going to strike, now would be the time. But there was no suspicious activity. No one sat in a car alone or hovered in the bland lobby. Nothing out of place or out of the ordinary.

Slowly, I breathed a sigh of relief. Of course, it was short-lived. "No keys."

I hadn't thought about that problem until I got here. I definitely didn't have a key stashed in a flower pot. I had no I.D. which was going to cause me no end of grief tomorrow when I tried to get into NSA headquarters. Just the thought of the paperwork I'd have to endure brought my simmering headache to a full roar. Red-badged.

There was no worse humiliation as an NSA employee.

"No problem." He opened up the back of the van and pulled out lock picks. The man certainly was prepared.

We moved cautiously, taking the steps up to the second floor. But no one lurked nearby.

"You want to use them?" He gallantly offered, but I'd rather see what he could do.

"Go ahead."

He made short work of my locks. With the same equipment, I might have gotten inside even faster, but not much.

After the lock clicked open, we assumed positions on either side of the door. I went low while he went high. I didn't want to notice the synchronicity in our actions.

We were inside.

No one hid inside the doorway or crouched behind the sofa. But I had a new set of problems. My apartment had been tossed. Neatly, efficiently tossed. "Dammit."

"What's wrong?" Lucas asked.

"Tossed."

He glanced around my neat, almost bare interior, taking in the leather sofa and blank walls. "Really?"

"Yeah." Everything was in place, however little things were just slightly off.

He didn't question, didn't disagree, he just cut right to the point. "Can I help?"

I ignored his offer. I was used to being alone. Solitary in both my work and home life.

Lucas Goodman and I had spent most of the last four days together. Surprisingly, having him around wasn't driving me crazy. I liked it. "So...when are you leaving?"

"As soon as you check out the NSA computer for information about Johnny."

I prowled my apartment, searching to see if anything had been removed. There wasn't much to take. The computer on the desk had no files. I used it for research then wiped the hard drive. Every single time.

I never checked on Bella here. Ever.

Methodically I opened drawers full of office supplies that I never used, pens, paper, highlighters while Lucas skimmed my bookshelves.

"Lot of biographies," he commented neutrally.

"I like to read about people." Even famous people's lives contained a normalcy missing from mine. "Family influence and dynamics."

I had none. No one to sway me, encourage me, or even discourage me.

On the other hand, I was keeping our country safe. And I was keeping Bella safe.

Lucas stilled. "Where's *your* family, Jamie?"

"Gone," I whispered, regretting the admission immediately. I yanked open the last drawer and there it was.

My badge. The badge I'd had on me when I'd been abducted. The badge with Staci Grant's name on it.

I didn't make a sound and yet Lucas picked up on my distress. "What?"

"Nothing."

He came up behind me, stared at the lone content of the drawer. "It's your *fake* badge."

I cleared my throat. It was the fake badge. One with another woman's name on it, yet they'd replaced it in *my* apartment. I didn't like the implications. At all.

I'd just filed the paperwork to inform the NSA personnel department of my change of address. Chances are it hadn't gone through yet. Only Carson knew where I lived. Unless he'd been compromised. Could that be why he wanted to speak in code on the phone?

Either that or someone, some agency, knew where I lived and that I was undercover as Staci Grant.

"How would your abductors know you were impersonating Staci Grant?" Lucas laid a hand on my shoulder.

I was rattled. "They knew who I was."

"In the warehouse?" Amazingly he knew what I meant. "And you're just getting around to telling me?"

"Maybe."

"So they kidnapped you, not Staci?"

"Yeah." All the information pointed to me. But I couldn't shake the idea that Staci Grant and I were connected some way I just wasn't seeing yet.

"Then we need to keep watch." Lucas stretched. His t-shirt pulled from the waistband of his jeans showing a thin strip of bare skin.

My mouth watered.

"Get some rest. I'll take a look at Staci's files for you." Maybe I'd find a concrete connection between Staci and myself. I held out my hand, wiggled my fingers.

Lucas rubbed a hand over his head. "Not without me."

Resolutely, I pulled out a chair, turned it around, and straddled it. "Let's get started."

* * *

MY HONDA WASN'T NEARLY as nice as Staci Grant's Lexus. I tried not to let the comparison bother me. For the most part, it didn't.

I had simple tastes. In my line of work, unremarkable

was necessary. But as I drove through the gates of NSA headquarters, I wished for the powerful purr of that cherry-colored Lexus, with the V-8 engine, leather-wrapped steering wheel, and smooth caramel leather seats.

The guard stopped the car, checked my license plate. I relaxed in the driver's seat, waiting for the okay. The complex wasn't exactly bustling at six in the morning.

While Lucas was in the shower, I had collected my mission evidence: the cup with the liquid from the syringe, the syringe, and I'd downloaded the scientific data from my abductors in the warehouse onto a new flashkey.

I had hoped to add the information from Staci but no matter how carefully I searched Lucas's pockets and the van, I hadn't been able to find the information we'd downloaded from Staci Grant's computer.

So I shoved the evidence in my leather backpack and left him in my shower with a note on the kitchen table. There wasn't anything in the apartment to steal and I was moving soon anyway. Plus what were the odds it would be that easy to get rid of him?

I glanced in my backpack one more time, making sure the cup was still there. Hopefully there wasn't any smell that would catch the bomb dogs' attention.

I still had Staci's badge and frankly, I loved her clothes. So I'd dressed in her linen palazzo pants, a fine amber color, and a long-sleeve wrap around top in white. I'd blown my hair dry into a sort of wavy, natural style and added a fair amount of makeup, swiping confident red lipstick across my lips.

I couldn't disguise that my eyes were bleary from lack of sleep and hours of staring at the computer screen. We'd never gotten into Staci's files and at five had given up. I had memorized my information on her and couldn't come up with any real leads on her password.

After parking, I headed for OPS 1. Using a phone in the lobby, I called office of the one techno-geek I actually knew by name. Fortunately, he was also the guy who had worked on that encryption program and he'd asked me out repeatedly.

I infused my voice with a friendliness I really didn't feel. "Hey, Zeke. Got a minute?"

After confirming he had time to see me, I headed for the High Security Portal and entered the glass booth. I was entering the complex with the Staci badge, my own was with Carson. I swiped my fake badge down the reader, and then wondered if my Staci badge had clearance. As soon as the retina scan started, I relaxed.

After the load cells measured my body weight, clearing me to enter the highly classified area, I stepped out of the portal and headed for Zeke's office.

He opened the door and ushered me inside, staring intently at me for a minute. "You aren't here to take me up on the date thing, huh?"

I gave him the 'don't ask' stare but surprisingly he held my gaze. And I really looked at him. He didn't look much like the geek he was. He was attractive, in that bulky, wrestler sort of way. Only about five foot ten, but very well-defined upper body and a really tiny butt. I knew he did some rock climbing. That was where we'd initially met. I'd caught his spot rope, saving him from a nasty fall.

"I don't date--"

"People you work with. I get it."

Actually no, but explaining that I didn't date at all just seemed to incite men to challenge. I'd learned that one years ago.

I realized I might have played it wrong. I needed to soften up a little if I wanted his assistance and purposely let my body relax.

"Don't bullshit me," he said brusquely, shoving his hand through his blond surfer dude hair. "Just ask."

My estimation of him went up another notch.

"Out in the Real World should there be a program with your encryption protecting it?"

His ocean blue eyes widened. "No way."

"It sure looks like yours." I hesitated, hoping he would ask to see it.

"Not possible." He crossed his arms over his chest, his forearms rippling with tension and his gaze cutting away from mine. "Can I see it?"

I hesitated for a minute. The vacuum sealed rooms were hushed, interrupted only by a slight hum from the heating and cooling system. If I appeared too eager he'd know he'd done exactly what I wanted.

He snorted in disgust. "Jesus. You're playing me."

I blinked. He was the second person in the last few days to get a line on my true motives. Was I losing my touch? "I'm trying to give myself a good reason to show you evidence."

"Just give me the damn file," he said. "Your secret is safe."

I needed confirmation but a big part of me still had a hard time handing the information over to him. I wasn't sure what was going on with Carson, so at this juncture, Zeke was my only option.

"Okay." I handed over the computer files from the warehouse. "Can you disable the encryption so that I can actually access the data?"

"If it's my program." He made a twirling motion with his hand. "Turn around."

"Why?" I pretended to be bewildered.

"Because I don't want you to watch me and then be able to disable any other files."

I huffed out a breath. "Jeez, you're a hard ass."

"I learned from the best." He flashed a smile at me, his perfectly aligned white teeth gleaming. Now he was trying to butter me up. It wasn't working. It really wasn't.

I turned to the side and listened to the tap of his fingers on the keyboard. My eyes shifted to the poster on the wall, 'Loose lips sink ships', obviously the marketing department had gone retro for the new set of reminders not to talk about your work. They'd also conveniently covered the poster in glass, so I could stare at the reflection of the computer screen. Carefully, I noted the keystrokes and path he took to disable the program. Just in case I needed the skill again.

"Son of a bitch," he ground out. "This is mine. Where did you get it?"

So either someone in the NSA was behind the kidnappings, which made no sense whatsoever, or someone had stolen our technology. Neither scenario gave me warm fuzzies.

I turned toward him. "You know I can't tell you that." My mission code was the absolute highest.

"We've got a breach." He stared hard at the screen, a confused frown on his face.

"I'll note it in my report." Later.

"Yeah." He stood, so close we were only about a foot apart. The clean scent of him filled my head as he placed a hand on my shoulder for emphasis and I felt nothing beyond the warmth of a brotherly touch. So I guess my recent obsession with sex was focused strictly on Lucas.

"This is a problem, Jamie." He looked completely freaked.

"I know. If you look the other way, can I use your computer to research some information?" That way the breach couldn't be traced back to me and when they traced it to him he'd have deniability.

He dropped his hand. "Yeah."

I needed to know the names and any other personnel information I could get on the abductees from the NSA. I knew a few were from the CIA so those wouldn't be accessible...unless I could somehow access the deeper layers of my mission file.

I thought for a minute. "Are you able to get into code Umbra files?"

Zeke reared back. "You want to break into code Umbra files."

Code Umbra files had extremely high clearance. Only a few people in the country had access because the information was so sensitive it usually had global implications.

"Yeah," I said softly, soberly.

"Is someone coercing you? Are you being blackmailed?" He stared at me intently, as if he could see straight into my soul.

I just looked at him. "You're kidding, right?"

"Right. What was I thinking? The ice bee-yotch doesn't have any vices, any friends or any damn vulnerabilities."

I thought about Bella. He was wrong. "Can you get in?"

"Are you *trying* to commit career suicide?"

I ignored him. "Why don't you go down to the cafeteria and use your employee code to buy a cup of coffee so if this is traced back to you, you can honestly say you had nothing to do with it."

"Fuck that." He pulled the chair out and slammed down into it. "Tell me what you need."

"You really can't look at the file."

"Fine."

I whispered the mission name.

He clicked away on the computer for a few minutes, furiously typing. He squeezed his eyes shut, like a little kid who really, really didn't want to see. "You're in."

"Thanks. I'll be out of your hair in a minute."

"You have more integrity than anyone I've ever met. I'm putting my whole career in your hands." He took in a deep breath, blew it out slowly and stood, keeping his gaze squarely across the room. "Don't screw me over."

"I won't." I memorized the contents of the mission file. I didn't have time to analyze the information now. Just the fact that I accessed the file was grounds for immediate suspension. I scrolled quickly through the information, one notation caught my eye.

# CHAPTER 19

S taci Grant had a file folder of the same name. What was the connection? What was 5491?

I had to look this up while I was still at headquarters. The NSA computers were unhackable. They weren't connected to the Internet. We had our own Intranet to share information with other agencies but if you wanted information stored at the NSA you weren't getting it anywhere but here.

I accessed Werz'it, our internal search engine and typed in 5491. Nothing. No records. No data. Nothing.

According to the system, 5491 didn't exist.

# CHAPTER 20

After he read my report, Carson requested I meet him in the hallway off of VTR–261.

A Vault Type Room. He didn't want me in his office. That news did not reassure me.

Carson was at the end of the long wide hallway. He strode toward me, his wing tips thumping along the carpet in a quick tempo, while his gaze swept up and down, looking me over.

The fluorescent light rippled over the creases in his bald, black head. "How are you?" He reached for my hand and squeezed. The demonstration of affection was huge, startling me. Carson was the closest thing I had to family, but he'd never shown me any physical affection. It was a line he never crossed.

He'd broken his pattern and I had to wonder why. As his fingers clasped mine, he visibly relaxed.

"Fine." I pulled my hand away. "But I have a lot of questions."

I strode toward VTR-261. The rustle of his wool

gabardine suit whispered along the deserted hallway as he followed.

"You should get the key." Carson grabbed my arm and dragged me over to the steel wall closet.

"Me?" I raised an eyebrow. Usually the person with the highest clearance entered their badge number and PIN to get the key for the restricted room.

"Mine might be coded." He took a cloth handkerchief from his pocket and wiped the sweat on his head.

It was sixty degrees in the hallway.

Carson believed if he requested the key our conversation would be recorded. I entered my information into the AKAM machine, and a robotic arm dropped the key into the retrieval bin.

I unlocked the door to the conference room. This whole mission stank to high heaven. Yanking out a wheeled chair from the small walnut table, I sat. "You read my report?"

Carson eased into a chair at the head of the table. He steepled his fingers, his manicured nails shiny in the low light, drawing my gaze to his hands. "I did. We also got some excellent intelligence from your ring transmission before you aborted. Talk to me."

It was in my report, but I felt compelled to repeat it. "They kidnapped me, not Staci."

"The evidence does seem to support that conclusion."

I watched him carefully as I dropped the large clue that someone at the agency had to be involved. "They were tracking me through my implanted beacon."

"Unlikely." His mouth turned down.

"But--"

"Accessing car rental records, calculating rate of speed and possible directions, they could predict your probable destination." He dismissed the idea. "That would explain the two men in San Francisco."

"I have an official bolt hole there."

He pressed his lips together and I knew I wasn't getting anywhere with that line of thought. My usually flexible boss was being completely inflexible and I had to wonder why.

"What kind of intelligence made you think Staci Grant would be next, not me?" I'd been so concerned about using a cover with ties to Georgetown, I hadn't asked many questions. I had just taken my mission parameters and run with them, busy making sure I wouldn't come near Bella. "Communications intelligence through email or signals intelligence through coded communications?"

Carson shook his head and withheld the answer.

"Commint or sigint?" I pressed, fisting my hands with frustration, feeling the pressure mount. I forced my fingers to relax.

Finally, reluctantly, he said, "There was a significant increase in chatter but I can't discuss the sources." Which meant it exceeded my security clearance.

I followed my hunch. "Why'd you choose me to impersonate her?"

Carson seemed surprised by the question and he answered slowly, "Your general build, language skills, your location, your...commitment to the team."

"What else do we have in common?"

"Nothing." He frowned.

"Tell me what happened to her."

"Staci?" The way he said her name seemed familiar, personal rather than objective. Carson shrugged, but I saw the evasion in his eyes. "She'd been doing work with a humanitarian organization responsible for removing land mines in Afghanistan when she was captured and imprisoned. There was an uprising at the prison and she was killed."

"You're sure?"

Sorrow spirited his eyes before they turned blank. "Oh yes."

"Someone is taking care of her house."

"Staci's?" For the first time I'd managed to surprise him. His eyebrows lifted into the furrows in his forehead. "How do you know?"

"I went there to see what I could find out about her." I got up and walked around the conference table. I trailed my finger along the gleaming polished wood. "Agents went into the house after her security alarm was disengaged."

"Really?"

"Yeah."

"Any idea why someone is watching her house?"

"I don't know." Carson brushed lint from his pants, contemplating my revelations. "Did you find anything?"

I thought about the secret computer room, the files I'd taken, 5491 in specific. I knew I should share the information with Carson but he was acting too oddly to trust him. Something wasn't right. "Someone is keeping up her house."

"To what purpose?"

"I haven't a clue." Someone else was also impersonating Staci Grant. But I wanted to hold that information in reserve.

He stared out the window. I glanced out to see what was so fascinating. Even through two panes of bulletproof glass, five inches of sound deadening space, and a thin skin of copper, all to eliminate spying or electronic eavesdropping, I could see it was going to be one of those crisp, clear fall days. A day where the wind would ruffle leaves and sing in the sky but nothing out there should take precedence over our discussion.

"Am I done being Staci?" The request came out more plaintively than I anticipated. There were certain things I liked about her, the car, the clothes.

"Yes." He nodded.

I removed the Staci badge from around my neck, dangling it from my fingers. "Do you have my badge?"

Carson slid it out of his breast pocket and pushed it across the polished wood.

I dreaded this next confession, because the consequences of losing the badge were extreme. I was going to have restricted access to the office until they could determine if security had been breached.

"They took all of my official weapons. GPS, firearm, Staci's badge," I confessed.

Now he frowned. "I don't like that your weapon is missing."

"Me either." Personally, I'd been more concerned about the badge. "Focus here, Carson. Something stinks. They took Staci's badge when I was abducted but I found it in my apartment."

"Well, of course you did. I put it there."

"You did?" Were my concerns about Carson off base? "You searched my apartment?"

"After we realized your abduction was different, I had a clean up team go over the abduction area. We returned Staci's car to her house and I personally put the badge back in yours."

"And searched my apartment," I said again, wanting confirmation.

"Yes. I made sure you didn't have any files there,

anything incriminating...in case someone else figured out where you lived."

He knew better. He'd taught me everything I know. "Of course not. Was anyone here unduly interested in my absence?"

"No. That's why I told you to come home the long way. Hoping for some sort of lead, but there wasn't anything." Carson drummed his fingers on the table. "Any tails after you left San Francisco?"

"The pursuit seemed to stop after Sacramento." We'd been off the grid. No credit cards. No rentals. Nothing to trace electronically.

"Do you have the evidence?" he asked abruptly. He added, "If we had the actual drug, we could get started on the analysis."

My purse, with the cup wrapped inside, rested at my hip like a holster for a weapon. I fingered the zipper. A twinge of guilt pricked at me. I'd withheld the scientist files from the warehouse. I wanted more analysis before I handed them over. I didn't put Barb in the report because I didn't want her on anyone's radar. I found myself strangely reluctant to hand over the liquid I had left. "My contact has already potentially identified the classification. Have you ever heard of gene therapy?"

"For treating cancer?"

"And other various conditions." I censored my words cautiously. "She believes the drug will alter brain function but she wasn't sure how."

"This isn't good."

Isn't good? It was a freaking disaster. Carson wasn't reacting the way he should. This potential threat to agents was huge, yet he wasn't throwing out hypotheticals or even speculating. Clearly, he was thinking about something but he wasn't sharing whatever he'd linked together.

I hesitated, feeling very unsure, my internal sensors going crazy. But in the end, I followed my training. Besides I'd be able to get the results from Barb. I flipped open the purse and extracted the syringe and other cup of the drug. "Here's the rest."

"Excellent job." Carson studied the evidence as I slid it across the table.

Carson peered at the liquid without touching the cup. "Why'd you abort?"

"It didn't feel right."

His perfectly shaped brow crooked. "You're resorting to fairy tales now?"

Impatiently, I said, "Something was off about the whole operation. My abduction was far different than the others, starting with the cross country relocation."

He tilted his head to the side, as if considering the information.

"Do you think they'll try again?"

"I'm...not sure." He reached into his jacket pocket and tossed me another ring, this one with an aquamarine stone. "But your abduction didn't conform to their m.o. I'd suggest you wear this."

"Same details?" Twist and press to activate the satellite audio transmission.

"Yes."

I slipped the ring on quickly, the heavy weight of the platinum band strange on my finger.

"I'd appreciate your expense report on my desk as soon as possible."

That was it? My mission was over? I hadn't discovered

who was kidnapping the agents. What if another one was abducted? "What about capturing the people responsible?"

"Your piece is done." Carson's tone was final.

"Let me keep working. There must be some link." I pushed, pretty sure I knew where my request was going, but I had to confirm my suspicions. I was going to keep working on it. With or without his permission.

"There's no link," he said sharply. "The information you obtained will be disseminated and collated with the information from the other abductions."

All the abductees had the 5491 designation but I wasn't supposed to know that.

I wasn't going to let this go. There was nothing in the general computer database about 5491. I didn't know if it was a classification, some sort of code, maybe a hire date or a training class code, but every name in the mission file referenced it.

What the hell....

"Do you know anything about 5491?"

Panic flickered in his eyes before being ruthlessly subdued. "Never heard of it."

He was lying.

Before he was contemplative and almost analytical about our conversation, but now there was tension. I wouldn't get any more out of him through direct questioning. And pushing him further might raise his suspicions. One other issue weighed heavily on my mind. "Do you know anything about my parents and a tie company?"

He carefully smoothed a hand down his tie. "I believe not."

He was lying. Again.

I could lie too. "I remember something about my parents having a fight...about a tie company."

"I'm sure it was nothing." He stood unhurriedly. "By the way, because you aborted your mission, you're required to have an extra psych evaluation."

It was standard operating procedure.

"I made an appointment for today at two o'clock."

I usually made my own appointments. The change in the routine bothered me. "Is something wrong?"

"No." He waved a hand dismissively. "But this is the first time you've ever backed away from mission parameters. I just want to make sure you're on top of your game."

Sports analogies.

Carson only used those when he was upset. It was his tell. He'd pushed me so hard to eradicate them that I'd always picked up on his only one.

I also realized he was trying to distract me from asking more questions. He pulled a dossier out of his jacket pocket, dragging my attention back.

"I've got the information you asked for on John Wishbone." Lucas's guy. I'd almost forgotten. A touch of guilt ran through me, but I ignored it. Lucas was not my responsibility.

"Anything interesting?"

"Well...he disappeared. No information about where or how. No evidence of foul play. It just looks like the boy took off."

In the company of Staci Grant. Who was dead. Carson had left a lot of information out of that run down.

"Now to the information about your new friend."

"Lucas?" In my report, I'd been completely honest about my initial contact and subsequent dealings with Lucas. However, I had left out my conflicting emotions regarding him. Something in my voice must have given me away.

"Have you formed an attachment to this man?"

"That would be ridiculous." It would be.

"And inadvisable."

Carson had taught me all I needed to know about espionage and developing assets while staying detached. He had indoctrinated me on the subject repeatedly when I had wanted to see my sister all those years ago.

"Here is what you need on him."

A moment's foreboding made me hesitate before I took the dossier from him. "He's told me quite a bit himself."

"Did he tell you he worked for the FBI?"

Of course he did.

"Did he also tell you he'd been the subject of an OPR review?"

Office of Professional Responsibility. The Bureau's own version of internal affairs. That's why Lucas hadn't wanted to discuss leaving the FBI.

"What for?"

"You need to address your loyalties here, Jamie."

I skimmed through the file quickly. "What does that mean?" I wanted him to spell it out for me, even though I'd already guessed.

"It means, he has a tainted record." Carson paused, his hand on the doorknob. "We just had a scandal with Agent Johnson dying by the hand of a double agent. Assistant Director Armbruster himself is handling that one. We can't afford another."

His words sounded like a threat. I wanted to be wrong. I wanted my suspicions to go away. But Carson was making it impossible.

"I'd hate for years of your work, your reputation, to be jeopardized by associating with someone with questionable ties."

I quelled the tremor in my hand, refusing to show any weakness, and repeated the question. "What does that mean?"

Carson opened the door slowly. "It means, you don't want to deal with an investigation of your own."

# CHAPTER 21

*J*'d had time to process the threat from Carson on the way home, and I wasn't happy.

I wanted to slam the steel door to my apartment, so I closed it with a gentle click. I wanted to rip something, someone, apart with my bare hands.

"What's wrong?" Lucas lounged against the generic white wall, the seemingly casual pose at odds with his coiled, tense body. He'd crossed his arms over his chest, the lean muscles corded and bulged from the short sleeves of the tight black t-shirt.

I pressed forward crowding into his personal space. The heat from his body surrounded me like a force field. He'd put my existence, my *sister* in jeopardy--by withholding the reason he left the FBI.

"Why did you leave the FBI, Lucas?" I asked evenly.

He blinked. "What?"

I broke away from him and stalked into my living room, knowing he would follow. "Answer the question."

"It's not something I'm real fond of discussing."

I wanted to chop his body into little pieces with my

hands. I wanted to jam his balls so far up his ass that he couldn't walk for a week. I wanted to...hurt him the way Carson's words had struck at me.

"Gee. Wonder why." My teeth may have been more clenched than I'd thought, for understanding dawned in his eyes. "Maybe because you were fired."

Lucas's face blanched. "Oh hell. I quit."

"Under suspicion." I wanted to prowl around the room. I longed to pick up one of my favorite books and hurl it at his head. So I forced myself to sit calmly on the tan sofa.

I took a deep breath. These feelings were inappropriate and counter-productive.

"The OPR investigation was a witch hunt."

Did he have any idea what associating with him for the past four days would get me if anyone at the NSA, besides Carson, found out? Automatic suspension. A check into my background, all the dealings I'd had for an indeterminate time prior to suspension. If I didn't have my job, my clearance, I couldn't protect my sister.

"They were looking for a scapegoat and I got elected." He dropped onto the sofa next to me, our thighs touching. "I finally quit when the stink started spreading to my friends."

"What kind of stink?"

"About eleven years ago, we'd had some success with an informant on a group of men who had ties to the first bombing of the World Trade Center. Before 9/11 someone higher up decided we didn't need the guy anymore." He stopped.

"So...."

"So I started seeing the guy on my own, compiling information, mainly in my spare time, about this group. And the higher ups caught wind of my obsession with the group and pretty much ordered me to stop."

"Of course you didn't." Look at how freaking tenacious he'd been about trailing me to find Johnny.

"No." His gaze cut away from mine, sorrow in his eyes. "I was supposed to let it go...instead I got a friend to check some things out for me."

"And the friend got in trouble?"

"The friend got dead," Lucas replied evenly. "He was in one of the towers when it collapsed."

I shut off the emotion at his obvious sorrow. I turned over his explanation looking at it from several sides. It made sense. And suddenly, information snapped into place. "Johnny's father."

"Yeah."

"That was a long time ago."

"I kept in touch with the informant. Some of the information he'd given us was dead on." Lucas clasped his hands together. "I still believe he could have helped nail some missing connections to al Qaeda."

"So why the OPR?"

"I used discretionary bribe money to pay the guy." He hesitated. "Technically it wasn't against policy, except that the someone I pissed off, wanted me to pay for disregarding his orders. So, they opened the OPR and started examining every single move I'd made. Which put my friends and colleagues into an awkward spot of having to defend me and worry about their own careers coming under scrutiny."

"Okay." Except that still didn't eliminate the inherent danger in associating with him.

"Your turn."

What was he talking about?

"Jamie Hunt." He said my name like a curse.

I'd held nothing back. I'd given him free rein of my mind. I'd taken him to Staci Grant's house. I hadn't lied to him.

In fact, I'd been more honest with Lucas Goodman in the past four and a half days than with anyone in my entire life--even before my world was shattered by a car bomb.

I wondered how he thought he could turn this confrontation. He couldn't win. He'd lied by omission.

In my line of work, I expected people to lie to me. Frankly I was more shocked when someone told me the truth. But I'd begun to trust Lucas Goodman and his breaking that faith wounded me.

Lies shouldn't hurt. They might get people killed but they shouldn't hurt. Yet there was an ache in my chest that sat like an elephant on my lungs.

I realized then, I wasn't really mad at Lucas. He'd withheld information but I'd known he wasn't telling me everything. Carson, on the other hand, had lied to me. On so many levels I wasn't sure where to start.

I shouldn't take my fear and anger and frustration out on Lucas. He didn't owe me anything. Not even the truth.

"That's me."

"No." He shifted on the sofa, opening his body language, spreading his arms, rolling his shoulders. "Question number two."

"Fine."

He watched me, carefully, intensely. "What is your real name?"

I'd given him my name. "We've been over this. Jamie Hunt."

"And you were lying," he said savagely.

"I was not."

"Jamie Hunt is a legend, a cover developed over years and years. You have another name."

I'd forgotten.

I'd had the name Jamie Hunt since I was fifteen years old, since the day I'd agreed to work for the United States government, since the day I'd vowed to protect my sister.

Anguish pierced my heart.

He meant the name I was raised with. I shifted my gaze to those biographies. I'd wiped that name from my memory.

He jammed his hands in his pockets. "Admit it."

"My name is Jamie Hunt."

In thirteen long years, no one had questioned my background. I wasn't about to reveal the details to a disgraced, ex-FBI agent.

I crossed my arms over my chest, drawing his gaze to my breasts. The action was unintentional and automatic. Distract the target away from their true purpose. Good thing my subconscious was paying attention.

"You weren't always Jamie Hunt."

And in that moment, I saw the hurt in his eyes. Even if I wanted to tell Lucas about my prior life, it was forbidden. "You investigated me?"

"You knew I would."

He got up from the sofa. "I told you. I can spot a fake background."

"You're off this time." I lied without compunction. Even if I wanted to tell Lucas my real name, I could never reveal anything which would link to Bella.

"What is your real name?" He wasn't going to give up.

But neither was I.

I answered the only way I could. "Jamie Hunt is my real name."

We stared at each other.

I'm sorry.

I could come up with several good stories. I'd told a number of fabulous lies about my background over the last thirteen years. A runaway girl escaped from tyrannical, overbearing parents. Traveling the world on a yacht, my whole family washed away at sea. An epidemic of influenza wiped out my whole village.

But I didn't want to lie to him again. "I can't."

His gaze was steady on mine. "Parents?"

"Told you before. Gone."

"Siblings."

I thought about Bella. So far out of my reach. Even when the ache to connect with her was so strong it hurt. "Not an issue."

"Then why keep it a secret?"

"I can't tell you."

He leaned in closer. Suddenly I could smell the musk of his scent, the heat of his body warmed me.

"I can't."

Some of my frustration must have made it through because he backed off. "I'll let it go...for now."

I gazed at my barren living room. Staci Grant's townhouse made me realize not everyone in my line of work lived the way I did. So sparingly, so blandly, so unremarkably.

Her house looked normal, like a photograph from one of my biographies. I found myself wanting to reach for that illusion of normalcy, to reach for that illusion with Lucas. Even though I knew it was false. I offered him an olive branch, small though it was.

"You want to know what I found out about Johnny?"

"Yeah."

I handed him the file. "It's more what isn't in that report than what is."

Lucas flipped through the pages slowly, his eyes skimming the meager contents.

"No mention of Staci Grant." He fingered the edge of the paper. "She should have raised a flag somewhere."

"I would have thought so."

"This is all you could find out?"

"That's all that was given to me."

"Really." Lucas picked up on my meaning. He tapped the file against his palm. "Can you get me more?"

I hesitated.

I shouldn't even be seen with him, let alone look into Johnny for him. But something strange was going on. Johnny and Staci Grant. Staci's 5491 file and mention of the same numbers in the mission file.

Staci Grant seemed to be connected to both of our cases. It wouldn't hurt to pass along any information I discovered. "I'll...see what I can do."

"Fair enough." And with that, he forgave me. I could see it in his gaze, hear it in his concession. An emotion I refused to identify trickled through me.

"Can I ask you a question?"

Lucas nodded.

"Were the people who kidnapped me FBI?"

"No." His response was emphatic.

"How can you tell?"

"The moves were wrong."

I knew exactly what he meant. Every law enforcement agency had their own training maneuvers and practiced team moves until they had them down pat. "Did you train in Hogan's Alley?"

"Yeah. And their routine was not anything we practiced."

"Did you recognize it?"

He hesitated. "Could have been DIA."

The Defense Intelligence Agency?

Lucas added with a shrug, "CIA, maybe."

"What would the CIA want with me?" And why not just go through official channels? It was a lot of effort to kidnap someone.

I stared at the biography of Ronald Reagan on my glass-topped coffee table.

"Maybe they're trying to smoke out whoever is impersonating Staci," he theorized. "And got you instead."

"Fishing expedition?"

"Yep."

But the chemicals in that syringe were real enough. And their intent to inject me certainly had been real. The old man had said, *the program is in place.* But just what was the program?

Were they looking for security leaks? Finding them among the kidnapped agents? Researching the efficacy of their drugs?

I thought about Agent Johnson's death. About Staci Grant's capture and death. Could they be the results of this program?

Upstairs someone dropped a heavy object, shaking the ceiling.

The sound jolted through me.

"We can't stay here," we said in unison.

"Took the words right out of my mouth." I grabbed my pre-packed 'gotta roll' duffel. "How long will it take you to get ready?"

"I'm already there."

"You could have left without me." After all, he had the data from Staci's computer. He didn't need me. But now I needed that data.

"No, I couldn't." His grey gaze was steady on mine.

He scooped up his black duffel. "We need to go to Staci Grant's office."

My heart jolted. At the university? That close to Bella? No way.

"It's the logical place to look next."

I deflected the idea. "What we really need is to figure out how to break into Staci's files." I'd effectively told him I needed to see her files too.

I needed to sit down with all the evidence files from my mission and to analyze the information I'd stolen from the NSA. If we could break into Staci's files maybe I could tie it all together. The answers to my questions had to be in that data somewhere.

Lucas slung the duffel over his shoulder. His black t-shirt rippled across the muscles in his chest. "I already found the closest library."

I'd been warned off associating with Lucas. If I left with him, I was making a choice. One that would jeopardize my job and my ability to protect my sister.

But strange things were happening. I couldn't trust Carson and the evidence pointed to someone within the NSA being involved.

Lucas had been honest with me.

I had to go with my gut and hope I wasn't making a huge mistake.

## CHAPTER 22

The library existed in a time warp. Or someone had gone for a totally retro 60's look.

Utilitarian Danish furniture in light wood held the books. In a reading area, chairs in orange, yellow and pea green circled square tables littered with periodicals. A rug with a psychedelic swirl led from the card catalogs to a rounder with tattered paperback books.

Card catalogs? We were in trouble.

"I should have worn my leather headband and striped bell bottoms," Lucas murmured.

I prowled through the stacks looking for a side room, any place, that looked more modern. Lucas shifted his black leather computer bag to his left shoulder.

Found it tucked away in a little corner.

Internet Computer Room.

Lucas beat me to the room with a stride to spare and pulled open the door.

A row of study desks with dividers had been converted into computer stations. We had the room to ourselves. I sat down at the first open seat. Lucas sat at the empty bay next to me.

I contemplated how to tell him to bugger off. It wasn't like me to be wishy washy and that annoyed the hell out of me.

He turned to me. "Promise me you'll share anything related to Johnny or Staci Grant."

He'd solved my problem for me. Which annoyed me even more. "Fine." As long as it didn't relate to national security.

The library computer was on and ready to go.

After plugging in the flash drive, I used Zeke's keystrokes and bypassed the encryption on the files taken from the warehouse. The scientists' files were set up numerically. One through ten.

Ten. Yet, I'd been told, there had only been six agents kidnapped. Seven if you included me. I mentally ran through the information I'd accessed in the mission file. They only referenced six agents.

I opened the first file. No identifying information beyond sex and age, everything else was codes and numbers. I studied the scientist information, mostly numbers. On a whim I did a search for 5491, but came up empty. Again.

It looked like it might be blood work analysis but I couldn't be sure. To verify my conclusions, I'd need another pair of eyes on this. And I knew I couldn't go to anyone at the NSA.

"I need a consult," I said starkly. It was possible since she had knowledge of the drug, she could extrapolate the information in these files. "You think Barb would do it?"

"She'll do it." Lucas rattled off Barb's email address.

I sent her two of the subject files taken from the

scientists with a request for explanation of the numbers and data in the file.

I wondered if I was completely destroying my career and my sister's life. But I needed to move forward with trying to discover who had kidnapped me. I also really wanted to know what chemical they had been going to inject in me.

I leaned over the partition to check on Lucas.

He had set up his own laptop and was busy clicking away. "What's that?"

"My people search program." His fingers flew over the keys. "I requested a full asset check on Staci a few days ago."

The disparity between my life and Staci Grant's had hit me hard and curiosity ate at my attention like a virus at a cell. I peered at the screen.

The asset check showed her debts. She owed three thousand dollars on the fancy plasma television in her living room and ten thousand to an art gallery in Washington, D.C.

"Huh." Who spent ten grand on art? "She's tossing around a lot of cash for a professor."

"Trust fund."

"How much?"

Lucas scrolled back up the screen and pointed to an account. "Preliminary asset search shows a net worth of nearly thirty million."

"Million?"

Lucas tapped his pen on the table. "So why did she work?"

"What else would she do?" *Sit around all day?* "She does, did, charitable work over in Afghanistan."

"You realize that was probably a cover."

Yeah. I knew it, but I hadn't been going to bring it up. "What else is on there?"

Lucas punched at the keys. "Besides the townhouse in Virginia, she owns a house on the Cape in Massachusetts and a beach house in the Bahamas."

"Bolt holes?" Pretty nice ones.

"Probably investments. If she has a bolt hole it would be hidden a hell of a lot better."

Lucas pulled up the specifics of Staci Grant's portfolio. Although her amounts were much higher, we'd invested in almost the exact same companies and funds.

"What?"

I hadn't made a sound. Hadn't moved. And yet he could tell something about Staci's portfolio struck me. "Let me get a closer look."

My investments were layered in pretty much the same manner. I had a balance between individual large cap and small cap stocks, stock funds, real estate investment trusts, bonds and bond funds.

As I trailed down the list, a growing sense of disbelief buzzed through me. With my index finger, I started at the beginning and scrolled down slowly. The list was alphabetical and long.

And identical to mine.

Identical.

My salary was decent. I had no real expenses. Most of the time I was on assignment. I drove an unremarkable car and lived in an unremarkable apartment.

Most of my money went into a numbered account and was then invested. In the event of my death, I'd instructed Carson to give everything to Bella, anonymously. Invent a long lost relative who'd died and ascribe the bequest to them.

As my life expectancy was never considered long, I liked to look over my expanding portfolio and hope that Bella would be able to do something wonderful with the money.

Lucas started to clear the screen. I put my hand over his. "Wait."

"What?"

Should I tell him? The hard strength of his fingers felt solid beneath mine. "It's exactly the same as mine."

He didn't insult me with platitudes. "Exactly?"

"My quantities are smaller."

"That goes beyond coincidence."

I agreed.

"Where do you get your advice?"

I hesitated. Here it got tricky. Carson's financial advisor invested the money for me. Carson had started the portfolio after my parents had died.

He'd also been lying to me. An insidious thought slithered into my mind like a snake. *What else had he lied about?*

"My handler takes care of it."

"His name?"

I couldn't give up Carson's name. I shook my head.

"I didn't think so." Lucas crossed his arms over his chest and tipped back in the chair. "So your handler advised Staci Grant as well."

I remembered Carson's seeming familiarity with Staci. At the time the sadness in his eyes had surprised me. Now I realized he'd known her a hell of a lot better than he'd let on.

I couldn't let go of the similarity. "Check when the account was started."

His chair dropped back down to the floor. "The trust fund comes from her grandparents and was started right after they were killed."

A cold chill knifed down my spine.

"What about her parents?"

"Died when she was a little girl." Lucas did some finger work. "She was raised by her paternal grandparents."

And right after they were killed, this account was opened.

Lucas pressed another button but I wasn't watching. I was remembering. I vaguely recalled Carson discussing this with me. He'd opened the account while I recovered in the hospital.

The annoying buzz of the fluorescent light pressed in on me, piercing my eyes. "How did they die?"

He glanced over at me sharply. "Her parents?"

"Grandparents."

"Coming home from a play on Broadway. Mugged and stabbed on the street."

Different but still as effective. Both dead at the same time. My blood chugged sluggishly through my veins. If anything, my heartbeat slowed. I forced the question through lips that felt numb, frozen. "Year?"

"1995."

I was afraid to ask but I needed to know. "Month?"

"Late October."

Same as my parents. The light bouncing off the glass window swirled, making pretty patterns in my eyes.

"Jesus, you're pale." Lucas hand came up to my neck and forced my head between my knees. "You gonna tell me the significance of that date?"

"What?" My head hung down, my gaze staring straight between the metal legs of the plastic chair as the blood rushed back in. I'd forgotten he was there. Forgotten where I was.

"What is it about late October?" His fingers, still clasped around my neck, soothed.

Everything within me tightened. I couldn't tell him. "It's nothing. I'm just trying to figure out the portfolio thing."

"You okay?"

"Yeah. Must be low blood sugar.

"Must be," he said derisively.

I lifted my head back up, my thoughts swirling in confusion and agony. Everything was upside down. I huffed out the breath I'd forgotten to exhale.

The rasp of our breathing in the little room was strained. I lifted my gaze to see his steady on me. As if he could hold in all of the bad stuff, keep it at bay.

He twisted toward me, framing my chair with his arms, caging me in the hard plastic. He curled one hand around my neck and pulled me closer.

The kiss was going to be a mistake. I knew it.

Even he knew it.

Awareness shaded his eyes as he drew me in. I could have pulled away, should have, but in that moment, I was so cold and so alone. I needed contact.

Human.

No. Sexual contact. I couldn't afford to need the comfort of human contact. But I would let myself feel through sexual contact.

Except when his lips touched mine, his touch wasn't hard or demanding but...gentle. He licked at my lips wetting them, inviting me to lick back.

I had to wrest back control, change the embrace into something I was comfortable with. I opened my mouth but instead of pressing harshly as I should have, I sucked lightly.

His teeth nibbled at the corner of my lips and I acquiesced, hoping for the violent thrust of his tongue. He confounded me again by softly tracing the outline of my lips then light as a butterfly kiss, he curled his tongue around mine.

I melted.

There was no other word for it. Desire puddled low and heavy in my body in an exquisite rush.

My hands gripped the rough edges of the plastic seat to keep from reaching for him. But my traitorous body shifted, my legs fell open bonelessly, inviting him, urging him to lean into the shelter of my thighs. Invoking promises of something I had no intention of delivering.

I wasn't a tease and yet I couldn't stop the acceptance, the reaction of my body.

His left hand slid along the outside of my thigh and up to the curve of my hip, anchoring me in the chair. His fingers squeezed into my flesh.

His assault on my senses kept going. He swept me closer, his knees scraping along my inner thighs. Though I clung tightly to the hard plastic my body betrayed me by straining toward the sheltering, all-consuming heat of his embrace.

His hands came up to cup my breasts, thumbs brushing against my nipples through the cool linen blouse while his mouth devoured mine.

He yanked me on top of his lap, my legs draped over his and my breasts crushed against the hard plane of his chest. The heat of his erection throbbed against my core. Blood rushed to fill my senses.

Oh, God. I wanted more.

I wanted to break the promises I'd made to myself and kept for all these years. Tempted beyond reason to relinquish my principles, the foundation of my existence, for the hot, slick slide of him into my body.

For Lucas, I just might let go of those promises and damn my 'one time only' rule.

That rogue thought shocked me.

I forced my hands to push him away, but my reaction was sluggish, slow, almost drugged. "No."

He stilled. His breathing harsh in the quiet of the room as his chest moved in slow, deep inhalations. His eyes burned, but not with the anger to which he was entitled. "No?"

"I...can't."

He freed me and I scurried back to my chair, refusing to think about how close I'd come to breaking my rules. And how much I'd wanted to. The yearning, for his touch, for his comfort, for surcease from my worries, was unbelievably strong.

He leaned his head back awkwardly against the chair and spoke without heat, "Damn your rules."

Again, he seemed to understand. Physical was easy. Sex was simple.

His understanding of me was at once terrifying and tempting. Someone who understood me.

The truth was in his words, making me yearn to deepen the connection he insisted we had. For him to understand me, that was the scariest thing of all.

# CHAPTER 23

We'd each gone back to our own little partition to work. About five minutes later, Lucas scooted back his chair. "I have a proposition."

My eyebrows rose.

He gave me a 'Not that kind' look.

"I need to get into Staci Grant's files to see if she has information about Johnny." Lucas said calmly, "I believe you can get in her head and figure out the password."

"What makes you think so?"

"You got into her attic room."

"True."

The only lead I had right now was the connection between abductees. The mysterious 5491. Staci had a file on 5491. If I could break her password, I might get the answers I was looking for. But Lucas didn't need to know that.

If I helped him I wanted something in return. If his program could find out that much information about Staci Grant, then he could use it to find Donald Christian. Worry about Bella had started to nag at me. Carson hadn't been honest. Which meant that I had to distrust everything he'd told me recently, including the status of Bella's safety. No matter how painful that discovery was, my first loyalty was to Bella.

"Okay. I want to...." *Need to.* "Find the right Donald Christian."

"Fair enough." Lucas clicked away at his keyboard. "I've already put in requests from another more extensive site, DMV pictures, any fingerprints, that kind of thing."

Excellent.

I had one other favor. I hesitated, weighing the stupidity of asking for advice against the strong need to get a second opinion.

Lucas drummed his fingers on the laminated desktop. "What else?"

Bella had indicated our parents had been arguing about a tie company. But I'd been thinking about her comment and wondering if she'd assumed it was a neckware provider.

There were several variations on the word tie. And then I'd been struck with the idea that maybe it wasn't a tie company but some sort of compensation or comm, communications.

"You ever heard of a communications system with the word tie in it?"

"T.i.e.?"

"Not sure." When I had asked Carson, he'd run a hand over his tie. A clue or misdirection? "It could be t-y, or t-I, or t-y-e, or t-h-a-i, I suppose."

"Tiecomm, tycomm, ticomm, tyecomm, or thaicomm." Lucas punched letters into his laptop. "No hits," then he paused. "Until I typed in ti comm."

"You got something?" I peered around the divider. The search engine asked if he meant TICOM.

"TICOM. Why is that familiar?" Lucas murmured far too close to my ear.

"TICOM stands for Target Intelligence Committee. It was created during World War II to capture German codebreakers and cipher machines."

"Right. The German codebreakers. We found their secret headquarters in the castle before the Russians, and snapped up the machines and personnel, effectively snapping up all that lovely Russian code at the same time." Lucas cocked his head. "If you knew that, why'd you ask me to google it?"

But I wasn't interested in TICOM. My parents weren't old enough for World War II. Yeah, my father was older but he was only ten when the war started. My mother hadn't even been born until the mid 50's. They couldn't have anything to do with German codebreakers, WWII, or the NSA.

"That isn't what I'm looking for," I said calmly, shaking off my unease.

"Huh." He leaned back. "Does it have anything to do with Staci Grant?"

"No."

"Then let's get back to work," he murmured. "We need that password."

Right. Staci's password.

"I've got to get into her head." I punched up Google. "I'll google Islamic Fundamentalist groups."

"Charities and churches." Lucas said, "Most terrorist groups' funding in this country is going to be under the guise of charities and mosques and sometimes churches."

"Yeah. I know." Up until September Eleventh, the government had hesitated about investigating charitable organizations. Because of our country's policy of separation of church and state, religious organizations had mostly been left alone.

Not anymore.

Holy.... "Over sixty thousand hits." I blew out a breath and glanced at the computer clock. I had about two hours until my appointment with the department shrink. "This is going to take awhile."

"We knew it wasn't going to be easy," he murmured into my ear. Something in his voice affected me at the cellular level, my body reacting every time. Lucas's scent floated over the smell of newly installed industrial carpeting and warm computers.

Nothing was ever easy. I scrolled through the articles looking to see what kind of results I'd gotten, searching for anything to decipher Staci Grant.

We had the room to ourselves with an almost nonexistent possibility of it being bugged, so we tossed out ideas.

"Staci Grant understood what Islamic militants wanted." If I wanted to get in her head, I had to understand too. "Let's talk it out."

Lucas got up and stretched. "Fine."

"There's a lot of articles about Muslims denouncing the September 11th attacks and defending Islam."

"Of course. Islam is a peaceful religion. Most Muslims don't want warfare." He prowled around the room.

"A lot of American citizens don't believe that."

"Yeah. The difficulty in explaining Islam from an American perspective is that it truly combines religion and politics into one." Lucas rubbed a hand over his mouth.

"No separation of church and state." Unlike the U.S.

"Exactly."

"That is where the breakdown in understanding

happens." I reasoned, "As a country, we've separated religion and politics for so long, it's hard to for us to see that Islam's basis is intertwined in both political and economic decisions which motivate religious—at least in our mind--action."

"Pretty much."

"Whereas they just believe they are protecting their way of life."

"A way of life infinitely better for those in power and those who would be hurt financially by a change in political climate from Islam to democracy," Lucas said drily.

Isn't that what everything boiled down to? Money and power?

"So what would she use as a password?" He dropped back down into the chair.

"We have to get into her head."

"We?"

I pressed my eyes closed. The implications of the word were frightening. I lifted my lids slowly. "We."

He smiled, a warm, intimate smile and longing unfurled within me. His knowledge of me was like a seductive lure. I felt my lips curve in answer, and I returned back to my analysis.

Staci's password wouldn't be anything standard. No birthday, address, phone number. Based on her house and her profession, Staci Grant had a sophisticated and complicated mind.

Lucas said, "She's got at least two passwords. The general one that is the same as her house alarm password. And another secret password for the deeper security--blocking the information we're trying to access."

The dichotomy would appeal to her.

The first level was her alarm password and accessed the

general information related to everyday life and her work as a lecturer.

For the second level, she'd use something more universal. But not easy. "The street recruitment work would be something that would be accessible by other agents in case anything happened to her."

"She isn't stupid."

The admiration in his voice shouldn't have irritated me, but it did. *I'm losing it. I'm jealous of a dead woman.* "I know."

I thought back to her townhouse. Simplicity hidden in extravagance.

"Something related to the job." I scrolled through websites looking for anything that stood out or triggered an idea.

I mentally sifted through the information I'd read on the websites. But like a tongue probing a sore tooth, my mind kept going back to TICOM. That's when it hit me.

"What about MARA?" I asked.

"Who is Mara?"

"It's an acronym. Like Hamas, the Palestinian organization." My excitement grew. "MARA for Mohammed Al-Rasheed."

Lucas looked thoughtful. "Mohammed. The prophet."

The messiah in Islam. It made a twisted and perfect sense.

"I like it," he said.

The more I mulled it over, the more convinced I became I'd hit it first try.

"We've got her files." I glanced around the public library. I didn't want to be looking at Staci Grant's files in a public place. "Not here."

"I agree." Lucas's computer chimed softly, drawing his attention away from me. "Huh."

That little word pulled me out of my excitement. "What?"

"Let me fiddle with this." He punched the keys some more. "I hope Donny Boy isn't too important."

"Why?" I refused to panic until I knew more.

"He's amazingly clean. I can't find much." Lucas punched at the keys some more. "Wait, wait. Let me look at another page."

I closed the file and wiped the library hard drive of my presence, focusing on the mundane, rote task while I waited for him to get to the point.

"He doesn't exist."

My heart grew cold. Earlier visions of weddings and houses and babies crystallized and shattered into tiny particles. "What do you mean he doesn't exist?"

But I knew.

"His records prior to a month ago are zero. Unless he just moved to this country and filed for a social security number."

I didn't think so. But I needed to make sure I understood clearly. "He's at Georgetown. There must be a record."

"No. There are two Donald Christians at Georgetown, but this email address for your Donald isn't related to either one. He just has the address doctored to look like he goes to Georgetown."

I blew out a breath slowly when what I wanted to do was hurl the monitor across the room.

Was he after Bella? I forced myself to calm down. It did Bella no good to make assumptions, but I sure wasn't buying coincidence. Maybe the agency had assigned someone to protect her, but that would mean she needed protecting. Shit.

Either way, Carson should know what was going on.

Lucas said, "If you want to know who he really is, then I need more information."

"That's all I have." I tightened my fingers so hard around the desktop my knuckles showed white.

"He isn't related to your recent problems, is he?"

I needed to relax, to make Lucas believe Donald Christian was not important. "No."

"I'll keep digging and see what else I can find out."

Good. He could keep digging. My gaze shifted to the clock, the tick of the second hand magnified in the silent room. It was one o'clock. Dr. Fitzhugh would be waiting. Time to go. Even if I didn't want to. What I wanted was to find this Donald Christian kid and beat the shit out of him.

"I have an appointment."

"I'll go with you."

"You can't."

"We go together."

I knew he'd argue. "It's a psych eval."

That shut him up.

"At headquarters?"

I could have lied to him, but somewhere, sometime I'd decided to trust Lucas Goodman.

"No. The Psychological Services Building is in Hanover."

"Want me to wait in the van?" We'd driven here separately. Lucas in his van and me in my car.

"Surveillance cameras in the parking lot."

"Is there security to get into the parking lot?"

"No." Suddenly I wondered why not. The intellectual and mental workings of an NSA employee contained a bounty of confidential secrets and if someone tapped the information, potential breaches in National Security.

Shouldn't that information be at Crypto City, guarded against as judiciously as actual international espionage?

I glanced over at him. "You still can't wait for me."

"Why?" he asked bluntly.

What the hell. "How familiar are you with the NSA?"

"I know a little."

"If an employee is discovered meeting with, speaking with, or exchanging information with a questionable person...."

"Me," he said flatly.

I inclined my head. "Their security clearance is taken away until it can be determined no breach has occurred."

"Son of a bitch." He slammed his hand down on the desktop, making his laptop jump. "The stink is here."

"Pretty much."

Lucas rubbed his hand along his thigh. "How about I find the library in Hanover?"

"Okay." I hesitated. I could bail on him. A week ago I would have. "I'll meet you there."

He didn't ask for my word on it. I could be lying through my teeth. He'd just have to trust me. Of course, trust is a two way street.

As he held my gaze with his, the hum of the computers perched on the cubicle desktops and low murmur of voices beyond the door faded. "I trust you."

I trusted him too. Sort of. The realization shook me. Trust was a power within itself and Lucas Goodman wasn't stupid.

I did trust him. Just not completely.

*I* didn't have time for a psych eval.

I strode into the tan brick building, wondering if their patient files were secure. Intense worry spread through me, spooking me, and I wished I had a weapon.

I sliced my badge through the magnetic reader, wiggled my fingers at the security camera. The door clicked open and I walked through the entryway into a waiting area painted a soothing sage green. Framed in brass, watercolors of lush flowers dotted the walls.

I saw Dr. Mary Fitzhugh every three months, regular as clockwork. But this session was a non-standard mission review, separate from my quarterly physical and psychological evaluation.

Security concerns continued to bother me.

No secretary waited behind the standard-issue office desk. A potted plant with big shiny leaves trailed over the Formica edge. No file cabinets flanked the walls. An appointment book lay open on the desk. Curious, I looked at the pristine white page.

Only first names.

So far, so good.

I wondered if the office had security cameras unobtrusively placed in the room. A protective seal coated the windows, keeping the sunlight out and prying eyes blind to the occupants of the waiting room.

If he'd been dead, George Thorogood would be rolling over in his grave at the Muzak version of *Bad to the Bone* piped into the waiting area.

The building had four floors and thirteen personnel. On the first floor there were three doors, all closed. Mary's was the one on the right.

Conflicting emotions caromed through me. I wanted to prowl the office, instead I perched on the desktop and surveyed the outer waiting area. I crossed my arms over my chest and wished I had my firearm. Any firearm. Instead of ceasing, the naked feeling I'd gotten when I entered the building continued to escalate.

I didn't need to be re-hashing my failure on the mission but the warning from Carson had been clear. I needed to pass this psych eval.

"Jamie." Dr. Fitzhugh's voice startled me out of my musings. "How are you?"

I straightened to greet the woman standing in the doorway to her office. A lavender cashmere sweater peeped out of the sleeve of her white lab coat as she held out her hand.

Not as good as I should be since technically it's between visits. I shook her hand quickly and dropped it. "Okay."

Her eyes displayed nothing beyond professional concern. She had to know why I was here, but she exhibited no shock that I'd disobeyed mission instructions.

"Why don't we go into my office, where we'll be more

private." She gestured toward her office with a smile and her iron will.

I wondered at her polite euphemism. Could the outside offices be bugged? In a permanent building like this, the walls could be hard wired. The solicitous way she handled me pricked my consciousness. Perhaps her insistence that we move to her office was more a way to put me at ease than I'd given her credit for.

Mary Fitzhugh was about twelve years older than me. I'd been her patient since the beginning of my association with the NSA. At first, I had wondered if they'd assigned her to me as an older sister figure but after our first few sessions she stopped attempts to forge a relationship beyond doctor/patient.

Still, I never wasted a source. And today she had 'good source' written all over her.

We walked into her office. I noted her pristine desk. The only file on it a thick one, presumably mine. A calculator, scotch tape dispenser, and ceramic vase with a fake flower were lined up on the credenza behind the desk.

I plopped down on a sofa upholstered in muted pastels while she took her customary chair to my right.

"So...what happened?"

I always tempered my responses during the sessions with Dr. Fitzhugh. Besides the fact I couldn't reveal exactly what happened or where I'd been, I hadn't trusted anyone for so long, being obscure came as second nature.

I realized long ago if I didn't present a composed picture, she had the power to recommend I be taken off active duty.

I couldn't bear that.

"I'm not sure. I was in the middle of a mission and

realized that something was off. So I ignored my original directive and got out."

"This is the first time that you haven't completed your assigned mission." Her tone seemed accusatory which had me going on alert. She was supposed to be an objective observer. "How do you feel about that?"

"It was unavoidable." I skirted her question. I never told anyone how I felt, especially not the shrink.

Mary Fitzhugh tensed. "You seem a little stressed."

I shrugged. I was getting a bad feeling about this. I hadn't shot anyone, I hadn't harmed anyone. I hadn't given away any National Security information.

Dr. Fitzhugh glanced down at a file. "I see there was a civilian man involved with this last mission."

Standard procedure dictated we document non-NSA personnel contact in a mission, but I had no intention of discussing Lucas with her. I stared, not commenting.

"Was he the reason you decided to abort?" She lifted a mug of steaming liquid to lips that matched the lavender of her sweater.

"Nope." I slid down into the comfort of the sofa, stretching my feet underneath the coffee table.

She put the mug down on the coffee table and made a notation in my file. My very thick file.

"You look tired."

"Twenty-four hour days on the road will do that," I quipped.

"Are you tired, Jamie?" The gentle voice always put me on edge. After she tried to lull you with the sympathetic tone, Mary Fitzhugh usually went for the jugular.

"Nothing ten hours of uninterrupted sleep won't cure."

"The anniversary of your family's death is almost here."

She leaned over and put her hand on my forearm. "Are you sure that didn't affect your decision making process?"

What?

Two things shocked me. She never touched me. Ever. Frankly I was uncomfortable being touched--which she knew. And she hadn't brought up my family in years. I had steadfastly refused to discuss them when I first started coming to her. Even then I'd sensed my conflicted feelings about their deaths could jeopardize my need to avenge them, my need to atone for not dying too.

I'd read enough psych books to know I had survivor guilt. I didn't need her telling me I needed to get over it.

"I know about anniversary reactions." I carefully removed her hand. I wanted to curve my arms over my stomach so I deliberately relaxed. "This wasn't one."

The pastel walls, designed to soothe, were suffocating me.

Did this mean she knew about Bella? Was the doctor trying to get me to acknowledge her?

"Do you think you exhibited any surprising weakness during your mission?"

I glanced sharply at her, my gaze focused on that little bit of lavender cashmere. The phrase mirrored what the white-coated man had said too closely. That unsettled feeling bumped up another notch. What the hell was going on here?

I deliberately answered her question incorrectly. "My eyes were a little hazy."

Her lips tightened but she didn't challenge me. She made a notation in that folder again. I moved imperceptibly closer, wondering if I could get a look at my file.

The phone rang in her office. We both ignored it. The

ringing continued. The phone had never rung during one of our sessions before.

"They don't seem to be hanging up." She looked distracted and slightly harassed. "Do you mind?"

"Go ahead." I gestured to the open door, hoping she'd leave my file on the coffee table.

"I'll be right back."

I had a really bad feeling about this. Phone calls during an eval session. Bringing up my family.

She took the file, but set it on the desk by the doorway. How could I steal that file? The blinds were open halfway and I stared out the window formulating a plan.

A van in the parking lot, idling by the front door, caught my eye. It hadn't been there when I'd come in fifteen minutes ago.

I didn't like it.

Federal buildings had strict policies about vehicles parked within a certain distance, and this truck was breaking every one of them.

The doctor was still on the phone at the desk in her inner office, her back to me. Something about this whole set up did not feel right. Again.

I jammed over to the file, flipped it open and grabbed the top few pages. Shoving them into the waistband of the tailored linen pants, I skulked toward the door.

I had to make tracks. Because if I wasn't mistaken, that van was for me.

CHAPTER 25

My hand was on my cell phone before I even got out of the office. The natural instinct to call Lucas stopped me cold. The fact that I instantly thought of him scared me. I didn't need anyone. Couldn't need anyone.

I couldn't rely on anyone but myself. And I'd better not forget that fact.

Get your head in the game, Jamie.

Deliberately, I put the phone in my pocket. I couldn't go out the front. Opening the back door would most likely trigger an alarm, unless I could figure out how to disable it. What if...? I strolled casually across the waiting room, crossing slowly in front of the entry door. The men in the van couldn't get into the building unless they had a badge.

Once inside the bathroom, I locked the door. A small window faced the back of the building. I gauged the size. It would be a tight fit. I figured I had ten minutes tops before I was busted.

Hopefully security hadn't wired the windows. Otherwise I was in deep trouble.

I ran my fingers around the perimeter of the metal frame looking for any kind of wire or security device. I found the wire within a few seconds. Shit.

I needed to create a diversion.

I peered through the frosted glass window, trying to picture what the back of the building looked like. Flipping open my cell phone, I dialed Yellow Cab and gave them the address of the office building one street over and two buildings down. Occasionally paranoia has its upside.

I slipped out of the bathroom. Casually, I picked up the flower pot and sauntered toward the back door. When I reached the double doors of bullet-proof glass, I heaved the ceramic pot across the empty lobby into the front entrance doors.

All hell broke loose.

The force of the impact set off the alarm system but didn't break the glass. The alarm blared. A mess of dirt and leaves scattered over the carpet. I slipped out the back door before Security arrived.

Now I knew what was out the back. As I assessed the blacktop driveway and chain link fence topped with razor wire, a car shot up to me.

I tensed, ready to flee.

Lucas popped open the passenger door. "Don't have much time."

Lucas. Again. "How'd you know?" I hopped in and slammed the door.

"I didn't. Just a feeling."

"Some feeling."

He grinned at me and tossed me a bag with a fluffy blond wig, a tube of lipstick, and rose-colored sun glasses. "Slide down."

"Yeah." I curved under the dash of the Toyota Camry and my relief and pleasure at seeing him tripled while I tugged on the Dolly Parton wig.

I stripped off my wrap-around blouse, leaving only the skimpy white tank top beneath. Although I tried not to let suspicion creep in, I felt it, crawling along the back of my neck. How did he always know when I was going to be in trouble?

"You seem to be making a habit of this."

"Same thing occurred to me." His gaze cut to me, lingering on my breasts. "Right place, right time."

The car moved sedately through the side end of the parking lot, away from the altercation at the entrance to the building.

"Stay there until we're past the fracas." Lucas pretended to slow down to look at the melee. "There's a leopard print blouse on the backseat. I'll grab it as soon as I can."

And then I realized he must have been close by all along. As in waiting, just in case.

"I would have thought they would make their move when you got here," Lucas said conversationally.

He was right and if I hadn't been so ga-ga over his appearance I should have clued into the same thought. Why hadn't they tried to get me on the way in? Why wait until I was coming out?

"Me too." I slipped on the pink wire-rimmed sunglasses and slopped on the coral lipstick.

"What happened?"

"I'm...not sure. But when I saw the van loitering, I knew it was time to take off." I wish I'd gotten the license plate of the van. "You didn't--"

"Yeah. I did." He gestured to the dashboard and I saw a

number scribbled on the rental agreement. He'd rented the car under James Koch. "We can run the plate later."

"We need to dump the car."

"I left my van at the airport." He flipped his blinker on and turned carefully. "We can ditch this and pick the van up."

So he'd dropped his van at the airport, walked to the rental car shuttles and picked up a car. With the timing, he must have left the library right behind me.

"You never had any intention of going to the library in Hanover did you?" I couldn't tell if I was happy or pissed.

"Backup. I was providing backup."

Checking up on me.

"Backup which you needed," he chastised. "Was it the same people?"

Carson, Dr. Fitzhugh, Lucas and I were the only people who knew I was going to be in the psych building this afternoon.

Lucas didn't have any reason to set me up. He had Staci's files. I should be suspicious, but it didn't fit. Even if he did have a disconcerting tendency to rescue me.

"You didn't call them, did you?"

He just looked at me.

"Never hurts to ask," I said. "You could have some sort of Munchausen by Proxy rescue thing going."

"What?"

"Never mind." Okay. Clearly, I was little bit rattled. "It was stupid to think that they were going to give up."

And I wasn't stupid. Dammit.

"But why not get you when you came out of headquarters this morning?"

I shook my head. "Too visible." The Crypto City police had surveillance everywhere. Plus I'd used Staci's identification to get into OPS, not my own. When I'd scanned out of the building with my Jamie Hunt badge, they might not have had time to catch me.

If I knocked out Lucas and myself, I was down to two suspects. Dr. Fitzhugh and Carson. And possibly Carson's secretary, if she made the appointment.

Three suspects.

I closed my eyes and walked back through my time in the building.

"Don't go on Highway 100 just yet." I slid up into the passenger seat, knotted the leopard print blouse at my waist, and strapped in. "Turn left and then left again."

Lucas did what I asked without question. A nice enough change. "Pull into that parking lot."

We waited. A Yellow taxi cab screeched up to the entrance then sat.

"Quick thinking."

I shrugged, uncomfortable with the admiration in his voice. "Not quick enough." If Lucas hadn't been there....

Everywhere I turned my world was crumbling. What the hell was going on? I watched but didn't see any suspicious cars waiting for me to come out of the building.

The cab driver honked.

When no one came out, he hopped out of his car and strode to the entrance. He didn't look annoyed. He looked ecstatic, like a government man about to nail his suspect. He jerked open the door and his jacket swung open revealing a shoulder holster with a weapon.

"Time to go." Lucas had seen the same thing I had.

"Let's wait."

The offices must have been bugged. Either that or they had tapped into cell transmissions and heard my call to the cab company. I rubbed a hand over my chest.

Lucas flipped open a cell phone and pretended to be talking. We watched in silence as the pseudo-cab driver got back in. The driver waited another five minutes then got out of the cab again, not even bothering to disguise his wrist radio.

He ran into the building then stomped out a few minutes later, banging the flat of his hand on the hood of the cab before getting in and pealing away.

"Let's get out of here." Fine tremors shook my body. "Nice and slow."

"In a minute."

I was sinking into quicksand and every time I nearly got out, some new tentacle pulled me back in. I craved a simple touch. Yet I couldn't ask. I couldn't show that weakness. Weakness was a tool to be used against you.

Wanting warmth, compassion could backfire on me in a heartbeat. I'd lived for years without comfort. Why was I now suddenly craving the unthinkable?

"I'm fine." The words were more for me than him.

Lucas's hand cupped my shoulder. Possibly the least erogenous zone on the human body and yet, everything in me stood up and took notice. I shivered. Involuntary and inescapable.

His eyes narrowed at my body's betrayal. Lucas yanked me toward him and unable to resist, I let him. He angled his head to the side, slammed his lips to mine.

This was no gentle kiss. No easy seduction.

I burned like the first time we'd come together. I reached for him as if possessed, clasped his jaw and devoured his mouth.

He licked and nipped trying to inhale me.

Everything within me combusted. My body was on fire.

Heat poured through me. I wanted him inside me. Now. If the console wasn't in the way, I'd be on top of him.

Now. Now. Now.

The word beat in my head, in rhythm with the blood pulsing through me, coursing, pounding, arousing.

I tried to pull him closer. The sharp edges of the papers from my file cut into my belly, stopping me. As much as I wanted to lose myself in the oblivion of his touch, we needed to leave in case they sent another team to investigate the area.

I untangled my fingers from his hair, pushed away from him, my back hard against the molded plastic passenger door. "We need to get out of here." My voice was steady, even, with none of my turmoil coming through.

"Right." He pressed his hands on the steering wheel gripping tightly. "You're right." But he didn't like it.

"In case they come back."

Lucas turned the car, taking the back exit from the parking lot, checking his rear view mirror repeatedly.

I had to get back in control, away from the spiraling emotions that had overcome me a minute ago.

"Did you bring everything with you?" I wanted to kick some ass. To fight, defend myself, my sister. But I didn't know who I was supposed to fight. The link was there. I just had to find it.

"Of course." He gave me a look and sped up the ramp toward the airport.

He really hadn't needed me. In fact, with the people chasing me, he'd be far better off nowhere near me.

"Why did you come get me?"

Lucas didn't answer. He concentrated on weaving in and out of the afternoon traffic, glancing frequently in the rear view mirror. My position afforded a view of his driver's side mirror. No one was following.

"Why?" Give me an answer, even if it's a lie.

His hand snaked out and grabbed my fingers. "Our connection."

I snorted.

"Jesus. I knew you weren't ready to hear that. Even when I know it's not a good idea, you push until I react. How the hell do you do that to me?" He laced his fingers with mine. It made me realize again, how seldom people touched me.

I'd been wrong. I didn't want to hear the truth. "You don't need me for anything."

"We've been working pretty well as partners," he countered.

"I don't do partners." Just like I didn't do relationships or friends. Or sisters, I mourned.

"You do now." His tone was merciless.

"Why?"

He switched lanes, exiting to the airport's short term parking. "We're linked. Somehow, someway. I can't let you go. This...thing between us is a gift. If I don't play it out then I'm squandering the gift to my life and yours."

"Life is a penance," I blurted. I kept my gaze on the steel and glass geometric design of the terminal. Life was like that building, constructed of solid beams and shatterable glass. The implacable and the fragile. I didn't have room for fragile in my life.

I left that to Bella. Bella whose life would be all the normal mine was not. Bella who would have everything that I couldn't. Bella who was telling family secrets to a guy who didn't exist.

Lucas screeched into a parking stall. "Who do you have to do penance for? Who, Jamie?"

I didn't answer. I couldn't. No one knew about Bella. No one but Carson and me.

Carson. Who may have betrayed me.

"Fine. You want me to leave you alone?"

My heart stopped then started beating in triple time. I did want him to leave me alone. So why was my body treating his words like a hostile threat?

"Tell me where to take you so you have someone, anyone, to help you."

My throat closed, burning with the need to cry out.

"Give me a name. Someone you can turn to."

I was silent.

He slammed his palms against the steering wheel. "You can't do it. You have no one."

I still didn't answer.

"I'm it, baby. Unless you can tell me where I can drop you off. Where you have some support. You're stuck with me."

"I don't need anyone." I forced the words out, my voice gravelly and rough.

"You think you don't, but you're wrong. We all need someone," Lucas said. "I learned that the hard way."

"I'll wait here while you go pick up the van." I made my voice as even as plate glass. "The hotel at the airport is our best bet. Even if they discover the rental, they'll expect us to go far away from the scene not stay on top of it."

"The skirt to go with that top is in my duffel in the back."

I nodded.

He pushed the keys under the front mat. "Are you going to be here when I get back?" His stark eyes were haunted.

"Yeah." Because he was right. I had no one.

Before, that knowledge had comforted me, filling up all the lonely crevasses inside of me, because if I had no one I could keep my sister safe. I watched Lucas drive away, and I realized I wasn't alone.

I had Lucas. At least for now. Maybe, just maybe I should accept his presence for the gift that it represented.

# CHAPTER 26

*S*how time.

I flipped open the two pages I'd taken from my psychiatric file. One had a list of unanswered questions. The other was the general information page. Quickly I skimmed looking for the critical data.

Family: deceased. No mention of Bella. Thank God.

I pulled out the cell phone and punched in Carson's number, keeping in mind if they were tracing me I wouldn't have much time before they could get a lock.

He answered on the first ring.

"Is this line secure?" I snapped out without saying hello.

"You can talk." He hadn't answered the question. "What happened?"

I tossed the pages on the driver's seat. Then I crawled into the back seat of the Toyota and unbuttoned my pants. "There were people waiting for me at the doctor's office."

"You got away."

"Yeah." While holding the cell, I shimmied awkwardly out of my pants, shoved them in the bag, and snatched up the only skirt in the duffel. Spandex.

"Good work."

A plane took off overhead—giving Carson a bead on my location. If I sat in the rental car long enough, would I see a black Suburban cruising the parking lot?

"Where are you?"

Not a chance. "I'll call in later."

"But Jamie--"

"Someone in the NSA has to be involved."

"In what though?" He sounded as frustrated as I felt.

"You need to bring the good doctor in, ask her who called during our session."

"Fitzhugh?" I heard the surprise in his voice. "I can't imagine...."

"Yes." Too much similarity existed between her questions and those asked by the white-coated man in the warehouse.

"I need to know your location." Urgency threaded his voice.

I couldn't trust Carson. Not after today. Not after now.

I'd called him hoping to be reassured. Hoping the vibe I'd felt this morning was just post-mission jitters. Hoping he really hadn't lied to me. But he wasn't reassuring me. "I'm fine."

"I don't want you out there without some kind of backup."

*Lucas* was my backup. I had Lucas. I couldn't tell Carson I was still hooked up with him, not after the way he'd threatened me this morning.

I must have hesitated too long.

"Jamie." He said in a stern tone, "Turn your ring on so I can track you."

The ring. Nope.

Lucas's van rolled to a stop three lanes over. He sat inside. Waiting. Time to go. "I'll be fine."

"But--" Carson sputtered as I cut the connection. I checked my surroundings, looking all ways before sliding out of the car.

With the duffel bag slung over my shoulder and my other hand resting firmly on the grip of the 9mm I'd found inside, I scooted over to the van.

Lucas pushed the door open. His eyes gave him away. He thought I'd be gone.

Another plane roared overhead. An Indian Summer breeze gusted warm air and swirled through the rows of cars in the parking lot. The van idled, the engine pinging. I trembled at the brink of this crossroads.

I needed to make a decision right now about what was going to happen next. I'd lived my life alone since I was fifteen years old. Depended on no one. Relied on no one. Except Carson.

And I couldn't trust Carson anymore.

I hopped inside and hoped like hell I hadn't just made the biggest mistake of my life. "We need to make a stop."

Lucas didn't argue. "Where?"

"Bus station."

He smiled, showing plenty of teeth and no warmth. "Careful. You're getting predictable."

We cruised through the parking lot toward the payment booths and freedom. Dr. Fitzhugh's questions about my family circled in my head like vultures waiting to attack. The need to check on Bella burned a hole in my gut. However, I wouldn't do Bella any good if I got caught.

"You want to get in back?"

"Yeah." Just in case the airport was being watched.

* * *

WHEN WE GOT to the bus station, I adjusted my skirt and climbed back up front.

"What changed your mind?" He wanted to know why I hadn't run. Yet.

"Question number three?"

He shrugged. "Why not?" He didn't think I'd be around for four and five.

"You did." After his speech about me needing someone. He understood me well enough to know his words, his beliefs would cause me to run fast and far in the other direction. Instead of making it difficult to leave, he'd given me the opportunity and the means to go. I could have taken the rental car, the 9 mm, and been long gone.

Lucas parked the van.

"Is it temporary?" He wanted to know if I was ditching him here.

"No." I opened the van door. "I'll be right back."

Lucas opened his door and hopped out, pressing the remote key lock after I'd jumped down.

I rounded the hood of the van. "You don't honestly think I'd take off now, do you?"

He gave me a steady look. When he spoke, his voice was even, unwavering. "I'll tag along."

"Lucas." I lay my hand on his wrist, the tendons and muscles rippled and tensed beneath my fingers. "You made your case."

He jerked to a stop. His gaze dropped down to my hand on him. "Really?"

I flushed, snatched my hand away. *Great move, Hunt.* "Let's get this over with."

"Are we leaving?"

"Nope. Just retrieving a little care package." One the NSA had no record of.

We walked through the doors together. The Greyhound station was the same as always. Even the renovations, additions of plusher seats and high tech lights, couldn't disguise the sense of hopefulness and hopelessness of the occupants.

Tired mothers with little babies, teenagers whose clothes looked lived in not just slept in, men with holes in their shoes more troublesome than the holes in their lives paraded through the wide hallways towards new places. A pall coated the air, not visible like the grime on the floors, but just as pervasive.

As I noted the updates, I sent a little prayer of hope their budget hadn't extended to the bathrooms.

I gestured to a bank of seats. "Wait here."

Lucas slumped in the already worn seat.

In the women's bathroom, I waited patiently until the third stall from the left was open. I locked the door, wrapped some toilet paper around my fingers and opened the receptacle for used tampons. I eased out the liner bag. And at the bottom, in a little magnet key case, was my prize. I retrieved the case, flipped the lid open.

The key was still there.

I slipped the key into my pocket, tossed the magnetic holder in the garbage, and hustled out of the bathroom.

Lucas was waiting outside the door. It stung.

He looked me up and down. "Itchy feeling."

Huh. Usually his itchy coincided with mine, but I wasn't buzzed. Had to point it out. "I'm okay."

"Humor me."

We watched the lockers for a few minutes, looking for anyone who looked out of place, but everything seemed fine.

The locker contents were personal, not company owned. No one at the NSA would know about this locker. No one.

The identifications and credit cards were purchased illegally and paid for in cash. There was not one link to Jamie Hunt or the NSA.

"Let's do it," he said.

I stuck the key in locker 105 and removed a duffel.

We both looked around. I still felt fine. "Back to the airport?"

"A woman who can read my mind." He grinned, his mouth curving in amusement, his eyes crinkling at the corners.

Not hardly.

* * *

As I SASHAYED through the hotel lobby, I tugged on the black spandex mini skirt. "What is your deal with spandex?"

Lucas ambled one pace behind me, both our duffel bags in one hand. "Condenses well and doesn't show wrinkles."

I tugged on the skirt again.

His arm curved around my waist, hot and strong. "And looking at your ass is a perk."

"Pervert."

"I am not."

"That's how it starts."

"My sex drive is perfectly normal." Lucas raised his brows and played along. He muttered under his breath, "Just frustrated."

Our banter carried us through the lobby and up to the standard room with two double beds. Lucas ordered dinner, while I went into the bathroom and ripped open the duffel from the bus station to review the contents.

Lucas hung up the phone and turned on the television to a music station to cover our conversation. He sauntered into the bathroom, rubbing his hands together like a madman anticipating mayhem. "What have you got? High tech scanners, listening devices, tracking equipment?"

"No toys," I said drily. I held up four driver's licenses. Three women, one man. Hair dye, hair pieces, facial modifiers, colored contacts, various fashion accessories, an instant camera, and credit cards.

He took the driver's licenses and studied them. "They made a mistake on two of the women. There's no way you could pass for five foot five."

Two for me, two for Bella.

"This guy's statistics will work for you," I said and tossed him a box of L'Oreal Ash hair color that would come off looking gray.

"So you go for older guys?"

"No one." Even when I wanted to.

"That one time only rule." Lucas fingered the glasses case. "So what's the deal with that?"

I selected an i.d. for a five foot five inch girl with black hair and bright blue eyes. "We can color our hair after dinner."

"It'll be just like a slumber party," Lucas mocked.

What the hell was he talking about? My face must have shown an absolute blankness.

He explained, "Stay up late and do each other's hair."

I carefully laid out the items we'd need on the bathroom counter, refusing to remember I hadn't ever been to a slumber party.

He touched my shoulder but I shrugged off his hand. I didn't need his comfort or his touch. He curved a hand around my waist, swinging me around to face him.

"I'm sorry," he whispered. His lips brushed mine ever so softly. I gave in to the need to touch him and let myself curve into the hard planes of his chest.

His hand cupped my jaw with infinite gentleness, a tender intimacy that shook me.

The soft assault on my lips, the gentle lave of his tongue against mine, the feather light stroke of his fingertips along my collarbone, the sensations that tumbled through me were foreign.

I held onto his shoulders gripping tightly, wanting our original urgent passion back, because that I understood. That I knew how to reject.

Temptation shimmered as possibility within me. I wanted to reach out and hold onto the illusion of this intimacy, this connection he was so sure we had.

A knock on our hotel room door saved me. I drew away, sliding my weapon from the thigh holster.

He cocked an eyebrow. "Is that a gun in your pocket or are you happy to see me?"

The knock came again. "Room service."

Lucas mouthed. "Stay here."

I slid behind the bathroom door, peering through the slit of space between the almost closed door and the frame, weapon at the ready, but the delivery woman never even looked.

The scent of grilled beef and garlic wafted to my nose. My traitorous stomach growled. The swish of the cart's wheels and the clatter of metal lids disguised the noise, hopefully.

"Boy, was I hungry," Lucas said in a Texas drawl and handed the server a tip. "Thank you kindly."

As the spring loaded door slammed shut, I eased out of the bathroom.

"Good thing she wasn't paying any attention. A little bit hungry, are we?" he teased.

I needed my toughness back. I couldn't let the insanity of the last few minutes overtake my good sense. I couldn't afford to have these feelings. Or this connection. I kept my mouth flat, my gaze hard. "Let's eat."

"Oh goody. Ms. Bad Ass is back."

I ignored him. If he knew how much I wanted to relax, wanted to enjoy his company, him, he'd never let up. "We've got work to do."

Lucas sighed. "Let's work while we eat."

He pushed aside the magazines on the desk and set up his laptop and we were ready to access Staci's files.

The password protect came up. "Let's see if this is it."

Lucas typed in MARA.

A message popped up on the screen. "Welcome Dr. Grant."

"We're in."

Lucas leaned forward in the chair, hunched over the desk, his gaze intent on the screen. I perched on the bed across from him. He angled the laptop so we could both see the screen and searched Staci's files, looking for Wishbone. The computer whirred as it cycled through all of the folders.

In my duffel from the locker, I had also kept a laptop. I set it up across from Lucas. The software on this one was a little bit out of date, but it would still work.

Lucas said heavily, "The computer search found a file on Johnny."

"That's great." I glanced across the wood desk.

He wasn't moving. He'd shifted his gaze to mine. "Let me help you."

I leaned across the space and pressed a button on his laptop to open Johnny's file and close our conversation. "Quit stalling."

He knew full well I was the one stalling. He reached out, covered my clenched fingers with his. "Let me help you."

"Looks like his mother was right to be worried." I deliberately opened my fist. "That's what it looks like on the surface anyway."

His gaze snapped to the screen, an instant hit of dismay obvious on his face. "Damn."

I scanned through the file quickly. Name, date of birth, ethnic background, parents's background, religious affiliation, school history, work history.

"Sounds like the same guy." I wanted his attention away from me, away from my problems.

"Yeah." Lucas opened the file of another 'recruit' and scanned through the details. Smart of him to check more than one file. As he skimmed through more files a commonality became evident. Many of her file subjects had family members killed by U.S. carelessness.

"You see it too?"

I nodded. "Common thread."

"Yeah." Lucas didn't look happy. Even though he'd found Johnny Wishbone, he hadn't 'found' him.

He was close to finding Johnny. Then he'd be gone. Whatever I could do to speed that along, I would. And if possibly I was going to miss him when he left, no one would know that but me.

Lucas just looked at me steadily, frustration in his gaze.

This information was basically a dead end. She had a file about Johnny on her computer but the file had no specific information. No details such as if or where he was sent, dates, assignments, incarceration.

"Maybe he was only a potential recruit." Not an actual recruit. "Maybe she just has files on anyone who comes to her attention."

I couldn't believe I was trying to reassure him. The chance that Johnny was mixed up in Staci's business was strong. It was more a question of whether she'd tapped him for a terrorist trainee or as an undercover CIA recruit posing as a terrorist trainee.

"Yeah. But then who really checked him out of the hospital? And where the hell is he?" Lucas rubbed the back of his neck. "I have a feeling I can't shake. Staci Grant is the key."

Since I'd seen his feelings in action, I didn't doubt his intuition was right.

*Not my problem.* I wouldn't let it be.

Lucas ticked off what we knew about the situation. "One. Staci dies in a prison camp. Two. Someone posing as Staci checks Johnny out of the hospital. Three. There is plenty of intelligence chatter regarding her. Four. Your mission is to impersonate her."

"Which turned out to be incorrect." I couldn't help but point out.

He kept going. "Five. Someone is watching her house. Six. Johnny is in her files."

Seven. She has a file related to my mission on her computer.

He was right. But I didn't have to like it. "I'm going to color my hair."

"Might as well do it together."

I sauntered to the bathroom as if the need to run from the room, from him, didn't burn in me.

First I needed to do some trimming. I snatched up the pair of scissors and started chopping in what looked like a haphazard fashion.

"You know what you're doing?"

"We get training in how to change our appearance."

"Ah." Lucas opened a box and pulled out the directions. "Trying to distract me by giving out classified information."

I ignored him. When I finished cutting my hair, I flushed the trimmings down the toilet in a few small batches.

He tossed the L'Oreal box at me. I ripped open the package and poured the clear fluid into the plastic bottle with the pitch black dye.

"You took the license of one of the short women."

Damn him for noticing. "She's eighteen. If anyone questions me, I'll tell them I grew."

"Still puts you in the category of standing out."

"I'll make it work."

"Bella is five foot five."

His words were so shocking, so out of place, I nearly bobbled the fluid.

I shook the bottle mixing the two chemicals and hoped he didn't catch the tremble in my hands. "Who?"

"You know who she is."

"I don't know anyone by that name." Not now anyway. The odor of peroxide ate at my ability to breathe. I tried to draw in air but my lungs had seized.

Bella. No one could know about Bella.

"It took me awhile, but I finally figured out Donald Christian was only your target because of his connection to Bella Holden."

Dammit. I'd thrown the piece of paper away.

"Her family died in a spectacular car bomb explosion." He wrapped a towel around my shoulders, his fingers squeezed in comfort before he let go.

"How terrible for her." *How terrible for me.*

"About the same time as Staci Grant's grandparents."

So he'd picked up on the similarity. Rage and fear roiled in my stomach, fighting like two cats, snarling and ripping at my insides. "You must have a really good memory."

Lucas dragged a chair into the small bathroom.

"She also has an investment account that mirrors Staci Grant's and yours." He hammered away as he pushed me gently into the chair. Lucas squirted the color on my shortened hair and started massaging the cool liquid onto the strands.

"Tell me who Bella is." Lucas met my gaze in the mirror, pinning me with piercing intentness.

I knew this interrogation technique. Wait. Stare. Intimidate. I'd perfected it at twenty.

I didn't speak. Couldn't.

All this emotion about my family and Bella, my disillusionment with Carson chipped away at me. On the television, Billy Joe crooned about walking alone on a *Boulevard of Broken Dreams*, the lyrics my one stark truth.

I walk alone.

"Obviously she's important to you."

I twisted the plastic bag up and knotted it on my forehead. Ripping open the box of Ash, I began mixing the colors, hoping he'd drop the subject.

"You kept one tall and one short i.d."

God damn him for noticing that too. "Never hurts to keep your options open."

With a jerky movement, he twirled the chair around straddling the wood with strong legs, the flex of his thigh muscles playing inside the soft denim.

I thought he'd finally dropped the subject of Bella. I thought he was relaxed, until I noticed his white knuckles and the tendons standing out on his wrists. "Right. Make me into Grandpa."

Then we'll talk. I could hear the words even though he hadn't spoken.

"Let me get a feel for your texture." I ran my fingers through his hair. An excuse to touch him. Even though his words terrified me, the small contact soothed me in some elemental way.

"You could always get a job cutting hair."

I hesitated, unsure I wanted to continue this conversation but curious to know where he'd go with it. "What does that mean?"

"You've been associating with me. Your career could be in jeopardy. Quit the NSA. Cut hair."

"I have no intention of quitting." I couldn't and keep Bella safe. Although now I might not have a choice.

"Why not get a real life?" Like he had. He left that unspoken. "Make connections. Live."

I couldn't help but attack. "Oh, like you are?"

"What's wrong with my life?"

"It's a fake, fringe life." I squeezed the plastic bottle spurting the coloring fluid onto his hair as my anger and frustration came bubbling out.

"Tell me."

"You pretend you're so involved."

"I am involved," he defended. "What about the guys in the restaurant, the men on the stoop?"

"Casual." I massaged the color into his hair and scalp with slippery plastic gloves.

"No."

"Yes. And if you were really that connected you wouldn't have been so reluctant to take this case for Johnny's mother."

"Bullshit." But I could see the guilt, the reserve on his face.

"Don't you lecture me about being involved. At least I'm honest about staying alone."

His shoulders tensed under the towel and he quivered with the need to get up and out.

I fumbled for harsh words, anything I could think of, that might drive him away before I let myself lean on him. Let myself deepen that connection I could feel and kept resisting. "If you'd really been involved with your life you wouldn't be sitting here with me right now," I said viciously.

"Not true."

"You'd be working any angle you could to track Johnny down." Instead of sticking with me.

He opened his mouth to fire back a denial but the truth dawned. "So involve me."

I wasn't sure what surprised me more, his agreement with me or his calm request.

"Involve me," he said again urgently.

I slipped the bag over his head and twisted the plastic up on his forehead. "No."

Lucas stood up, stood before me, the solemn reserve on his face striking fear. I wasn't even sure what I was afraid of, him agreeing to leave or him insisting on staying.

"Let me in," he urged.

I pressed my lips together. I wouldn't, no, couldn't.

Lucas said reluctantly, "Donald Christian is a government cover."

"What?" My greatest fear had materialized. Jesus, could he drop any more bombshells?

"He's been getting weekly deposits of two grand."

"When was the first deposit?"

"Exactly two weeks ago."

The day after he 'met' Bella. Shit. Shit. Shit.

I tried to assimilate the new information Lucas had tossed at me like a matador waving a red blanket at an angry bull.

"And you're just now getting around to telling me this."

My God. Were they paying him to watch her...or recruit her?

I'd asked Carson about Bella and he'd been evasive and dismissive. No need to worry. I should have known. I should have known. My hands balled into fists, hot and ready to pound something. Someone.

Why hadn't he brought this up sooner?

"I'd hoped you would confide in me," he said, answering my unspoken question reluctantly. "Hoped you'd ask for my help."

"I don't need your help." I couldn't afford his help. It was imperative I touch base with Bella. Now. I wished I could go see her, visually confirm her safety but it was too dangerous. I could tap into the cameras at her dorm. It was risky but, in that moment, necessary.

He already knew she was important to me. I'd thought as long as I kept her identity a secret, she was safe.

"Yes. You do." He caught my bicep as I brushed past.

The clock radio buzzed. Time for me to rinse.

I unclipped the plastic bag, tossed it into a garbage bag from the duffel, and bent over the sink. Lucas pushed away my hands, rubbing his fingers through my cropped black hair, slowly washing away the dye. I wished I could wash away my worries as easily.

So far all of my information had come from Lucas. Maybe he was playing me. If he was, I'd fallen right into it.

"I can practically hear the synapses firing in your brain," Lucas said grimly.

I didn't answer. I'd already given away too much. Time to start acting like the independent, aggressive agent I was.

I ignored him and dried my hair.

"I can help you." Lucas made one last stab at trying to

insinuate himself into my world but it wasn't going to work. Nothing he could say would sway me.

I was on my own.

He wrapped the thin white hotel towel around my head.

I tried to get past him, but he curled his fingers around my bicep and pulled me close. Leaning into me, he brushed his mouth against my ear...and dropped another bomb.

"Bella's name is in Staci Grant's files."

# CHAPTER 28

*J* couldn't move. Couldn't breathe.

As Lucas rinsed his own hair, I stood frozen. I knew it was a mistake to let him know how much that revelation rocked me but I couldn't seem to pull it together.

Bella was supposed to be safe. Untouchable. I'd spent the last thirteen years of my life making it so.

A phone rang.

The sound jerked me out of my fog and I reflexively drew my weapon out of the holster. No one was supposed to know we were here.

I blinked.

"It's my cell, Jamie." Lucas stood in front of me, hands raised. His voice rumbled in a soothing, calming tone. "My cell. We're fine. You're fine."

My hand tightened around the grip. Bella. I had to protect Bella.

"Bella's fine right now."

I lowered my weapon slowly. God, I was a mess. The events of the last few days jumbled around in my head, too much to assimilate. Every time I turned around some new betrayal punched at me.

Lucas pressed a button on his cell phone, not taking his eyes off of me. "Goodman."

My arms hung at my sides as I stood in front of him, lost and more alone than I'd felt since age fifteen. The weight of the 9mm pulled my hand down like an anchor setting a ship and I sank onto the floral bedspread.

"Hey." He still watched me. "It's Barb."

He turned slightly, his profile stark in the muted light. I wondered if he wanted a more private conversation. Maybe. I couldn't bring myself to move.

"Great," he murmured into the phone and beelined for the night stand at the side of the bed. After pulling out a pen, he scribbled on the complimentary hotel paper.

"What?" Lucas gouged the pen into the pad.

She must have the final component of the drugs in the syringe. I couldn't bring myself to care, not at this moment. Too many disasters in too short of a time. Bella, connected to Staci Grant, was the final straw.

Lucas's hand was white as he wrote down whatever Barb told him. The hard ballpoint scratched audibly in the small room.

Mental note. Make sure to remove that pad when we leave. Lucas had probably made an impression on all the pages in the little booklet.

"Uh-huh. Okay. Thanks, babe. I owe you one. Watch out."

He pressed the off button but didn't move.

"You okay?" he asked.

I wanted to laugh. Okay? No. I hadn't been okay for years.

Through it all ice trickled through me. *Bella wasn't safe.*

*Bella wasn't safe.* If she was in Staci Grant's files something was terribly wrong. Carson must have known Bella was on some agency's radar and he hadn't said a word.

Betrayal ate at me like acid at skin. I wasn't okay but I needed to know what Barb had to say.

"What was in the syringe?"

He didn't answer.

Nothing could faze me now. I waited, instinctively knowing Lucas needed time to sort it all out. We weren't going anywhere tonight.

"The data files you sent were the final piece she needed to put it all together." Lucas said cautiously, "The chemical was an antidote."

That shocked me out of my stupor.

"An antidote?" All along I'd been under the assumption that the final component was the DNA altering drug she'd referenced. But if it was an antidote....

I'd unthinkingly crouched into a fighting stance.

"It seems to be an antidote to the drug she told you about before."

What did that mean? Had I already been injected with the original drug? Why give me an antidote if I hadn't?

"So they weren't going to inject me with a DNA altering drug." They were going to inject me with an antidote. Shit.

I needed to lash out at something, punch something. I clenched my hands into fists and started a series of Krav Maga punches and warm up kicks.

Lucas fell into a neutral stance. "Apparently not."

My suspicions were growing. Before Barb went to work in the private sector she'd done classified work for the government. That was handy wasn't it? "Her connections to the drug seem awfully convenient."

His palm slapped at my leg as I lashed out with a knee

strike tactic. Then Lucas responded calmly to my snarl. "We're lucky she'd done some assistant work on the Human Genome project."

He blocked my kick and struck out with his own. I chopped his foot and executed an arm blow that he managed to evade.

"Again, awfully handy." Perfect Barb.

Lucas stepped forward into my next move, somehow knowing what I planned. I dropped into position for combat neutralizing grappling.

Lucas mimicked my stance. "That's why it took so long for her to figure it out. The components didn't add up. Whatever you sent her clicked everything into place. She realized the drug would counteract or negate the impact of another drug."

The play of his biceps and deltoids mesmerized me as I assimilated possibilities. If they had been going to inject me with the antidote....

He performed an intricate technique to grab me in a choke hold, but I couldn't bring myself to care.

"We need to find out more about the original drug," he said with vicious precision, his forearm strong and tight across my neck.

"And whether I received an injection of it." I finished for him. Had I? What did this modifying drug do? Had it impacted how I was doing my job? What was the intent of the drug? And what was the intent of the people administering it?

I broke his hold. And I realized he'd let me.

"This may not be the best time to mention it but Barb would like to look at any other data you've got."

I moved away from him, kicking out again, performing a defense against multiple assailants, my arms and legs striking out as if I could knock down all the unseen enemies coming at me. Kicked as if I could decimate the last few days. As if through sheer brute force I could change the chain of events that brought me to this hotel room.

"You studied Krav Maga," Lucas said.

I recognized the attempt to distract me, and for a moment, I let him. All NSA field agents were trained in a variety of defensive techniques. I just happened to prefer the Israeli Army fighting moves. More pain. "Yeah."

It was unusual that he also knew the moves but Lucas continually surprised me. I wouldn't ask.

He offered. "There's a studio near my apartment. I know the owner so I have a built in sparring partner."

Lucas grabbed my ankle. I thought about doing a mid-air twist and breaking his hold but my heart wasn't in it.

He let go of my ankle, his right arm wrapped around my shoulders and pulled me tight against his chest. I let myself sag against him, my forehead resting along his cheek. His left hand cupped my head and he pressed a kiss to my temple. The gesture was sweet. Nothing I usually wanted or needed.

"We'll figure it out."

For the first time the word 'we' didn't scare me.

I allowed myself one more second to regroup in the comfort of his embrace.

"We?" I said in my toughest voice.

"We."

I could either chose to trust him or leave.

I reviewed everything that had happened since I'd met him. I'd been kidnapped. I'd confiscated a syringe full of an antidote to a DNA altering drug.

I'd been followed, lied to, and betrayed by the very government I'd served for the past thirteen years. I'd probably been injected with a drug that manipulated my genes but I didn't know in what way, possibly impacting my reactions to everything. So not only couldn't I trust my handler or my government, I couldn't trust myself.

I took a deep breath then spewed the information in one long exhalation. "*Bellaismysister.*"

"Holy shit."

"Succinctly put." My heart pounded as if my adrenaline had kicked into fight or flight and refused to surrender. I hadn't spoken those words aloud in thirteen years and claiming her as mine kindled something giddy within me.

Lucas shoved me onto the bed and pushed my head between my legs. "My God."

"I'm okay." My voice was muffled by the quilted bedspread.

"Stay there for one more minute until my heart rate settles back down."

"I wasn't going to faint." I pushed up against his hand indignantly.

"Right." A faint sheen of sweat covered his face. "You were whiter than the sheets."

He sank down next to me. His arm curled around my shoulders and he pulled me against his side. The scent of warm male and hair color chemicals tickled my nose. Heat poured off of him, seeping into me, the smooth skin of his bicep hot against my frigid back.

When had I gotten so cold?

I tried to shift away from him but Lucas held me tight. "Stay." He stroked his hand lightly down my arm.

When had I last been comforted by someone? My mother, perhaps, over some silly indiscretion or teenage misunderstanding.

We sat, the only sounds the murmur of the shower next

door, the soft huff of our breathing, and the smoky, jazz lament of Diana Krall from our television radio.

Thankfully he didn't ask me anything else about my sister. Just saying the words aloud was all I could handle right now. But I'd have to get to it soon. I took a deep breath unsure if I could even voice the request. I whispered, "I need your help."

With Bella. With everything.

The head rush hit me harder this time. Stars danced before my eyes. My life had spun completely out of control. I couldn't count on myself anymore. I needed help and that need was as foreign as the comfort he'd offered.

I'd turned him down before. Now I didn't have that luxury. For Bella I would do anything. I risked a glance at Lucas.

He still hadn't answered.

I said it again, louder. "I need your help."

"I know." He rested his chin on my head. "You've got it."

"Thank you."

I pushed away from him eager to put space between us, to establish that line again. The line of separatism. The line of control.

I had to check on Bella, had to reassure myself that for this moment, this night she would be okay. As if by seeing her, even just her image from a security camera, I could cast a spell of protection upon her.

Lucas seemed to understand I needed to be alone while I did it.

"I'll rinse my hair." He grabbed some things from his bag and headed for the bathroom. "After I'm done, I'll set up our nighttime security."

I cautiously tapped into Georgetown's security webcams.

Her dorm entrance was fairly busy at this time of night. I watched while Lucas took his shower but there wasn't any sign of her.

So, I accessed her account. She wasn't online and it was early. I tracked back to her last posting. She was going to bed. She had a mid-term tomorrow.

I tapped the screen lightly. *Keep safe, baby girl.*

Bella was safe. At least for tonight. But I still couldn't relax.

I ripped back the covers of one of the beds just as Lucas stepped up behind me. "I'd think that after our sparring you'd realize that's a dangerous place to stand."

Tension ratcheted through me twisting fear and anger into a tight ball in my gut.

He touched my shoulder. "Let me sleep with you."

Sex would be good right now.

I twirled, snaked my arms around to the hard planes of his back, bumping us together. He slanted his head and pressed his mouth to mine. But his kiss was too nice.

I wanted hard and fast and rough. I didn't want time to think about breaking my rules. I wanted oblivion. I rubbed my breasts against the mucles of his chest, willing him to ignore my lack of desire and take what I offered.

But he refused to give in and pulled his mouth from mine.

"I'm not talking about sex." Exasperation laced his words. "Let me hold you."

Bad idea. Terrible, terrible idea. A mistake in every way. I didn't want comfort.

Then I thought about all I'd learned today and the fight went out of me. We'd only be sleeping for a few hours anyway.

"Fine."

He cupped his body around mine and the sense of coming home struck me with such force I wanted to tighten and defend against the threat.

I pulled away, climbed in the bed and turned to face the wall, unable to watch as the mattress depressed beside me.

I willed my body to relax.

"Just for a few hours." Lucas pressed a kiss against the back of my neck. "Then we'll figure it all out."

There was that word again. We.

I'd never get used to it.

# CHAPTER 29

Dawn light filtered through a sliver of open curtain. I awoke instantly, alert to my surroundings. I hadn't thought I would sleep but apparently I'd fallen off within moments and slept. Deeply.

Lucas had wrapped his body protectively around mine. His left arm draped over my waist, his hand rested possessively below the curve of my breast. His fingertips brushed against the soft cotton t-shirt, my body tingling in response to the heat coming from him.

The white sheets cocooned us in a haven of warmth and softness. The urge to linger in that sanctuary, to take advantage of Lucas's early morning erection, spiraled through me. I'd read about the phenomenon but never actually encountered one. After all, I never slept with anyone, ever.

He was awake. I could tell by the cadence of his breathing he was waiting to see what I would do, letting me have the control. I appreciated the gesture. But it scared me too. I didn't want him to understand me. Especially after only a few days.

I let myself savor the sensations for one more moment, then curled away from him. "We need to get up."

He squeezed me in a one armed hug then let go, rubbing a hand over my spiky hair.

"We need to lay out *everything*." Go over all the events of the last week. And make a list of what we needed to accomplish. First, and most important, was Bella.

I had to assure myself she was okay, needed the cyber-check like an alcoholic craving a pull of liquor.

"Anything I need to disable before I go online?"

He punched a few buttons and deactivated the jury-rigged alarm system. If anyone had managed to track us, they hadn't attempted to access this room. Unless they were waiting for us to leave.

Lucas hopped in the shower while I got online. I found Bella in her favorite chat room. She was chatting with a girlfriend, GirlyQ. I'd checked out GirlyQ a few months ago. Nice girl, conservative family from Pennsylvania. She spearheaded a campus group for organic living.

Bella hadn't gone to bed last night. She'd gone out with Donald Christian, the liar.

GirlyQ: So when do I get to meet him.

Bella: I want to keep him to myself for a little longer, but I took a picture on my cell when he wasn't looking. <g>

A photo would be a goldmine. Come on, baby. Show me this guy so I can nail his balls to the wall.

GirlyQ: Come on. Dish.

Bella: Got to run. I've got to go to class. I'll send it from there. Later.

No! I screamed silently. I needed to see that picture. Now.

I tracked over to the webcam screen and watched Bella rush out the front doors and down the wide cement steps.

She was okay...at least right this minute.

I slowed my breathing, taking a long inhale and a deliberate, measured exhale. My normal patience was gone, replaced by the urgent imperative to protect my sister.

I'd spent the tail end of my childhood and my entire adult life in service to this country to see her safe yet suddenly that safety was threatened.

"She okay?" Lucas spoke from behind me, startling me.

Instinctively, I reduced the screen so he couldn't see Bella. "For now."

He knew I couldn't talk about her so he distracted me. "Did you send the rest of the data to Barb?"

With everything else that had happened, I'd forgotten. Quickly, with no hesitation beyond the simple momentary pause before hitting the send key, I emailed all of the scientists' files to Barb with a short note. Hopefully she could use the data to make sense of their research.

"Let's get to it." He rubbed my shoulders. "We've got until eleven to check out but we need to be gone before then. Just in case."

I nodded. We couldn't afford to stay in one place for too long. Sitting ducks got shot, no question.

I clicked on the television to cover the sounds of our conversation and thought back to the day we met, the day I was kidnapped. "How long were you following me that first day?"

He shrugged. "Most of the day."

"Only one day?" I went back over the two days I'd shadowed Staci Grant's life.

"Yeah."

"So someone was watching me for longer than a day."

"What?"

"I made an assumption." I blew out a breath. Once I'd hooked up with Lucas, I assumed he'd been the one watching me the whole time. Never assume anything until verified. I'd broken my own damn rules. "Give me your timeline."

"I saw the credit card activity, caught a red eye, got in that morning, rented a car and started tracking Staci, you, about an hour later."

But I hadn't noticed him until about four that afternoon, which told me I'd been distracted that day. I'd sensed I was being watched. I should have caught him tailing me, I thought with disgust.

"Don't sweat it. I'm good," he said, without an ounce of humility.

I couldn't let that go by. "I was distracted."

"How come?"

"I...." I'd been tired, coming off of a two week stint of listening to tapes, analyzing data. The mission details had been sketchy, due to the security clearance there was information I hadn't been given. "I had a weird feeling about the job."

Lucas made an encouraging noise and took out the clothes from my duffel. He kept the 'older man' clothes and tossed the 'teenager' clothes to me. "Why?"

I paused. This was a moment of truth.

Consulting with Barb and Zeke, I'd only given them pieces of the data with no way to put it all together unless they collaborated.

When I took the mission data out of headquarters, it had been cause for suspension, an intermediate to serious infraction.

Associating with Lucas, same thing.

But, telling Lucas about this mission was career suicide.

My mission was VRK. Very Restricted Knowledge. Only four or five people in the world had access. One was the President. Revealing this information went against everything I'd been taught, against every rule I lived by.

But something was wrong. Most importantly, Bella could be in trouble. And no one else was telling me the truth.

"Jamie?"

I carefully laid out the makeup and other items on the dresser in front of the mirror, then related all of the facts and information about the mission before I could change my mind.

Lucas stopped threading his belt through the khaki loops. "Other agents have been kidnapped?"

"Yeah."

"So why were you impersonating Staci?"

"There was chatter about Staci but my handler wouldn't specify beyond that. Staci's dead, but only a few people know that. So there I was."

"Don't leave out any detail."

Lucas knew about Bella. No other secret was worth keeping. "My handler lied to me."

"What a surprise. Someone in the espionage world lying."

He could mock all he wanted but to my knowledge it was the first time Carson had lied to me. Although he'd evaded answering a few times before.

"How did he lie?"

Before answering, I popped in contacts, changing my eye color from hazel to bright blue. "I asked about intelligence and he told me it was classified beyond my clearance level."

"Is that normal?"

"Depends on the mission. This particular mission has a very high clearance level."

"How high?" Lucas's eyebrows rose.

"Pretty much the highest." To ignore his dawning understanding, I picked up the black eye liner pencil and outlined my eyes in kohl, Goth-style.

Of course, Lucas didn't let it drop. "Thank you."

I shrugged him off.

"I know what happened before you were abducted." Lucas sent me a heated look. "What went on in the warehouse?"

In my mind, I went over everything that happened from waking up in the Suburban to busting out the delivery door. "Two people in lab coats, man and woman. They both said they wouldn't hurt me. She seemed determined. He came off as fanatical."

Lucas wound a tie around his neck and began the process of knotting it.

*Never influence the data with your own conclusions. You taught me that...obviously Agent Hunt's physical abilities are fantastic. Can't wait to get her in the lab, run some tests.*

"Their words indicated scientific research." The idea of being a lab rat made me shudder.

"Research for who or what?"

*Do you feel you have any weaknesses?*

"The old guy wanted to know what it would take to betray my country." At least...that's what I'd assumed from his comments about women's weaknesses.

Lucas snorted. "With you? Nothing."

As long as they didn't know about Bella, he was right. Although technically, I was betraying my country right now. *Focus on what you can control.*

I layered my lashes with mascara until they were thick.

"They tried to use you." *We won't hurt Lucas, as long as you come out.*

"Me?"

"Yeah. They told me they had you...wait, they had Lucas Smith."

"So, they didn't know my real name." Lucas tossed me a pair of jeans. "But they knew I existed."

I thought back to that moment. They had known about Lucas and wanted me to give up, to come out, to keep him safe.

*Our research shows that a woman's weakness is caring about the fate of others, most especially a threat to someone they care about. Why isn't this working with you?*

"They threatened to hurt you."

"Good thing I wasn't really captured." He smiled.

As I wiggled into the tight jeans, I agreed. I hadn't had any proof that they would not hurt Lucas. I hadn't hesitated. I would have let him die before I betrayed my country. The thought settled in my stomach like a lead weight.

Lucas touched me briefly, gently. "Hey. I'm fine."

I looked into his eyes. I wouldn't make the same decision today. Another frightening thought. I would come up with a creative solution instead.

I strapped a black leather, metal-spiked bracelet around my wrist. "There might have been collateral damage from the other kidnappings."

"Collateral damage, meaning other people related to the kidnap victims are killed?" Lucas responded slowly.

"Yeah." I thought about it for a moment. "Except, nothing in the mission file indicated that was the case."

I thought over the facts I did know about the kidnappings. "There were two events that happened prior to the known kidnappings. Staci Grant was killed in Afghanistan and Brad Johnson was murdered by a suspected double agent. I made the assumption that Staci and Brad Johnson hadn't been kidnapped."

"They could have been the first victims and you just didn't know it because they died."

Except that Staci Grant was captured long before the kidnappings started. And Agent Johnson died a week ago, again before the kidnappings started. "Those events happened before the kidnappings started," I said again.

"Unless you don't have an accurate start date." Lucas said, "Maybe there have been other victims who haven't admitted to being kidnapped."

I mulled that over. It was possible. Strict procedures were followed if an agent thought they might have been compromised. But what if they didn't tell anyone?

Lucas snapped his fingers. "What if the agents weren't killed because of the kidnappings but because of the original drug?"

"Something in the original drug causes them to get killed? That doesn't make any sense either." I went through their words again. "Huh."

"What?"

"The man in the warehouse referenced weaknesses. Twice." Lucas would qualify now.

Why hadn't I picked up on that earlier? The guy kept talking about weaknesses. *Do you feel you have any weakness?*

Lucas snapped his fingers. "Trying to find the weakness caused by or enhanced by the original drug."

It made a scary kind of sense. "A gene manipulation drug that enhances a person's weakness?" I shuddered. Knowledge of a specific agent's weakness would take the guesswork out of trying to find ways to compromise or capture the agent. If that information became available for sale, the potential for exploitation in the espionage world was huge.

"How could a drug be administered without agents' knowledge?" I strapped another leather and spike accessory to my right wrist.

I came up with various delivery methods and then discarded them while I methodically packed away the dye boxes and the plastic bottles, tying everything into the plastic CVS bag and shoving it in the duffel. I'd dump the bag away from the hotel.

Lucas packed clothes into his duffel as he worked out his thoughts. Neatly and efficiently. "Shots."

"Possibly."

"How often do you get vaccinated?"

"I get standard inoculations once every three months."

"How many?"

"Since I never know where I'm going or when, it's like a cocktail...."

"That's what Barb called the liquid in the syringe."

A cocktail. It made a sort of crazy sense. "Why not wait, give the second injection, the antidote in the next round of vaccinations?"

"Exactly. Administer the antidote the same way as the original drug." Lucas mused aloud. He pulled the instant camera from the side pocket of the duffel. "Lower profile. No one would have ever known."

"But if the side effects of the initial drug were that catastrophic, wouldn't you want to eliminate the problem, inject the antidote, right away?"

Catastrophic effects...like being killed by a suspected double agent as Brad Johnson had? Carson had insisted that Agent Johnson didn't have anything to do with this problem. But I'd already determined Carson wasn't being truthful.

"But who knew about the weakness? And how did they find out?" I wondered.

Lucas tossed me a black leather dog collar and a belt of chainlinks. "Mission debriefs."

"Yeah. Maybe." My voice was muffled as I tried to fasten the dog collar around my neck. "But that's more of an autopsy of what went right and what went wrong. If several agents were doing something wrong don't you think there'd be more rumors about it?"

"Maybe." Lucas's fingers brushed the back of my neck as he took the body decoration from me. "What happens after a mission goes wrong?"

"Easy. Just like today...." I trailed off. The shrink. Dr. Fitzhugh who used a phrase similar to the one the man in the warehouse had used. "Psych evals."

"I ran the license plate number from their van," Lucas said.

"Any leads."

"Fake registration."

I knew it wasn't going to be easy, but couldn't I catch at least one break? I squirted gel onto my hands and scrunched my hair into short spikes. "Let's run a check. Maybe the name will connect to something else."

"It wasn't a government car," Lucas said thoughtfully.

I'd picked up on that too. At least not one overtly connected to the government. "Did you get anything from the warehouse?"

"Nothing. I was too busy getting shot at." His eyes lit up with mischief.

He'd missed being in the field. "Adrenaline rush got to you."

"Hell yes." Lucas slid the aviator-style glasses onto his nose. "What about the papers you took from the doctor?"

I slicked black lipstick over my lips. I should have known he'd noticed.

"I only took two." The top paper she was consulting from and the initial client information file.

"Anything?"

"The paper she was making notes on didn't look like the other notes in my file. This has specific questions. How did you feel? What kind of response time did you have once the threat perception kicked in? What went through your mind? Any perceived weaknesses?"

I thought for a minute.

"But nothing about vaccination or inoculation dates." I blew out a breath.

I had to work on the theory that I'd been given the original DNA-altering drug. All the hypotheses in the world were just that, educated guesses.

Lucas motioned for me to sit. "Say cheese."

I frowned, just as he snapped the picture. He set the developing film on the dresser and handed me the camera.

I thought about the 5491 file. All the people abducted had that designation but I still didn't know what it meant. I hadn't looked this morning when Lucas was in the shower. I'd been too busy checking on Bella.

Did I tell Lucas about it? I didn't think I had a choice.

"Staci Grant has a file on her computer, 5491, that might have something to do with my mission." I fiddled with the camera, looking at the mechanisms instead of Lucas.

"What does 5491 stand for?"

"I don't know."

I looked through the view finder at him sitting on the bed. He'd even used his body language to change his age, hunching his shoulders and putting a sag in his lips. I snapped the picture.

He straightened up immediately. "Let's see if we can get into that file."

"Okay." We accessed Staci's files, plugged in two levels of passwords, and clicked on file *5491*.

If I could figure out the relationship between the NSA mission file, the scientist file and Staci's file I might be able to connect them all together.

His computer made a little bell noise. "Access denied."

Dammit. She had a third level of password.

I wanted to check to see if Bella had uploaded the picture of Donald Christian. "I need to check online."

Lucas waved me off and started the process of glueing our new pictures onto the fake driver's licenses.

I checked and sure enough the .jpg file was there. I clicked on the file and the picture began filling in on the screen.

Waiting, I grabbed a bottle of water out of the mini-fridge and took a swig.

I turned back to the screen as the picture began to solidify. I took another gulp then choked on the cool liquid.

"Lucas."

"With you in a minute." He was bent over the dresser, carefully applying the top layer of covering with the holographic image on it.

"Now."

Something in my voice must have clued him in and he turned.

"Holy shit. Is that recent?"

"Yesterday."

"Where'd you get that picture of Johnny?"

"You're sure that's him?" The guy wasn't looking straight at the camera, it was a half front/half side view.

"I've known his family for years."

I gestured toward the screen with the half empty bottle. "That's Donald Christian."

I watched realization dawn. Johnny Wishbone and Donald Christian were the same person.

# CHAPTER 30

Second story work was not my favorite. I regarded Staci Grant's bedroom window from the brick walkway and prayed we'd find answers. Some clue to her third-level password. I needed to know what the hell 5491 meant and Lucas needed answers about Johnny.

The sooner we got answers, the sooner I could get Johnny away from Bella. Lucas convinced me Johnny wouldn't hurt her. So I reluctantly agreed to wait until we could discover why Johnny Wishbone was pretending to be a student at Georgetown before I approached him.

Before I told him to stay the hell away from my sister, before I broke him in half and buried his body where no one would ever find it.

Possibly I hadn't mentioned that part to Lucas yet.

"Ready?" Lucas murmured into his tiny mouthpiece.

The words echoed in my head as the earpiece broadcast the sound.

"Yeah." I touched a finger to my ear. The white one piece work suit, with Mel's Window Washing printed in water blue on the back, hung limply on me. We'd agreed I would go through Staci's things, while Lucas stayed outside and squeegeed windows, keeping an eye on the alley behind the house.

We'd left the van, complete with a magnetic sign advertising clean windows fast, parked one house over from Staci's backyard. That didn't sit particularly well with me but the van needed to be easily accessible. Just in case.

We'd picked up a ladder at the Home Depot in Halethrope. Lucas propped the ladder against the house and we climbed to the second story quickly. He soaped up a window while I jimmied open her bedroom window using new magnets and double stick tape, and climbed inside.

Then I hustled to the bedside table and pulled out the remote. I punched in the code for the hidden door and waited to hear the slight slide of the door opening. Instead, I heard nothing.

I punched in the code again.

Still nothing.

Listening intently, I heard no other movement in the house. Maybe whoever kept watch on the house had changed the code. But that didn't make sense. The men who had come in last time didn't know anything about the secret doorway.

Maybe the door had gotten hung up on something. I walked over to the closet and slowly opened the doors. Nothing moved.

As the closet door swung open all the way, I realized why I hadn't heard the secret door slide.

Both doors were already open.

Before I could retreat, a man stepped out from the same place Lucas and I had hidden the last time.

"Drop the remote. Keep your hands where I can see them."

I kept silent, judging my options, as I knelt down slowly and placed the remote on the carpeted floor. It would be stupid to go for the weapon at my ankle.

Lucas's coveralls rustled in my ear. "Find anything?"

"Who are you?" The man with his cold gaze trained on me held an American-made weapon like he knew what to do with it. He stood about six foot three with broad shoulders tapering down to a narrow waist, hair military short, clothes black and nondescript, his ethnicity a Hispanic/Anglo-Saxon mix, facial features sharp and unremarkable.

Until you looked at his eyes.

"Who is that, Jamie?" Lucas must have picked up the guy's voice on his earpiece. Sensitive suckers.

"I don't suppose you'd believe...a window washer?" I hedged, wondering how the hell I could get out of this. I let my hands dangle at my sides trying to look as non-threatening as possible.

If anything the guy straightened more, his body alert and ready.

Lucas said, "Shit. I'm coming in."

"No," I said at the exact same time as the guy with the gun.

"What are you doing in this house?" The guy in the doorway stepped toward me.

"Are you in trouble?" Lucas barked.

This is why I didn't like working with a partner. I reassured Lucas first and hoped the guy with the gun wouldn't make any unexpected moves. "Trust me."

"Nope." Closet man narrowed his gaze. "I won't ask again."

I assessed my position. He was too far away to disable with a well-placed Krav Maga kick. The damage his weapon could do at the range of six and a half feet was significant, assuming he didn't miss. And based on his confidence, he wouldn't miss.

This could work to our advantage. We'd wanted to find something, anything that would give us a clue to Staci Grant's private password. A big clue stood right in front of me.

When dealing from a position of weakness, it could be beneficial to give something up. We needed this guy. "I'm looking for information about a young man Staci Grant recruited and I believe it's here."

"This is a private residence not an office," he parried.

I nodded my head toward the open stairway. "The files up there are private."

He stiffened.

The air behind me shifted and shimmered. Dammit. Lucas hadn't listened. And gun guy had figured it out.

"What is this--a goddamn party?" the guy said gruffly.

"Ramirez?" Lucas called from the beyond the open closet door.

"Holy shit. Goodman?" The guy's focus shifted behind me. The barrel of his weapon dipped to point at the floor.

Lucas trod past me, ignored the weapon, and grabbed the guy in a bear hug. "How the hell are you?"

Ramirez slapped Lucas on the back. "What the f—heck are you doing breaking into Staci's place?"

"Ah...missing person case."

"B & E suddenly become the new Bureau approved way to get inside a building?"

Lucas stepped back and looked uncomfortable. "I...left. Last year."

"The OPR smear." Ramirez looked regretful. "For what it's worth, I thought you got a raw deal, man."

"Thanks."

They were both verbally dancing around the real issue and we didn't have time. The surveillance out front could well do some sort of hourly rotation. "We need to get into her files."

Ramirez stiffened, going back on alert in a heartbeat. "She with you?"

"Jaime meet Jordan Ramirez."

Jordan Ramirez noted Lucas hadn't given my last name, just as I noted Lucas failed to tell me how he knew Jordan Ramirez.

I inclined my head.

"Staci isn't here right now," he said, as if she'd gone out for a jug of milk.

"Staci Grant is dead," I said gently.

"No. She isn't."

"Ramirez...." Lucas placed a hand on his shoulder, but Ramirez shrugged it off.

"That may be the common theory but I don't believe it."

"We don't have time for this," I said sharply.

Jordan Ramirez glanced at the military dial watch on his wrist. "You've got thirty minutes before he makes rounds again."

Lucas looked even more uncomfortable. "What are you doing here? How did you know Staci?"

"We're...friends." Jordan Ramirez had been more than Staci Grant's friend. Theories clicked through my brain at top speed.

"Did anyone know?"

Jordan Ramirez's gaze snapped back to me. "Our relationship was, is, private."

Lucas straightened, as the possibilities fired between us.

"No one?" I persisted.

"I never told anyone." Ramirez flipped the safety on and tucked his weapon into the waistband of his jeans. "And Staci wouldn't."

"What do you think?" I directed the question at Lucas, but I knew we'd found the key.

"It's worth a try." Lucas glanced at his friend. "If it's okay."

"We have to find out what's going on," I murmured fiercely.

Being part of Staci Grant's files, in my book, placed Bella in clear danger. Johnny was in Staci's files and hanging out with Bella under an alias. At this point I didn't know what that signified. Staci had information on 5491 that I needed in order to figure out what was going on with the NSA, the kidnapped agents and me. "I need in those files."

Ramirez watched our exchange with a puzzled look.

"We need to find a recruit of Staci's," Lucas said.

"What kind of recruit?" Ramirez asked, not giving anything away.

"Her agency recruits." I looked at him steadily. "The ones she recruited for the U.S. Government."

No one mentioned the CIA.

Ramirez aimed a look at Lucas. "You trust her?"

Shit. I was on uncertain ground here. I intended to get into Staci Grant's files with or without this guy's permission. But wasting time to take him down would be an annoyance.

"Yeah. I trust her," Lucas said softly.

I let out the breath I'd instinctively held. An emotion, elation maybe, seeped into my blood fizzing like a lack of oxygen.

"I can't help you. I...can't get into those files." He hadn't approved. It was clear in his body language. He'd wanted nothing to do with Staci Grant's job.

"I think I can."

"Right." Jordan Ramirez laughed, but it was far from a happy sound. "Did you know her?"

I stepped toward the attic office. "No, but...."

He stretched his arm across the doorway, barring entrance. "I've been trying for weeks and can't get into her private files. What makes you think you can?" Fierceness shimmered off of him.

In that instant, I knew Staci Grant had one more thing for me to be jealous of. This man had loved her. So much so that he wasn't willing to accept her death.

"Let her try." Lucas surprised us both. "Her record is pretty good."

Jordan Ramirez reluctantly dropped his arm. I bolted for the stairs. The clock was ticking.

Jordan and Lucas followed. They spoke in low tones but I ignored them. When I got upstairs the computer was up and running. "You've been working?" I asked slowly.

"Only in her regular files. I've been...tracing every one of her students. Looking for answers."

Answers to what? And did he really want to know?

"Trying to find her," he said.

But Staci Grant was dead. I sat down at the computer. "What is your middle name?"

"Mine?" Jordan Ramirez lifted his eyebrows.

"Yours."

"Angelo." He rubbed his fingers up and down his arms. "She wouldn't use me. Our...thing was casual."

Jordan Ramirez wasn't telling the truth. If it had only been casual he wouldn't be here, trying to find Staci Grant and prove she wasn't dead.

He clarified. "Besides, I've already tried my name."

But Lucas had caught on. "Initials. Just like the other."

I typed in JAR. The computer hummed in the silent air as we waited tensely. The system beeped: Access Denied.

"When did you meet?"

He rattled off a date and I added that to the initials.

Then the computer dinged. "Welcome, Dr. Grant."

"I can't believe she used my initials." Jordan Ramirez wrapped hard fingers around my bicep. "How did you know?"

I started to shrug him off with a glib comment, but he deserved more. "We're a lot alike," I murmured.

"Great. Maybe you can tell me where she is." He bit the words out without any heat, just sadness.

These files, her secret CIA recruit files, had to give me answers to why Johnny Wishbone was pretending to be Donald Christian. And why Staci Grant had recruited him. And why Bella was in her files.

Staci Grant was dead. But maybe I could help Jordan. If our suppositions were correct, it was possible she'd had the DNA altering drug.

She might have died *because* she'd had a DNA altering drug. "Had she been acting differently before she left?"

He thought back. "She'd become obsessed with her grandparents's deaths. She started going over the old police reports, looking for something but she wouldn't ever say exactly what."

That had hurt Jordan Ramirez.

Then I processed what he just told us. Her grandparents, who had died in a single violent act.

Like mine.

"What did she find out?"

He shrugged and wandered toward the window. "She didn't say."

And that had hurt him even more.

I ran a search on files, typing in Johnny Wishbone's name. Waiting, I stared at the black and green screen as the computer scrolled through files at lightning speed.

"She ever mention anything about TICOM?" Lucas's casual question jerked me back to their conversation.

"TICOM? Isn't that from the second World War?" Jordan frowned. "She's only thirty-two."

"You realize those files are still sealed?" Lucas's statement was again casual.

"So they're still sealed," Jordan said. "Where's the connection?"

"Don't know yet."

"I can't believe there is any connection between the Target Intelligence Committee, from World War II, and Staci."

The computer dinged. I clicked open the file on Johnny Wishbone and sent a copy to the printer. Then I typed in my sister's full name, hit enter and waited. The need to know what information she had about Bella burned like acid etching stone.

The computer dinged again. My heart stopped with fear.

I'd faced down crazy killers, scientists with syringes and the death of my family, but right this moment I was terrified to look at that file.

I needed to send the information to the printer but my hand shook too badly. I clenched my fingers into a fist and hoped no one had noticed.

Lucas leaned over and hit the print button. He'd noticed.

I opened the file on 5491, the computer whirring as the file loaded. I hit the print button.

Jordan Ramirez sighed and looked out the window. "Uh-oh."

Crap.

"This is another reason I don't believe she's dead." He waved toward the street below. "We've got company."

# CHAPTER 31

*L*ucas swore. "Forgot about the ladder."

I said drily, "Our friends are back?"

"Yeah." Jordan pressed a button under the desk top.

The hidden closet door slid closed. I wondered how long we'd have to hole up here before the butthead twins left.

"Let's go." Jordan motioned.

"Where?" Lucas whispered. We'd all heard the alarm go off and the heavy tread of feet. They'd make a beeline for Staci's bedroom because of the ladder.

"This way." Jordan flipped open a keypad along the shared wall then silently punched in a code. Suddenly a pocket door, well-hidden in the wood paneling, slid open.

I snagged the printout from the printer and stuffed the papers into my jumpsuit. Couldn't figure out why we should hide in a small room when we had the whole attic but I filed into what I'd assumed was a hidden room.

Except we stood in a mirror image room, set up with a large sparring mat, a weight bench and stack of towels. Similar to Staci's without the computer.

"Where are we?" Lucas asked.

"My place." Jordan closed the door and peered out the identical round window.

"You live right next door?" I assessed the concealed door. "You sure no one knows about this?"

Jordan's mouth flattened into a tight line. "We put it in together."

"You and Staci?" Lucas said.

"Yeah."

His appearance in her house when we were here was awfully convenient. "Why was the door open in the closet?"

"Because I knew someone had been in the attic. I hoped they would show up again." He bared his teeth, but it wasn't a smile.

Lucas said, "Damn. I hate to be predictable."

"Never that, buddy. Anything outside tie to you?" Jordan interrogated. "Fingerprints?"

"Gloves." Lucas held up his hands, still encased in latex. "Magnets came off after I came in."

"With the exception of the ladder, her house is undisturbed."

My mind raced. Jordan Ramirez truly believed Staci Grant was alive. "Why would they keep such a close watch on her house?"

Maybe they were waiting for one of Staci's recruits to show up. Or maybe they were waiting for her impersonator to show up. Or maybe Jordan Ramirez was right and they were waiting for Staci.

As we proceeded down his carpeted stairs, he shrugged. "As far as I know, the agency has the same files in the office that she does here. But a week after she was reported dead, they started 24/7 surveillance on her house."

"Constant?"

"Two guys during the week. One on weekends."

There had to be a reason. No department would waste those resources without just cause. "If she was alive, wouldn't they know?"

I glanced around at his living room. Besides the fact that the house was in a fancy neighborhood, on the inside his place looked a lot like mine. Nothing personal. No pictures. No mementoes. At the bottom of the stairs, Jordan paused. "She is alive."

"But...."

"Someone completely trashed her house in the Bahamas."

"That doesn't mean she's alive," I said softly.

"She's alive," he repeated tersely.

Lucas spoke into the tense silence. "I saw the report. It...didn't look good."

"I saw the pictures." Jordan Ramirez stalked into his kitchen. The fierceness of his response struck something within me. His intensity reminded me of my need to protect my sister.

"The body," he swallowed. "Was missing a scar."

Jordan Ramirez wouldn't be anymore help. He was operating on passion not evidence. We needed to get out before we drew any more unwanted attention.

"Time to motor," I said briskly.

Lucas glared at me.

I checked the backyard. The single man—if Jordan had been right about the surveillance schedule—was still in Staci Grant's house. If we waited much longer, he'd have a clear view of us and the van. "We have to go."

Jordan Ramirez visibly shook off his funk. "She's right."

Lucas pulled a white card out of his breast pocket. "In case they decide to check up on Mel's Window Washing."

Jordan Ramirez examined the card. "Nice work, Goodman."

"I try." Lucas clamped his hand on Jordan's shoulder. "Keep in touch."

"If you find anything...."

"You'll be the first to know." I shoved Lucas out the back door.

"Did you have to be so harsh?" Lucas sniped as we hustled down Jordan Reynold's sidewalk.

I knew he didn't understand and I couldn't take the time to care. "Candy coating reality isn't going to help him."

"What if he's right?"

"He's not." I wanted to believe Jordan Ramirez was a sap, a sucker, a total emotional nutcase. But I tripped up over how much he loved Staci Grant. And his refusal to believe she was dead.

He wasn't a sap. He loved.

A lump grew in my throat making it difficult to swallow. Again I couldn't help but make the comparison between Staci's life and my own. If I died there'd be no one to search for me. No one to mourn me.

I'd be just an anonymous footnote in Bella's life.

Bella was in danger. Even though Lucas believed Johnny wouldn't hurt her, this feeling of impending doom wouldn't leave me. I had to protect her. First, I had to obliterate this emotionalism before the liability got Bella and me killed. Focus and focus hard.

"I put business cards in the houses on this side of the street. Maybe they'll believe what they see." Lucas started the engine as I hopped in the passenger side. "After all, we didn't trip the alarm."

The back door of Staci Grant's house burst open, just as we drove down the alley.

The guy spoke into a microphone at his wrist. He wasn't running for his car. "We better hope they don't have another team waiting."

"Two car surveillance detail. On a dead woman's house? What are the odds?" As soon as Lucas completed the turn, he pressed the accelerator down.

"Nonexistent. No one has that kind of budget." Even the NSA had to answer to Congress for budgetary concerns now. I stripped the white jumpsuit off my arms as Lucas took the turn onto the cobblestone street slowly.

"You pick the damndest places to undress." Amusement lit his words.

Adrenaline fizzed through me, his mood infectious. "Yeah, that's me. A total exhibitionist," I deadpanned.

He let loose a laugh from deep in his belly. Laughter creased his face.

The tires jiggled over the uneven cobblestone.

I leaned over and started unzipping his jumpsuit. "Can't keep your hands off me."

"In your dreams," I said roughly.

"Oh, yeah." The appreciation and memory in his voice gave me pause.

"We're going to have to ditch the plates and get rid of the magnet." Almost at the intersection, I saw what we needed. "Turn into that alley."

A row of buildings with narrow yards and detached garages bordered the alley.

Lucas swung left. "What now?"

"Over there." I pointed to an open garage.

Lucas eased the van into the garage. I hopped out, tugged the cord, pulling the old manual door closed with a screech. Hopefully the owners didn't hear the door close. We didn't have much time.

I pulled the magnetic signs with Mel's Window Washing off the van while Lucas switched the magnetic license plates. We moved in concert, stuffing our signs in the back and pulling the white jumpsuits down our legs.

I hopped on one foot, tugging off the suit. Lucas balled his up and tossed it in a wire bin in the back.

I yanked off the white painter's cap I'd been wearing and clipped it onto the metal grid bolted on the floor and ceiling, then fluffed my dyed hair.

He grabbed another sign from a storage rack like the kind that hold baking sheets.

"That Goth look is growing on me." He grinned as he slapped up a logo for Artistic Signs on the side of the van. He ran his fingertips lightly along the underside perimeter of the van's bumper.

I climbed into the rear of the van.

Lucas paused, his hand still on the bumper for a minute.

"What?" I sat up on my knees. "Tracker?"

"No. What are you doing?"

"One of us should get in back."

He yanked me to him, our hips flush and angled his mouth over mine for a quick, hot kiss. I ripped my mouth from his. "We've got to go."

"Yeah, but I should be in the back." Lucas yanked up the garage door. He scrambled in back and pushed me through the barrier separating the driving section from the back. "Haul ass."

I reversed out of the garage and went back the way we came. Waiting for a break in traffic, I watched the cars go by, but no one suspicious passed. We crossed the street with Staci's rowhouse. With any luck, I'd catch a glimpse of the guy I'd seen outside the house.

But no one was there. And no one was following us. I

turned the van sedately onto the cobblestone street and headed for the freeway.

"That was too easy," Lucas commented, his voice muffled from the barrier of the curtains.

I agreed. "Tracking device?"

"Nothing underneath," Lucas said.

I turned again, racking my brain for another type of tracking device that could be planted easily. "Still no one following. Any ideas?"

"Not enough time for anything fancier. With the exception of the few minutes we were all in the closet, Jordan or I had the van under constant watch."

I hesitated. "Can we trust him?"

"No reason not to." Lucas's voice was muffled by the curtain. "Maybe they don't want us."

"Then who are they waiting for?" The question bugged me. Staci's impersonator? Staci? Which brought me back to the file with Bella's name on it. Had Staci tried to recruit Bella? I couldn't get a handle on the situation. The urge to touch base with Bella, warn her somehow, was incredibly strong.

"Call her." He shoved his cell phone through the curtains.

"What? Who?"

"Your sister."

Was he crazy? I couldn't call her.

"Here's my cell. Call her." His disembodied hand waggled the phone at me.

I glanced at the thing as if it were poison. I couldn't call her. How the hell could he even suggest such a thing?

Because he didn't know.

"I can't." I'd meant the words to come out forceful, direct. But it was a whisper. My hand reached out without my permission to take hold of that phone. I deliberately curled my fingers into a fist. I couldn't.

"Why not?"

A huge lump grew in my throat. I'd given up the right to see her, talk to her, long ago. "I can't."

"Jamie?" I heard the question, the confusion in his voice.

"She thinks I'm dead."

"Well shit." Lucas was silent. "Why?"

It was a question I'd never asked. When they had come to me in the hospital, I'd been scared and heartsick with grief. I'd never thought to really question why Bella had to believe I was dead.

"It made sense at the time."

"Does it make sense now?" Lucas asked gently.

I wasn't sure anymore. "I...don't know."

Lucas climbed through the curtain and slid into the passenger seat. He put his hand on my knee, the gesture ripe with comfort.

I flipped Lucas the papers with the information from Staci Grant's private files. "Look and see what you can find about Johnny."

"Here we go." He rubbed his hands together. Lucas was silent for a moment, then he muttered, "Just his general statistics. Nothing new here."

"What about recruitment notes?"

"Let me read."

I kept trying to look over at the papers as we sat stalled in the late afternoon traffic. He skimmed the papers without reading aloud.

"I'm waiting here."

He cleared his throat. "Sorry."

"Just read the notes." I squeezed the steering wheel. I

hated feeling impotent, hated just sitting here doing nothing while he scanned through information. I sighed. Information he needed to track down his friend's son. Although, Johnny/Donald was toast if he hurt Bella. In any way.

"It's all here. She's got the MICE acronym and her analysis of what would work best for Johnny."

Money, Ideology, Compromise and Ego—the cornerstones for espionage recruitment. "What did she put in the file?"

She has analysis of each method and Johnny's personality.

"But she dangled the big carrot. The one that hooked him. Revenge."

She'd used exactly the same technique Carson had used to recruit me. Exactly. Did they have a damn script? *Son of a bitch.* "What about Bella's file?"

"Isabella Gertrude Holden."

I swallowed and wondered if I was really ready to hear what was in Bella's file.

"Parents: deceased. Mother: Elizabeth Lilly Holden, nee Kaplan, diplomat. Father: Richard no middle name Holden, diplomatic spouse."

I cleared away the sadness.

"Money. So noted that Bella doesn't need money." My heart wrenched. My parents had plenty.

"She inherited her parents's estate," I said.

"*Her* parents?" He lifted an cyebrow.

I pressed my lips together. It helped to distance from her even in that little way. "Our parents."

"Does that bother you?"

"What?"

"Your sister got everything. Money, stuff."

I shifted my gaze back to traffic. "What am I going to do with money like that?"

"What do you do with your paycheck?" Lucas asked.

"Daily expenses." So what if a good portion went into an account for Bella? If anything happened to me, she'd have another layer of cushion to take care of her.

"She also inherited her aunt's, my mother's sister's, farm in Virginia. That's where she went to live after they died."

"So your sister is loaded."

I'd never really thought about it that way. She had enough money that I'd never have to worry about her financially.

I shoved away the unpleasant memory of her comments about the day we'd all died, about seeing the car explode. *Nothing years of therapy couldn't fix.*

He looked down at the notes.

"Ideology." Lucas took a deep breath. "No chance of her having a love for her country. The files says Bella has a distrust of the American government. She blames them for not protecting your family, for allowing their deaths."

Sorrow pierced my chest. "Compromise?"

Lucas said, "Again nothing fit there."

The last was ego.

"Ego," he said calmly. "Ego probably has a better recruitment success rate on guys than girls but Staci seemed to think ego was not the way to play your sister."

But when I put it all together, fear coalesced. "What was Staci planning to do?" And had someone else taken up her trade?

I must have uttered some sound because Lucas gave me a sharp look. "Where's the fear for yourself?"

"I can take care of myself." I dismissed his concern with a wave.

He skimmed through the rest of Bella's papers. "No contact yet."

Shit.

Until Lucas confirmed it, I'd held out hope that maybe Staci had been providing some sort of protection for Bella. But the details in the file killed that dream. She had considered trying to recruit my sister.

If Staci wasn't already dead, I'd kill her myself.

I held onto the words, no contact yet, like a Mecca pilgrim clutching a prayer rug.

I forced myself to move onto the other file we needed to look at. "Can you read the 5491 file?"

"Sure." Lucas looked at the file while I drove through the streets, turning left and left and left. Watching for tails.

Lucas was silent.

"What's it say?" I hated not being able to look with my own eyes. Even though I'd retain the information just as well if I listened to it from him, I was still relying on his perceptions, his intonations, and his paraphrasing.

"It's a chart of names and dates."

"Read it out loud, please."

"Brad Johnson, Staci Grant, Jamie Hunt, Luna Sunlight a.k.a. Sunshine, Ezekial Hawthorne, Isabella Holden, Katerina Wolf." Lucas continued to rattle off names but I'd stopped listening.

I knew several of the names. Zeke, Brad Johnson and I had worked for the NSA. Staci was CIA. I maneuvered through traffic but my attention was focused on Lucas.

"The second column seems to be their parents or grandparents names, the third column are dates. Huh."

It was frightening but I knew that little sound and it wasn't a good sign. "What?"

"The dates are all very similar."

A cold chill skittered over me. "When?" But I had a feeling I already knew.

"Late October 1995."

The same time my parents were killed. So everyone in the 5491 file had relatives who were killed around the same time. What the hell?

"Did you know that Bella has been receiving regular payments to her savings account since your parents died?"

So was I. A sense of foreboding swept over me. A sense that I didn't really want to know the answer. "Insurance."

"Staci Grant receives the same payments."

I could see where this was leading. My skin chilled, as ice trailed down my spine. "From the same bank?"

"Yeah."

"Can it be traced?" Maybe this was the connection I could use to tie us all together.

"Bank is in Bermuda."

Even if we got an account number there was probably no way to find out the owner's name. Virtually untraceable.

I turned the van onto the highway automatically checking my surroundings, looking for tails, looking for followers. But we were clean.

Staci Grant, Bella and I were receiving money every month from an untraceable account. Could the others in the 5491 file also be receiving payments?

All of the abductees were also connected to 5491.

But how did those two facts connect to each other? Only one person might have the knowledge we needed to put it all together.

Carson Black.

It was Saturday. He might be in the office but he was most likely at home. If I wanted to get answers, I would have to surprise him there. I didn't want him to have time to prepare.

"I need to go to my handler's house in Virginia." The statement came out flat. "You want me to drop you off?"

"Not a chance." He put his hand on my thigh, his fingers burning through the worn denim, and squeezed. "Haven't you figured out I'm in this for the long haul?"

# CHAPTER 32

$\mathcal{C}$arson lived on a five acre parcel in rural Virginia. About sixty miles from the office in distance and a universe away in lifestyle.

I turned down the private single lane and drove along the decorative wood rail fencing that bordered their property. An explosion of fall color, trees brilliant with orange, red, and brown leaves framed the driveway.

When we reached the stone posts and wrought iron gate, I stopped. An intercom system sat on a post, easily reached without getting out of the van. I pushed the call button, spoke my name and waited.

Lucas said softly, "Want me to get in back?"

I thought about how much he'd helped me in the past few days, thought about all the things that were going wrong that I had no control over, and I thought about Carson's threat. "Nope."

"Why, Jamie. How...lovely." The lilting Southern voice of Carson's wife, Antoinette, came over the system.

"I, we, came to talk to Carson."

"Honey, he isn't here."

The element of surprise was gone. We'd wasted our trip. I'd done a quick check and he hadn't answered his office or his cell phone. So where was he? Dammit.

"Is he planning to stay at the office or should we wait for him here?"

"He's out of town." Her unspoken question was loud and clear. *Why didn't you know that?*

Time for damage control.

"Darn. I haven't been in for the last few days. I've been out of touch." I backtracked to cover myself. "Did he leave a number?"

"You'd better check at the office for that." She hesitated. "Y'all want some refreshments since you came all this way?"

Antoinette wanted to check out Lucas.

"Love to." The light on the security comm went off.

I knew she couldn't help us. Carson would never share his work with his wife. But her offer was perfect.

The wrought iron gate opened pendulously. I drove up a long winding drive to a modest, ranch-style house.

"You realize their security system will get us on tape," I said.

He shrugged. "As long as you're okay with it."

I left the window down as we made the drive. Birds twittered. A lawn mower droned somewhere close by, the smell of freshly cut grass drifted in the air. A tinge of woodsmoke curled lazily from their stone fireplace, wafting toward us.

I'd spent more than a few weekends at this house during the beginning of my training. The scents, the sounds spiraled me back. Carson and Antoinette had tried to give me a safe haven, but I'd been miserable, struggling to understand all that had happened to me and my family.

We rolled up to the ranch house. The facade was

Connecticut blue stone with small columns supporting the roof of the covered porch. White mullioned windows gave an impression of welcome. Low to the ground and simple, the landscaping left no place for anyone to hide.

"Bullet proof glass, reinforced steel supports, and no outside cover. Nicely done," Lucas murmured.

Antoinette hovered in the open doorway.

A trim, black woman in her mid-thirties, she exuded a monied, finishing school poise. She managed to wear trendy clothes with a style only someone very comfortable could carry off. She had beautiful, light brown skin. Ringlets of crinkly black hair cut in a chin length bob framed high cheekbones and slightly slanted eyes the color of a mossy swamp.

I recalled the first time I'd met her. Only twenty-two to my fifteen, she'd still managed to make me feel unpolished and gawky.

As I jumped out of the van, I remembered my spiked hair, black-ringed eyes, and ripped jeans grunge look.

"Why Jamie, this is a new look for you." She smiled politely as she clasped my hands in her perfect, french-manicured fingertips and kissed both my cheeks, European style. "How are you doing, sugar?"

"Fine." I fought the urge to shove my short, unpainted nails behind my back.

"I'm Antoinette." She held out her hands to Lucas and tilted her head in a manner innately flirtatious. Yet I knew she meant nothing by it. Antoinette was devoted to Carson. "Who might you be?"

I answered, knowing Antoinette would understand the need for first names only. "This is Lucas."

"I don't mind telling you, it's a pleasure that Jamie has finally brought someone home."

A deep red flush burgeoned from my belly up to my face. I couldn't remember the last time I'd blushed like that. When I was fifteen, maybe.

Lucas raised an eyebrow at me, but when he turned to Antoinette his answer was smooth. "She waited until she found the best."

Antoinette laughed appropriately. "She has...discriminating tastes."

Lucas slipped his hand into mine, reinforcing her impression we were a couple. "Yes. She does."

"Goodness. Where are my manners? Come in, come in." She led us to a great room with a giant fieldstone fireplace. Logs crackled and snapped in the grate. Before I could step all the way into the room, she pulled me aside gently.

"Does he know what you do?" she whispered.

I nodded.

"I'll go get some iced tea. Be at rest," she called out.

"What's wrong?" Lucas asked as soon as Antoinette left the room.

I crossed my arms in front of me, rubbing my biceps with cold hands. My world was falling apart and coming back here reminded me of the most miserable time in my life. But I couldn't tell Lucas that. Couldn't share with him. Especially not in this house. The beginning of the life I lived now. "Old memories."

Antoinette swung back into the room carrying a large silver tray with a pitcher of tea, three glasses, lemon slices, sugar, and spoons. She set the tray down on the cocktail table and started to pour. "So, how did you two meet? Or can you not tell me." Her whole face lit up, eyes sparkling with mischief.

"On a job," I answered slowly. "We're actually still not

done, which was why we stopped by to see Carson. I had a question for him."

About Staci, me, Bella, and all those other names on the 5491 list. And how they related to the kidnappings.

About my sister.

Then I wondered if Carson had ever brought Bella here. No. He'd promised to keep Bella out of this life. Carson wouldn't have brought attention to Bella by linking her with him in any way.

"I can't tell you how nice it is to see you, Jamie. Seems like forever since you were here." Antoinette poured the tea then handed glasses to us both.

Almost a year ago. "Last Thanksgiving."

Lucas waited until Antoinette sipped her tea, then he took a healthy swallow. I let the conversation flow around me as Lucas and Antoinette made small talk.

"How long have you known each other?" Lucas's question surprised me out of my funk.

"Going on thirteen years." Antoinette must have decided Lucas was okay because she answered truthfully. "I remember the first Thanksgiving Jamie spent with us. So quiet and so reserved."

"Yeah. And she's such a chatterbox now," Lucas said drily.

Antoinette laughed with delight. "Oh, but she is so much more talkative than she was then."

"You must have been pretty young," Lucas commented.

"A new bride. My first Thanksgiving disaster." She waved a hand in front of her face, a delicate flush on her cheeks. "Lordy, that turkey was burnt to a crisp on the outside and raw and pink on the inside."

It occurred to me then, I must have been a big intrusion

on her life. Newly married, with a heartsick teenager horning in on their first holiday together. "I never really thought about how much of a nuisance it was for me to be here."

"Oh, sugar. You were in so much pain. I didn't mind." Antoinette said, "And I think it helped Carson. He was pretty torn up over your parents's deaths."

Lucas perked up. Not visibly. He still relaxed on the sofa but suddenly he was more alert, more focused on Antoinette than a minute ago.

"I didn't realize he knew my parents."

"Oh, I don't believe he did." For a moment, Antoinette looked flustered. "I didn't phrase that right. He knew how much you were hurting. I've never minded taking care of y'all."

Y'all implied more than one person. A warning bell went off in my head. I'd only come for Thanksgiving. Never Christmas or Easter or Fourth of July. Could it be that I wasn't the only one Carson had taken in?

I forced myself to relax and sink back into the floral chair. "You are a saint to put up with all of us."

Antoinette looked amused. "Not me. Carson is the saint."

I wanted to fish, but couldn't put my finger on the right method to not spook her. Finally I decided to go with the direct approach. "It's too bad about Staci."

A sad look crossed Antoinette's face, her bronzed-glossed lips turned down. "A tragedy. That's what it is. Carson is still torn up over her passing."

Lucas took a sip of tea. "Some people don't think she's gone."

Antoinette shot a sharp look at Lucas. "You knew Staci?"

"A few years ago. I used to be FBI." He wisely left out the part where he'd been investigating her.

Antoinette shot me a look, as if to say, *Is that advisable?* "They're mistaken. Carson seems very sure."

"Is Katerina one of the other girls?" Lucas asked casually.

He had an innate ability to identify what track I was on. If he could figure out my next question, he knew me too well.

"It isn't appropriate for me to say," Antoinette said sharply.

"Oh, sure." Lucas smiled easily. "Just curious if I knew any others."

I played the hunch that had been bothering me since we'd talked to Jordan Ramirez. "Antoinette, did we all have links to TICOM?"

Her brow crinkled. "I don't believe I'm familiar with that term." And she wasn't. It was plain to see.

"No big deal. Just something that popped into my head." I stood up casually. "We should probably get going. I'll just have to ask Carson my question when he gets back."

"If I speak with him, I'll let him know you stopped by." There was a stiffness in her posture that hadn't been there when we'd come in. And she fairly hustled us out.

It couldn't be helped.

At the door, I turned and impulsively gave her a hug. "Thank you for taking such good care of me for all these years. It's just now occurred to me that it couldn't have been easy for you," I whispered.

She held onto me for just a second, squeezing gently. "My pleasure."

Lucas and I strode to the van together, as he said, "Time to motor."

I nodded, mulling over the information Antoinette had unwittingly supplied.

"How long before your boss connects with us?"

"He doesn't usually do field work. We should make contact sometime tomorrow."

"He'll have had time to marshal his thoughts, guard his defenses."

I turned the key and the engine rumbled to life. "Yeah."

As I put the van in gear, he said. "She'll repeat our entire conversation."

I strapped my seat belt, thinking it through. "It's probable we're on their video surveillance."

Lucas turned on the GPS system.

I thought about the glasses of iced tea. "It's also probable she'll turn your fingerprints in for testing."

He glanced over at me. "Good thing I'm on file."

Yeah.

"Why are you smiling?" Lucas asked.

"When she does, it'll be on record that you, Lucas Goodman, were in their house." And then if Carson wanted to screw me, he'd have to screw himself as well.

"What's so great...." Realization hit him. "You have a devious mind."

"It's working in your favor." And mine.

"Will she be that suspicious?"

"After living with Carson for the last thirteen years, probably," I said cynically.

"You were fifteen when you first came here?" Lucas burst out.

I can't believe I'd let that slip.

"Never mind." Lucas fiddled with the radio. "What's wrong?"

Our whole conversation with Antoinette bothered me. "There were others like me."

"It would be interesting to find out if they have the same deposits to their bank accounts as you and Staci and Bella have," Lucas commented.

And if they were all in Department 5491. Did that mean they had all been kidnapped? "Yeah." I headed toward the highway.

"Question number four," he said slowly.

That meant he thought the question was important. "Maybe."

"Where did that TICOM question come from?"

I thought about not answering. But since he'd asked Jordan about the committee, the World War 2 events kept nagging at the back of my mind. Was TICOM somehow connected? Maybe Lucas would see something I couldn't. "Just fishing. Sometimes you just have to toss the bait in and see what happens."

"Yeah." Lucas was quiet for a moment. "But what does TICOM have to do with you? Or Staci Grant?"

"Number five?"

"Nope. Four is a two-parter."

"I don't know." I connected the dots slowly. "How could Carson have had anything to do with my parents's death? And why?"

"He definitely did. You heard what Antoinette said."

She said Carson had felt responsible for my parents's deaths. But why? My parents didn't have anything to do with the NSA. Besides, Carson would have only been a junior director at the time.

The waning fall sun dipped low in the sky. It was early evening. I had a feeling Carson would be calling me fairly soon. "We need to get rid of this van. Antoinette would have recorded the plates."

"Yeah." He ran a hand over the dashboard, a funny look on his face. "I know."

I could tell he didn't want to leave it. "It's only temporary."

He inhaled slowly, then patted the dash. "I know."

"Let's head for McLean." I can't believe I was letting him get to me over his sentimental attitude toward a hunk of metal. "I've got credit cards to go with our current licenses in the duffel."

"Gotta love that duffel," Lucas said.

"We need a hotel." The vision of Lucas in a bed flashed through my mind.

He punched in a website, looking for possible hotels. "I thought you'd never ask."

# CHAPTER 33

The proprietress of the small bed and breakfast led us up the stairs. "I hope you two enjoy your room. You've missed the afternoon cordials and hors d'oeuvres."

Damn, just what I needed. A cordial.

I took in the old fashioned wallpaper, fussily painted chair rail and molding, and wondered what the hell we were doing *here*.

"We had a late lunch." Lucas's voice rumbled from the vicinity of my forehead. His arm curled around my shoulders and held my brunette pageboy wig-covered head snuggled up to his chin, effectively blocking both my face and his.

His wool sweater made me itch. I rubbed against him, the sensation of his hard chest against my softer and more sensitive breast reminding me of another itch. One I had no intention of scratching, but an itch getting harder and harder to ignore.

"Here's your room." The older woman pushed open the door and stepped back to let us enter. She sent a warm smile to both of us. I couldn't be sure but she might have winked at Lucas. "You two enjoy your impromptu stay."

We'd taken the time to change our appearance to look like her typical customers. I'd wiped off the Goth makeup and removed the bondage jewelry. Now I wore boot cut jeans, a conservative pale yellow sweater, and pearls. Lucas had dressed in khaki pants and white button down pressed with sharp creases. His hair was still gray but he'd lost the glasses and slicked his hair into a younger looking style.

Look at us. Two harmless tourists. In Virginia to take in the fall color. If questioned, hopefully all she'd remember was our story of impulsively heading to the country from the city.

"Thank you," I said huskily, annoyed not all of the huskiness in my voice was feigned.

"Breakfast is served between seven and nine."

"We'll be there." Lucas pressed a kiss to my forehead, the warmth of his breath feathered against my skin.

As she tottered back down the hall, Lucas reached out and closed the door gently.

Without trying to appear as if I were jumping away from him, I jumped as far away as I could. "What are we doing here?" I whispered.

"This bed and breakfast was about as far from a chain hotel as you could get."

From a hiding standpoint, it was perfect. We hadn't had any tails since we lost the guys yesterday at Dr. Fitzhugh's office. Unless the people after us had unlimited manpower, they didn't have the time or the resources to canvass every small hotel in D.C. and surrounding area.

"You're right." But I didn't have to like staying in a romantic place like this.

After dumping his van at Dulles, we'd used the new i.d.'s

and gotten a rental car. We were Sherry and Bradford Hayes. Thank God she hadn't asked to see my driver's license, because on Sherry's license photo, she still looked like a Goth Queen.

"It's clean." He reached into the leather duffel and pulled out a salami. "How about some dinner?"

My stomach growled. Loudly.

"I'll take that as a yes."

I wondered where we were going to eat. The website had billed this as cozy and quaint...with internet access. They had the cozy down pat. The room was dominated by a mahogany highboy and gigantic matching bed. With barely two feet on either side of the bed, the room had no space for any other furniture, say a chair or a sofa. A tiny window seat decorated the dormer window, one side of the bed held a small night stand, and a brick fireplace was tucked into the room's corner.

The bed was it.

Lucas spread out a towel on the gold duvet cover near the foot of the bed. "Picnic first."

Lucas laid out the salami, cheese, and crackers along with a Swiss Army knife. He whisked a bottle of Chardonnay from the bag as well.

"Where'd you get that?" They sure as heck hadn't sold that at the gas station mini mart.

"The proprietress. They keep a stash of bottles refrigerated for just such a situation as we find ourselves in."

"What? Running from an unknown government agency while trying to figure out which one and why?"

He put a hand over his heart and the other swung into the air. "Weary, but impulsive travelers with a yen for romance."

"Give me a break. Did she really fall for that?"

"It worked."

No, I thought, as I watched him smile, that's not what worked.

Lucas zeroed in on the one thing guaranteed to get me to do what he wanted. "You won't do your sister any good if you aren't at your best. Eat."

I tensed again, then focused deliberately on relaxing my shoulders. Lucas came up behind me and kneaded gently, his thumbs pressing into the tender spot between my shoulder blades.

"Jesus, Jamie. You're so tense." His breath tickled the back of my neck, sensitizing my body. In that moment, I wanted nothing more than to lean back and let him shelter me.

But my focus right now had to be my sister. Had to be finding a way to get Johnny away from her. And finding a way to keep her safe. She'd left for the farm alone.

She should be safe for the weekend.

I sliced the cheese and salami while I got my emotions under control.

"I need to find Johnny." Lucas poured the golden Chardonnay into crystal wine glasses. Where had he gotten those? "As much as you want to protect your sister."

"Do you think Johnny has anything to do with the kidnappings?" I worried.

"Johnny is just a kid," Lucas said firmly. "Maybe a little mixed up but I don't believe he's involved in anything of this scale."

A feeling of sympathy rose in me for Johnny Wishbone. He'd been lured to the job almost exactly the same way as I had.

Lucas slipped his hand into mine and tugged me toward the bed. "Talk to me. Maybe it will spark something."

"I understand Johnny." I understood that wish to prove yourself at any cost. "He wants to succeed. He wants to show them they didn't make a mistake by recruiting him."

"So what is he going to do now?"

I knew what my next step would be. Get closer to the target, Bella, and reel her in. "God help Johnny Wishbone if he hurts my sister." I hopped up on the bed and sat cross-legged, the fluffy down comforter bunched uncomfortably under my knees.

"He won't. I know this kid." Lucas swung up next to me. He propped the pillows up against the headboard and prompted me to lean back.

I shook my head.

He grabbed both wine glasses and handed one to me.

"You *think* you know this kid." I took a sip of the crisp Chardonnay. "He isn't that kid anymore. There's this moment...an instantaneous rush of confusion when you're asked to do something that goes against the code of behavior you grow up believing is right."

I stared at the cream lace curtains, a filmy shade between inside and outside, distorting, concealing both sides from the other. "But you do it. And you don't look back." I drew my gaze away from the curtains, down to the lush cotton spread. "Because you can't."

"What did you do?"

"I did what had to be done." It wasn't the answer he wanted but the only answer I could give.

Because you close everything off. Close it off so it can't hurt you. And never look back.

"I don't believe he will. But...we won't let him hurt her," Lucas said softly. He bumped a cracker loaded with a slice of salami and cheese into my compressed lips. "Eat this. Please."

I opened my mouth, let him feed me a cracker.

The furnace kicked on, the radiators hissed with steam, filling the silence. Lucas pulled his laptop out of the duffel. "Let's find Johnny."

I welcomed the chance. If we found him, then I could get to him make sure he never went near Bella again.

We spent the next half hour going over every piece of information we had about Johnny Wishbone/Donald Christian. He had no known address, no phone number, no utilities. He had a fake email account and an untraceable cell phone number which he never gave out online.

Finally we struck pay dirt in an email about attending a lecture tomorrow.

"Perfect." Lucas searched the Georgetown University website, pulling up the details of the lecture. "We've got a time, noon, and place, McNeir Auditorium."

"What if he doesn't show?"

"Then we wait for another opportunity."

We were so close. "Maybe we should go now."

Lucas glanced at the watch on his wrist. "We've got over twelve hours until the lecture. If we loiter, campus police will be all over us."

I picked at the bedspread, pulling at a loose thread. "I'd rather go now."

"We draw more attention to ourselves if we leave now."

True.

He slid his long fingers along my jaw, traced the curve of my ear and curled around my neck. Slowly he eased toward me then, gently, gently he pressed his mouth to my cheek, in a kiss so tender it took my breath away.

He eased back to his side of the bed. "What if I rig a way to track Johnny so we can find out if he moves before then?"

"Great. How?"

"I'll tap into his email. Every time he communicates, an alarm will go off. We get a bead on where he's going and then we'll know if he changes plans in the next twelve hours."

He looked so pleased with himself. And it was good. Really good.

"Let's do it." Of course the alarm only worked if the kid actually sent an email to change his plans.

Lucas held up a hand. "I know it's not foolproof but it's a hell of a lot better than sitting in the rental car outside the auditorium all night."

"Okay."

Lucas set the laptop on the minuscule night stand and started finessing the keys. Within a few minutes he'd pressed the sleep button.

"It'll go off loudly enough to wake us."

"So that's it. We should connect with him...tomorrow."

# CHAPTER 34

Reality hit. Lucas had found Johnny. Which meant he was leaving. Gone. History. *Sayonara. Adios. Auf Wiedersehen. Adieu.*

An ache burned low in my gut. I'd gotten used to having Lucas around, used to bouncing ideas off of him, used to him giving me comfort, support and friendship. Used to *him*.

I didn't do relationships. Didn't know how. My relationship growth had been stunted at fifteen while in the burgeoning stage of understanding how a man and a woman fit together.

But I realized, for the last few days I'd actually been making a stab at it. And I'd liked it. Probably more than I should have. There it was. I'd liked it. I liked him.

I liked Lucas.

Wine clung in my throat like tiny razor blades.

Lucas put his hand on mine. "I'm not leaving."

Of course he was. Everyone left. Wasn't that how it worked? I'd served my purpose. Time to move on. It wasn't a question of if, but more like when, he would leave. I knew the score, knew because I'd been the one doing the leaving since I was twenty.

I couldn't say all the things bunched up in my throat. So I said the obvious, "You found him."

"And I'll deal with him."

I tried to drag in air but somehow breathing was difficult. My chest hurt, as if my lungs had shrunk to the size of a pea and couldn't hold any more oxygen. I curled my toes into the rich cotton and took another sip of wine to avoid commenting.

"I'm not leaving," he said it again. But I didn't believe him.

I might do the initial leaving but no one ever came back. Everyone left me sooner or later. I knew that. I was comfortable with that. I understood and handled it.

But his words opened up something inside me, a hope unfurling cautiously. Because I didn't want him to leave.

I didn't do begging but for a moment, I wanted to. Resolutely I pressed my lips together. The two feet of quilt between us yawned wide like the chasm of the Grand Canyon. Impassable. Unsurmountable.

Until Lucas leaned across and dragged me into his lap. His arms circled around me, and pulled me onto his thighs.

He took my wineglass and deliberately, slowly placed it on the bedside table. His fingers tunneled through my hair holding me in place, holding me still. His other hand came up to rest on the curve of my hip, the heat burned through the heavy denim of my jeans.

His mouth possessed mine. With heat, with fire, with absolute intensity. Lucas kissed me as if he couldn't ever let me go. This was not the kiss of a one night stand.

It was a kiss of intimacy.

He knew me. He understood I had an ironclad defense against a kiss that ravaged.

I controlled the tone of my sexual encounters. Our first time together had been quick and furious and frantic. If he had attempted the same physical contact, rejection would be easy, the embrace simple to deflect.

This was something completely different.

I couldn't bring myself to stop him. His fingers feathered across my cheek, the tender erotic brush sent a shiver through me.

He stroked his hand down the outside of my thigh. The simple caress shouldn't have had any effect but as he spread his fingers wide my body clenched in anticipation. His thumb slid along my hipbone then brushed lightly against the zippered placket. The touch, through two layers of clothes should have done no more than annoy, but my body remembered our second time, the clever slide and press of his fingers. Instinctively, my hips rose forcing the palm of his hand hard against the ridge of my pubic bone.

He felt so damn good. I stifled a moan as he pressed his hand upward, skimming the heel of his hand along the sensitive path to my navel.

I still gripped his shirt, bunched between my fingers as if I was a virgin waiting for her first sexual encounter. I tried to focus, tried to remember why this was a bad idea. But as his fingers traced over my collarbone and cupped my breast, my thoughts drifted away like smoke.

"Let me in." His voice was husky, the soft rumble reverberated through me sending ripples of sensation over my skin.

He trailed wet, warm kisses along my jaw. His tongue slid down the curve of my neck as he rubbed his thumb along the valley between my breasts. Each time his hand swept closer to the part of my body aching for his touch.

I held my breath until finally he curved his hand around my breast. He squeezed gently and I let the air out on a sigh. His fingers teased my nipple, playing with the hard berry.

I hooked my arm around his neck and pulled him closer. Tracing the curve of his ear with the tip of my tongue, triumph surged through me when he groaned.

With my teeth I nipped my way down his neck. Tunneling my hands under his cotton shirt, I pressed my palms to his hot muscled chest. His stomach contracted against the scrape of my nails as I slid my hands down toward the waistband of his khakis. His erection pulsed against the strained zipper.

As if choreographed, together we rolled until he lay on top of me, his rock hard erection wedged into the tight v of my legs. He linked his fingers with mine and stretched out over me.

Oh, we had way too many clothes on. Arousal swept through me. My panties were wet and my hormones were locked and loaded.

"Nice weapon," I murmured.

I flashed back to our first meeting and insight blinded me. The absolute insanity, the absolute weakness I'd felt. The crazy insane attraction that had struck like a lightening bolt.

"Weakness," I murmured.

"What?"

"You're a weakness."

For a moment, Lucas looked pleased.

But I'd already segued to the next thought. Weakness was the word the warehouse guy had referenced. Twice.

I jackknifed into a sitting position, the bed squeaking as it rocked.

"Not now." He scooted up, leaned his head back against the headboard and sighed. Heavily.

The mood was broken. I kept recalling what the old man in the warehouse had said. Weakness. Lucas was a weakness. The guy in the warehouse had thought so. Why was that?

People in my line of work, people in my position, couldn't afford weaknesses. "We need to call Barb," I said.

"If you insist." Lucas dialed his cell, then handed the phone to me.

"Barb. Good. We caught you."

"You helped Lucas with his problem?" Barb asked. She sounded tired.

"We're really close to finding Johnny."

I watched Lucas grabbed the pillow, turned it up on its side to use as a cushion, then leaned back against the iron bedframe. "Say hello." I handed him the phone.

"Hey babe."

Barb, the babe. I tried not to let the little surge of jealousy in but it snuck under my defenses.

"It's late." I heard her say, then her voice became indistinct. Lucas responded slowly to whatever she'd said, "Uh, yeah, it's late here." Guess old Barb knew we were together. He handed the phone back to me.

"Tell me what else you've been able to find out."

"What do you know about chromosomes?"

"We've all got twenty-three pairs."

"Right. Each chromosome has different functions." She paused. "After looking at all of the data, it's clear that the drug targeted chromosome 11, possibly the D4DR gene sequence. It looks like from the blood work that the alteration or manipulation worked differently on the different people."

"What would the alteration do?" My brain clicked along at coming up with multiple scenarios—all of them bad.

"Well that particular sequence is believed to be responsible for confidence and fear levels."

"Give me some ideas."

"Without talking with the people involved it would be difficult to predict exactly what would happen."

"Try."

"We're really just learning about the DNA strands. The Human Genome Project identified DNA sequences where there were mutations and changes but most body actions and reactions seem to have multiple DNA controlling strands. Take auditory processing for example--"

"Quit hedging and tell me what you really think."

"I think that if it worked on the confidence center in the brain that it probably produced an extremely high level of confidence which would translate to an enhanced level of performance."

"What's the downside?"

"If you are afraid of something it probably produces a debilitating level of fear."

Could that be why I was so off balance? Why I'd had this unusual and extreme reaction to Lucas Goodman? The knowledge gave me some comfort. The weakness was drug induced.

Until now I hadn't really believed I'd had the drug. But the reality hit home.

"So if someone is given the original altering drug do they need the antidote or would the drug naturally work its way out of their system on its own?"

"It looks like this produces a permanent change."

"So anyone injected with the original drug would need this antidote?"

"If I'm reading these DNA blood work-ups correctly."

Shit. I had to focus on those kidnappings. The scientists had files on ten people but there were only seven known kidnappings, including mine. I needed to figure out the identity of the remaining people.

"One more thing."

Those words were never a good omen. "What?"

"I don't know if it matters or not but all of the subjects have similar DNA."

"I thought all humans are 97% similar. I read that...somewhere."

"True." Barb hesitated. "But the three percent that determines where people evolved from is not always similar and all of these people—with the exception of the child are the same. Their ancestors were from Germany."

"Back up, back up. Child?"

"Unh-huh. I double checked the birth dates because the data surprised me." Barb reaffirmed, "One of the subjects is a five year old child."

Who the hell would give a drug like this to a kid? Fanatics.

Then the other part of what she'd said registered. "Germany?"

"Looks to be." Barb answered. "I had to do a little digging but I found the international database and compared the strands. Every single one is descended from that area."

"We're talking thousands of years back. Right?"

"Sometimes but based on the mutations, probably in the last two or three generations."

That wasn't right. My parents weren't German. My mother had been Spanish and Dad was Scandinavian.

"Thanks."

"You take care of Lucas," she admonished.

I pressed the off button. Thought about Barb's information. No wonder I was so damned off balance.

"We'd better get some sleep." I lifted the covers and got underneath.

"Right." He stretched out on top of the quilt and closed his eyes.

Lucas knew I'd use the drug as an excuse.

I lay there, my mind racing with thoughts and possibilities. I didn't like the idea of this strange drug coursing through me. But it was nice to finally understand why I'd been feeling this way.

"Go to sleep, Jamie."

But my mind wouldn't shut off. I kept going through everything that had happened in the last few days and, I had to admit, with the exception of my reaction to Lucas, nothing else had seemed out of whack.

I must have dozed off because the chime of the computer interrupted my light sleep. I leapt off the bed and looked at the computer screen. "Shit, shit, shit."

"What's wrong?" Lucas sounded as alert as I was.

"Johnny a.k.a. Donald changed his plans."

Lucas muttered a soft curse. "Where is he going?"

My heart stopped in my chest as I read the final line of the email. "He's going to see Bella at the farm."

Panic zoomed through me with the speed of a heat-seeking missile. I ran for my duffel bag, finger combing my hair.

"Calm down."

"He isn't getting anywhere near my sister." Dammit.

"Jamie." He curved his arm around my shoulders, pulling me back against his hard, lean body.

My chest heaved as I tried to draw in enough air. I targeted what I knew would appeal to Lucas rather than my initial panic about my sister. "We know where the bastard is going to be."

"I'll go get him," he said.

I had to go. I shrugged out of his hold and yanked on my jeans.

"I thought your sister doesn't know you're alive."

The sweater I tugged over my head stopped me from answering right away. When I yanked the wool to my waist, I stared at him, my eyes burning with fatigue and anguish. "I can't let him near her."

Lucas sighed and pulled on his khakis. "Okay. Let's make tracks."

An overwhelming relief cascaded through me. All these emotions. This was all a result of that stupid drug. As soon as I made sure Bella was safe, I was going to get that antidote.

*A*lmost there.

Tension ratcheted through me as we passed the post office near Bella's farm. "Right at the next stop sign."

"How come you're so familiar with the directions?"

I'd memorized the way to Bella's home when she'd come to live here long ago. I had only allowed myself to come here once. I'd sat in my car, stared longingly at the old house and wished for a different life. But Lucas didn't have to know that.

We drove through the tiny town in the pre-dawn darkness. Old fashioned street lamps threw beams of yellow light on carefully maintained storefronts and trendy little boutiques and restaurants.

It was picture perfect.

"Stay on this road for the next ten miles."

The car twisted and turned as fingers of light spread across rolling green hills. The roiling in my stomach took new and violent rolls as the road dipped and curved.

A low stone fence separated the rustic road from the lush, verdant expanse of Bella's farm. At the top of a hill, we had a perfect view of the house and driveway one hill over. I pointed to where I wanted Lucas to stop. "We can wait right here. Pull off onto the gravel."

"Can we see the house from here?"

"Yeah. Up on the hill."

"You okay?" He switched off the ignition and killed the headlights.

"Fine." Or I would be, as soon as Johnny Wishbone/Donald Christian tried to approach the house and we nabbed him. Once he was in our possession we could find out what the hell he'd been doing with my sister.

Lucas reached in the back and pulled a pair of binoculars out of his duffel.

I needed to pace, to run. Something to ease the tension and fear screaming through me.

I sat perfectly still.

Lucas cleared his throat. "Nice place."

"Yeah." It was. I wanted to look through the binoculars, to catch a fleeting glimpse of Bella through the window. I wanted it so badly I clenched my teeth until my jaw ached.

"He's already here."

"What?" I snatched the binoculars from him and jammed them against my eyes.

We were too late. There it was. Sitting in the driveway.

A car. Not Bella's S-type Jaguar. An innocuous Ford Escort. The perfect college car. The perfect government-issue car. I'd had one myself when I'd been going to classes at SpyU.

My blood congealed in my veins. My fingers clenched the binoculars so tightly I thought the plastic casing might crack. My breath stalled in my throat, a lump so huge I didn't think I'd ever breathe again, blocked the passage of air. Anger, frustration built like the pressure in a shaken coke can ready to spew.

I had to focus, had to think. I needed Bella to be safe from Johnny, from the government that wanted to use her the way they used me. But all I could do was stare at the simple car. That car represented danger.

"I have to go in." The words came out as a whisper. I couldn't seem to make my voice any louder.

"Just me." Lucas pried my fingers off the binoculars and held onto my hands.

"No." What if the kid went crazy and went after Lucas? He wouldn't be expecting it.

He knew my logic. "Jamie. I know this kid. I'm his godfather, for Chrissake."

"You don't know what his mission parameters are."

"I'll be fine."

I ignored him. "We need to go now. Before he does anything to her." Convinces her to throw away her life, to work for the agency, to give up all the things I'd given up to secure her future.

"Watch through the binoculars."

I didn't trust him not to be swayed by this kid. I didn't trust anyone but me to get rid of Johnny and eliminate the threat. "I'm going."

"This isn't a good idea. Your sister thinks you're dead."

"I realize that." She wouldn't recognize me. "She hasn't seen me since she was five years old."

If she did somehow recognize me, shock would be her first reaction. And I realized, I might finally see my sister, touch her, hug her. Joy burst in me like fireworks on July fourth.

"Stop smiling," Lucas said harshly.

"I can't." My cheeks refused to listen even though I knew Lucas was right. "Let's go."

Lucas didn't start the car.

Now that I was here, all my resistance was gone. Bella was only a mile or so away. The temptation to reach out to her, to connect with her was immense. "I know this isn't the greatest idea--"

"This is a train wreck." But he started the car, then crept down the road at a snail's pace.

"Hurry."

"I'm giving you time to change your mind."

"No. Go faster."

Lucas inched up to a whole ten miles per hour. As we wound up and down the drive, every light in the house blazed like a welcome beacon. Warmth poured from the dormer windows shining down onto the ever-lightening yard.

He pulled up behind the Ford Escort, blocking its path. "In case they try to bolt."

Bella wouldn't, but Johnny Wishbone might. I inhaled a long calming breath.

Lucas pulled his Glock from the pocket in the duffel. "Weapon?"

I didn't want to take a firearm near Bella's house. Didn't want to bring the violence of my life into hers. Yet...what if Johnny Wishbone forced the issue?

I debated the pros and cons in my head.

"They're going to notice us sitting here." Lucas huffed out a sigh and handed me a Sig Sauer P226.

We opened our car doors simultaneously and closed them with a near silent thunk. On the way to the door, I touched the hood of the Escort.

Warm. He hadn't gotten here much before us.

As I tiptoed toward the wraparound porch, I was struck by an unusual hesitation. Maybe this was the wrong thing to do.

"You could wait in the car," he murmured. "I've got a listening device."

Then I could at least hear Bella. But if anything happened I'd be too far away. I shook my head.

Lucas moved up to the leaded glass doorway with its fancy scrollwork and flimsy security. By silent agreement, I stood two steps to the right on the side opposite the hinges, while Lucas stood in front of the oval glass.

He pressed the doorbell.

I heard Bella's giggle before Johnny/Donald shushed her. I visualized their positions in the house, listening to their footsteps as they strode to the door.

Lucas stood in military at-rest position. His hands, with weapon, clasped behind his back.

"Who's there?"

Stupid kid shouldn't have even come to the door. He should have made reconnaissance from another vantage point. If Lucas had been an assassin, they'd both be dead.

"It's six o'clock in the damn morning," Lucas snarled. "You shouldn't have answered the bell."

The door flew open. "Lucas?" Surprise, astonishment lit the kid's face.

I wanted to pivot and scare the crap out of him. But I didn't want to frighten my sister, so I snuffed the impulse to swing my weapon up to his nose and stayed still.

Lucas slid his gaze to mine, transmitting that he could keep the kid from coming outside.

I nodded.

"Donald. Do you know him?" Bella's voice hit me. I hadn't heard her speak in forever. Once, years ago, Carson had given me a tape of Bella, a school speech about improving the food in the cafeteria.

Oh God. My sister.

"How are you kid?" Lucas asked Johnny.

I could feel the 'oh shit' moment hit and Johnny's instinctive move to shut the door. Lucas saw it and angled his hip to block the door from slamming shut.

"We need to talk."

"Uh...." Johnny's gaze bounced from Lucas's leg and back to Bella and back to Lucas. Something must have snapped into place because the kid recovered. "This isn't a real good time."

"No shit," Lucas said drily.

"Donald, who is this guy?"

Johnny gave Lucas a pleading, 'Don't blow my cover' look.

Lucas tucked his weapon into his right hand and held out his left. "Lucas Goodman. Friend of the family."

Bella hesitated then extended her hand toward Lucas. "It's a little early for a social call."

"This isn't social." Lucas still hadn't moved his leg. He held his right arm behind his back awkwardly.

"If you don't move your leg, I'm calling the police."

"Bella, no. You don't understand," Johnny/Donald stopped her.

"Make me understand quick."

Pride flowed through me. My baby sister was no pushover.

"Lucas is a former FBI agent. It's fine."

"FBI?" Bella still sounded suspicious.

I recalled the file. Bella had a distrust of the U.S. government. Shit. Maybe we should have factored that in before we knocked on the door.

"Yeah." Johnny cleared his throat. "I just can't figure out why he's here."

"Maybe you should have called home, *Donald*," Lucas said.

Johnny straightened and took a step backward.

"You told me your parents were dead." Bella's voice had risen.

"They are." Johnny gave Lucas another look.

*The liar.* I thought Johnny's mother might have little something to say about that.

"We should have this discussion in private." Lucas motioned to the car.

"Yeah. Good idea."

I hated staying hidden still able to watch but what I really want was to be there in the kid's face, scaring him.

"I'll come with you," Bella insisted.

Not a good idea.

"I'd prefer to keep the conversation private." Lucas's tone was firm and inviolate.

"My house, my rules."

You go, girl.

"Bella," Johnny placated. "Maybe I should talk to Lucas alone."

Lucas shifted slightly toward me. It was a mistake.

"Who else is out there--skulking?"

"Excuse me?" Lucas was unfailingly polite, but Bella refused to back down.

"Who else is out there?" She flipped on the overhead light, pushed her way out of the house and onto the porch. I stepped back into the shadows.

"Who are you?" she demanded. "And what the hell is going on?"

Bella faced me, demanding answers.

*I'm your sister. I love you.* I held the words captive. "I'm...a friend."

She raised her arm, the small .38 special weapon visible in the glow of the overhead light. "Move slowly. Step into the light," Bella said harshly.

I couldn't stay in the shadows now. Even though I knew it would be the prudent thing to do.

Lucas's hand jerked up swiftly, weapon cocked. "Drop it."

Slow as molasses events unfolded before I could move. Her weapon on me, Lucas's weapon aimed at Bella. Johnny tensed, ready to charge Lucas.

"Stop." I stepped into the light.

Bella's hand dropped. Her skin lost color and her eyes widened and darkened in her pale, pale face. She looked at me with total bewilderment.

"Mama?"

# CHAPTER 36

"Shit." I heard Lucas whisper in a far off, hazy sort of way.

My vision fuzzed, tunneling to grey at the edges. The light from overhead must be about to fritz because a loud buzz sounded in my ears and I couldn't seem to hear anything else. I couldn't move, my feet cemented to the wood porch, as I stared at my sister.

Bella thought I was Mama.

I looked like my mother? I didn't know that. I...didn't realize. How could I? I had no pictures of my family, only memories. Memories which I'd locked away years ago as too painful to contemplate, too agonizing to remember.

"Who is she?" I saw Johnny's lips move, but I couldn't hear him.

"You look just like her pictures, but you...you can't be her." The weapon hung limply from her right hand. "Mama's dead."

Lucas said softly, "Give Donald your weapon, honey."

"Who is she?" Johnny asked, louder this time.

"She won't hurt anyone." Lucas shifted closer to me.

312

Don't bet on it.

Johnny reached slowly for the .38 special, peeling Bella's fingers from the weapon. Lucas held out his hand palm up, and Johnny flipped the barrel down to hand it over. Lucas tucked the gun away.

"You and Donald should go inside," I directed Lucas.

"I'm not going anywhere," Johnny said belligerently.

Bella stood unmoving. The light fell over her pale head illuminating her white blond hair like an angel's halo.

*My little angel*, Papa had always called Bella.

Confusion darkened her cornflower blue eyes. "Who *are* you?"

I'd imagined this moment so many times in the darkest hours of the night, lying awake wherever I happened to be, lonely, always alone. I'd dream and imagine deep in my heart that Bella and I could be a family again. Sisters.

I'd developed an instinct about when to wait, when to stay silent. Usually, I cultivated silence letting the potential asset work through what I'd given them. I knew when to press and when to back off. But my instincts were a mess. I wasn't trying to use Bella, wasn't trying to coerce her.

Bella tilted her head to the right, a tiny frown pushed her eyebrows into a V as if trying to place me, as if she should know me.

The glow from the open doorway highlighted her cheek. Suddenly I was fifteen again and teaching Bella to read. She'd tilted her head in that exact manner when she was five and sounding out some new word.

Too many images from the past bombarded me. And I found myself wanting to help her understand this moment, just as I'd helped her sound out her words.

"Come closer." Bella's voice was rough with confusion.

I stepped slowly toward Bella. I had to tell her. Years of

holding my identity inside were hard to break. The thought of saying my name out loud was terrifying. I'd rather face a loaded syringe than speak my true name.

"Who are you?" she demanded.

Not in front of Johnny Wishbone. I jerked my head at Lucas indicating he get Johnny out. But the kid refused to budge.

"I'm not going anywhere." Johnny planted his feet and glared at me.

If I wanted this reunion, this connection, I had to speak out now. I cleared the ball of emotion from my throat. Exhaling slowly I released my fear, my apprehension.

"It's Helena."

As I moved, Johnny edged closer to Bella.

"Helena?" Bella squeezed her eyes shut. "That can't be. She's dead."

"No. I'm not." I halted, not saying anything else, giving her space, giving her time. Bella would accept the truth faster if I didn't try to persuade her.

I could feel Lucas willing me to look at him. The need to check in, to get his reaction was extreme but I couldn't look away from my sister.

Finally she moved. She lifted her hand. Fingers shaking, her whole body shuddering, she traced my features with her fingertips.

Hope and a profound sense of relief burst in me like a giant bubble.

Lucas flanked Bella, his instinct to protect me. Not her.

No one spoke. Dawn trembled in the sky, a morning dove cooed its early call, somewhere far off in the distance a truck rumbled along the lane.

"We should take this inside." Lucas's gravelly voice interrupted Bella's stare.

She blinked. "It really is you?"

I saw the acceptance. "Yes."

"You aren't dead."

"No."

She lifted her hand, swung her arm back. In disbelief, I watched the blade of her hand come toward me in slow motion. Staring in horror, I waited for the physical blow to hit me.

But it never came.

Lucas chopped Bella's wrist, breaking her momentum, forcing her to take a step back.

I stood frozen, already crushed, waiting for another blow. Of all the scenarios I'd imagined when I thought of this day, physical assault wasn't on the list.

"How could you do that to me!" Bella wailed, crossing her arms over her waist.

To her? I thought of my life for the past thirteen years. About everything I'd done. All for love of my little sister.

"*For* you." I tried to swallow. "I did it for you."

"Right." She laughed bitterly. "Growing up an orphan was a great experience. Watching my whole family explode and burn to a crisp in front of me was fantastic."

Her words hit like punches, pummeling me.

"That's enough," Lucas said harshly.

"Who the hell are you?"

"Your sister's friend."

"Well you know nothing about it, so back off."

Lucas crowded into her space getting right in her face, using his physical presence to intimidate.

Years of thinking of my sister's protection kicked in, instinctively I interceded.

"Don't," I said roughly. But the hand I placed on his

forearm was gentle, soft even. With an ease that surprised me, I pleaded silently for his understanding.

His muscles tensed, but he backed off.

"I can't deal with this right now." The melodramatic statement drew everyone's attention back to Bella.

Johnny curved his arm around Bella. "Lucas. Ease up, dude."

I glared at his arm around her. "Who are you to talk?" I sneered.

"It's a little too late to start acting like a big sister." Bella's stab hit its mark with deadly accuracy.

I drew in a sharp breath. "Maybe. But your boyfriend here has been lying about his name, among other things."

Bella gasped. "What?"

Johnny glared at me. "I don't know who the hell you think you are."

"You should have gone inside with Lucas when you had the chance." I grabbed his wrist from her shoulder and twisted him into an arm lock. We didn't have much more time. "Who are you working for?"

"Working for?" Bella snatched ineffectually at my arm. "He's a student, Helena."

The sound of my name on her lips was weird. Foreign. Surreal. "I don't use that name anymore," I said quietly.

"It doesn't matter what name you use." Bella fell into a fighting stance. "Let go of him."

"That's enough," Lucas reprimanded. "Inside."

He had the same itchy feeling I did. "Now."

I squeezed Johnny's wrist then let him go.

Bella stomped her foot on the old, painted porch. "What is wrong with you two?"

Johnny shook out his arm, then tugged Bella toward the door. "Going inside is a good idea."

Lucas hustled everyone into the house.

"What is this about?" Bella asked petulantly.

The itchy feeling didn't go away when we got inside. Lucas made a quiet motion with his index finger against his lips.

I agreed.

He leaned over and whispered in Johnny's ear, asking if he swept the house when he'd arrived.

Johnny shook his head, No.

"Hey, babe. I have a present for you in my bag." He unzipped the bag and pulled out the bug wand. "Trust me. You're gonna love it."

"What is that?"

I strong armed Bella, wrapping my hand over her mouth and my arm around her waist from behind. A part of me wept as I realized my fantasies of a reunion with my sister were just that. Wishful fantasy.

This travesty of a hug was as close to Bella as I was likely to get. Ever.

Her body tensed as Johnny quietly and efficiently checked the room, while Lucas looked for hidden cameras.

"It's clean."

Interesting. With the amount of buzzing between Lucas and I, it surprised me the room wasn't bugged.

I held on for one more second then let my sister go.

"What the hell is going on?" Her voice and her posture were considerably subdued. She'd finally clued in, something was seriously wrong.

"I'm sorry." Johnny apologized to Bella as he unzipped his bag and put the bug wand away. "I never meant--"

"Who are you working for?" I repeated the question.

Johnny shot a glance at Bella. "I...can't say."

"Protection or recruitment?" I balled my fists and stepped toward him.

Johnny looked at me, then Lucas. "Protection."

"Okay." That was something. Protection. "Any problems?"

"No. As a matter of fact, nothing at all. I think I'm about to be pulled."

"Why?"

Bella was absolutely silent, staring at Johnny in confusion. He wouldn't return her gaze as he said, "It was only supposed to be a short term thing. The assignment actually went a little longer than I'd originally been told."

"You're sure there was no recruitment directive."

"Positive. Protection only."

A frigid chill scuttled up my spine. Had I compromised Bella's safety by coming here? Had my concern for her overridden good sense and years of training?

Lucas rested his hand on my shoulder. The heat of his palm warming my frozen body.

"You're protecting me?" Bella dropped into an overstuffed chair with giant cabbage roses.

Johnny cleared his throat. "Yeah."

I looked away from their private conversation. Johnny was in deep shit, which was fine with me. We were in the living room. The walls were painted a cheerful pink. The chairs were puffy, upholstered with a floral pattern. What caught my attention was the bookshelves. There were lots of biographies. Some of the same ones I had read.

"Is Donald your real name?"

"Uh, no."

"What is it?"

"I...can't say."

"Won't, you mean." Bella shot him a bitter look.

"Can't. Bella. I'm sorry." Johnny eased onto the puffy arm of Bella's chair and threaded his fingers through hers. "I want to, but--"

"So what was the last two weeks?" she spat.

"I really like you--"

"Sorry to interrupt your lovefest, but I need to ask you," I jabbed a finger at Johnny/Donald, "some questions about Staci Grant."

I blocked out Bella's reaction to me. I blocked out her rejection and the invisible wounds. And I focused only on the one thing I could do. Protect Bella.

# CHAPTER 37

Johnny's eyebrows rose. "I don't know any Staci Grant."

"Cut the crap." I bent down until I was eye level with him. "Who was the woman who checked you out of the hospital? And is she the one who recruited you?"

Johnny looked at Lucas for help. I could see him out of the corner of my eye. Lucas stood with his legs apart, arms crossed over his chest.

Johnny sighed. "Staci Grant. She's the one who wanted me to watch over Bella."

I kept perfectly still, my gaze unwavering. "The real Staci Grant is dead."

Johnny frowned at me. "Then who was that in the hospital?"

"You tell me. Staci Grant died weeks ago in Afghanistan." I let that fact sink in. "Have you ever met in person before?"

"No." He kept his eyes steady on mine and I actually believed him. He hadn't shifted his body or his gaze away.

I could lie without compunction but somehow I didn't think Johnny Wishbone was there yet.

"What did she look like?"

"About your height, light skin for a black woman."

"She's white."

Johnny shook his head. "This woman is definitely black, probably a mix though. She had dark curly hair, but not kinky like a 'fro."

"Eyes?"

"Deep brown."

"Shape. Color can be changed."

"Oh, right." He looked flustered--as well he should. "Deep set, slight tilt."

"Why did she hire you?"

"She said Bella might be in danger but she was still working on why."

"Why you?"

"She said I was as ready as she could afford and trust."

"What was the plan?"

"She was going to eliminate the threat and then Bella would be safe."

Ironic that the Staci Grant impersonator was trying to keep Bella safe. Why? "Do you have a contact number?"

"No. She calls me."

"Next time--get a number," Lucas said. "And call me on my cell. We need to talk to her."

Johnny nodded.

"Something to remember, kid. Never trust anyone. Not even your friends."

I could see Lucas's words hit Johnny. "So this was just a test?"

"If it was a test, you failed," I said. "You gave up information."

Lucas looked at Johnny. "Call your mother. Explain something."

"Your mother?" Bella's voice rose. She snatched her fingers away.

Johnny frowned. "I left a note."

"Where?" Lucas asked.

"In the hospital bed." Johnny glanced at Bella. "I said I needed to get away for a few weeks and not to worry."

"She didn't get it."

"It's just a few weeks. It's not a big deal." The kid said with the arrogance only youth can pull off.

"It is if she files a missing persons with the police."

Realization dawned. "That's why you tracked me down."

"Yeah. This isn't a game."

"I thought it was a test."

"And if you pass, what happens?" Lucas asked.

"I go to the next level."

"What does that mean?"

"She recommends me for all of the testing, evaluations, and a training class."

I didn't give a shit about his career path. "She show you any i.d.?"

"Uh, no." Johnny had the smarts to look embarrassed.

So this stranger impersonating Staci Grant, without i.d. to back up her claim, had asked him to look after Bella. Even if, in some bizarre twist, his recruiter was actually Staci Grant, their contact didn't make any sense. Staci identified the recruits. Someone else made contact so Staci's cover stayed intact.

Unless his operation was supposed to be the first contact of recruitment for Bella. "If you try to bring my sister along with you, I will hunt you down. Are we clear?"

Johnny swallowed audibly. "Yeah."

Bella jumped up from the floral chair and glared at all of us. "I am in control of my own destiny. No one tells me where to go or what to do."

"Consider yourself lucky you have a choice." I averted my gaze to the fireplace. The mantel was littered with pictures. In all sizes and colors, pictures crowded the ornate strip of wood. Pictures of our family. Pictures I hadn't seen in thirteen years.

Lucas put a hand on my arm. "It's time to go."

"I know." I wanted to stay, to make sure nothing ever hurt her. But I wouldn't be welcome.

The itchy, twitchy feeling was back. We needed to split. Johnny was here. And Lucas and I would be close.

I said to Bella, "I have to leave."

"You're good at that," Bella said bitterly. She twisted away from me, her arms wrapped tightly at her waist. "Leave."

I had one last chance. "I thought you never go away angry."

Bella whirled around. "You...spied on me? How dare you!"

I stared hard at my sister for one long moment, taking in her straight streaked blond hair, clear innocent skin, and eyes the same color and shape as my father's, sparking with anger all the way down to her bare feet and her pale pink toenails.

Suddenly everything I'd done, every action I'd taken for the last thirteen years seemed wrong with no way to go back and change it. Even if I wanted to. I'd done everything for her. "I did what I had to do."

Lucas's hand was warm and comforting on my arm, as

if he knew how difficult those words were. He alone understood the sacrifices I'd made for my sister.

I shot Johnny a hard look. "Keep her safe."

"He's not staying here either!" Bella yelped.

Johnny started, "Bella, wait, let me explain...."

"It's either him or me," I barked in a hard voice. I wasn't leaving her alone.

She wouldn't even look at me, her lips scrunched in a pout. "Him."

Her choice had been easy and automatic--no hesitation at all. She didn't want me. I'd take out that pain and examine it later but right now I had to get out.

We'd sit in the car and watch for the rest of the night. Bella was fine. John Wishbone had been watching over her and he'd seen no threat.

I walked out the door, knowing I'd never be back.

Stopping on the steps, I remembered the last time I'd been at the farm, when I'd been ten, maybe eleven. I still remembered the way the wraparound porch welcomed visitors, the way the white picket fence curled around a yard filled with flowers and statues and fountains, the way the birds twittered and the fireflies buzzed lazily in the twilight.

I remembered playing hide and seek with my brother in the summertime, scrunching under the heavy stone benches in the gazebo or squeezing between the raspberry vines and the fence.

I rubbed my arms gently.

The scratches from those long ago days had hurt. Now I understood those angry red slashes were simple wounds that healed easily. It was the scrapes and scars you couldn't see that hurt the most.

Lucas drove away from the house, along the winding drive. "You okay?"

"Fine."

"We'll sit and watch the house."

"Yeah."

He parked in the same spot, about two miles in distance and a lifetime in experience, as we had less than an hour ago. Half hour tops. Amazing how little time it takes for your heart to shatter.

I leaned back against the head rest, stared at the grey fabric ceiling of the rental. Maybe I should have tried to argue my case to Bella, but explaining my actions contradicted the way I'd lived for the past thirteen years. And I really don't think it would have made any difference.

"Don't." I heard his voice through a fog. "She'll understand when she's older."

I laughed bitterly.

Lucas leaned toward me, his hand on mine, staring intently at me. Willing me to believe. "At least she'll have the chance to grow old. Because of you."

Right. Focus on the salvageable.

I closed my eyes, closed him out.

"You did everything you could. She isn't going to comprehend the sacrifices you made right now. She's still just a kid. A kid who got to experience a full childhood."

Lucas's arguments made sense but I remembered her face as she raged about being an orphan. The rough anguish in her voice. Maybe I hadn't done the right thing.

I'd never know.

The roaring in my head grew. Until I realized, it wasn't my head. I snapped my eyes open as Lucas whipped around.

Shit.

Each action seemed to flash and freeze, like watching motion through a strobe light.

An SUV barreled up the driveway going at least sixty.

Lucas was already turning on the engine.

Four black clad figures, heads covered with balaclavas, spilled out and ran toward the house.

We roared down the hill, the farm house was out of sight for seconds, then came back into view.

A flash bang boomed and flared. The front door swung open.

Our engine strained, ripping the shocks as we took the dips too fast.

They carried the limp bodies of Bella and Johnny out of the house, rolled them into the van.

No blood. No blood.

"Probably tranqs," Lucas said grimly.

The SUV sped down the driveway.

"Standard training exercise from the Farm." In exercises they didn't use live rounds.

Lucas swerved onto the narrow driveway.

The SUV barreled towards us, headlights blinding.

We drove straight at them on the narrow road.

"In a game of chicken we're going to lose," Lucas commented.

"I know."

A weapon appeared outside the passenger window aimed straight at us.

"I'm going to have to give soon."

I thought of Bella and Johnny rolled in the back like sacks of garbage and how they would fly if we hit. "Go now."

Lucas jammed on the brakes and swerved to the right.

The muzzle of the weapon flashed twice.

No sound. Silencer. But the bullets were real.

"Shot the tires." The car jerked, his forearm muscles

straining to hold it steady as the car bumped over a tree root.

I heard the thud as his head hit the roof of the car.

We clipped the side of a tree. My head slammed into the windshield.

I lay against the seat, my head resting on the cool glass of the passenger door, in the grip of fear so intense it left me immobile, watching the SUV speed away in the side mirror hanging awkwardly from the car.

I couldn't do any more than stare in horror as the SUV disappeared. Could it be that in trying to protect my sister, I'd done the exact opposite?

They had Bella.

# CHAPTER 38

Rage howled through me.

I didn't even realize I was screaming until Lucas laid his hand on my shoulder. "Jamie. Stop."

He unclipped the seatbelt, ran his hands over my body. "Are you okay?"

"Did I cause this?"

"I don't know."

"We didn't leave any tracks."

"Shit. You're bleeding."

I swatted his fingers away from a lump on my forehead. A warm trail of blood trickled down the side of my face. "We've got to see if they left a ransom note."

"Honey. They don't want ransom," he said gently. Lucas opened the driver's door and eased out.

"They have to want something." And whatever it was I would move the universe to give it to them and get Bella back.

The passenger side of the car was crushed against the tree. I crawled over the driver's side and he reached in to help me out of the car. I stood, swaying woozily. "Got to get moving." My throat was sore, scratched. I couldn't quite figure out why.

We tramped toward the house. Lucas was favoring his right leg. And my vision had the tendency to separate into two images. "You okay?"

"I'll live," he said. "Let's find a ride."

"We'll take the Jag." I said fiercely, "We've got to get them back."

"We will."

We limped up the porch steps. The only indication that something violent had happened here was the slight scorch mark on the door frame and some trampled grass.

Lucas pushed open the door and we paused, gazing inside. Nothing in the entry was disturbed.

"How the hell did they find her?"

"I don't know." Lucas said, "The bigger question is why take her?"

He took my hand and squeezed, the sides of the ring cut into the skin on my finger.

The ring.

"Your ring?" Lucas asked.

"Dammit." The satellite transmission ring Carson had given me, supposedly for my protection. I ripped the ring off then twisted and pressed the stone twice and screamed into it. "Damn you, damn you, Carson. Did you put a GPS transponder in this?"

Lucas looked at the ring, then stared at me. "You think they tracked you through this ring?"

I nodded and viciously twisted the ring back to off. "He must have put a tracker in it so he could track me." The last ring hadn't had a tracker, but they hadn't needed one.

They'd used my implanted beacon. I swayed, trying to piece it all together.

"They went toward D.C.," Lucas said, as we limped down the hallway to the kitchen.

"I saw."

"Plates on the SUV?"

"Dealer plates," I responded tersely. "Nothing to trace."

We stepped into the homey kitchen, where the lights still blazed. The scent of brewed coffee overlay the slight odor of gun oil and sweat. One earthenware mug sat on the oak farm table. The other lay on its side, the liquid dripped through the seam between table leaves to the pine floor below.

Plop. Plop. Plop.

"We'd better get out of here before they send a clean up crew," Lucas said.

I was tempted to stay behind, get picked up by the cleaner crew. But the chances they would know anything about where the extraction team took Bella and Johnny was minuscule.

I pawed through the drawer in the kitchen searching for the keys to the Jaguar. I couldn't wait to get to Carson. See his face when I ripped off his balls and shoved them down his throat.

"Jesus, you're bloodthirsty."

Lucas slung an arm around my shoulders and pressed a kiss to the side of my head that didn't hurt. "Let's get out of here before you use your secret decoder ring to set up a meeting."

"This isn't some joke."

"I know." He stopped, gripped my shoulders, his gaze boring into mine. And there I saw the anguish and the sorrow. "I know."

"I'm sorry." I'd lead them to Johnny too.

"We'll get them back."

*  *  *

THERE WAS nothing menacing about the crowded little donut shop a few miles from NSA headquarters.

It was Sunday morning so the inside of the shop was packed. Kids dressed in sports clothing, families decked out for church, a few couples with coffee and papers crowded the tables and counter. Due to the Indian Summer, the tables outside were still set up. While anguish and fear warred within me, I sat composedly at a small bistro table on the sidewalk, waiting for Carson.

Lucas had my back. He was on the bus bench about ten feet away with a clear shot, if necessary. I had an earpiece so he could alert me if it looked like anyone was moving in.

I didn't think there'd be any kind of attempt to attack me in such a public place. But clearly I'd been horribly wrong numerous times lately.

I'd threatened Antoinette so I knew Carson would show.

Carson slipped into the chair across from me, right on time. I'd already ordered his latte.

He picked up the paper cup, took a sip while he surveyed the bruises on my face. "What the hell happened?"

I knew he was rattled because of the profanity. Tough. I looked him in the eye and deliberately twisted the ring off my finger then set it down on the table between us.

"Who knows about Bella?"

"No one."

"Why would Staci Grant hire someone to protect Bella?"

"He frowned. "Ridiculous. Staci doesn't, didn't know Bella."

"Did you bring Bella into the NSA?"

Carson took another sip of his latte, stalling. "Of course not, that was part of our deal," he replied calmly.

"Then who kidnapped her?"

Carson blanched. "Bella's been kidnapped?"

"Was there any chatter that indicated another kidnapping?"

"None." He rubbed a hand over his mouth. "That doesn't make any sense. All of the abductees were in the espionage community."

Someone had taken Bella and Johnny. If their abduction led back to me, then the mission was likely where this mess started. "Would she have been kidnapped because I kept investigating?"

"You kept investigating?" His hand trembled slightly before he carefully set the cup on the bistro table. "I told you to drop it."

But I hadn't dropped it and the more I investigated, the more links there were between me, the abductions, 5491 and Bella. "Why did you want me to drop it?"

Carson stared across the street, avoiding my accusing gaze. "David Armbruster closed the investigation on Agent Johnson's death. Apparently Johnson had files on the people who'd been abducted. Although we weren't able to determine why they were abducted, everyone in his files is accounted for."

This whole setup stunk and I didn't understand why Carson would just...roll over. "Don't you care why they were abducted?"

Carson's gaze cut to my left as he stared intently at the logo, a steaming cup of coffee, on the shop's window. "The agents are on administrative, low clearance desk jobs until we can determine the impact of the abductions."

"The reason for the abductions is equally important."

"Armbruster wanted the matter dropped. We've got to do some serious damage control after losing two agents in the last month," he snapped.

"We didn't lose them. They're dead." I thought about the scientists's file. "The third component in the syringe, which they were going to inject in me, was an antidote to a DNA- altering drug."

Carson tried to shut me down. "Our lab results were not conclusive."

"I took files from the warehouse. The files were encrypted with a program developed by the NSA. The files contain DNA analysis of ten people. The agents were originally injected with a gene manipulation drug." I spewed out before he could stop me. "I believe when problems became apparent, they abducted the agents to administer an antidote. Until me, they'd been successful."

"Is this true?"

"It's a theory." With plenty of evidence to back it up.

A fine sheen of perspiration misted his forehead. "How many agents were in the files you took from the warehouse?"

"Nine adults, ten subjects in total." I wanted the details from him. Something was terribly off balance here.

Carson's face reflected shock. "You never told me you had this intelligence."

"I didn't trust," *you. I still don't.* "The NSA. Let's focus on the problem at hand. Bella."

Carson expelled a sharp breath. "You are really on top of your game, Jamie."

I noted the sports analogy again. Carson's tell. He was nervous, unsettled.

"Those agents need to be monitored for any adverse affects from both the original drug and the antidote." I slapped my hands on the table, enjoyed the pain stinging my palms and the subtle flinch of Carson's shoulders. I wanted answers. "Is there any way Bella could have received the original drug?"

"I can't imagine how or why," he answered faintly.

"Could it be because she's part of 5491?"

If anything, Carson got whiter.

"All of the abductees related to my mission are designated 5491," I hammered at him.

He pressed his lips together.

I leaned toward him, letting him see the fury barreling through my numbness. "Tell me."

"It's classified."

"I don't care." I had nothing left to lose. "Someone has Bella."

His gaze darted around the café, noting the patrons. The buzz of morning conversation and the clink of silverware on ceramic would muffle our voices. He canted toward me and spoke softly, "That's a special department. Funding from various agencies filter through to 5491."

"What's the funding for?"

His mouth tightened, deep lines scored his face with worry. "This could mean my job."

"I don't give a rat's ass about your job." I hissed. "This is Bella's life." *My life.*

"Monthly reparation payments for the descendants of certain agents killed in the line of duty."

I processed that information but only came up with more questions. Line of duty? I received those payments but..."What does 5491 have to do with my family? My parents didn't work for the NSA."

But he didn't answer.

If I followed the logical chain of information, I had to ask, "Tell me about TICOM."

He jerked at the request. "TICOM?"

"Don't act stupid," I accused.

Carson rubbed his hands over his face in a gesture of total defeat. "TICOM was an operation during World War II."

"I know that." I gulped more black coffee and forced myself to remain calm. "Skip to the important parts."

"You know the joint U.S. and British forces captured the castle in Saxony, Germany, confiscated the cipher machines, and took the German codebreakers captive?"

I waved him on. "Yeah."

"After they were captured, those codebreakers disappeared."

"We eliminated them?" The idea that the U.S. had been so brutal against non-combatant enemies was shocking. Disgust flashed through me, but I kept coming back to one thing. "What does that have to do with my family?"

"We didn't eliminate them," Carson replied calmly. "We picked their brains and, after the war was over, we gave them new identities in countries far away from Germany."

Realization dawned. "So that's why parts of the TICOM operation are still sealed from anyone, even Congress, reading them."

He nodded. "To keep those German codebreakers--and their families--safe."

I couldn't put together what this had to do with me and Bella.

"Your father was a Nazi codebreaker."

Papa? That couldn't be right.

"He wasn't old enough." My father had only been ten

during World War II. Besides he wasn't German, he was Norwegian.

"Yes he was." Carson rebutted, "It was a time of turmoil. Passports, identification could be changed, recalculating nationality, age."

My father was a Nazi? My father was German? He had been involved in the war. It didn't seem possible. I tried to process everything. My entire life was a lie. My family's entire life was a lie. My father….

*Focus on the bigger picture, Jamie.* The information seemed so bizarre, so huge, and even though other evidence seemed to support the idea, the small details kept getting in my way.

"But...why keep those people secret?

"We were uneasy allies with Russia. The Germans had cipher machines for Russian code too. We wanted those Russian codes." He sat still, speaking quietly, "It's my understanding we also didn't want the Germans revealing our code to the Russians."

"Weren't they worried about the codebreakers eventually returning to Germany?"

"Any return to Germany was against the agreed upon negotiation terms."

I was still trying to figure out the ramifications of this information. "What if they tried?"

"Sleepers were in place to stop that from happening."

"So...if a codebreaker broke the terms of agreement, the sleeper was activated."

"Their directive was to eliminate the rogue codebreaker," Carson finished for me.

I didn't say anything, too stunned to process all the information he'd just thrown at me.

"Sleepers are insurance," he said patiently.

I knew that too.

Suddenly I recalled Bella's revelation. I clamped a hand on his wrist in a grip so tight, my fingers turned white. "My parents were arguing about TICOM the day they were killed."

Carson fell silent but there was a look of anguish on his face.

"What?" I demanded an answer. I thought about Department 5491. Reparations, making amends for a wrong, to descendants of agents killed in the line of duty.

Carson had become my mentor, the only authority figure in my life. The look on his face made me want to turn away, to close my eyes and go on without the knowledge he had.

"A sleeper cell killed your family."

I sat immobile, unable to take it in. A sleeper. Killed. My. Family. A giant ache settled in my chest. I had to focus on the here and now. Focus on what you can control.

"That issue is dead." Like my parents. Focus on now. "Why did they take Bella?"

"There's no reason for it." Carson frowned, paused.

His attitude was far too casual for me. My heart thudded, ba-boom, ba-boom, like a car stereo too heavy on bass drums, shaking my frame, rattling my composure.

"Did the agency do this?" I demanded. "You owe me at least that much."

"No. I would know if this had something to do with the NSA." Carson put on his best authoritative voice, "I'll do some checking. Call me as soon as you find her, I can send in an extraction team."

Not a chance in hell. I wasn't letting him, or the NSA, anywhere near Bella.

"Anything else you can think of?"

"Yes." Carson wiped his fingers fastidiously on a paper

napkin. He leaned over and whispered in my ear, "Don't ever threaten Antoinette again."

I couldn't summon any emotion beyond one thought. *Now he knows how it feels.*

But, I wasn't any closer to finding Bella.

# CHAPTER 39

I sat, thinking about all of the information Carson had revealed, all of the things he was still hiding.

Lucas's voice sounded in my earpiece. "Jamie. We've got someone showing too much interest in your table."

For a moment, I forgot what I was supposed to do if Lucas contacted me. What was the signal? My brain fogged. Could I freaking take any thing else?

"At your two."

I snapped back to my surroundings. I had to rescue Bella, and I couldn't let Lucas down. I fiddled with my fork in the prearranged signal that I understood his message, then slowly moved my hand to my lap. I eased my gaze toward the spot Lucas had indicated.

Zeke Hawthorne, the NSA programmer, was across the street, staring into the window of a bike shop but he wasn't moving. As camouflage went, his sucked. He wore a bright red sweater, rumpled, and his hair normally a charming curly mop looked like he'd been on a three day bender.

His hands were in his pockets. Didn't look like he had a weapon but it paid to be cautious.

The microphone clipped in my bra would send my response back to Lucas. "I know him."

Lucas's voice came low and gentle in my ear. "Friend or foe?"

"I...don't know anymore."

"Best guess."

"Friend. Maybe." I drained my coffee. "I'll circle around and pick the guy up."

"Meet me one block over at our rendezvous point."

I crossed the street, heading for Zeke. He didn't run when he saw me. In fact, he smiled. "I guess I wasn't too hard to spot." He gestured with self-deprecation to his clothes.

I ignored the obvious. "What are you doing here?"

"Carson didn't see me," he said hopefully, eyebrows raised, a small grin playing around his mouth.

"He saw you."

But I hadn't. I'd been so shocked by Carson's revelations I hadn't even noticed him until Lucas pointed him out. That kind of mistake could get me, and Bella, dead.

Get your head in the game, Jamie.

I ignored the flat line of Zeke's mouth. "What are you doing here?"

"I came to see if you needed any help."

"Cut the bullshit." I made my voice hard, mean. "You look like hell."

"I wanted to help." He rubbed a hand through the mass of tangled hair. "This has to do with the kidnappings, doesn't it?"

I regarded him warily. "What do you know about them?"

"I...hear things. And I wrote the program remember?"

"You looked at the files I accessed?"

"Hell yes. I thought maybe I could help."

His answer was a little too offhand, forcing me to think. I connected the dots. Ezekial Hawthorne was on Staci's 5491 list. Zeke. Another TICOM descendant.

The sound of Lucas's cell phone ringing blasted in my ear. Loudly.

"Hello," he answered. Then Lucas whispered to me, "Listen up. We've got contact."

To hell with propriety, calmness, not drawing attention to myself. I took off across the street, not bothering to say goodbye to Zeke.

"Yes, this is Ms. Hunt's secretary." Lucas's voice sounded in my ear. My secretary?

I pumped toward our rendezvous point, vaguely registering that Zeke was following. Dammit. I wanted to hear the other end of this conversation.

"One moment and I'll put you through to her."

I was breathing fast as I approached the Jaguar. Lucas was leaning against the doorframe. I ripped the phone from Lucas's hand, took a second to try to slow my breathing. "Hello."

"Ms. Hunt?" It was a man's voice.

"Yes."

"And how am I to be sure this is you?" The brogue was back.

"You're approximately five ten, portly at about 180 pounds, grey hair and you walk with a cane."

He let loose with a deep belly laugh. "Excellent. I've a proposition for you."

"Where are they?" Too eager. Too eager. Shit.

"Ah now, we'll be getting to that later. I'm sorry for the mishap. Clearly I'm entertaining the wrong young couple," he said it as if he'd picked up the wrong brand of hot dog at the store. "Luckily for them, Mr. Christian knew how to get in touch with you."

Thank God Lucas had given Johnny his cell number.

"They'll be returned," he paused. "After we meet."

The lunatic. Much more dangerous than the syringe lady, Susan. And he hadn't said *how* Bella and Johnny would be returned.

"Will Susan be there too?"

"She goes where she is told." His voice was no longer jovial.

"Where and when?" I wanted to be able to play off Bella's abduction, play it cool not frantic, but my heart hammered so loudly in my ears that I could barely hear. My throat constricted.

He was a fanatic and until I figured out his main goal, he was the most dangerous man on the planet.

"Not so fast," he said laconically. "You're a sharp one. We need to set some ground rules."

"Go," I forced out through numb lips.

"We'll meet later today." He coughed, a raw, hacking, bark. "I'd hoped to be done before now. Unfortunately, I've an appointment I must take care of first."

"Place."

"I'll call you at four forty-five." He paused again. "Come alone and bring the key fob."

Fuck. I didn't have the key fob. But I had the files. It had to be enough.

"Is that why you've been after me?" I decided to let him know that I had accessed the information. I couldn't be a total wimp, he'd get suspicious. But I couldn't push too hard either. "To get the data back."

"Very good. You are proving to be extremely intelligent."

I could practically hear him rubbing his hands together. "Just what I need. Be at Reagan National Airport. I'll be in touch."

Smart place. Access to planes, bus, Metro, cabs. I wouldn't be able to give a partner enough warning.

"Bring the antidote," I said.

"You are in no position to make demands, Agent Hunt."

Lucas's phone beeped in my ear as the old man broke the connection.

I came back to my surroundings with a blink. On the sidewalk, Lucas had Zeke in an arm and head lock. Zeke stood, his posture relaxed, face stoic, but the line around his lips was white with tension. "You can let me go now."

"Who is this?" Lucas jerked his head toward Zeke, not loosening his hold.

"Zeke meet Lucas. Lucas meet Zeke." I tucked his cell phone into my pocket. I wasn't letting go of my only link between Bella's kidnapper and me.

"Who are you?" Zeke shrugged away from Lucas but his stance was anything but conciliatory. "Jamie doesn't work with a partner."

I wasn't about to expose any more about Lucas to anyone at the NSA. I dismissed his question with a dead-eyed stare. "Why do you look like you slept in your clothes?"

"I fell asleep in the chair in my office, looking out for you," he said grumpily.

"Why?"

"I'm beginning to wonder the same thing."

"How did you know about the meet with Carson?"

"Jamie. I'm the one who remotely turned on the tracking device in your ring. I was worried about you." Zeke looked uncomfortable for a moment. "After you, uh, sent your message to Carson, I relayed the information to him.

Uh...I'm not sure what happened, but whatever it was is probably my fault."

The buzzing in my head was getting louder. "You set me up?"

"Not intentionally. I was trying to help," he laughed bitterly.

"We need to get out of here," Lucas said grimly.

He was right. We'd been in one place too long.

"What's the plan?" Lucas asked.

"Later."

Zeke planted his feet, legs spread wide. "Let me help."

"No."

"Someone stole my encryption. I'm as invested in this as you are."

Not even close, buddy.

"You need someone technical," Zeke said desperately. "I might be able to trace the cell transmission. Find out where the call originated."

That caught my attention. But still I shook my head no.

"I was kidnapped too," Zeke blurted.

"What?" That stopped me.

He looked miserable. "A few weeks ago."

"And you didn't tell anyone?"

"It's complicated." Zeke fisted his hands and looked me square in the eye. "I have a natural resistance to truth serum drugs. They don't work on me."

"So....what?"

"I know I didn't give them my encryption program." Zeke said fiercely, "I know I didn't."

Not that he remembered.

"I have the right to help you get these guys. I want to know how they got my program."

We stood there, all of us silent. I was processing. Thinking.

"He's got a point," Lucas said after a minute.

"Are you crazy?" I hissed. "I can't take him along."

"We've got two hostages, Bella and Johnny, and at least two combatants, Susan and the old guy. One hostage is awake, right now. But what if they're incapacitated when we get there."

"I'll figure it out."

"You can't do this alone," Lucas insisted.

"Watch me."

"You need backup," Lucas said. "We're in this together."

"I'll hurt you." I hurt everyone. Even when I wasn't trying.

He looked at me steadily. "Maybe. Maybe not."

My conscience wouldn't let me take him up on the offer of backup, even though I was tempted. Unbearably so.

"I...." I looked at him, at the sincerity and the acceptance in his eyes. I really didn't want to hurt him.

Lucas threaded his fingers with mine, his hold gentle and implacable. "I'm willing to take that chance."

My throat tightened, my heart slowed, the ba-bump echoing in my ears. He understood me so well. A me that hadn't existed a week ago. He'd found a tender, softer me. Nurtured me, cared for me, and protected me. I couldn't shut him out, couldn't turn him away.

Then he used the argument that swayed me every time. "Do it for Bella."

Bella.

Zeke watched us volley back and forth.

"You don't know anything about field work," I said to Zeke. One last desperate attempt.

"I could be the control."

"I work alone." But I was weakening and they both sensed it.

Rage was not my friend. The last time I'd gotten angry, my family had ended up dead. I needed calm, cool planning and execution.

I couldn't seem to erase the picture of Bella as a hostage. And every time I did a savage need to strike out filled me. I couldn't afford the anger. I didn't have any training at hostage rescue and Lucas was right, one against two, with an additional two incapacitated hostages, were bad odds.

If I accepted the help, it would be possible to rescue Bella. I just...had to relinquish my aloneness, my solitariness, in order to get this done. If I didn't, Bella had a much smaller chance of survival.

I blew out my breath, realizing for the first time since I'd seen that SUV driving away, I could breathe. "Okay."

"And we know someone with hostage rescue experience," Lucas enticed. "Someone who also has a vested interest in rescuing those hostages."

Although I'd trained for plenty of situations, I had no practical experience in hostage rescue. "Who?"

"Someone who would love to get Johnny's information about Staci."

"Who?" I demanded.

"Jordan Ramirez," Lucas answered simply.

# CHAPTER 40

*H*ow the hell had I ended up with not only a partner but a team?

I stalked around the shabby motel room, scuffing at the mud brown carpeting. We still had a whole freaking hour until the instructions for the meet came through.

We'd turned on the television to a music channel but some idiot had put on rap music.

Lucas and Zeke were in a deep conversation, bonding over some stupid listening gadget they'd picked up. Zeke's head bobbed with the beat of Nelly. There sat the idiot.

Jordan Ramirez sat in the chair by the desk, eyes closed, his body so still he looked asleep. But his eyes moved at a rapid rate beneath the closed lids and I knew he was mentally going over our plan, visualizing the take down-- even without knowledge of the meeting place's floor plan.

"What the hell are we doing here?" I snarled. I gripped the cell phone in my hand so tightly my fingers were sore.

Ramirez unfolded gracefully from the chair as Zeke hopped up and practically ran for the door. "We'll, uh, go next door and pick up some food. Bad idea to run an op on an empty stomach."

Ramirez silently prowled toward the exit. Pausing, hand on the knob, he assessed us both with a long look, gave one wry shake of his head. "We've got an hour. Get it together."

Great. I'd turned into a raving lunatic. I had a plan. I had gadgets, weapons, partners. I shuddered. What I didn't have was a place or a time. And every moment Bella was in the madman's clutches, I worried.

Lucas stood slowly, treating me like I was fragile, breakable. "Try to rest."

With gentle hands, he kneaded the rigid muscles in my neck then pressed a kiss to my hair like a father comforting a child.

But I wasn't a child. I didn't want tenderness. I wanted oblivion. And I had to get rid of this rage.

I shoved his hands away, ripping at my clothes, stripping off my tank top with hasty fingers, baring my breasts.

"Jamie." Lucas tried to put my top back on.

I said grimly, "We've spent too much time in hotel rooms wasting opportunity."

Life had kicked me in the ass one too many times. I wouldn't regret this. I grabbed his hands and jammed them on my breasts. My own hands massaged the thickening bulge in his jeans.

Visual and tactile stimulation. I'd have him where I wanted him in another sixty seconds.

My nipples stabbed into his palms. I could see his helpless reaction in the way his hands curved around me, his thumbs brushed against the stiff peaks. And still he was too gentle.

"What about your one time only rule?" I heard his desperation.

"Fuck my rule." I fisted one hand in his hair and slammed my mouth against his. With the other hand, I popped the snap on his jeans and forced the zipper down.

His hips bucked as my hand curled around his cock.

The fog surrounding me thickened. I wanted hot, raw sex. I wanted to forget the last few hours. The last few days. My whole life.

"I refuse to hurt you," he murmured vehemently against my open mouth.

But he would. Everyone did.

Lucas whirled me around and shoved me up against the wall of the motel room. He used his teeth to nip down my throat. With firm hands he squeezed my breasts pushing them up to his mouth. He feasted, nibbling, sucking until I thought I would explode from the sensation of his slightly rough tongue against the sensitive tips, and the soft brush of his hair against my jaw.

He scraped his teeth along the path to my belly button as he slid to his knees. His hands played with my nipples while his tongue painted patterns on my stomach, his weight against my legs anchored me to the wall.

But what held me captive against the ancient wallpaper in mud brown and orange was my own vulnerability. My own need to hold on to our connection.

He dragged his hands down to my waist and ripped at the zipper of my jeans. The soft scrape of his beard scuffed erotically against the sensitive skin of my belly before his tongue probed the thatch of hair protecting my sex.

My hands hung limply at my sides. I may have started the game but Lucas was halfway round the board and I hadn't made a move.

He pulled my jeans down to my knees and braced his forearms against my thighs. With his thumbs, he spread me open wide and like an ice cream cone, he licked me up in one long stroke.

All my blood rushed south. I thought my knees would give way. I'd lost control of this encounter. "Move to the bed."

"Nope." Lucas shook his head back and forth, the stubble of his beard brushed against me. My blood throbbed and pulsed.

I was so turned on I couldn't breathe. The air in the room seared my lungs as I tried to draw in oxygen. I could make him move. "I know at least ten defensive moves that could have you on the floor in two seconds."

"But then we'd miss all this fun." His teeth scraped against me as he spoke. Then he turned his head sideways, opened his lips and sucked my clitoris into his mouth like a grape.

"Jesus," I gasped.

He relentlessly, rhythmically sucked at the knot of nerves and sex until I came in an explosion so hard, fireworks blurred my vision.

With a gentle lick he teased my still sensitive body. I whimpered as internal contractions milked a phantom cock. The sound galvanized something within me. I didn't want a phantom. I wanted him, inside me.

I wasn't going to be the only vulnerable one in this room.

Lucas knelt in front of me. His jeans spread wide, an impressive erection filled his boxers and the tip of his cock peeked out the top. He glanced up at me, his hair mussed from my hands and a smug smile on his face.

"What?"

His grey eyes sparkled as he swirled his tongue over his wet mouth. "Yum."

I shoved my jeans down around my ankles, pushed them off with my toes.

"Your turn." I slid slowly down his body my hips and stomach rubbing over his chest, the hard points of my nipples stabbing into him. The wet heat of my open legs caressed the head of his cock, still trapped in the confines of his jeans, as I sank to my knees.

I held his wrists in a loose cuff. Then I pressed his hands against the wall, forcing him to keep his hands off. "No touching."

I wanted him as hot and helpless and breathless as he'd had me. I eased my palms over the hard muscles of his ass and gently scraped his jeans down to his knees. Pulling his hips to mine, I tilted my hips up slightly and encased his shaft in the triangle between my legs, touching but not penetrating. Wet rain from my body slicked his erection as we rocked together. He dropped his head back and a long, low groan came from his throat.

The compulsion to let him slam his body into mine was overwhelming.

The muscles corded in his arms as he strained with unbearable tension. "Let me in."

I cupped his testicles drawn tight with arousal. The scent of sex hung in the air. That unmistakable mingling of male and female. The instinct to tense, to keep him out was strong. This willing surrender of my body went against everything my mind wanted. My body wanted his heat but also his strength.

I wanted him.

Not just sex. Him. The traitorous impulse invaded. I wanted all of him. Impossible. His gaze burned into me willing me to let go. To let us take each other.

"Now."

He slid his palms up my back tracing the line of my spine. His arms banded around me, cradling me, pulling me up. He pushed off his jeans as his mouth covered mine. The kiss was urgent, insistent, erotic.

We tumbled to the bed in a tangle. He ripped open a foil packet and covered his erection. Finally, he speared my body with his.

He touched me deep inside, in a place frozen from lack of use, encased in a shield, so hard it would never crack or melt.

Yet I felt as if I could melt. Become soft, pliant, needy in a matter of moments just from the intimacy of his lips against mine. The heat of his arousal burned away the last of my resistance.

The press and slide of his weight on top of me, covering me, protecting me, roared through my blood. My hips slammed into his, our bodies colliding with erotic slipperiness. Fierce heat incinerated us as we soared over the edge of sanity.

Impossibly this joining was more intense, more memorable than our first time. And I wanted, as before, to just lie in this bed with him. Be with him. To hold on to this exquisite feeling for a little longer before reality intruded.

We lay there, chests heaving, his weight upon me no longer a protection but a burden. Already my thoughts intruded, rejecting this neediness I seemed to feel. I understood anger. Understood revenge. I didn't understand this need inside of me, clawing to get out, clawing to hold on to him as tightly as I could and never let go.

Mentally I squirmed, antsy, anxious to put distance between us. Searching for a way to stop the neediness from overwhelming me.

And I found my answer in Bella.

How could I have done this, taken this refuge, this respite while Bella was a prisoner, trapped and afraid—because of me?

He heaved a sigh then rolled to the side, yanked my body flush to his, and jammed his mouth on mine. Hard.

Here was the heat, the anger, I thought I'd wanted earlier. But I couldn't go back. Not now.

He said, "Bella isn't in more danger because of this."

I pressed my palms flat against his shoulders trying to shift away.

"You aren't bad for taking this release."

But how could I find pleasure right now?

"I'm sorry," I ground out. Apologizing was foreign to me. "I can't do this. It's not fair to Bella."

"Not fair to Bella?" he said musingly. "I've been thinking about your relationship with Bella."

I definitely didn't want to talk about that. "No thanks."

"Oh, this needs to be said." He kept his hands on my body, but his touch was gentle now. "You told her you'd done everything for her but that isn't really true, is it?"

I jerked back. The sentiment was harsh, judging, totally at odds with the tender caress of his hands.

"What are you talking about?"

"You didn't cut yourself off from her, from everyone just for Bella's protection."

"Of course I did."

"Be honest, Jamie."

This abrupt stranger baffled me. "I was honest."

"Bullshit. You haven't been honest since you were fifteen years old."

I hadn't realized how much I'd started to depend on Lucas's support and understanding until it was so suddenly ripped away.

His pulse beat in his throat, his voice raw as if ripped from his gut. "If you didn't get close to anyone, then *you* couldn't get hurt again. All that posturing about protecting your sister. You were protecting yourself."

His accusations stripped me bare emotionally, as bare as I was physically.

"If no one gets close, then it can't hurt when they leave. Or die."

Was he right? Anger fueled the hurt burning in my chest. For his understanding of me, completely and thoroughly. The need to lash out, to wound him consumed me. "Yeah. Well, everyone does leave. Everyone does die." My heart cried even as I forced the words through lips stiff with pain and distress. I knew my words would push him away, I knew it. Just like I knew him.

Everyone leaves me. He would too.

"Yeah...I guess I'm gone then." His rejection was absolute. His words gutted me with astounding accuracy. Pain, intense and insistent, rolled through me.

I'd thought Bella's rejection had hurt. But my relationship with Bella was merely a fantasy...something I'd built in my own mind.

My relationship with Lucas had been real, solid, a bond that had strengthened by the minute.

Until I ruined it.

Silence overtook the room. We had nothing more to say.

"We'd better get dressed," I said. "Ramirez and Zeke will be back soon.

Lucas rolled away from me and I slid off the bed quickly.

I dressed quietly, picking up clothes strewn all over the hotel room. The lack of control I had granted myself just a short while ago appalled me.

My thoughts arrowed back to the last time I'd dressed in the half light of the partially open bathroom door. The last time I'd stolen away before temptation won and I lay back down to revel in the comfort of his arms.

As he lay in the hotel bed sheets, he looked tired. Circles of exhaustion rimmed his eyes. His hair was wrecked, mostly from my hands fisting in its silky texture.

His arms were roped with muscles and dusted with blond hair. Strong arms that held me with tenderness, even when I demanded rough. Cradled me when I needed comfort.

And I had severed that connection, like a scalpel through flesh, cutting it out, ridding myself of the weakness.

I'd gotten what I wanted, what I needed.

So why did it hurt so much?

Five more minutes until contact.

We'd picked up Lucas's van from Dulles because we'd needed the gadgets and the surveillance capabilities. As soon as we'd parked the white van in the Reagan National Airport parking lot, Lucas started checking the equipment one last time. "Ready?"

I tumbled out the back of the van. Zeke sat in the passenger seat with Ramirez ready to drive.

I adjusted the mini-microphone/transmitter situated just below my throat and disguised to look like a button. The device had a range of three hundred yards and matched the other buttons on the white shirt I wore underneath the yellow Izod sweater. Hopefully the outfit made me look approachable and harmless.

"Check," I whispered. Fall had hit with a vengeance and my warm breath puffed white.

Zeke sent one click to the listening device disguised as an earring. He'd tracked my voice. One for yes. Two for no.

Lucas stepped out of the back, touching his ear piece. "We've got reception," he said tersely.

Lucas stepped toward me, rubbed his hands along my biceps and eased me into his arms awkwardly. I tried to step back but he held on to me too tightly. "Just for a minute, please."

Ramirez and Zeke turned away to give us privacy. The tension between Lucas and I had been clear. Since they returned from getting food, both men avoided us.

Lucas had cut me open with his words in the hotel room. I knew the only reason he'd stuck around was to rescue Johnny. Otherwise he'd be long gone.

"Be careful." He looked as if he wanted to kiss me. But then he let go.

"Always am." I forced the words out.

This had to work. Gratitude and regret weighed heavily on me. *Thank you.* A sudden urge to shelter in his arms shook me. I had forfeited that right. "Keep safe."

"Stick to the plan," he cautioned.

"We've been over it multiple times."

"Just don't do anything hotshot."

"Me?" But the expression on his face compelled total honesty. "I would never jeopardize the hostages."

"I know." Lucas brushed a hand over my hair, then pulled back as if he'd breached some invisible field.

I eased away from him, walked around to the passenger side of the van, and flipped open his cell phone. My contact point with the psycho holding my sister and my link to my crew. "Are you tracking?"

"I've got you," Zeke said through the open window, then nodded toward a handheld device. "You realize if we can use trilateration to track your location with this, they can too."

"It's a risk I'll have to take."

Lucas frowned. "What if they block the signal?"

"We should still have some time to pinpoint her location." Zeke punched a button on the tracker. "We just need to hope they're so busy with the phone they don't notice the low level frequency of the button."

"Just record everything." I wanted this guy caught. "And get my--the hostages out alive."

Ramirez was silent through our exchange. And for a moment I wondered what was going through his mind. He looked at us, his mouth a flat unsmiling line.

He was waiting for a woman who might never return and his only concrete lead, Johnny, depended on this rescue. He nodded once, then gripped the steering wheel.

Lucas's cell phone rang. The rasp of my breathing was harsh in the silent night air. What if they'd hurt Bella?

A lifetime of worrying about her safety and protection washed over me. I took a deep breath and answered. "Hello."

Without hesitating, the older man said, "Take the Metro and get off at the Foggy Bottom station. The trains run every fifteen minutes. Call this number when you're street side."

I repeated the information back to him, watching Zeke's fingers fly across the laptop keys. He'd start tracking me right away. He'd been right. We'd needed him.

"You have the key fob?" The man on the phone asked arrogantly.

"Yes." Not a complete lie. I had the files but not the actual key fob.

"You have thirty minutes." The line clicked off.

I'd need to hustle. If I missed the train I'd be late. And with traffic, Lucas, Zeke and Ramirez would be lucky to be at the station before me. I didn't have time for any more goodbyes. "Get them." I gave them a thumbs up and ran for the Metro station. Rather than wait at the machines, I bought a MetroCard illegally from a guy on the way down.

I made my way to the entrance, my heart pounding so loudly people at the Pentagon could probably hear it. My adrenaline spiked.

*Pull it together, Jamie. Or you won't do Bella any good.* I paused at the escalator for a calming moment. Taking one more slow inhale, I headed down. I'd be out of pocket while underground, the transmission capabilities on the button would be muted in the train tunnel, but there was no choice.

If Bella's kidnappers grabbed me in the station, Lucas and crew wouldn't have any warning for at least twenty minutes--until they expected me to arrive at the Foggy Bottom station and I didn't show up.

Zeke would still be able to pinpoint my location through the GPS on my cell phone.

I waited, still and watchful, on the platform for the next train. The new lights eliminated hiding places in the corners, so I carefully studied fellow passengers looking for potential threats. The Metro system had too much security in the stations and on the trains to make an abduction probable. The lights flashed on the granite platform edge indicating the train was arriving. I checked my watch. Five minutes had passed.

The ride took about twelve minutes. In that time, nothing major happened. Two teenagers, baggy pants, gold chains and Redskins caps argued about the noise from the one's iPod, creating a distraction while a third lifted a wallet from a pair of tired tourists.

I mentally shook my head at the couple's lack of safety sense. I couldn't afford to get involved. I kept my back to the security cameras and held tight to the cell phone.

After the chime sounded and the doors slid open, I

casually stuck my foot in the way of the third teen. She went flying, took a rolling dive and the wallet fell onto the granite platform. The tourists started yelling.

That ought to keep everyone busy and, hopefully, keep eyes off me as I strode toward the exit.

When I emerged outside, dusk was turning into early evening, that hazy time between the waning fall sun and the blanket of dark night. I headed around the corner, sat on a street bench, and dialed the man's number. He answered on the first ring and immediately asked for my location. So he wasn't watching. Or at least that was what he wanted me to believe.

The man's voice was tense with anticipation. "Walk two blocks down the street and you'll come to the Presidential Suites hotel. The downstairs restroom is off the pub. Pass the doorman and go directly to the restroom. No dallying."

Once I hung up, I repeated his instructions for my listeners but didn't get an answering click, which meant they weren't in range. Shit. I didn't see the van anywhere and finding parking was going to be a nightmare.

We'd debated whether one of the team should get on the train with me but I felt it was more imperative that my partners stay hidden. Now as I kept a slower pace than I wanted while walking toward the hotel, I wished I'd listened to Lucas.

As I made the solo walk, I wished I'd listened to him about more than op details.

At the hotel, the doorman opened the heavy brass door with a flourish and tipped his hat. The lobby was small but ornate. Persian hand-knotted rugs lay scattered across worn marble floors. In the fireplace, logs crackled and sparked. A settee and two wing chairs were grouped around an extravagantly carved coffee table with a large arrangement of exotic flowers spiking from a ceramic urn. Sconces adorned the walls, throwing off muted light and casting a warm glow over burnt orange walls and ornately framed portraits of former presidents.

"The lobby of the Presidential Suites is beautiful," I said out loud, hoping for some confirmation they had a lock on me.

No answering click.

No one paid any attention to me as I headed toward the public restroom off of the pub. I opened the door cautiously then whirled inside. Against the far wall, adorned with satin wallpaper, stood an Asian woman.

It was her. Syringe lady, Susan, from the warehouse. "What a surprise." One step closer to Bella.

Her features tightened. She looked tense and ill at ease. She held out a shaking hand, palm up. "Give me the key fob and you can go."

I stared at her hard, wondering what her gig was. She hadn't called me. The man had. I glanced around casually as if taking in the pink granite counters and solid brass fixtures. "Funny. I don't see any hostages."

"I'll let them go," she said. "Just hand it over and leave."

*Not a chance.* "What about the old man?" I leaned back against the cream-painted doorframe, crossed my arms over my chest.

"I'll deal with Liam." She firmed her lips together and then steadied her gaze on mine. "Trust me," she implored.

Liam. The old man's name was Liam. The scent of roses hung in the air along with wisp of disinfectant, making me nauseous. Something was really off here.

"Pass." I straightened abruptly and Susan took a nervous step backwards. "Let's get this over with."

"Fine."

"Where to?"

"Elevator." She gestured for me to go down the hall first, then followed.

I noted she stayed a fair distance away from me. I supposed I could take her out now, force her to tell me Bella and Johnny's location. But the area was too public and I couldn't jeopardize their safety.

I stepped into the elevator, moved to the back corner, pressing my shoulders against the elegant wood paneling. A sign over the call panel indicated floors five through eight were under construction.

Susan ignored the sign and requested the fifth floor. I noted she kept her face in shadow, away from the security camera in the elevator. Neither of us spoke.

The doors dinged open and I arched a brow at her.

"You first." Susan said, then directed. "To the end, last suite on the left."

A tinge of smoke scented the hall. Visqueen hung from the ceiling, blocking off the hallway on the right. Susan stayed about ten feet behind me. Far enough so that when I stood in front of room 501, and hoped my backup heard me, I murmured, "501 blues."

No click. Dammit.

I had to give them some time before I accepted I was on my own. The plan was to let my abductors become complacent. I would be cooperative and gather evidence against the kidnappers. Zeke would man communications and make sure we got the audio evidence to nail these guys while Lucas and Ramirez rescued Bella and Johnny.

Susan stood behind me. "Open the door."

Tentatively, I turned the handle. The door swung open slowly.

"Come in, come in," the old man said from the sofa. His

cane leaned against the cushion and he held a Sig Sauer with a silencer in his hand.

I stepped warily into the suite, Susan lingering behind me. The hotel was clearly set up for two room suites with a living room and kitchenette in one room and a separate bedroom with a door that closed. Both rooms had access doors to the main hallway. The bathroom was to my immediate left. The living room and kitchen were bisected into two separate areas by forest green carpet and a neutral tan tile.

The kitchen had a stove, refrigerator, and sink, all in almond, in a compact triangle design. A breakfast bar in tan Granite gleamed under a trio of single lights hanging in a straight line.

The living area was directly in front of me, with a settee sized sofa, coffee table and two wing chairs. An armoire presumably held the television although the doors were tightly shut. To my far left was a connecting door. I could only hope Bella and Johnny were through that door.

The old man reclined in the corner of the sofa, dressed in Southern casual; a lightweight Seersucker suit in cheerful mint and white stripes couldn't hide the miasma that coated his features.

He nodded to Susan, who stood a good six feet behind me. "Frisk her. Make sure to check for everything. Not just standard agency-issued weapons," his voice was raspy with a slight wheeze.

They weren't going to make any mistakes this time. Neither was I.

I replayed his words. *Not just standard agency weapons.* Did that mean they were familiar with agency issue? Interesting.

Susan tentatively took a few steps toward me. She was the weaker link right now. And just because I was going to

be cooperative didn't mean I would roll over and
play dead.

"You can't shoot me. Hotel security would be here in a
heartbeat." Effectively, I let Zeke know they had a weapon. I
took two more steps into the room, moving as if to go
around the wing chair, shifting closer to that bedroom.

The gun came up a notch. "No. The fire last week
damaged the upper floors and half of this floor." He
smirked. "We're alone."

Susan followed me, easing closer. I could see her in my
peripheral vision on the right. Several times, her head
shifted to the weapon in his hand.

"Sorry," she murmured as she cautiously started patting
my biceps.

I held my arms away from my sides, widened my stance
and waited until I could see both of their eyes, watching for
any flicker or evasion. "Where are the hostages?"

"All in good time." The old man smiled a jovial,
conspiratorial smile, but his eyes looked sunken and his face
was pale. Despite the apparent bulkiness of his body, the
skin on his head was shrink-wrapped to his skull and his
cheeks had a hollow dip to them.

As Susan retrieved my blackjack from my belt loop, she
glanced furtively toward the partially open door to the
bedroom area. I tensed in readiness. I couldn't seem too
anxious about the hostages, or he'd understand how much
they meant to me.

I stretched my neck as if working out kinks and tried to
get a glimpse into the other room but the door was only
open about six inches.

Susan faltered as she found the knife in the sheath at my
ankle. While their gazes shifted to the wicked blade, I had

one quick glance into the room and then I casually returned my focus to Liam.

I had barely been able to see into the bedroom. A four poster bed with a canopy had two bodies stretched out and tied to the bed posts. But I saw one bare foot with pale innocent pink toenails.

Another tiny detail had me rejoicing. I'd seen the subtle, slow rise of the covers indicated they were breathing. Something within me eased. Bella was nearby, and she was alive.

Susan reached into my pocket and found the phone. As she pressed the button to turn it off I realized she had forgotten to step out of my range of motion.

The temptation to head butt Susan, use her as a human shield and rescue my sister bubbled up. I could do it. Susan was tentative. Liam was old and obviously sick. My muscles actually twitched with anticipation. My heart beat slowed to a steady, reassuring thump.

Screw Lucas. Screw Ramirez, and Zeke, and Johnny. I didn't need them to rescue Bella. \

I didn't need anyone.

# CHAPTER 42

$B$ut...even if I did overpower Liam and Susan, we wouldn't get everything we came for.

If I went rogue, went alone, I was guilty of the hurtful things Lucas had said. Protecting myself.

I'd given an unspoken promise to Jordan Ramirez that we'd find out what we could about Staci. And Lucas had trusted me to help him get Johnny.

I had to let go and trust they would show up. But it didn't mean I would be a doormat. "Hmmm. You think you missed any?" I taunted.

Susan found my gun and the ten clips wrapped around my waist, paling at the amount of firepower I'd brought. Score one for me. I'd wanted them so focused on the weapons they'd overlook the transmitter.

There was also an added bonus if they missed one.

Susan had placed each successive find in a bag on the floor. Though I kept my gaze on the firearm in Liam's hand, peripherally I noted she slipped my Glock into the back waistband of her pants, underneath her black twinset cardigan.

"No keys," Susan said tensely.

The flash key was hidden in the collar of my shirt.

"Tie her to a chair," he said. "And make sure her hands are behind her back. Securely."

Susan dragged a ladder back chair from the kitchen area, the legs screeching over the tile floor until she reached the edge of the carpet. She pushed me gingerly into the chair, curved my arms around the wood back, and cuffed me. The plastic restraints pulled at my deltoids.

"Where is the key fob?" he demanded.

Time for me to push back. "All in good time, Liam."

"If you know who I am," his smile disappeared, "Then you know, you don't want to mess with us."

But I had no idea who these two really were. "Who are you?"

Neither responded verbally. But syringe lady pulled out her trademark. I eyed it warily. "What's in the syringe?"

"Something to keep you docile and forgetful," he said.

Could it be the antidote? I'd been so focused on my sister, I'd forgotten the other reason I'd come here. I wanted that antidote.

I stared determinedly at the long thin needle as she tiptoed cautiously toward me. Whatever they had given me had messed me up badly these last few days. I needed to return to my calm, controlled and unemotional world. I needed to get rid of this ache in my heart from Lucas. Like a magic pill, one shot from the needle and it would all go away.

I needed my old life back.

But even as I had that thought, I knew I didn't want it back. That Jamie was alone. The new Jamie had...a team, friends, a lover. Not just a one night stand.

The tiny prick shouldn't have made me flinch.

As the cool liquid squirted into my veins, I relaxed. One way or another it would all be over soon. Almost immediately, the Sodium Pentothal and Rophynol effects began to skew my perception. To throw them off guard, I started asking questions, praying Zeke was getting the transmission.

"What were you going to do with the information you collected? Sell it to the highest bidder?"

"Of course not."

Susan flipped on the lights over the breakfast bar and the bright fluorescent beam bored into my eyeballs, driving imaginary nails through my skull. "Don't believe you. That information would be a gold mine on the international criminal market."

"Our goal was not espionage," the old man snapped.

I said slyly, "But you could make a fortune."

"I don't want money."

"What do you want?"

His eyes lit up. "To make a lasting contribution, a legacy."

"What legacy?" I could see the pride in his face, hear it in his voice. He wanted to brag. And I could hope this stall was completely recorded. *Come on, asshole. Tell Jamie all.* "Go ahead."

"I'm a scientist." He wheezed out a cough which turned into a long hack, his face turning a violent shade of purple. When he was composed again, he said, "I've developed a drug that enhances the performance of field agents."

I blinked, feeling the drugs wind through my system, my arms and legs becoming fluid and boneless.

"You could be the first in a new group of über-agents. Better counter-terrorism, better armies, better intelligence, safer country." His voice trembled with self-congratulation. "Stronger in every way."

"Huh." Hadn't affected me that way, but I couldn't make my mouth form the words.

"Like steroids for agents. Without the negative side effects like liver disease, structural changes in the heart, thickening of arterial wall, kidney problems, or even depression."

Susan butted in. "But there's a problem."

"We can fix it. I know we can," the old man said fiercely.

"What problem?" I tried to ignore the way the tan and green stripes on the wallpaper were undulating.

"We didn't have this problem in the rats. Of course, it was difficult to quantify because we couldn't tell..." He hesitated. "The human body and brain are amazing. There is so much we still don't know."

"What. Problem." I repeated.

"It's minor." Liam dismissed my concern. "I've already modified it again to reduce the problem. We just need more tests."

"On *people*," I said snottily. Tests of a drug with a problem. That sounded great. We were all giant lab rats.

"DNA is tricky. We isolated the strand we thought controlled confidence, but it turns out several strands on different chromosomes are affected—which in turn affects the brain." Liam had a faraway expression in his eyes.

He wasn't really looking at me and the temptation to just bust out and get my sister washed though me again. I had to wait, keep them talking. "How does it affect the brain?"

Susan shot me an annoyed look. "Even though the drug works brilliantly on confidence levels, it also enhances the brain's perceived weaknesses."

I shook my head, trying to clear it, and tried to

unobtrusively peek through to the bedroom again. "Explain."

"Say you had a mild case of anxiety for...going out in public."

"Agoraphobia."

"This drug magnifies the fear to the point where it's debilitating and you can't even leave the house." Her voice broke.

"We'll figure it out, lass." The old man's voice was actually gentle and a slight pity coated his gaze.

That was a relief. That explained why I was crazy to see Bella even when I knew it was a bad idea, explained my sudden inexplicable attraction to Lucas. What it didn't explain was who was behind the kidnappings and experiments. There had to be a government agency involved. "What branch of the government are you working for?"

Of course, they didn't answer.

"Why kidnap us to give the antidote?"

At that Susan moved behind Liam and put her hand on his shoulder, effectively moving herself out of the range of the weapon. "Don't tell her."

He shrugged off her hand. "She won't remember it anyway, lass. Not much time left."

Okay. If they wouldn't tell me why then maybe how. "How did you get the manpower?"

Susan's gaze skittered toward the other room again and for a moment, I wondered why, but the thought floated away.

"That isn't important," Liam snapped.

"Then how did you find me?"

Susan purposefully turned her back on the other room. "We calculated probable locations and used separate intelligence branches, so no one noticed a pattern." She paced the floor.

"You had access to my tracking beacon." Which meant they had access to NSA computers. Could they be working for the NSA? But we didn't have a scientific branch.

Liam said with admiration, "Until you cut it out. Very clever."

I knew I needed more information. I just had to focus. Ask the right questions. Stall until my backup got here. If they got here. "So why didn't you abduct me again when I got back to D.C.?"

"We couldn't find you right away." Susan answered slowly, "We had the wrong apartment information."

So the NSA must not have entered my change of address into the company personnel files yet. But that also meant Susan had access to those files.

Suddenly neither was talking. Time to take another tack. "How was the original drug administered?"

"The original drug was mixed in with the quarterly vaccinations," Liam responded.

"Aha." We were right. We, I loved that word.

But there was no we anymore. I'd messed it up. A giant hole opened inside of me, swallowing me up and making me disappear until there was nothing left this horrible wrenching aloneness.

"Why not just inject the antidote during the next round of vaccinations?"

Susan said, "The problem was getting bigger. Agent Johnson had a need for an ultra adrenaline rush. He kept putting himself into extreme situations."

I thought about the blank paper with the list of questions I'd pulled from my file. "So you decided to use Fitzhugh to get information?"

Liam shrugged. "I can't perfect the drug if I don't know how the agents feel."

"We feel annoyed someone is using us as guinea pigs."

He waved my comment off. "Think of it. We enhanced behavior and attitude by triggering a switch in DNA strands. The long term applications are immense."

"This is ground breaking work," Susan confirmed.

"The nano-technology we used as a vector to deliver the drug worked," he said elatedly. "The possibilities are endless. Behavior modification, DNA alteration, gene therapy to treat Parkinson's disease, Huntington's disease, sickle cell anemia...the opportunity to stop, even cure, cancer is within reach."

I decided to jab at him. "Who are you trying to convince?"

"I don't have to convince anyone."

My head started to loll but I forced it back up. Anger burned away some of the drug's effects. "Ten people were given the original drug. How'd you pick them?"

Liam pressed his lips together. "We needed a good cross section of test subjects. Unfortunately they all had similar genetic backgrounds which probably skewed our results."

He hadn't answered my question. I shifted in the chair, looking for relief from my burning muscles. "How many got the antidote?"

"Seven."

I calculated slowly, my brain full of cotton. "Three left."

"Two are dead."

So Johnson and Staci had been given the drug.

Susan wrung her hands. "The negative effects...."

"Are intriguing," he said, the faraway look back. "We just need to fine tune the drug a little."

The coldness of that statement edged down my spine.

He didn't seem to feel responsible for the consequences of giving the drug to unsuspecting agents. The drug had left them vulnerable, and two had ended up dead. "You don't feel guilty about their deaths?"

"You, of all people Jamie, should know they were in a very volatile and dangerous profession. Their sacrifice will benefit their country, possibly all of mankind." He gestured grandiosely, flinging his arms wide.

I tried to track everything, think through all of their revelations but I wasn't processing quickly enough.

Seven had the antidote. Two were dead. They'd accounted for nine of the ten. That left one.

That left me. "So I was the last one?"

"The last one for what?"

"To get the antidote."

Liam frowned. "I hate it when the drugs cause babbling. Why would I give *you* the antidote?"

Adrenaline and anger burned some of the fuzziness I was feeling away, but I kept my language slurred and short. "'Cause that DNA drug seriously messed me up."

The old man thumped his cane on the floor. "You never had the original drug."

# CHAPTER 43

"Then why the hell am I here?"

Liam looked at me scornfully. "Two reasons. We need that key fob back. It has the blood data on the change in DNA blood cells from the injected subjects."

I snorted. "You kept that DNA information on portable storage? What about your main storage center?"

"We had a virus. Quite the irony." Liam chuckled, the amusement turning into a wheezing cough. "So you investigated the information on the key fob?"

"Yeah. Us secret agent types get a little nuts when someone tries to inject us with unknown stuff. We investigate."

I hadn't had the drug. That fact kept circling in my head, distracting me. But I needed to focus on keeping them talking so the others could get Bella and Johnny out. They would have access either through the bedroom door to the hotel hallway or down the fire escape.

I still couldn't hear anything from the bedroom. But Jordan Ramirez had carefully explained the first rule of hostage retrieval was to try to get in and out undetected.

"What agency are you working for?" I tried again.

There was a sudden clicking in my ear. It took me a minute to identify the morse code. It had to be Zeke. Every code geek learned morse code as a beginning basis of ciphering before moving on to more and more complex systems.

Zeke repeated the sequence again. -.-. -.. -.-.

-.-. C -.. D -.-. C

C.D.C. The Center for Disease Control?

I couldn't process the information bombarding me. I hadn't had the drug. If I hadn't had it, what was all of the emotional stuff with Bella and Lucas?

And if I hadn't had it..."Why did you kidnap me in the first place?"

"It was originally a mistake." Susan walked over to the sink and got a glass from the cabinet. "We'd gotten a lead on Staci Grant, thought maybe our information about her death was wrong."

"Staci Grant is dead," I interrupted her.

"She might not be. And if she isn't, she needs the antidote." She filled the glass with tap water and then took the drink over to Liam. I noted how she made sure to stay out of the path between his weapon and me. "Anyway, somehow the wires got crossed and they picked up you instead."

"I guess that solves the mystery of why you had guys on Staci Grant's house the whole time." I wriggled my fingers to see if she'd left me any maneuvering room in the cuffs. Some. Not enough to free my hands.

"Staci Grant's house? No. We weren't watching her house." Susan had moved back into the kitchen area and began to pace back and forth, her low heels click-click-clicking on the tile, annoying me. "Our guys noticed the

watchers. That's why they grabbed her...you at the
strip mall."

"Huh." I tried to process everything. "Why did you first
give me oxycontin?"

Susan spun to face the old man. "You gave her your
own drugs?"

He leaned back into the corner of the sofa cushions, as
if trying to shift away from her. "Last minute changes. We
had a small window of opportunity and I had to use
something on hand."

His drugs. Oxycontin was used to alleviate chronic pain.
What was wrong with him?

Zeke could hear me--but did they know where I was?

"Why Seattle, why not right here at the Presidential
Suites?" A big, fat clue for the boys in the van.

"I was in Seattle." Susan evaded my gaze.

The old man piped up. "Once we figured out we had
you, I thought to myself, Liam my boy, here is the next
generation. Look at you, you're smart, extremely gifted
physically. You're the best to begin with and, if we add this
new enhancement, you'll be unstoppable."

Irritation welled up within me. "But you were going to
give me the antidote. I stole that syringe."

"You stole a syringe with the antidote?" He whipped his
head toward Susan. "Why would she have an antidote,
Susan?"

"Liam," Susan started to placate.

"Why did you have an antidote with you, Susan?" Liam
snarled.

"You were going to give her," Susan gestured toward me,
"the new drug." She took a step toward him, toward the
sofa. "We'd been told to stop. It wasn't working."

"So you prepared an antidote for the new vaccine?"

"As best I could. Then, if you injected her, I was going to give her the antidote right away." Susan reiterated, "We were told to stop."

Liam said coldly, "I need those new results. The new vector method was working. We'd identified the other gene sequence to target. We are close."

"No, Liam."

I didn't like the sound of this. While combating targets took the heat off me, the situation was becoming more volatile. I really wished he'd put down the weapon.

"Who told you to stop your program?" My voice was more slurred than I'd anticipated. Shit. My resistance to the drug was weakening again.

Susan blinked, her gaze shifted back to me looking as if she'd forgotten I was there.

"We're so close," Liam said desperately.

"The tests were too dangerous," she countered. "For everyone."

"Who said?" I asked again, like a dog with a bone I thought if they would just tell me who told them to stop then I would have the final piece of the puzzle.

Susan's gaze cut to the connecting door. Was the third person in the bedroom with my sister? Shit. I'd assumed she and Johnny were in that room alone.

How much time did we have left?

We needed the name of the last agent. I had to start working like the über-agent he thought I was. "Who hasn't gotten the antidote yet?"

Susan pressed her lips in a flat line and crossed her arms over her chest. "It doesn't matter."

But it did. I needed that information. We had to get that agent the antidote.

I was so busy trying to stay alert it took a moment to

register that someone else was in the bedroom. They were here. Relief rushed through me.

My brain finally clicked on. I remembered the list had identified nine adults and one child. "The child."

"What child?"

"The child is the tenth subject." I would have snapped my finger if I could have. "What kind of sick bitch gives a child an untested, unstable drug?"

Susan broke, tears leaking from her eyes. "I would never have given my daughter the drug. Her father did it."

Shit. "The tenth subject is your child?"

Susan nodded, misery in her eyes.

I had to find a way to diffuse the tension. I raised my eyebrows and glanced back and forth between Liam and Susan. "Liam, you dog."

"Not mine." Liam snorted. "I would have never wasted this DNA drug on a child."

Nice attitude. "So the reason you need the key fob?"

"All of our data results are on that key. The information is critical to getting the antidote right." I heard the desperation in her voice, saw it in her plea.

"Are you saying the antidote doesn't work?"

"We're waiting for the next round of blood tests and psych evals to confirm its efficacy," Susan sniffed, wiping the tears from her face.

"You aren't sure," I said flatly. Shit.

"Not sure enough to give it to my daughter." She was getting agitated again.

"Why'd you take hostages?"

"Another mistake. We had your position. When they went in they found two people so they took them both."

Liam had his weapon up again.

I glared at him. "Uh, could you put down that weapon?

Guns in the hands of amateurs make me nervous. You know they get antsy and pull the trigger. Very messy." Must be the Sodium Pentothal taking over.

"Shush."

"What if I brought backup?"

"You didn't bring any backup. Your file indicates that you always work alone."

"Always work alone," I said morosely. My head sort of lobbed as I shook it. Alone. I'd been alone forever. Except for one short incredible week. The future stretched before me, a barren wasteland. "I'm always alone."

I still hadn't seen or heard Lucas. Since the transmission about the CDC, Zeke had also been suspiciously silent.

"Where are the hostages?" Shit. I shouldn't have brought them up, shouldn't have reminded them that I cared.

Susan said, "She didn't believe you would come for them."

I felt as if a knife twisted in my gut, sorrow at how much I had messed up with my sister. "I'm a mean woman and she knows it."

Liam shifted awkwardly to the edge of the sofa. "I can't wait to see how you react with this new drug." He eyed me as he heaved his bulk up from the sofa. His gun hand didn't waver but I wouldn't take bets on his accidentally pulling the trigger. "You will be a fascinating subject."

I didn't back away, even though I wanted to. Instead, I crossed my legs and slouched back in the chair, letting the drugs she'd given me make my muscles lax. I waited for him to come closer, praying the weapon muzzle that I'd seen in my peripheral vision sticking through the bedroom door was from one of my crew and not an unknown third kidnapper.

Keep his attention on you, Jamie. "Who told you to stop?"

His eyes froze.

Oops. Wrong thing to say.

"It's of no consequence." The old man set the weapon on the coffee table and pulled a syringe from the pocket of his seersucker jacket.

Susan shook her head. "No, Liam."

The old man thumped toward me with intent, the syringe gripped tightly in his pudgy hand. In an uneven gait, he came closer, the unmistakable hospital smell overwhelming.

I watched his eyes, waiting for the indication he really was going to inject me. There was no remorse or regret in his gaze. He wasn't just determined--this was a man with nothing to lose.

Susan cried, "Liam. Don't."

She glanced toward the bedroom again, then pulled my weapon from the back of her pants. Shit.

"Please. Don't make me do this." She didn't seem to be talking to Liam anymore as she pointed my weapon at him.

If she fired and the bullet went through soft tissue, I was going to have a hole in me somewhere. Assuming she didn't completely miss him and hit me instead, which was a distinct possibility because of the way her hand was shaking.

A sound rustled from the other room.

Liam didn't pause, but kept coming toward me. "We've got to keep the experiment going. It's my only chance...."

I heard the whoosh of the silencer only after he started falling, two neat holes appearing just above his ear. Brain matter splattered all over Susan. Well-placed, extremely accurate headshots. And they hadn't come from Susan.

Susan ran to the kitchenette area, her face was stark white, and threw up in the sink.

I knew the shots hadn't come from my team. We hadn't brought live rounds, only tranquilizers, which meant either she or I was the next target of the unknown gunman.

Fatalistically I waited for the next bullet to strike. My only regret was not telling Lucas how much he meant to me.

# CHAPTER 44

Fuck that.

I wasn't giving up without a fight. The shots had come from the bedroom. I threw my weight to the left, falling, hitting the hard tile floor, my shoulder bearing the brunt of the fall. Then I started inching my body toward the bedroom, using my feet against anything I could push off of to inch along the carpet.

I heard a thud as Susan's body hit the floor. This time there was no silencer. Different weapon or different shooter?

The hard Berber carpeting was rough beneath my cheek, my shoulder ached, and I'd lost the feeling in my left hand. Please don't let my faith have been misplaced. Let the second shot mean Lucas was here.

If he wasn't, I'd failed. Everyone. My sister. Lucas. Myself. Again.

But I wasn't going to lay there and wait. I scooted along, ignoring the throbbing in my shoulder.

Then I felt Lucas close, and saw his Nikes and the frayed hem of his jeans. My head swirled as he righted the chair.

He used one hand to hold my wrists while using his knife to slice at the bindings. "You okay?"

"Cold. Shoulder aches." I twisted my head side to side. My vision was a little blurry. "I...might have knocked my head when I fell. Bella?"

"She's fine."

Relief fizzed through me and my dizziness increased. Bella wouldn't want to see me, but at least I knew she was safe. "Johnny?"

"Fine, too." Lucas admonished me as he untied my ankles, "You promised no heroics."

"I kept that promise." Mostly.

"You call taunting a madman safe?"

"I'm fine." I tilted my head toward Susan, then straightened it quickly as I saw stars. "Is she...."

"Tranquilized. She'll wake in a cell."

When she woke, we would have the final answers about how the subjects were picked and how the CDC had access to the NSA information.

"Good." My circulation restarted with a frenzy, my blood tingling. "Where were you guys?"

"We got held up by your boss." He massaged my raw wrists.

"Carson?"

"Yeah. He intercepted us when we were coming in the window of room 505." Kneeling in front of me, Lucas rubbed up and down my arms with a gentle, impersonal touch. "Otherwise we'd have stopped whoever shot him." Lucas jerked his head toward Liam. "By the time we got to 503, the shooter was headed down the stairwell."

"He's gone."

I heard the soft pad of footsteps behind me as someone

came through the connecting door. Then Zeke was standing in front of me.

"He was dying." Zeke said, "Liam Odette, used to be in bio-terrorism at the CDC, but he was replaced a few months ago after being diagnosed with inoperable lung cancer."

"That's why there was no time." I shook my arms out, bringing the circulation back with a vengeance. "Who shot him?"

"Didn't get a clear look." Zeke's gaze cut to the blood spatter on the wing chair, then shifted away. "Ramirez went after the shooter."

"Did the hostages...see anything?" I asked, praying my sister hadn't witnessed Liam's death.

"They were blindfolded. They never saw any faces," Lucas replied. He stood up and held out his hand. I reached out ignoring the ache already pounding through my bones, and let him pull me gingerly to my feet.

Zeke said, "We've got a clean up crew on the way. Should be here any minute."

My hand was still clasped in Lucas's. Relief poured through me. Bella was okay. And suddenly I realized I'd been willing to trust Lucas with Bella's life. Why wasn't I willing to trust him with my heart?

Before I could confess, Bella rushed up to me, her fist against her lips.

"I'm sorry." I had to get that out first. "My intent was to protect you from this world."

Lucas dropped my hand as Bella flung herself at me and wrapped her arms around my waist. "*I'm* sorry. I shouldn't have...I was so upset...."

I shrugged as if joy wasn't streaming through me like the

drug in my bloodstream. But I couldn't quite make myself believe what I thought I was hearing.

She squeezed me tight. "I'm sorry. Don't go away again. Please."

I stared at Lucas over her shoulder, asking silently, 'What should I do'?

'Hug her back', he mouthed.

My arms came up slowly, tentatively. I wrapped them around her and hung on for dear life. It was everything I'd wished and hoped for in the dark of the night when I'd been alone and lonely.

And it wasn't enough.

She was warm in my arms. I was tired, sore, overwhelmed with information and thrilled. I knew I should leave it. But…"Maybe we could…get together…do…something." What did sisters do together when they were adults?

Bella nodded against me. "I'd like that."

Yeah. Me too. A family.

"Oh." Bella stepped back. I covered her eyes before she could look at the mess Liam Odette had made in death.

"I forgot." Bella blinked against my hand and tried to push it away. "Shouldn't we go untie Uncle Carson?"

"Go ahead." Lucas explained to me, "We put him in the chair next to the bed."

As I let her go, Bella looked at me one more time and squeezed my hand. Maybe she was just as unsure as I was about what to do next.

*Uncle* Carson? I'd deal with that later. "What's Carson doing here?"

"Apparently he came to help," Lucas said. "But since I wasn't sure whose side he was on, I voted to tie him up and we brought him next door with us. I didn't want him out of my sight."

"You got the drop on Carson?" I smiled. "You really need to be more specific about what you did for the FBI."

Lucas sidestepped my request artfully. "He insisted he had only been trying to get evidence against whoever was behind the kidnappings. But he did admit...reluctantly, that perhaps he'd left you to twist a little too long."

I said, "It's good he's here. We're going to need his help to get this straightened out."

My heart pounded, pouring adrenaline and hope through my bloodstream. Lucas hadn't left yet.

I needed to tell him--

"Shooter's gone. Got the weapon." Winded and shaking his head, Jordan Ramirez ran back in the room.

"That looks like mine." It had the same custom grip and it had been missing since I'd been abducted. Who was the shooter?

"You'll figure it out," Lucas said.

You. Suddenly I hated that word.

I turned and looked back toward the bedroom. I could see Bella, working Carson free of bungee cords. "I appreciate your help," I said, turning back to Jordan.

Jordan Ramirez eyed me for a moment, then nodded. "Thanks for the lead on Staci."

Lucas gestured toward Johnny, who stood in the doorway, his eyes blank with shock and horror as he stared at Liam Odette's body. "Did he give you any good information?"

"I showed him a picture of Staci."

"Was it her?"

"He identified her features but insisted she'd had much

darker skin. At least I've got a starting point." Ramirez curled his fingers around mine. "Thank you."

The distress in his eyes was easy to see. Why hadn't Staci contacted him? Why had she let him believe she was dead?

As best I could, I answered his unspoken question. "I guess you won't know until you find her."

He was definitely going looking. Staci needed that antidote.

"Yeah." His face grim, he nodded abruptly. "I have to go."

I hoped, for his sake, he found her soon. "Good luck."

Careful not to disturb any more of the scene than necessary, we walked toward the bedroom. The odor of gunpowder and death hung in the room. This mess was going to be a long string to unravel.

When we reached the doorway, I stopped, turned toward Lucas. Who still hadn't left. Everything was different. I was different.

I'd finally connected with my sister. It wasn't perfect, but it was a start. I stood looking at Lucas, the strong line of his jaw, the softer slash of his mouth, and the absolute love in his eyes. "I don't want to go back. I want to go forward. Go small."

He lowered his brows in a perplexed frown. "Small is...good."

I needed a hug. Needed to hold on to him. More than I needed anything in my life before this moment.

I wrapped my sore arms around his waist and rested my head over the reassuring, steady beat of his heart. "You haven't left."

"Ah...not yet."

I held onto him tightly. My heartbeat syncing in time

with his. Hoping he'd understand all the things I wanted to say but didn't know if I could get out.

Lucas curled his arms around me. "One question."

I cleared my throat and stared up into his eyes. "This is number five."

"Yeah."

"You sure you want this to be your last question?" I was struck by the vulnerability in his gaze. "Maybe you want to... keep one in reserve."

"Reserve," he repeated slowly. "As in...stick around for awhile?"

"Yeah." I looked at him steadily, hoping he could see the acceptance in my gaze, hoping he'd stay, hoping he wouldn't leave. "Unless you're dying to ask this last question."

"You just answered it."

"Good."

I could see the kiss coming. Knew it wasn't a mistake. It was right. His mouth brushed mine with tenderness we both deserved.

"I have this on tape you know." A smile brightened his face, joy shimmering back at me.

"I'm under the influence of truth serum." I might just keep it my little secret that I'd had resistance training.

He laughed. "Good point."

"So, you have one question left, better think long and hard before you ask."

It was as close as I could come to voicing out loud that I wanted to explore the connection between us. That maybe I finally understood, my needing him wasn't a weakness, having Lucas around made me stronger.

But he understood.

He knew me.

* * *

Is STACI REALLY DEAD? Click here to find out.

THANK YOU, thank you for reading BLOWBACK!!

If you enjoyed Jamie and Lucas's story, I would appreciate it if you would help others enjoy this book too. Here are some suggestions.

Good: Lend the book to a friend

Better: Recommend the book to your friends

Best: Leave a review at Amazon, Apple Books, Kobo, BN, Goodreads, Google…basically any place they sell or review eBooks. Every review helps my work get out to other readers and I cannot even express how much it means to me when you let people know you liked my work. Readers have so many choices nowadays and limited dollars to spend. It can be difficult to take a chance on a new author even if the premise sounds appealing. By reviewing books, you give other readers insight into the story world and help them make informed purchases.

THANK YOU, thank you, thank you for your support!!

P.S. Would you like to know when my next book is available? You can sign up for my new release email list/newsletter at Lisa's Confidants

<u>Family Stone Box Set (Stone Cold Heart, Carved in Stone, Heart of Stone, Still the One, & Jar of Hearts)</u>

<u>The Nostradamus Prophecies</u>

<u>View To A Kill #1</u>

Never Say Never #2

<u>ALIAS</u>

Stalked (ALIAS #1)

Hunted (ALIAS #2)

Vanished (ALIAS #3)

<u>Billionaire Breakfast Club</u>

His Semi-Charmed Life (Camp Firefly Falls #11 and Billionaire Breakfast Club #0)

Everything He Wants (Billionaire Breakfast Club #1 The Jock)

Queen of His Daydreams (Camp Firefly Falls #23 and Billionaire Breakfast Club #1.5)

Excerpt from Betrayals

## ANOTHER BLACK CIPHER FILE

Disinformation n. Deliberate spreading of false information
with intent to mislead.
August 31
Afghanistan

Something snuffled in the corner.

I curled my arm protectively around the meager bowl of
whatever they'd brought me. No stinking rodent was going
to touch my daily ration.

The dank smell of urine-soaked sand, feces, and human
sweat filled the fetid air. A thin layer of grit and despair
coated everything, including my tongue. I vowed never to set
foot on a beach again.

Probably wouldn't anyway. As I was likely to die in this
godforsaken rathole of a prison. I scooped the cooked until

mush food into my mouth greedily, careful not to spill a single grain.

Hard to believe a month ago Jordan and I had been dining on spice-rubbed porterhouse and chipotle garlic mashed potatoes in D.C.

That life was long gone. The contrast between then and now was laughable.

Then I'd dabbed daintily at my mouth with a soft linen napkin. Now I lapped the bowl with my sand-coated tongue and carefully sucked on each dirt-crusted finger.

If malnutrition didn't kill me, the germs probably would.

I could hear the woman, our chef, server, and general attendant, coming. But I wasn't finished.

*Fuuuuuccckkkkk.* I screamed the expletive silently. I'd learned brutally fast that cursing in this prison, especially from a woman, was taboo.

One by one, the locks clicked open. I huddled over the tiny tin bowl, licking with short, frantic strokes, trying to eat it all before she took my food away.

My arm chains clanked as they swung together, ringing in the silence. I ignored the extreme stabs of pain in my left arm.

The woman scurried in furtively and eased the door closed.

This was a change in routine. Subtly, I shifted to a higher state of alertness. The bruises, aches, and burns from the last 'change in routine' still hadn't healed. I was pretty sure the radius bone in my left forearm arm was broken.

Fortunately not the ulna and fortunately not my shooting arm. I hadn't had a beating or torture session in a few days. They'd left me alone.

"Miss," she whispered in Pashto.

I didn't answer. I didn't know how much they knew

about my background and I wasn't about to give anything away.

"Miss." This time she whispered in Dari.

I remained silent.

"Miss." Next it was Modern Standard Arabic. Something must have flickered in my eyes because she continued in Modern Standard. "Come. I will let you go."

My brain whirred. It had to be a trap. Let me go and then follow me. Thinking I'd lead them to whatever they thought I had.

Common torture tactic. Slowly break down all barriers to civilized behavior until the prisoner was more animal than human. Then dangle the carrot of freedom and watch the animal lunge for it.

If I was in their shoes, that's what I would do.

I sat quietly, waiting for her next move.

She started stripping off her burkha.

That wasn't right. A woman showing her face, her arms, her legs was not tolerated. Especially not in front of the prisoners. Walking around without the covering meant certain death.

Maybe that was the test.

See if I'd react with compassion. Would I think of someone else before myself? I analyzed each possible reaction and action for this situation.

One. Take the burkha and take my chances. But what about the woman?

Two. Help her put the burkha back on. And stay.

Three. Stay still and do nothing.

Inaction was always my least favorite response. And I'd been trapped in this prison for two weeks.

As she lifted the veiled hood from her face, she was crying. They'd coerced her into doing this.

She knew as well as I she'd be dead if she set foot out of this cell without the covering.

"Put the burkha back on," I whispered in Pashto.

"They are going to kill you." The rough wool tangled in her hair, muffling her voice.

And what do you think they're going to do to you?

I wanted to be free, but not at the expense of this woman. I wrapped my arms over my chest, stifling a gasp as the wrist cuff banged my injured forearm. "Go back to your duties."

"My slavery." She spit. Kneeling beside me, she jiggled the key to open the shackles. "You must go."

The glob of mucus lay in the middle of the sand and dirt floor. "No."

"They killed my *xawand*." She stood in the middle of the room, proud and fierce, dressed exactly like me in a grey cotton shift. "They killed my *mashums*."

Her husband. Her babies. Her family.

I understood that kind of loss.

I understood the rage and the grief. I understood the unquenchable lust for revenge. I'd used the emotions on more than one occasion to recruit agents for the CIA.

Because the same had been used on me.

Excerpt from Stone Cold Heart

The first novella in a series featuring the Stone Family siblings, Jess, Connor, Riley and Jack….

Family Stone #1 Jess

In the early evening dusk, Jess Stone lay on her stomach in the twenty foot high rubble of a demolished church, underneath a black and gray city-scape tarp intended to camouflage her position. A sharp-edged chunk of debris dug into her lower rib cage, the scope of the Remington M24 cool and familiar against her face.

Her standard uniform of jeans, running shoes, and plain black t-shirt rendered her just another anonymous and transient relief worker...which she was actually. A black baseball cap hid her distinctive multi-hued blonde hair. The paper mask kept out the contaminated dust from the destroyed buildings but did little to stem the overwhelming stench of decaying bodies.

Tanks rumbled through the destroyed coastal town, their public address system blasting warnings for citizens to stay in their homes, curfew was in effect. The threat was a joke. Ninety percent of the people in the town didn't have homes left. Those who did were terrified to go back inside. In the fetid, humidity choked air, the tent cities erected in the parks and on the beach were seething masses of the injured and shock struck.

The substandard construction in the small country had never been enough to withstand the angry might of Mother Nature. Buildings had toppled like a stack of Tinkertoys, and left crumbling cement walls with twisted rebar poking out of the jagged ruins like a skeletal hand.

Trapped in the concrete pieces that littered the ground, the heat from the tropical day seared through her thin sturdy clothing. The stank of the raw sewage that ran in rivulets through the streets overpowered the salt-laden breeze off the ocean. People, covered with the grit of pulverized buildings and humans, shuffled along with blank vacant stares. Two weeks after the quake, still in shock, their lives decimated first by nature and then kicked and beaten by the ineffectiveness of a flawed relief system. Hundreds of humanitarian agencies had descended on the population duplicating efforts and yet completely missing the need in other areas. The government was ostensibly trying to coordinate the effort, however the mass chaos was undeniable.

Through the Leupold Ultra M3 fixed power sight, she tracked the movements of Henri LeRoy, leader of this tiny island nation, violator of human rights and dignity, and all around poor excuse for a human being.

Sickness roiled in her stomach. The power bar she'd eaten for breakfast threatened to add to the rubble pile as she tried to figure out how in the hell she'd ended up here. Back behind a sniper rifle with the power over life and death trembling in the muscles of her right trigger finger.

Dammit. When she'd decided to take control of her life and quit the FBI, she hadn't wanted to do this any more.

She'd wanted to be a simple relief worker. She'd wanted to connect with her family, brothers and mother.

But that bitch, fate, had slapped her upside the head and now here she was, where she'd sworn she never wanted to be again. Looking through the scope of a high-powered rifle, with a crystal clear head shot and a murky sense of right and wrong.

With little fanfare, she could blast LeRoy's brain matter all over the silk-covered walls and the antique Louis the XIV scrolled chairs in the receiving room of his ridiculously elegant weekend mansion which, since built properly, had sustained minimal damage. Her muscles twitched with the knowledge and acceptance that with one slow slide of her finger, the despotic, amoral leader would be history.

Jess didn't want to kill him, didn't want to be directly responsible for another death. She didn't want this choice. She'd given up this kind of life. She'd left the FBI after a series of high stress cases to get away from the doubt and guilt that had crippled her. To make her own decisions about right and wrong rather than carry out the commands of her bosses.

But if Henri LeRoy lived, chances were astronomical that many other citizens would die.

And yeah, she'd probably been manipulated into this. Actually no probably about it. Assassination had not been listed as one of her duties when she'd joined Global Humanitarian Relief. Damn her brother anyway.

But now all she could do was lay here in the desecrated

remains of the former church and hope that her special skill set wouldn't be needed.

Fortunately, she was secondary backup.

And unless several things went horribly wrong, she would break down her weapon, get back to the relief aid encampment, back to actually helping people, and be out of here without ever firing her rifle.

Then she could hand out seed packets to her heart's content and figure out what she was going to do next. If she'd stay with GHR and her brothers, or go. First, she had to get through the next two hours.

But if something did go wrong...she prayed that if she was called upon, she could make the right decision. Make the shot. Cold zero.

USA Today Bestselling Author Lisa Hughey started writing romance in the fourth grade. That particular story involved a prince and an engagement. Now, she writes about strong heroines who are perfectly capable of rescuing themselves and the heroes who love both their strength and their vulnerability. She pens romances of all types—suspense, paranormal, and contemporary—but at their heart, all her books celebrate the power of love.

She lives in Cape Ann Massachusetts with her fabulously supportive husband, two out of three awesome mostly-grown kids, and one somewhat grumpy cat.

Beach walks, hiking, and traveling are her favorite ways to pass the time when she isn't plotting new ways to get her characters to fall in love.

Lisa loves to hear from readers and has tons of places you can connect with her. It's a wonder she gets any writing done at all....

Be Lisa's Friend on Facebook
Follow Lisa on Twitter

[Become a member of Lisa's Confidants](#)
[Visit Lisa on the Web](#)
[Follow Lisa on Pinterest](#)
[Follow Lisa on Instagram](#)
[Email Lisa](#)
[Be Lisa's Friend on Goodreads](#)
[Like Lisa on Facebook at Lisa Hughey Author](#)

ACKNOWLEDGMENTS

So many people had a hand in the final version of this book that it is probably impossible to name them all, but I'll try. I started with a glimmer of an idea and a stack of research books about the NSA. Years later, this book is finally being published. The glimmer grew into a trilogy and Blowback is the first in the Black Cipher Files.

Thank you to all of the early readers, Danielle Girard, Jean Brashear, LGC Smith and Sophie Littlefield. A huge thanks to Alicia Rasley for her editorial input and for always teaching me something new about writing and my
own work.

A giant hug to my critique group, Trish Cetrone, Cyndy Rymer, LGC Smith, Adrienne Miller, and Sophie Littlefield for nurturing me through the entire writing, agent finding, submission process and your support when I decided to go a less traditional route.

Thanks to the Pens Fatales, Sophie Littlefield, LGC Smith, Rachael Herron, Juliet Blackwell, Martha Flynn, Adrienne Miller, and Gigi Pandian, for their encouragement and cheering up when I needed it. A very special thanks to

Martha Flynn and LGC Smith for the final read through. And an extra squeeze for Martha for helping me navigate this journey. I am blessed to have the friendship and support of such amazing women.

Finally, a billion and one hugs and kisses to my family. Kids (for all the times you dealt with, "Mom's working, can you make your own dinner?") I like to think that rather than being neglectful, I was teaching self-reliance. Thank you for helping me reach my dream.

And to Jim for always believing that this day would come.

www.ingramcontent.com/pod-product-compliance
Lightning Source LLC
Chambersburg PA
CBHW032200180726
48284CB00001B/121